More Than Luck Required

A Journey of Healing, Hope, and Love

Connie Morgan

Black Rose Writing | Texas

ISBN: 978-1-68513-609-3
LIBRARY OF CONGRESS CONTROL NUMBER: 2025933036
PUBLISHED BY BLACK ROSE WRITING
www.blackrosewriting.com

Printed in the United States of America
Suggested Retail Price (SRP) $22.95

More Than Luck Required is printed in Garamond Premier Pro

*As a planet-friendly publisher, Black Rose Writing does its best to eliminate unnecessary waste to reduce paper usage and energy costs, while never compromising the reading experience. As a result, the final word count vs. page count may not meet common expectations.

PRAISE FOR
MORE THAN LUCK REQUIRED

"Author Connie Morgan weaves a profound tale of love and loss with a pinch of fantasy in her glorious debut, *More Than Luck Required*. Morgan's writing is clean and crisp, catching the reader unprepared for the emotional rollercoaster of finding love again, only to ponder the risk of heartbreak!"
–Barbara Conrey, *USA Today's* best-selling author of *Nowhere Near Goodbye* and *My Secret to Keep*

"*More Than Luck Required* by Connie Morgan is a charming and heartwarming tale of how a group of people can reclaim happiness after insurmountable challenges. Readers who enjoy a wholesome and hopeful tale will certainly love this book. I highly recommend it."
–Diane Nagatomo, author of *Finding Naomi* and *The Making of Us*

"There's no escaping heartbreak. Three wounded characters are each grieving in differing circumstances, and each has a new chance at love—if they accept it. Will they break through their shells of resistance and fear to find love and even romance? Fans of Colleen Hoover's *Hopeless* series will love Connie Morgan's novel of three scarred souls taking the ultimate risk."
–Jann Alexander, author of *Unspoken: A Dust Novel*

"I enjoyed the writing style, which evoked emotions within me and enabled me to be fully engaged from beginning to end. I loved how the characters each have a unique backstory and distinct personality."
–5 Star *Reader's Favorite* Review and Award

"The subtitle of the book is "A Journey of Healing, Hope, and Love," and author Connie Morgan delivers on all three fronts. Without revealing any spoilers, I will say this is an immersive, romantic read about characters we are happy to root for. Thanks to the characters' strong spirits and the help of a loveable supportive cast, I enjoyed the ride from start to finish."
–Ruth F. Stevens, award-winning author of *My Year of Casual Acquaintances*

Cover Symbology

People often link daisies to fresh starts and give them to those facing hardships. In Celtic mythology, God would comfort grieving parents by covering the land with daisies when a baby passed away.

More Than Luck Required

CHAPTER 1
LORA

Orca Park, Washington State

Situations that tug at your heart make you cave. Dad probably asked over fifteen times to put her past behind her. Consistently, her response was to leave the room.

His deathbed summons was an act of desperation. The plea from his watery, sunken eyes held her to him as he'd made his final request. His raspy voice wobbled while his icy fingers held her hand. Emotions had clogged her throat.

That day, her love for him wouldn't allow her to leave.

Yet, every day since, she regretted the promise she'd made.

With a firm flick of her arm, her empty softshell suitcase bounced off the wall of the closet. To make room for her mom's suitcase, she kicked it into the corner. She likely over-packed for a three-day stay.

Okay, Dad. I'm here to figure this out. Return to a more normal life.

She pushed on her low back to stretch her spine. Today...yes, it would be today, she'd begin her monumental task of rebuilding her life—though she had no clue how she'd go about doing that. To attack the tension in her upper back, she shifted her shoulders from side to side as she grimaced.

Heck, if only this were a vacation. God knows she *desperately* needed one.

That three-month grace period she'd given herself to grieve had long ago expired. Not following through on his request gnawed at her daily. Unfortunately, all those excuses she'd used piled on the guilt.

And darn it, guilt was as familiar to her as putting on her shoes every morning.

Across the room, Mom unpacked in that slow, deliberately precise way she did when something bothered her. It was unlikely she would speak her mind, though.

Undoubtedly, Mom's distress probably came from her. During the last half of their drive, she retreated into herself to brood, closing off conversation.

Great! Something else to feel guilty about.

To distract herself from her negative mental chatter, she walked over to gaze out their third-story window at the Pacific Northwest beach she loved. They'd vacationed there annually until she left for college. After that, summer jobs made it impossible to return.

She slowly released a deep sigh. It hadn't been fair to close herself off like that. Yet, as the mileposts ticked by, dread consumed her. It shouldn't have surprised either of them that she'd be moody over her purpose for coming.

This wasn't how she wanted their first mother/daughter trip to start.

It'd be best if she ditched her anger toward Dad. It was stupid and useless. He'd asked because he loved her. There wasn't anything wrong with his not wanting her to live her life alone. He meant well, but hadn't he realized how miserable she'd be, trying to find some sort of redemption for something she felt responsible for?

She bounced the side of her fist on the windowsill, fighting thoughts of premature defeat. *No, a promise is a promise, Dad.*

A normal life.

What was *that* supposed to look like for someone who lost almost everyone she loved, and what defined her? She had cherished being a wife, mother, and homemaker. What remained after didn't seem to matter much. Dad hadn't understood it wasn't just *what* she lost that prevented her from moving on; it was the *how.*

Could she ever move forward if she couldn't forgive herself?

She pulled her focus back to the sliver of beach visible beyond the cliff and the massive blue sky that covered the vista. This saltwater beach had a special energy she wanted to feel and absorb. It called to her. Could it provide the direction she needed to move forward?

"Got ourselves a nice day for early spring. Ready for the beach, Mom?"

Mom briefly assessed her with eyes void of emotion.

"I'll change my shoes and get my coat," Mom said, blinking, as if my words brought her back to the present.

Trickles of concern surfaced as Mom returned to her slow-motion mode while putting on her shoes. *Something* is going on with her.

As they walked out the door, a heavy sigh slipped from Mom's lips. She followed two arms-lengths behind, with a heaviness settling in my chest.

By the time they reached the lobby, her heart rate rocketed. That hyper-speed beat accompanied thoughts of what she needed to accomplish over the next three days. Automatically, her mind searched for excuses to stall the process.

Dad's request felt like a nagging heel blister, the kind that, no matter which shoes you wore, it always made its presence known.

When they reached the back side of the inn, where the steps down to the beach were located, she glanced toward the flower bed lining the back wall. One lone white daisy in a sea of green stems tugged her lips into a smile. The first bloom of the season. During their summers there, cheerful white daisies with yellow centers would fill that bed. Those dancing daisies always made her smile and would raise her above any teenage angst.

Her eyes went back to her mom. There was a heaviness in her stride. Her mom's slouching shoulders worried her.

What's troubling her?

Booking this trip came from an out-of-the-blue impulse. She'd hoped Orca Park would be a place she could clear her head. She'd thought having Mom come along might be good for her, too. Maybe she'd been wrong?

When she reached the top of the stairs, she paused before descending. A generous inhale brought the nostalgic aroma of sea air—that mixture of beached marine life and salty brine carried along through moist droplets she could both taste and smell.

As she reached the last step down, the old wooden plank creaked its resistance. When her right foot landed on dry sand, the tightness in her jaw released. As the left foot joined the right, she enjoyed the sinking sensation as the sand rose to cradle her shoes. Her lips curved upward as her body released a silent *ahh*.

When she extended her hand, her mom reciprocated with hers. As they walked away from the inn and the waterfront, facing homes, they continued to hold hands. The beach terrain changed as they moved closer to the water's edge. The soft, sandy upper beach transitioned into rocks, driftwood, and slippery algae-covered surfaces.

She squeezed her mom's hand. "Is it too soon to come back to the memories we made here with Dad?"

Mom stopped. Her chin dropped to her chest. When she spoke, her voice broke. "I wanted…I wanted my mind to go to the happy times we'd had here, but—" She shook her head as her eyes glistened with emotion. "After Dad's diagnosis, we came here to talk about what was ahead of us." Her nostrils flared as she sucked in a breath.

"Oh, I…I didn't know. I shouldn't have asked you to come."

"No, sweetheart, I wanted to. One thing your dad considered unfinished was helping you move on from what happened to Maggie, and what you went through with that *husband* of yours." She shook her head. "I've been so angry at Frank."

"Mom, I *hated* disappointing Dad, but it was the headspace I've been in. I couldn't—well, the only way I could keep it together was to wall myself off."

"Yes, I know. But Dad's not being able to help you grieved him so much. He always had a gift for helping young people. However, you were *so* resistant. I know a dying request was…unfair, but he didn't know what else to do. You'd given him no other option."

Mom stepped in front of her. "You've suffered too long. When you wanted to come here, I agreed because I thought coming here would lead to a breakthrough."

She raised a questioning eyebrow. A breakthrough? Here?

Mom smiled. "Your dad and I used to say this beach was your *discovery* place. As a kid, you'd take these long beach walks thinking about the school year you'd completed. Then you'd conjure up elaborate plans for what you wanted for yourself in the coming year."

"I remember that." She had recorded those grand plans using purple and teal gel pens in her pink floral journal. "Maybe that's why I felt compelled to return."

"Back then," Mom tugged her hand to start them walking again, "your beach sessions kept you focused on what you wanted to achieve. I was hoping you could establish that type of intention again, to help you move beyond your past. You've done a wonderful job turning the Goldens' business around, but you need more than work in your life."

What Mom said made her stomach churn. It was true; her future would be bleak if she kept doing what she had been doing over the past four years.

As they continued walking, her energy drained away. She couldn't deny it. Her life was pretty empty.

Better add curing loneliness to her *to-do list.*

"Mom, I have been lonely, especially this past year. They say grief gets dialed down with time, and it does. It has. Instead of pain, I've felt...*gratitude* lately. I'm grateful I had the experience of being a mom, even if it was—" Tears banked behind her eyes. "For such a short time." She pulled her lips in while taking a deep breath to regain control. "Some women never even get that. Yet, no matter how I try, I haven't been able to shake the idea that I could have prevented her death."

Mom narrowed her eyes. "Don't do that to yourself! Frank did such a number on you. Blaming you was so unfair."

"Maybe, but I can't seem to let it go. And if I can't, I won't be able to make the changes Dad wanted for me. Interacting and opening up to people makes me anxious. Vulnerable. Eventually, my past would come out, and once they knew, I'm pretty sure they'd judge me poorly."

"You've got to trust people will be more empathetic. Couldn't you go back and reconnect with your old friends? God knows they tried with you. Yet you wouldn't let them in. People cared about you. They still do, even though you've cut yourself off from everyone."

"I'm not sure reconnecting is right for me. I don't think people will be as empathetic as you believe." She averted her eyes, not wanting her mom to see what they held. "At Maggie's memorial, I overheard a few friends say I should have been watching Maggie, and *never* should have taken her to a construction site."

She felt pulled to look at the response on her mom's face when she said, "Jeanette was one of them."

Surprise bloomed on Mom's face. "I can't believe Jeanette would have said that."

Jeanette's comment had surprised her, too. What her best friend said had crushed her *and* continued to haunt her. She came to believe that if Jeanette blamed her, *anyone* would.

"The thing is, Mom, what they said, I had already said to myself. I'm sure others would think the same thing."

"I'm disappointed in them, especially Jeanette. People always look for someone to blame. Lora, honey, it was an *accident.*" Her tone then changed to a plea. "Don't do that to yourself."

They strolled for a while longer in silence before Mom spoke again. "I guess now I can comprehend why you pulled away from everyone. What was said must have hurt terribly."

"It did. Now you can see my moving away and keeping people at a distance seemed safer. If I told someone about my past, I'd be the next bit of gossip they'd run to tell their friends about."

"To deal with all of this might be challenging, Lora. However, you made a promise to your dad. Don't waste more years coming up with excuses and secluding yourself from so much of life. Maggie's death and Frank's falling apart weren't your fault. You've got to let that sink in and truly believe it."

"I know."

Mom stuffed her hands in her pockets with a look of frustration. "I suppose you think you're unworthy of being loved again." She shook her head. "That's not true."

When she remained silent, Mom took her hand and shook it. "Dad and I—" She blinked, then swallowed. "We've wanted you to have a happier, more meaningful life. Whatever that might look like for you."

Intellectually, she recognized the sincerity in Mom's words. Her cheeks moistened with tears. She would do her best...for Dad. She really would try anyway.

Mom scooped her into her arms. That tenderness brought a full-on cascade of tears. Mom held tight until her tears subsided.

"Sweetheart, everything will get better if you only try. You *are* worth whatever fight is ahead of you. Get to the other side, so you remember what an amazing woman you are. It would be a shame to continue hiding yourself from the world. You have so much to give with that marvelous brain and heart of yours. You are only thirty-four. There's still time for another family."

Mom stepped away. "I'm not the one to help you get to where you need to go. Dad's and my suggestion of counseling is still a good one. You've spent a long time not budging from the shell you've built around yourself. You'll need support taking it down."

Her head throbbed like a stubbed toe. So much crying seemed to have swollen her brain. She couldn't think of what to say or do. The only thought coming through clearly was that her agreeing to Dad's dying request gave him peace of mind before he passed.

Mom patted her arm. "I'm returning to the inn. You continue your walk. How about doing an adult version of what you did as a kid?" Mom kissed her throbbing forehead.

A whiff of Mom's vanilla cream lotion brought comfort. When Mom stepped back, her eyes revealed the hope she carried.

Watching Mom walk away constricted her throat. Disappointing Mom would be unacceptable.

Mom's all she had now. Her Pacific Northwest family had gone from five down to three and then from three down to two.

She flung her arms behind her back, gripped her wrists, and continued in the direction they had previously headed.

After filling her lungs with air, she pushed out a burst of frustration. Well, *of course,* she'd constructed a shell around her. She needed some kind of protection after being forced to sell her home and return to work—all the while feeling gutted by grief.

She stomped down the shoreline until her breathing returned to normal.

Her protective shell?

As she stopped to stare out into the inlet, her mind filled with an image of her mother sitting at the kitchen table nicking miniature walnut-like seeds.

"Why are you doing that?" she'd asked.

Mom replied, "This helps the nasturtium seeds take in water and nutrients so they can soften and let the life inside them emerge."

Humph. The life inside her had become so stagnant that she was probably *rotting* on the inside.

She called out softly, "Oh, Dad, what you want for me seems unattainable."

As she shoved her hands into her pockets, she resumed her walk.

Hmm, come to think of it, her shell had weakened or maybe at least cracked some recently. Hadn't she become more friendly with her barista and chatted more with her hairdresser and the cashier at the Thai restaurant she frequented? It took some finesse to keep the conversation away from herself, but the exchanges were pleasantly worth it. Her former self enjoyed chatting with people. It had always felt like a fun exploration.

How far could she go when connecting with others without revealing too much? Trickier, she supposed, when deepening friendships or becoming romantically involved.

She sank onto a hunk of driftwood, then gazed up at the sky. As she listened to the lapping waves, her eyelids lowered and her body slumped. She was so...exhausted.

When a chilly gust of wind hit her cheeks, her eyes opened. How much time had passed? The weather had shifted. Clouds with gray, menacing underbellies had swallowed the azure sky.

Unwilling to abandon the beach, she stood, tucked her hands into her pockets, and continued walking.

Emotionally, she was stuck. Frank's angry, vicious words tethered her to her assumption of guilt over Maggie's death. It seemed impossible to see it any other way. Though lately, a nagging feeling told her to seek the truth.

Whether or not she wanted to, it was time to re-examine the day of the accident and what happened after.

Her tears were back. She blinked them away while focusing on the incoming waves to prevent her shoes from getting wet. She hardly registered the distinctive plop of a Chinook salmon cresting the frigid waters. However, movement drew her eyes to the pursuing osprey plunging its talons into the sea.

She groaned. If she could only believe her parents. They'd always been steadfast in labeling what happened as an *accident* and *not* her fault. Failing to do so would prevent any type of future happiness.

Picking up a few rocks, she hurled them one at a time into the bay, watching them disappear into the depths. The sensation provided some release, so she scooped up another handful. This time, she used her whole body as she pulled back her arm to thrust the next three stones farther out into the inlet.

As each stone left her fingertips, she yelled, "Please don't let me be alone! Please don't let me be alone! Please...not alone." By the third callout, she was in tears and panting for breath.

Spent, she stared out at a lone cargo ship, appearing small and lost in the vast blue-gray waterway as it moved across the horizon.

She hadn't allowed herself to blubber like that for years. With a shudder, she lowered her chin and wiped her tears with the back of her hand. After a gulp of air, she pushed her shoulders back, readying herself to resume her walk. Searching into her pockets, she found the remains of a used Kleenex and blew into a salvageable corner before continuing down the shoreline.

To release leftover emotion, she kicked a piece of driftwood in her path. It moved a smidge, enough to divulge what was underneath.

"Ah, what do we have here?" Dad always said the first person to find sea glass was in for good luck.

Her cheeks lifted into a genuine smile. Some luck would be a blessing.

She picked up the blue glass and rubbed it between her fingers to wipe away the sand. Then she tapped it above her heart before putting the tumbled bit into the pocket of her jacket.

Her insides vibrated with anticipation of the inevitable changes ahead of her.

I need you, Dad. I don't know whether I'm brave enough. This all seems impossible.

Her pace slowed as she continued walking along the water's edge, her eyes focusing on each footfall. As her strides lengthened, her heels dug deeper into the sand. Ideas of how to change her life began to take shape.

The easiest place to begin would be at work. Fewer hours would allow her to implement changes in her personal life.

When her gaze lifted, she saw the fallen Douglas fir tree blocking her forward motion. "Oh, no!" She glanced behind her. The shoreline had narrowed considerably.

The tide was coming in. Fast.

She checked her cell phone; no bars. The digital clock showed she had strolled for over an hour. With trembling hands, she stuffed her cell phone back into her pocket. Her pulse raced.

This was so stupid of her.

Now what?

She faced the fallen tree, part of which stretched into the sound. The uprooted tree hung at the edge of an embankment, approximately five feet higher than the shoreline. When she glanced back at the narrowed strip of coastline, it too had an elevated embankment. Above that, scrub brush transitioned into a dense forest that climbed steeply in elevation.

Rooted in place, she decided heading back the way she came was out of the question. She scanned the embankment. Was that a narrow path? She ran back to check. Animals could have made it...or maybe humans?

Yes! This might work. While on a boat ride as a kid, she'd seen occasional houses on top of the cliff. She trotted onto the path, making her way inland. Maybe she'd come across someone who would help her?

As soon as she reached the edge of the forest, icy raindrops hit her cheeks. Even under the tree canopy, the early spring rain soaked her light jacket, pant legs, and jogging shoes. She pushed her wet hair from her face, wishing she had paid attention to the warning in those darkened clouds she'd seen earlier. Not checking the tide table was another mistake. She hadn't planned on being gone so long.

The farther into the woods she went, the more her breath caught in her chest. Nightfall was approaching, and the temperature was dropping. She shivered. Her damp clothes shrouded her in a chill. She had no choice but to keep moving.

Mom would be so worried by now.

She stumbled, then tripped on a tree root and fell, scraping her left hand and knee. Remaining on all fours, she closed her eyes to focus on slowing her rapid breathing. With a groan, she heaved herself up to a stand.

Locating the path had become a problem. Her cellphone battery was low, so she used the flashlight feature sparingly. She needed to be careful. If she broke a leg or injured herself, she might never make it back to civilization. Her racing heart and rising panic confirmed that her situation was bad. Another stupid accident. Yet this time, she'd put herself in danger.

She blew into cupped hands and cinched the bottom of her jacket, though she gained little warmth. Trudging onward, she cursed under her breath. It was getting too dark to see.

"Finally!" With the urge to do a happy dance, she tramped out of the forest onto a gravel road.

That elation quickly faded, seeing she had another choice to make. Go right, hoping to find a waterfront home, or left, to locate the main road leading back to the inn.

Turning right, she walked a few yards, then laughed in relief. Her heart leaped as she spied a split-railed fence lining one side of the road ahead. In the distance was the roof of a building. Her steps quickened as shaky laughter spewed from her lips.

Upon hearing the downshift of a diesel engine, she skidded to an abrupt stop. It sounded like it was behind her. Yet, the rain and wet, dense foliage could muffle and redirect the sound.

Before she could determine what to do, headlights were upon her as a truck came around the corner. With frozen fingers that ached to bend, she reached into her jacket pocket for the sea glass. Once found, she closed her eyes as she rubbed the smooth surface for luck.

With her arms tight to her sides, she leaned forward to see who might be inside. Her breathing had become rapid and shallow.

No, this was not good—a lone woman on a road in the boondocks, about to flag down a vehicle. Her heart thundered against her chest as the truck neared.

Who could be in that truck? A good neighbor? Or a serial killer?

As she swallowed what little saliva remained in her mouth, she decided that whomever it was, they would be her best chance at making it back.

After a humongous gulp of air, the tightness in her chest released. She stepped into the road and raised an arm.

CHAPTER 2
COOPER

As Cooper turned off the rural road onto his quarter-mile driveway, he blinked. As he leaned into the steering wheel, he squinted to identify what was ahead of him. His eyes sprang wide. A rain-drenched woman stood in the middle of the road, waving an arm. That made little sense. His home was off a dead-end road, miles from town, used only by a few scattered neighbors.

"What's goin' on here?" He swung his head toward his fifteen-year-old daughter, Emma. "Trouble, most likely. I don't recall seeing an abandoned car." He switched on his high beams for a second. "Seems to be alone." He pulled up beside the woman, whose wet, filthy clothes were molded against her slender body. "She's been out here a while."

He rubbed a hand over his jaw. "Could this day get any better?"

His day had started badly when he had to fire one of his crew. With a piece of broken equipment and now one man short, he'd be behind schedule for weeks.

As he rolled down the window, the woman stepped back. Seeing the apprehension in her huge blue eyes, he turned on the cab's overhead light. Maybe seeing Emma would lessen her concerns.

"Hey," he said, leaning out the open window. "Looks like you might need some help."

"If you would—" She halted, then rattled on. "I'm desperate to get back to the Sandpiper Inn. I went for a walk on the beach, lost track of time, and didn't notice the tide coming in. My mom's probably worried sick about me." The woman frowned, glaring at her phone. "My cell phone is useless out here, and the battery's almost dead."

Emma scooted forward to peek around him and chirped, "Hi!" waving with a bright smile.

Nudging Emma back, he said, "I'm Cooper Martin, and this is my daughter, Emma. We live in that house up the bend. Why don't you call from there...let your mom know you're okay? We've got groceries in the back that'll need to be unloaded; after that, we could take you into town."

His jaw tightened. What had just dropped in his lap would ruin his plans for his evening. He'd have to skip a few things from his tonight's to-do list. Stupid woman. She shouldn't be out here. It's too easy to get lost in these woods. He yanked his baseball cap off and raked his fingers through his hair. Just his luck.

His voice was gruff with concern when he said, "You should consider yourself lucky you found your way to us. Every year, some—" To stop himself from lecturing her, he cleared his throat. "Ah...somebody gets lost in these woods." He'd wanted to say, some *dumb-ass,* but she didn't seem in the mood for a scolding.

The woman pursed her lips and nodded.

"Best you dry off while you wait." He watched her consider his offer, though he knew there wasn't a better alternative.

When she raised her head, her eyes rose upward for a second. Then she sighed, squared her shoulders, and trudged toward the passenger side of the truck.

Clenching his teeth, his foul mood grew. He figured it probably showed on his face. As he waited for her to climb into the truck, he strummed his fingers on the steering wheel.

The woman looked pretty pitiful as she slumped into the seat Emma vacated when she scooted onto the console.

He jutted his jaw and shook his head, sighing. She probably wasn't too happy about the situation, either. Actin' like a knucklehead wouldn't help this woman *or* his predicament.

Emma held her backpack snug to her chest and turned to him to mouth, *Be nice,* as she playfully jabbed him in the shoulder. She pivoted back toward the stranger. With a cheerful voice, she said, "I turned up the heater, though we don't have far to go."

"Thanks. I'm Lora Hamilton, by the way. Sorry to inconvenience you." Her eyes closed as she settled into the seat.

Yeah, she might be feelin' vulnerable taking a ride from strangers. Man up, and be a Good Samaritan.

The woman, Lora, leaned forward, extending her hands toward the warmth of the heater vent. A smile of appreciation lit up her face...until she glanced down at her feet. As she lifted one muddy shoe, she groaned, then snuck a peek at him, as if to gauge his reaction to the mess she'd made on his floor mats.

He shrugged in what he hoped was a never-mind-it-happens gesture. Then he put the truck in gear to drive the rest of the way home.

Once parked in his driveway, he glanced her way to see her reaction.

Her hand had flown to her lips.

His house was impressive. He and Karen had built where the view was the most picturesque. They'd compromised on the house design, combining the two architectural styles they loved—the Pacific Northwest coastal style with a 1930s Sears Craftsman design. The exterior was cedar vertical board and batten siding with off-white, cottage-style window casings. Karen had drawn up the landscape plans. She'd layered down from the existing tall evergreen trees to Japanese maples, and then added rhododendrons, native plants, and grasses. The rear of the house opened to the Puget Sound inlet, with the sky as its backdrop.

Dark clouds parted, and light streamed down on the roof. Lora kept her fingers pressed to her lips, taking it all in.

"Emma, why don't you take Lora inside and show her the landline? I'll carry in the groceries."

"You have a beautiful home, Mr. Martin."

"Thanks. Please call me Cooper or Coop."

Lora jumped down from his relic of a pickup. He'd bet money she would wonder why he wasn't driving something classy to match the stature of his home. Holding back a chuckle, he watched Lora struggle to close the old Dodge's heavy metal door after Emma got out.

He'd never get rid of this old boy. The truck was a piece of memorabilia from his dad. By driving it to work every day, he gained the desired anonymity from the success of his business.

While Emma gave Lora instructions, he listened, noting how grown up his daughter had become. Emma was his world. His number one pride and joy. She'd be off to college soon, something he resisted thinking about. A life changer for sure!

Emma waved the woman toward their back door. "Right this way, Lora. Our phone is above the kitchen desk. When you're done, help yourself to the utility room bathroom. Use whatever towels you need from under the sink. I'll get you one of my old sweatshirts and a pair of socks. Oh, there's a small hairdryer in the drawer you can use."

"May I have a glass of water?"

"Sure, we also have an instant-hot water thingy. I could make you some hot chocolate."

"Water for now, please, but cocoa later?"

After unlocking his custom truck bed cover, he rushed to scoop up as many grocery bags as possible. With his long legs, he caught up with them at the back door. Lora took off her muddy shoes before she entered.

When Lora headed for the kitchen, Emma nabbed him in the hallway. "Dad, what about my plans for tonight?"

"I'll handle it," he muttered.

Satisfied, she hurried off to grab a glass of water for Lora, who drank it down in a few steady gulps.

He was curious about this woman, so he took his time putting away the first load of groceries.

Lora announced, "I don't have the resort's phone number with me."

"No problem," said Emma. "I'll look it up on my phone. We get lousy reception. Only one cell service works out here." Emma shook her head in disgust. "It drives my friends bonkers!"

He considered offering Lora the use of his cell phone, but he wasn't feeling very generous. The situation still ticked him off. This woman's stupidity had disrupted his whole evening. End-of-the-week burnout was a real thing for him. He'd planned to finish up a few work matters, then chill before he needed to pick Emma back up.

He left to get more groceries. When he came back in, Emma said to Lora, "Give me your phone and I'll charge it while you're waiting." As Emma searched for the charging cords above the desk, Lora peered at the family photos on their bulletin board. Her gaze held the longest on the one of himself, Karen, and Emma as a toddler, taken before Karen became too ill for outings.

Lora pointed to the picture. "Is this your mom?"

"Yeah." Emma grinned broadly, throwing her braid over her shoulder.

"She's very pretty. You have a nice-looking family."

He left for his last bit of groceries. It was odd having Lora in his home. There hadn't been a woman other than his mom in their home for years. Maybe that was why he was so curious about their mystery visitor...although the circumstances making her a visitor still churned his gut.

Dumb woman. She's no *visitor*; she's an annoying rescue.

Back in the kitchen, he slammed the bag of apples onto the counter. He couldn't let go of what *might* have happened if *they* hadn't come along. He needed to tamp down his anger.

His eyes met Lora's over the island's marble countertop. As their gazes held, his mind blanked.

Pink-faced, Lora was the one to break eye contact. Sputtering, she said, "Before I dry off, I'll call my mom." As she lowered her gaze, his eyes followed. A puddle of water had pooled at her feet.

"Sorry. So sorry," she said with a flushed face.

He threw a kitchen towel her way. "No biggie. We've had worse."

She took off her socks, dried her feet, and then rolled up her pant legs before she plopped the towel down onto the floor. Then she glided the towel back and forth with her foot to soak up the water.

As he watched, he pictured his wife doing the same thing. He shook his head to rid himself of the image.

As Lora made her call, he remained close by, eavesdropping as she explained to her mother what had happened.

CHAPTER 3
LORA

In the utility bathroom, Lora searched through the drawers to find the hairdryer. As she plugged it in, Emma knocked, then opened the door to hand her some dry clothes and a hot chocolate.

"Thanks, that's so kind of you."

Emma's cheeks turned rosy as she ducked out quickly.

Eager for the warmth, she sipped the steaming liquid before she pulled off her clammy, wet pants. First, she took a towel to her legs, then blasted them with warm air from the hairdryer. She did the same to her top half before wiggling into Emma's sweatshirt. Next, she rubbed down her hair with the towel and grabbed some Kleenex.

With a glance in the mirror, she groaned. "Omigod! I'm a mess." Kleenex won't fix this. She wet and soaped the corner of the towel to attack her dirt-streaked face. When finished, she stood back and examined her glowing pink skin.

"Oh, goodness!" Her hand flew up to muffle snorts of laughter. Stretched across her chest were the faded faces of a popular boy band. The sweatshirt was too small, though she appreciated the warmth and Emma's kind gesture.

As she pulled on Emma's purple unicorn socks, her lips turned up into a smile. She felt better already.

She hung her pants on the sink's edge, then took the hairdryer to them. Emma's colorful socks caught her eye. Emma was so considerate for someone her age. Would Maggie have been as kind if she had reached her teen years? If a toddler's sweet, kindhearted disposition could have predicted what she would've been later, then yes, she would have.

That thought warmed her insides. These *Maggie moments* came randomly. Luckily of late, they came without her chest tightening or tears welling up. That was good, since those thoughts and images kept her daughter alive for her. With less pain attached, it became easier to feel close to Maggie.

She'd hidden her *Maggie moments* from others, along with everything else she assumed people would judge her poorly for. Most of her new acquaintances didn't even know she'd been a mother.

Now that her pants were dry, she tackled her hair. While blow-drying, the wet strands lightened to a pale honey blond, which fell easily to the blunt bob style she'd worn for years.

Splotches of heat rose on her cheeks, remembering how Cooper had acted like she was a nuisance and a numbskull for getting lost. She'd sensed he'd even wanted to lecture her.

The jerk!

To dry the back of her hair, she swung her head down with a huff. What was that moment in the kitchen about? Okay, sure, he was kind of handsome. Not gorgeous, but he had great hair, and...sure, some might consider him cute.

Once finished, she swung her head back up. Why was she even thinking that way? She worked in a warehouse full of men, and she'd never paid attention to their looks. Enough of this nonsense. She tugged the sweatshirt down so the bottom edge would at least graze her waistband.

While she wiped down the bathroom, she told herself not to give Cooper another thought. She'd be out of his hair in no time!

She squinted, making her brows scrunch. Could this *minor* attraction to Cooper be connected to those recurring lucid dreams, starting after Dad's request? In those dreams, faces remained unrecognizable and names unsaid. She awoke smiling this morning, recalling feelings from those fleeting scenes; the sense of belonging from casual chatter around a full dinner table;

contentment from being held in a man's arms; and arousal from a finger slowly meandering down her naked belly.

The corners of her lips curved crookedly before she shook her head. *Not ready to go there.* That kind of intimacy with anyone wouldn't work out.

However, could the pleasurable nature of those dreams signal her wounds were healing? Or had she given herself permission to want a fuller life? *Hmm.* Lately, it seemed she'd been gifting herself a wish for what she might have again.

Her heart thumped wildly as a warning entered her mind. If she didn't move forward now, she'd be stuck. She'd never get back to the person she'd been or have a life that meant something to her. If that was even possible?

Done with cleaning up the bathroom, she placed the dirty towel on top of the washing machine before returning to the kitchen.

Would Cooper's wife arrive home while she was still there?

Emma stood beside her father, repacking cookies into smaller Tupperware containers.

Her eyes wandered around the open-concept kitchen. The kitchen was a cook's dream. A glossy bisque subway-tile backsplash complemented the cream-colored cabinets. They'd chosen high-end stainless-steel appliances, oil-rubbed bronze hardware and light fixtures. She coveted the enormous porcelain farmhouse sink. It didn't hurt that all the rooms faced a wall of floor-to-ceiling windows, which took advantage of their spectacular view of the Puget Sound.

When she turned back, she caught sight of Cooper's smug smile. How irritating. To hide her frown and the heat on her cheeks, she turned her head. What an arrogant twit.

She tamped down her disdain before she turned back again. "Someone must be a wonderful cook by the looks of this amazing kitchen."

"Well," said Cooper, nudging his daughter. "Emma's mom was a terrific baker. Looks like Emma has inherited her talent. Lucky me! Emma keeps me well-stocked with cookies and cakes." He smiled down at his daughter, who returned a matching affectionate smile.

Their exchange cooled her temper.

"However," said Cooper, "I am the chef in this household."

At the mention of food, her stomach grumbled loudly. Her hand flew to her belly, attempting to stop the embarrassing gurgles.

"Emma, put some of those Snickerdoodles in a baggie for Lora to eat along the way." Cooper gave her a wink. Heat scorched her cheeks.

As Emma handed her the cookies, she asked, "May I use one of these plastic grocery bags for my wet clothes?"

After Emma handed her a bag, she headed back to the utility room to take care of her wet clothes. Her mixed opinion of Cooper confused her. "Whatever," she mumbled with a shrug. It would be best if she tried to be grateful for his help. Other than that, no more mental energy needs to go his way.

She knew she had a pattern of being slow to trust, and she resisted making new acquaintances. That was her strategy for never reaching the *sharing phase*.

Yeah, but that was probably something she needed to change.

***

After they all climbed into the truck, she asked Emma, "You're going out with friends tonight?"

"Yeah, we're going to a movie. It's the newest Jacob Murphy movie, cuz that's my friend, Ivy's favorite actor. Well, for now, anyway. We rotate who picks the movie between me, Ivy, Sam, Gary, and Lisa. We started a once-a-month movie night in the fifth grade. I'm *almost* a sophomore now. Sometimes we rent, and sometimes we go to the movie theater. Tonight, Dad's dropping me off at Ivy's house; then her mom will take us to Sam's."

"Long-lasting friendships can be the best. I went from elementary to high school in the same town. Sticking to one spot can make the teen years easier. Though I suppose it could go the opposite for some kids." Her brows knitted. "I don't know about you, but friendships change during middle school. You know, the boy thing, competition, and cliques separating kids from one another."

"Yeah, that happens. Even in our group lately, as boyfriend/girlfriend stuff creeps in."

"Hey! None of that boyfriend stuff," proclaimed Cooper. He made a face emphasizing his position. "Emma's pretty busy with school, friends, volleyball, soccer...and taking good care of me, of course."

They turned onto a gravel driveway. A woman and a teenage girl stood leaning against a battered older sedan.

"I'm sorry. I'm sure I disrupted your plans."

"No big deal," said Cooper. "I usually provide most of the transportation and host both girls' turns for in-home movie nights. Ivy's mom doesn't mind driving occasionally."

After Emma jumped out, she walked to the driver's side to hop onto the running board to give her dad a goodbye kiss on the cheek. Grinning, she said, "Now, leave some of those Snickerdoodles for me, Dad."

"Nah, I'll have 'em finished off by the time you get home." As a parting gesture, Cooper patted her arm. "Bye, Chickpea."

Emma peered around her dad. "Nice to meet you, Lora."

"Nice to meet you, too. Thanks for the cookies and the clothes."

Emma waved and headed toward her friend.

"She's a sweetheart, Cooper. You're a lucky guy to have a daughter like Emma."

"You don't have to tell me."

She watched the girls hug. Though these girls are neighbors, a quarter mile apart, the difference between their two homes was noticeable. A glowing yard light at Ivy's home revealed a modest, single-story home suffering from neglect. There was a broken front porch railing and a moss-covered roof with weeds growing up from the gutters. Someone had patched a broken window with cardboard duct-taped to the outside frame. Tucked along the side yard were a few abandoned cars with blackberry vines twining through their fenders.

The rumble and vibration of the truck startled her out of her thoughts as Cooper backed out of the driveway. Gad! She was still snugged up beside him.

She froze. To give Emma an easy out on their quick trip there, they'd suggested she sit in the middle. Good grief, she hadn't slipped back into the passenger seat.

When Cooper swung his arm behind her to back the truck up, she sucked in a breath. *We're too close.* Would she look silly sliding off the console now? Her cheeks heated. This situation was far too intimate. What should she do?

His breath skimmed her neck. She shivered. That shiver morphed into an electric current that zinged down her spine as her right shoulder bumped into his hand. She leaned forward to put some distance between them.

Drat! Her borrowed sweatshirt was inching up. With one hand, she tugged it down. *Gad. Why was she getting so worked up? It's gotta be because she hadn't been this close to a man in years. That had to be it.*

Shoot! If she moved over now, he'd know how uncomfortable she was. That would be embarrassing. Yet, what would *not* moving say? She set her jaw and slowly slid into the passenger seat. Her cheeks burned. She was reacting like a hormonal preteen. *Wow! Schoolgirl feelings were weird at thirty-four.*

She turned to the side window to curse under her breath.

Was Cooper single? He'd used the word *was* when referring to Emma's mother.

Why should that matter? She'd never see him again after today.

She snuck a glance his way. Why was she even entertaining thoughts about his appeal?

She opened the bag of cookies and started munching. "These are so good!" she exclaimed as remnants of the cookie sprang free from her lips. "Oh, darn!" She quickly swept crumbs from her chin and pant legs.

Cooper chuckled. "Yep. One of my favorites." With his eyes on the road, he drummed two fingers on the steering wheel. "Tell me about yourself, Lora. A knight-in-shining-armor should get to know the damsel he rescued."

She paused, considering what to reveal. It wasn't likely she'd see him again, so there was nothing to lose. Biting her lip, she focused on taming her breathing. It wouldn't hurt to share a little...as an experiment, to see how it goes.

With her head held high, she opened her mouth to speak; no words came out. Instead, her stomach did a belly flop. When she could talk, her words spilled out in rapid succession. "I work as an office manager for a large candy-distributing company in Tacoma. You name it, my hands are in it." She giggled at the candy jar reference. "I'm a divorcee." She swallowed. "We had one child—she died in an accident when she was almost three. My dad died seven months ago."

Cooper's brows furrowed while he remained silent. She tugged down the sweatshirt again, waiting in the uncomfortable silence. Would he ask more about Maggie? She fumbled to close the Ziploc bag with the remaining cookies, though she was dying to stuff her mouth with another.

Sighing heavily, she crossed her arms. "I'm fed up with the life I've been living." She let out a nervous little snort. "I think I want a do-over!"

Cooper kept silent, his eyes on the road. What was he thinking?

She exhaled warily. With her voice lowered and the pace of her words slower, she said, "Emotionally...I'm wiped out. I'm working way too many hours. I need to make some changes." Her throat tightened. She squeaked out, "Change is difficult, even when you want to head in a better direction."

Cooper's silence dragged on. Finally, he shook his head and said, "Man, you've had it rough."

The tension in her chest released in one quick *swoosh*.

With kindness in his eyes, Cooper looked her way. "I know the pain and exhaustion that comes with tragedy. My wife, Karen, died of pancreatic cancer when Emma was about two and a half. It was devastating. Emma forced me to keep the course, though. My mom moved in shortly after Karen's diagnosis. She's been my rock." Cooper slowed the truck as they came closer to town. "My dad died when I was in college. That's another story."

The tone in his voice told her there was some unpleasantness attached.

"Got anybody in your corner, Lora?"

"No," she said, picking the cuticle on the side of her empty ring finger. "Not right now. I'm close to my mom, though I've tried not to turn to her when Dad got sick. She's had enough to deal with."

She looked up to gauge Cooper's reaction. Nothing showed on his face. Feeling flushed, she leaned farther back in her seat.

When she recognized the inn was nearby, she faced Cooper. "Thank you for telling me about your wife. I am sorry you lost her, especially when Emma was so young. That's heartbreaking. For what it's worth, you must be a pretty terrific dad, because Emma's a sweetheart."

Cooper smiled warily. "Thanks, though I have to give credit to my mom. She acted as a surrogate mother to Emma, along with being a bus driver, a cook, and a therapist to me. She gave me the time I needed to continue building my business. I wouldn't be in the place I am today, nor would Emma, without her involvement."

His acknowledgments put her at a loss for words. His humble gratitude was endearing. Unfocused and lost in the privacy of her thoughts, she stared out the window.

Cooper cleared his throat as they pulled into the inn's parking lot. After parking, he turned toward her. "This might sound a little out of the blue. I'd like to invite you and your mom to dinner tomorrow night. It's Saturday night—game night. My mom will be there, and Emma usually has her friend Ivy over. She's the girl from the house we dropped Emma off at." He cleared his throat again. "I'm a pretty good cook, so the meal should be tasty. Mom makes the salad, and Emma always makes an amazing dessert."

Excitement leaped into her chest before she could tamp it down. She clasped her hands, trying to lasso the turmoil of dual desires. "Oh, we couldn't intrude."

"I kinda expected that from you, Lora. I'll just have to pull out the payback card to get you to say yes. The knight-in-shining-armor's code of rights declares the rescued damsel must grant him the pleasure of having her as his dinner companion."

Immediately, her belly did a strange gymnastic routine.

If she accepted, someone might ask uncomfortable questions, or her mother might let something slip.

Then she saw Cooper's charming grin as he awaited her answer. She blew out her tension. It would be...nice to go. Her mom might like the family, and his mother would be there. Mom had said we should say *yes* to new experiences more often.

With a nervous laugh, she conceded. "Okay, what can we bring?" She fumbled around with the cookie bag, already thinking she'd made a mistake.

"How about a bottle of red wine and a competitive spirit? The girls take game night pretty seriously."

CHAPTER 4
COOPER

As soon as Cooper's eyes fluttered open, he questioned his invitation to Lora and her mom for dinner. Since he'd already planned a feast to impress the fair damsel, he might as well go ahead with it.

A yawn stretched open his mouth. Falling asleep had been difficult last night. He kept picturing Lora's big doe eyes. Sad, beautiful eyes. She could use a friend. Nope. He wouldn't let it go further than that.

***

As he drove to the inn, he tapped his fingers on the steering wheel, humming a Blake Shelton tune. Before he left, Emma had teased him about putting on cologne and scrubbing the mud off his shoes.

Mom had better not make a big deal about him inviting Lora over, either. It wasn't a date. Lora's mom was coming too.

After he knocked on room 314's door, Lora swung the door open. He stood blinking as he took in her transformation. Even drenched, she was attractive; now she was gorgeous. With makeup, her eyes were enormous. His heart hammered against his chest.

She appeared happy to see him. Since she was wearing a classy sweater and tailored gray slacks, he stopped himself from saying—*Damn. You look fine.*

So, he changed his approach and teased. "Ah, this damsel *is* the fairest in the land." He bowed, grateful to receive the merriest of laughs.

"Come in and meet my mom, Cooper." Lora stepped back, holding the door open wide.

He walked into the room, unable to wipe the goofy grin from his face.

"Mom, this is Cooper Martin, my knight-in-shining armor. Cooper, this is my mother, Rebecca Wilson."

He bowed again and stepped closer.

With a wicked smile, Rebecca playfully curtsied.

He extended his hand, and Rebecca's joined his. Her hand was small and fragile, though he sensed amazing strength there as well. She was clearly where Lora's good looks came from. Something was appealing about these two women.

With a smile that didn't quite reach her eyes, Rebecca said, "I hear you're an excellent cook. I hope we're not intruding on family night."

"Not at all. We're looking forward to having new competitors in tonight's game. Fair warning! My girls are cutthroats. And as far as my being an excellent cook, I'll let you decide that later."

Rebecca's smile grew. "Oh, I bet you're too modest. As for being competitive, I might give them a run for their money." Her eyes sparkled at the challenge.

Twenty minutes later, as they rounded the bend in his driveway, Rebecca gasped. She probably thought that since he drove an older pickup and displayed a certain amount of casual, country-boy charm, he wouldn't be living in such an expansive home.

He rather liked people having a lowered expectation of him. It kept people from trying to reach into his pockets. Giving to the community on his own terms was fine. Yet, he was diligent in not making the same financial mistakes as his father.

Lora said, "Your home's quite beautiful, all lit up for the evening, Cooper."

The house was glowing with well-placed up-lighting. Tonight, the sky was deep blue-gray with sparse clouds drifting across the evening sky. As he parked the truck, a great blue heron caught their attention as it crested the rooftop. The bird glided through the air with its long legs extended back and its neck tucked along its spine. They all sat in silent awe.

After he assisted Rebecca down from the cab, he held his hand out for Lora. When their hands met, her eyes widened. She pulled back. He blushed right along with her, reacting to the electrical current that passed between them. Stunned, he stepped back and pointed toward the front door, wanting the ladies to go ahead of him. As he followed, he stuffed his hands into his pockets.

This could be dangerous.

As the three of them walked into the foyer, the rich aroma of a tomato-based meat sauce enveloped them. The scent mingled with loud music and roaring laughter coming from the kitchen. Astonished, he and his guests stopped in the middle of the great room.

His apron-clad mother swished about the kitchen, using a long loaf of crusty bread as a microphone, lip-syncing to a catchy tune. Her backup singers were Emma, wearing printed leggings and a denim shirt, and Ivy, wearing all black with her face half-hidden by teal-tinted, deep-angled bangs. The girls were holding wooden spoons up to their mouths, taking on the role of his mom's backup singers.

He called out in a booming voice, "Hey, ladies, we have company! Alexa, lower the volume."

Everyone in the kitchen froze. Instead of showing embarrassment, they looked at one another before bursting into laughter.

"Oh, hi, Lora," said Emma, putting her wooden spoon on the kitchen counter. Then she nudged her friend. "This is my friend, Inez Victoria Young. We call her Ivy. She wants to change her name when she gets older, though she can't settle on anything yet." Emma rolled her eyes and poked at her friend.

Ivy did her own eye roll while waving a little, *Hi.* With a tone of disgust, she said, "It was a sick joke to name me after my grandmothers. I am officially going to change it when I turn twenty-one." Then, one hand went to her waist as she popped her hip in dramatic defiance.

"And," announced Emma, swooping an arm out toward her grandmother, "this is my nana, Claire Martin."

Claire's cheeks were flushed from the exertion of her performance. Her stylish salt-and-pepper cropped hair and multicolored tunic made her appear younger than her years, even while wearing her grandmotherly-style apron. Following the girls' theatrics, Claire extended her apron and performed a little curtsey, accompanied by a confident nod.

"Nice to meet the two of you," Claire said, shaking hands with Rebecca first.

"It's nice to meet you. I'm Rebecca, Lora's mother. I loved your musical performance." She paused nervously, twirling her wedding ring. "Thank you for the generous invitation." She nodded toward the kitchen stove. "By the aroma, we'll count ourselves lucky. Dinner smells delicious."

Mom turned toward Lora. "Lora, it's nice to meet you. I heard about your rescue all afternoon. It's rare for Cooper to become a hero so easily. A few of his rescues have been pretty arduous. I don't know if he told you. He's part of our local search and rescue team." She winked at him before turning back to Lora. "I'm glad they found you safe and sound. Being lost out here could have had a tragic ending."

Lora's cheeks turned pink, and there was a subtle shift in her expression.

I wish Mom hadn't brought that up.

Thankfully, Mom changed the subject. "Tonight, you're in for a treat. Cooper made his gooey lasagna. I've made my famous blackberry vinaigrette for our tossed salad, and Emma outdid herself on a new dessert recipe. So, I sure hope you brought your appetite."

Lora's smile appeared forced. Was Mom making her nervous?

"Right now," said Lora, sounding artificially chipper, "it seems like it's been a long time since lunch."

Mom's keen eyes looked puzzled over Lora's behavior.

Lora fidgeted before turning to Emma. "What game are we playing tonight?"

"Royal Rummy. Nana used to play it as a kid. It's more fun with a larger group. We play for pennies. Dad got you a roll when he was in town today. We'll have to decide whether we're going to play as individuals or on teams."

"Well, I'm starved." He headed toward the oven to pull out the lasagna to cool before slicing. "Let's decide all that after dinner."

While he worked in the kitchen, he noticed Rebecca placing a hand on Lora's arm before whispering, "Are you okay?"

He attempted to hide his eavesdropping as Lora scanned the room for observers.

"I'll be okay. Just some nerves creeping up. Don't tell them about Maggie or Frank. Okay, Mom?"

"I don't imagine the topic will come up. Nothing to worry about. Just try to enjoy yourself."

He wondered briefly why she would be concerned if Maggie and Frank came up?

He finished what he was doing in the kitchen, then invited everyone to gather around their enormous round walnut dining table.

Lora seemed to relax with all the lively chatter and laughter accompanying their meal. Most often, she quietly observed the group's interactions as if she were processing and evaluating, though it didn't seem she was being judgmental. She looked content as her gaze roamed over the group.

He couldn't keep his eyes off her. She often blushed when catching him watching her, though she would smile back. He wanted to know more about her. How had those hurtful parts of her past affected her?

The girls' banter pulled him away from his preoccupation with Lora.

"The movie last night was disappointing," said Ivy. "Jacob is *so* predictable. In every movie, he's being his normal self." She let out a heavy sigh while tossing back her bangs with an outstretched ring finger—a reflex he'd seen her perform a thousand times.

"Yet we—*you* keep picking his movies," said Emma, giving her friend a repugnant glare. "You know you have a crush on him *and* his predictable personality." Emma looked at Lora. "The movie was a comedy...as always." She turned toward her grandmother. "Pass the French bread, Nana. Please."

To draw Lora out, he asked, "Lora, what movies have you seen lately?"

She blinked a few times. "Um...well, I haven't been to a movie theater in years. If I have time in the evenings, I try to read. A guy at work loaned me *The Boys in the Boat* since it's historically connected to my alma mater, the

University of Washington. It's been slow going." She tilted her head. "I'm liking the second half better than the first, though."

"I read that. You'll like the ending. Funny. I went to U-Dub too. Did you ever watch the crew race?"

"No. Now I wish I had. The book helped me understand what a grueling sport it is. Then there's the dedication needed for the crew to...well, mesh together to become a synchronized team. Impressive." She turned toward the girls. "The wonderful thing about books...they wake you up to what you didn't know."

"I would agree!" shouted Claire. "Sorry for switching topics. Dessert now or after a few rounds of Royal Rummy?"

"I'm stuffed. Let's wait," said Emma. "I think we should play in teams, one person from each age group on each team."

He scooted his chair back. "Sounds good to me."

As everyone advanced to work on dinner cleanup, Lora gave her mother a reassuring smile before offering to help. He assigned her sink duty.

He nudged her arm and smiled down at her as he handed over the dirty lasagna pan. His breath hitched as she returned a dazzling smile. She held his gaze for a few extra beats, blinked, then ducked her head. Lora's face seemed to reveal everything she felt. Yet she confused him. Most often, around him, she was a mixture of awkwardness and anxiety. Although she presents as strong and competent at other times.

Was he making a fool of himself around her? By the sensation in his gut, and the fact he couldn't stop watching her, he probably was. Was that primitive male-female dance starting up between them? From his side of the dance, it probably was. He wouldn't allow himself to take it any further, though.

Don't overthink it. Just enjoy their evening together.

When they returned to the table, he pulled out Lora's chair for her. He noticed his mom and Rebecca raising their eyebrows at each other. Lora must have seen it too, since she'd stiffened.

Mom better not tease him later.

Teams were picked. Lora, his mom, and Emma were on one team. He, Rebecca, and Ivy were on the other. Halfway through the game, they stopped for dessert. The scorekeeper announced Lora's team was up by eighty-four cents.

After Emma served her dessert, she waited for someone to take their first bite.

Lora purposely took a big, appreciative bite. "Yum! Emma, this dessert is—" She closed her eyes briefly to savor the taste. "One of the best I've ever had!" Then she raised her fork. "For a new recipe, you nailed it!"

Emma beamed. "Thanks. Like my mom, I love baking. I've been going through her recipe collection. She kept tons. My goal is to make every recipe she marked in her cookbooks—all before I graduate from high school."

He patted his still flat belly good-naturedly. "Oh, boy. I'd better double my time on the treadmill."

"I'll save you, Mr. M," said Ivy with a dramatic flair. "Send them home with me."

He was enjoying how comfortable Ivy was with their guests. To an outsider, the friendship between the two girls might appear unusual. Ivy expressed her artistic side in colorful ways through hairstyles and clothing. Emma was more preppy, blending in with peers who were athletic or academically inclined. Regardless, Ivy was like an extended member of their family.

After gathering the dessert dishes, they returned to their game. By the end of the evening, the victors were himself, Rebecca, and Ivy.

CHAPTER 5
LORA

Lora accepted Cooper's offer of a tour of the house. As they followed the girls upstairs, Cooper explained, "I've set Emma up with as much technology as she needs to do school work and keep in touch with her friends...knowing I can't keep her all to myself."

Emma bounced on her toes when they entered her bedroom. "I've redecorated my room into what I call modern farmhouse chic."

The room had sufficient space for two twin beds, two dressers, and a computer desk with a printer stand. A bulky grocery bag sat on top of one bed.

Ivy must be staying over. Most likely, she was a regular.

With fake disgust, Cooper said, "Emma came up with the design plan last year. Just an excuse to go antiquing, seems to me." He grabbed Emma around the neck and gave her a knuckle-rub on the top of her head while Emma feigned distress.

While she meandered around the room, she pointed out Emma's innovative use of repurposed items, which gave Emma ample opportunities to tell stories about each object.

This family stirred long-forgotten emotions. Mostly a sense of serenity, similar to what happens when a puppy settles on your lap and falls asleep. It had something to do with watching their warm connection and how their acceptance of her put her body and mind at ease.

A pile of stuffies in a corner basket caught her eye. She walked over and stood in front of a white kitten with shiny blue acrylic eyes peeking out from the group. Slowly, she extended her index finger and brushed the kitten's nose. "Seraphina," she whispered. She tilted her head away, not wanting anyone to see her quick wave of sadness.

Before she turned back, she forced a smile back onto her face. "Nice job with the room redo, Emma."

Emma bounced on her tiptoes again. "Now come see our *creative space*." Emma glanced at Ivy, designating her as her partner in their creative endeavors. Ivy was now slumped down on a bed, avoiding eye contact. Ivy's mood had shifted.

Emma scrunched her face before she pivoted to leave the room.

Once in the next room, Cooper said, "I set the budget, but Emma took the lead in both rooms."

"Nice, Emma. Such a well-organized and beautifully designed space. Kudos for keeping it relatively neat for a room designated for creativity." She noted the pride on Cooper's face.

"Emma likes to plan things out and has an eye for color and layout," said Cooper.

"Check this out, Lora." Emma strolled over to one of the two workstations. "This is Ivy's mixed-media work. We looked on Pinterest for ideas, though she's got a real knack."

Ivy stood beside the doorjamb with her head lowered. All her happiness and vivaciousness from earlier were gone. To give Ivy space, she turned her attention to Emma, who was holding one of Ivy's projects.

"Nicely done, Ivy. Love the color choices. You have a unique style in your work."

Ivy didn't offer an acknowledgment. Was she uncomfortable having people look at her work? How sad. Ivy deserved recognition. She had talent, possibly even a great deal of it.

Ivy's passion for creativity showed by the number of completed art projects lining the wall.

Cooper's phone rang. "Excuse me for a minute." He stepped into the hallway to take the call.

Ivy's mood filled the room with tension. Wanting to ease whatever was bothering Ivy, Lora walked over and placed a gentle hand on Ivy's arm.

"I know it's hard to show your work to others, but...your pieces *are* wonderful."

Only minimal recognition showed on Ivy's face.

She patted Ivy's arm, letting her fingers linger for a moment, then wandered away.

"Ivy, you have an artist's eye for composition. I've always liked mixed-media creations. What you've done incorporating pages of books into your design is special. It's another form of repurposing, isn't it?"

Ivy affirmed with a slight nod.

"You know, I'm seeing more art galleries showcasing this type of art."

Ivy's face lit up. "Do you think I could sell these?"

"Probably. Bazaars and local shops would be the place to start. Or even sell online. If well-received, try making contacts in a retail store. It's certainly worth a try."

Ivy's smile rewarded her efforts to draw her out. Emma appeared pleased with the change as well. Ivy's shift in mood felt like a minor victory.

Her interaction with the girls was enjoyable. Young people were so energizing. When she returned home, she'd consider getting involved with teens. Teens could be the solution for livening up her life. Of course, she'd have to reduce her work hours to do so.

"Emma, this room is amazing—every creator's dream. How about you show me some of what you've made?"

"Well, Dad bought me some supplies for jewelry-making two birthdays ago. I've been experimenting with using old pins and earrings Nana gave me. I'm sorta trying to make statement pieces. Finding the right pieces to combine is hard. So is finding the time to work on them." She scrunched her face. "I think I like the *idea* of designing the best. The soldering is not so fun."

"You taught yourself to solder?" She picked up one piece for closer inspection.

"Dad showed me the basics. YouTube helped too. Though it's harder than it looks."

"Well, keep at it. It probably requires practice, though I think you've got something going here."

She pretended to think something through. "Hmm, I have some birthdays coming up and need gifts. Emma, would you mind if I bought one of your finished lapel pins? And Ivy, would you mind selling the canvas with the key on it?"

Both girls whooped with delight. Cooper entered the room again, chuckling at their antics. When he caught her eye, he nodded his appreciation. Obviously, he'd realized she was trying to support the girls' endeavors.

Watching Cooper talk with the girls made her heart thump. How she wished she could have had more children. She agreed with what Cooper said of having Emma—kids give you a reason for getting through hard times. Cooper appeared so comfortable around teenage girls. They were obviously comfortable around him. It showed that he cared about Ivy. It was fortunate Ivy had them in her life.

Funny. Something about Ivy pulled at her heartstrings.

Though Ivy was a girl of minimal means, she had the talent to create art out of anything. However, making inroads into an art career could be difficult. She wished she lived closer to help Ivy make her mark.

Cooper interrupted the girls' exuberant discussion about having a craft booth at a bazaar. "Now hold on a minute. Before this budding business venture takes over all your spare time, I want you girls to remember homework comes first. I don't want your grades dropping by taking on something like this." He clearly looked at Ivy, who hung her head.

"Okay, Dad. Ivy and I will talk about that."

Then Emma turned to her. "Lora, how much do you want to give us for the pieces?"

She grinned, loving the girls' enthusiasm for making a buck. To provide them with some business experience, she explained how to price their work. She was more than fair with her purchases, which elated Ivy in particular.

Afterward, Cooper took her downstairs to see his office. When they entered, he said, "Thanks. That was a nice thing you did for the girls."

"It was my pleasure. I'd forgotten how much I enjoy being around teens. In college, I volunteered at an after-school DECA club. I loved the teenager's enthusiasm and boldness for trying new things."

She'd been well-liked in the club and found teaching a version of what she'd learned in her college classes rewarding. Years later, she'd even received a letter from a student saying she had inspired him to enter business school. It was rewarding to know she'd made a difference.

Though those days weren't that long ago, the tragedy had eroded her previous opinions of herself. Emma and Ivy were nudging out some memories of past positive experiences. That felt like a blessing.

She clasped her hands behind her back and walked around Cooper's office. "Oh, this is cozy...though masculine, too."

"I try working late afternoons from home to give Mom more time off." He glanced around the room. "My office at work is pretty primitive compared to this." He nodded toward an enormous mahogany desk. "My crew would harass me if I had stuff like this at work."

She let her fingertips bump along the spines of what were mostly business reference books on the bookshelves. "From the looks of things, you're doing okay for yourself."

Cooper half-smiled and moved behind his desk to close his laptop. "Being in an economically depressed area, I'm proud we've been able to employ eleven full-time workers and four part-timers. We've expanded our sheet metal business by offering services and products that weren't available in this area before. We even registered a few patents for some unique pieces of equipment."

She leaned her back against the bookcase as they talked about labor shortages and training staff.

He sauntered around to the front of his desk. "In the past few years, we've landed a few out-of-state contracts. Now, I'm exploring what it would take to go international by transporting containers from the Port of Seattle or even Tacoma."

"Sounds interesting. What are your plans for making that happen?"

"I'm in the beginning stages of researching my options."

She pursed her lips. "I know a guy who's high up in a Tacoma shipping company. If you'd like to run your ideas by someone, he'd probably be willing to chat with you."

"That would actually be great. The timing is perfect." He stared at her for a few seconds. "Lora, you surprise me. And though I hate to admit this, your business savvy is a bit intimidating. In my field, I don't come across many women...or anyone like you."

She turned away, not wanting him to see how his comment pleased her.

She took a book from the shelf and acted like she was interested in the topic, giving her a moment to compose herself. Then she said, "Over the past four years, restoring order to the company I work for has provided a substantial number of educational opportunities. They were on the verge of bankruptcy. What I didn't know, I had to learn quickly. It was a desperate situation."

"Wow, they were lucky to have you. Hey, I'll definitely take you up on your offer to arrange that networking opportunity." He jotted a note on a pad. "Funny I met you as I was exploring if this idea could get off the ground."

"Next week, I'll give Ted Fogarty a call and see if he'd be willing to talk over your plans."

"Here's my card. Have him call or text me to set something up." He appeared to contemplate something as he gazed at her.

Goosebumps rose on her arms. As the evening progressed, Cooper revealed more attractive aspects of himself, which changed her initial opinion of him.

He seemed like a pretty amazing guy.

***

When they made their way back to the kitchen, their moms were sitting at the kitchen island, laughing while sharing a second piece of cake.

Claire looked up in surprise. "Oh, you caught us! This cake was so delicious, we *had* to have a second piece." Claire gave Mom a conspiratorial nod.

"Lora," said Mom, "Claire invited me to attend her quilting group tomorrow afternoon. They meet at the community center near where she lives. Afterward, she'll show me her adult housing complex. Would you mind my being gone all afternoon?"

"Not at all. You'd enjoy that. Claire, Mom's a beautiful hand quilter. Put her to work if there's a project."

"Nice to know. I'll reserve a spot around the quilt frame for her."

There was an awkward silence as she and Cooper stood in front of their moms, who seemed to be waiting for something to happen.

Eventually, Cooper comprehended his mother's not-too-subtle messages she'd been sending with her head and eyes.

"Um, Lora," said Cooper. "Looks like you're free for lunch and a tour of the area then. I could give you a local's point of view."

Before she replied, she glanced at her mother, who nodded her approval. "Um...sure, sounds great."

Her stomach fluttered as reality hit. Maybe she shouldn't go. What would they talk about? Would he ask her more about her past? The moms had put him on the spot. He probably felt pressured into asking? This surely wouldn't be a *date,* date?

"How about I pick you up at 1:00 pm, Lora? That way, we'll miss the after-church crowd."

"All right then. Sounds like a plan." She glanced at her mother, then at the door, trying to communicate that she was ready to leave. Her mother didn't notice. She walked to the kitchen counter and picked up the girls' carefully wrapped packages that they had brought down. To get her mom's attention, she had to resort to clearing her throat.

No reaction.

Frustrated, she turned toward Cooper. "Would the kind and generous knight please escort these two damsels back to the inn for an evening's rest?"

Chapter 6
Lora

Lora pulled her newspaper up higher when her mom became unusually chatty during breakfast. Since living alone, she wasn't used to disruptions during the quiet start of her day.

She yawned, having trouble focusing on what she read. Last night, she'd spent too many hours staring at the ceiling, going over everything that had happened at Cooper's.

In anticipation of his arrival that afternoon, she'd already lost her appetite.

Mom clunked her coffee cup onto its saucer. "Wasn't last night fun? Cooper's a terrific cook, and Emma would make an excellent pastry chef if she goes in that direction. Betty Leonard's granddaughter attended culinary school, and she's done well for herself."

"Hmm, bet they're proud of her."

She yawned again; her brain was mushy.

"Lora?" Her mother's voice grabbed her attention. "You should give yourself a pat on the back. You did beautifully last night. Your first social outing. How was it for you?"

"I was nervous at first, although I enjoyed my time with them, especially the girls. They were so much fun." The experience had boosted her self-confidence. Moving forward now seemed more attainable than she'd expected. The desire to build a more meaningful life was gaining steam.

In quick response to that thought, all buoyancy fell away. The familiar urge to suppress happiness took hold. Did she have the right to seek joy? Her little girl would never experience the type of excitement Emma and Ivy had exploring their future possibilities.

If she had taken that away from Maggie, how could she ever deserve to be happy? Frank believed her neglect contributed to Maggie's death.

Her jaw set. She was doing it to herself again. Whenever a bit of lightness came into her life, guilt and bitterness fought for dominance. That deep bitterness was a poison, killing the person she had once known herself to be. Bitterness was an ugly attitude she detested and fought.

To release the darkness inside, she drew in a long breath, hoping it would hold back the tears threatening to spill. She forced her focus back to what her mother was saying.

"And that house!" Rebecca steepled her fingers. "You know...Cooper hasn't dated a lot since his wife died."

When she didn't respond, her mother *harrumphed.* "Well, you seemed to like him. Didn't you?"

"Yes, Mom," she said in a low, cautious tone. "I like him. Don't get ahead of yourself. He's a great guy, and I'll enjoy his company today, but contact will most likely end after our trip." She flicked her head to confirm the finality of what today would bring, then returned to reading her paper.

"*Hmph,*" muttered her mom. "Claire's been a lucky lady to be involved in Cooper and Emma's lives. However, she's focusing on herself now. Nothing wrong with that in my book."

She peered over her paper

Mom raised an eyebrow. "Claire's sure a ball of energy. Imagine the age she was when she had to fill Karen's shoes. Toddlers can run you ragged. I remember when Maggie—" Mom stopped abruptly and sighed. She squeezed her hands together as she paused for a moment. "Maybe it's kept Claire young, though?"

Did Mom perceive her as being too fragile even to bring Maggie's name up? Over these past four years, that was likely the impression she gave.

Mom smoothed her fingers over the table. "It sounds like Claire's adult housing hosts functions to keep the residents active and social. That's nice.

I'm looking forward to my tour today." Mom glanced out the window at some seagulls. "I miss Carol. I don't begrudge her for moving close to her family. Yet, it's difficult to replace a friend you've had for almost thirty-five years."

"I know you've missed her. Especially after Dad became ill."

"Not having her made getting through it even harder. Carol had always been my go-to person for emotional support. She's a bright cookie. There's something to be said about having a friend who you—" She aimed her eyes at her coffee cup. "I've been writing emails to Carol. They've sort of become my form of journaling...about the transition I'm in. It's been therapeutic." Mom smiled shyly.

"Mom, I am sorry I haven't been emotionally available to comfort you more."

"Lora, it's healthy for both of us to have our separate support systems. What's going on in your life will always be a generation or more apart from what's going on in mine."

"But Mom—"

"Lora, we both have things we need to figure out...separately. I want you to be happy, and I know you want that for me, too." Her mom looked deep into her eyes to convey her sincerity. "You, my dear, are just getting back in touch with the woman you used to be. That makes me so happy."

They clasped hands.

Mom hesitated before she spoke again. "You know those emails I mentioned? Well, I gave Carol permission to share them with her new friends, many of whom are dealing with their own life transitions. They...well, they liked what I wrote and want more on the topic. They suggested I write a blog to help more women our age."

"Yeah?"

Mom withdrew her hand and twisted her wedding ring. "I've been thinking about it." She brushed an invisible crumb from her blouse and fussed with her collar. "Before I married, I'd wanted to write for the newspaper. It was a dream I let go with marriage." She looked up with wrinkled brows. "What do you think? Should I write a blog?"

She sat back. This could be good for Mom. "Blogs can be an enormous commitment. Yet, hey, if it's something you'd like to do, go for it! Do an online search for how to get started. I'm not familiar, though I'll help in any way I can. Heck, you should let me read some of what you've written. It might help me with *my* transition."

There was so much she didn't know about her mother. A blog. Imagine that.

"Mom, we have time for a quick walk on the beach. You up for it?"

"Always."

***

The tide was out, offering lots of beach surface to explore. She and Mom took separate, meandering paths down the shoreline. When she glanced over, Mom's posture was relaxed and her face looked content. So different from when they'd arrived.

Looks like coming here had been the right choice for them both, after all.

Immediately, sadness slammed into her chest. During her terrible time grieving the loss of Maggie, she'd never considered the impact Maggie's death had upon her parents. Especially her mom. Mom had had a special bond with Maggie. An apology was in order. Though Mom probably knew she'd been incapable of extending any comfort to anyone back then. Her grief, Frank, and then problems at work consumed her. Her anguish had blinded her from noticing anyone else's struggles.

With a heavy heart, she walked to Mom's side, took her hand, and gave it a little squeeze. When she leaned her head on Mom's shoulder, Mom reached over and patted her cheek.

For now, that communicated enough.

***

After their walk, she fidgeted as Cooper's arrival neared. She'd primped a little by reapplying her makeup, brushing her hair, and changing her shoes and top.

Now she couldn't sit still and started tapping her foot on the floor. Calm down. This isn't a big deal. Consider it practice for the future.

She jumped up as soon as she heard the knock. When she opened the door, her heartbeat sped up at seeing his approving smile. It had been a long time since she'd received a smile like that from a man. It felt amazing.

"Hi, I'll get my coat."

She texted her mom.

ME: LEAVING. HAVE A WONDERFUL TIME WITH CLAIRE. I'LL TOUCH BASE CLOSER TO DINNERTIME.

Today, Cooper drove a six-passenger SUV. "This is the rig Mom and I use to transport kids to events. I've been to all of Emma's games. She made the soccer team as a freshman, and next year she'll be trying out for the volleyball team. She's shorter than most of the girls, yet she's fast and plays strategically. That makes her a valuable player."

"I bet she's great." She enjoyed seeing his pride.

Cooper beamed as he talked of his daughter's athletic abilities. "She can be aggressive on the field or court, though that's not her general nature."

She playfully slapped his arm. "So says a dad with humongous pride for his daughter." Her cheeks heated, thinking he might take her actions as flirtatious.

Without knowing why, pride in Emma washed over her. She had taken to Emma instantly, so maybe that was the reason.

"Really, Cooper, it's terrific she's doing so well. The friendships among team members can be a valuable buffer from all the chaos going on during high school." That was how it was for her, anyway.

Cooper's sheepish smile quickly faded into a scowl. "Yesterday, you said things change in middle school. They do in high school, too. In this town, unless kids get scholarships, a lot of Emma's classmates won't make it to college. I'm worried about what will happen to Ivy." He strummed his fingers against the wheel. "I don't know about you, but college was one of the best experiences in my life."

She nodded in agreement. College memories brought a fleeting smile to her face. She'd met Frank during their junior year. Their youthful confidence bubbled over, believing they were equipped to create an amazing future together. They had never expected what was ahead of them.

To block the pain of her past, she attempted to live in the present. She wasn't always successful, especially during downtime. Now she questioned whether closing herself off from all of her memories had been a good idea. By not staying connected to her past, she'd lost valuable parts of who she had been. Before the accident, she'd had some amazing life experiences. By not allowing herself to hold on to those positives, her self-esteem had suffered.

Her trauma had kept her stuck in black and white thinking. She evaluated herself to be more unworthy than worthy. In doing so, she deemed herself undeserving of anything good.

If she couldn't reclaim her view of herself as a valuable, lovable human being, she would cower from life again. *Normal* would then be impossible to reestablish.

While she fought for herself, she'd have to expect setbacks. Guilt and sadness had the power to overtake her.

As Cooper's SUV took a hard bump over a pothole, it shook her out of her thoughts.

Cooper asked, "You okay? Been kind of quiet."

"I'm fine. You were mentioning your concern for Ivy?"

"Yeah, we saw some big changes as she entered middle school. Ever since, she's been riding the fence between having friends with kids who have goals and those headed for trouble. When she dropped out of sports, she went Goth, or grunge, or whatever they call wearing mostly black and ripped-up stuff." He made an *I-don't-get-it* gesture. "She's a good kid. The girls are like sisters."

"I saw that by the setup in Emma's room. It's nice you've made a place for her in your home."

"Ed and Judy, her parents, have struggled after Ed's car accident. Then he lost his job. A few years ago, Ivy's older brother got into trouble." Cooper drummed his fingers on the steering wheel. "Ivy's been moody lately. Things at home might be tough."

She liked Cooper even more, seeing how he cared so much about Ivy. "I'm sorry to hear that. I was wondering what was going on after seeing the condition of her home."

"Yeah, sad situation. Ed and Judy were high school sweethearts. Judy dropped out when she got pregnant. Ed graduated and had a job at the mill before the economy tanked. Ivy's been coming to our house almost every day since grade school. As a little tyke, Ivy made a shortcut through the woods to get to our place." He chuckled. "She reminds me of an oyster—hardened on the outside and mushy on the inside. It's impossible not to care what happens to her."

"She seems very sweet. But I see her closed-off parts. Gosh, that girl has impressive artistic talent, though."

"Yeah, she does." He scratched his head. "Emma said Ivy's been acting like a different person at school lately. Yet, around us, she's mostly a pleasant kid." He raked a hand over his chin. "I take that back. She's been defiant a few times lately, to Mom and to me."

It was clear Ivy mattered to him.

"Teenage life can be tough," she said, imagining it would be difficult for Ivy to navigate two households that functioned differently. She would hate for Ivy to alienate the Martins.

"I've stopped Emma from visiting much. Judy's a decent gal. I see her often at the Starfish Diner, where she works. The poor gal's been lookin' pretty beaten down these past few years. I imagine her job is the only thing keeping her family financially afloat."

She touched his arm. The desire to comfort him felt natural. It seemed like there were no barriers to openness and authenticity between them.

"Ivy's lucky to have your family in her corner. You're helping her see there are other types of family life."

She wouldn't ask, but was Ivy safe in her home? Her stomach churned as disturbing images tried to invade her thoughts. She distracted herself by gazing out the passenger window. As she breathed deeply, she clenched her right hand into a fist and pulsed her fingernails into the soft pad of her palm. Sometimes that worked to keep her brain from going where she didn't want it to.

When able to speak, she said, "You know, sometimes kids need a place to test boundaries. At Ivy's age, I suppose some defiance is normal as she tries to become her own person. She might not know how or when to do that, though."

The trees' changing height and shape were revealing their nearness to the coastline.

"I hope she gets through the next few years and sees a future she wants to head toward."

"Me too. Most of the time, we enjoy Ivy. So, for now, we're ignoring the behavior. If it gets out of control, we'll address it. Not being her actual parent, it's hard to—"

"Have her toe the line with any authority?"

"Yeah." He said, with tenderness in his voice.

When she spotted the Sea Breeze Restaurant ahead, she exclaimed, "I know this place! I read about it in a magazine."

The award-winning building had dramatic sweeping roof lines replicating a tall ship's sail. The restaurant sat on a cliff, with jagged rocks and scrawny fir trees flanking the building. As they walked to the entrance, the wind whipped her hair, and a saltwater mist moistened her cheeks.

Once inside, the restaurant's ambiance was as cozy as she'd expected. Someone had cleverly decorated the walls with old fishing paraphernalia. A cheerful hostess greeted them, wearing a white nautical blouse and a long, dark skirt reflecting the historical period when tall ships commanded the sea. The hostess escorted them to a booth facing the water. They sat across from one another.

They both ordered Cooper's favorite—fish and chips. The lightly battered halibut was crispy on the outside and tender on the inside.

Their conversation flowed easily. Cooper asked about her father. To her surprise, she laughed while telling stories of her dad's experiences in the fire service. With Cooper showing genuine interest, she relaxed and enjoyed herself.

"Tell me about your dad, Cooper."

"My dad was what you'd call a man's man. After high school, he worked on an Alaskan fishing boat, then came back here to open a hunting and fishing store. Dad's store was a hit in this community. He sponsored tournaments, that kind of thing. Everybody loved Joe Martin." With affection in his voice, Cooper said, "I loved him, too."

"I'm sure you miss him."

Cooper peered into her eyes over his glass of water. For a frozen moment, it appeared as if he'd lost his train of thought. Then he blinked and put down his glass.

"I attended college on a baseball scholarship and studied business, intending to take over Dad's store someday. When Dad died in a boating accident, we discovered the store was heavily in debt. Poor business decisions. Mom, who had never worked outside the home, had to take over the store. She insisted I finish college. By graduation, the store was doing okay, so I started an apprenticeship in my uncle's sheet metal business in Eastern Washington."

He drummed his fingers on the table. "Later, I took what I'd learned and started a sheet metal business here. I had a lot of help getting my business off the ground. I've been lucky. With my business affairs, anyway."

She nodded her sympathy, knowing he was referring to his wife.

After eating his last French fry, Cooper grinned sheepishly. "They have an amazing wild blackberry pie here. Share a piece?"

"I'm stuffed. Though who can pass up pie?" She loved listening to Cooper's stories. He had good reason to be proud of his daughter and his business success. She no longer saw him as arrogant. There was a lot to admire in this man.

As he spoke, every nuance in his expressions and how his restless hands assisted his communication captured her. She sensed he liked her—even knowing of her divorce and having lost her daughter. This gave her hope that maybe someday her past wouldn't be an obstacle to finding love.

Of course, Cooper didn't know the horrific details of the tragic event. If he did, he might change his view of her. As her pulse sped up, she tucked her hands under the table, squeezing her fingers. A reminder. She couldn't let her past take away her enjoyment of the present.

Cooper signaled the server and ordered a slice of blackberry pie à la mode. When it came, he fed her the first bite.

Her cheeks heated with pleasure from his gesture. "Oh my gosh, this is delicious."

He slid the pie plate toward her. She grinned as she cut a heaping forkful, then tried to balance an equal amount of ice cream on top. With one hand under the overloaded fork, she turned it around to reach across and feed Cooper the next bite. She giggled as he lifted his eyebrows.

"You're right. This is good stuff." Once they arrived at the last bite, his eyes twinkled as he offered it to her.

She giggled again. "This damsel has eaten far too much. Would the kind knight please accept the last tasty morsel as a token of her appreciation?"

With mirth in his eyes, he quickly stuffed the last bite into his mouth.

Their lighthearted banter provided a bit of a thrill. She was actually flirting!

"Cooper, the lunch and your company have been wonderful. Thank you for giving me the chance to experience this place. Please finish telling me about what happened next in your life."

He put an elbow on the table and placed a hand under his chin. "Hmm. Well, after my business took hold, I married Karen. We'd met at U Dub, yet we didn't get serious until one of her friends moved to this area and she started visiting frequently."

With a cocky smile, he said, "I think she had a crush on me. The attractive man that I was." He turned his head to give Lora a profile view while wiggling his brows.

She cracked up. "Well, naturally." It felt so good to laugh.

"Karen was the love of my life. We had the same dreams most young couples do. Emma came along quickly, and things were going well for us...until her diagnosis." He chewed his lower lip. "Mom sold the store and moved in to take care of both Karen and Emma. My business was expanding rapidly. I still regret not being around as much as I should have been...for all of them."

"I am so sorry, Cooper. Your mom is an amazing lady. Last night I saw how close you all are."

"We are. However, last year, Mom moved into her own place. She still picks Emma and Ivy up from school if Emma doesn't have practice. On my late nights, Mom gets our dinner ready. Otherwise, I take care of things." He wiggled his eyebrows again. "Hence my master chef skills."

"Ha, ha!"

"Mom unselfishly gave us a lot of years. I can't thank her enough."

"Oh, I think she probably got something out of it, too."

"Lora, I'm no saint. I should have done better in dealing with Karen's illness." He squinted and leaned back in the booth, twirling his fork on the tabletop.

His brow creased when he paused the spin. "I've read that kids will have to revisit the grief of a major loss at various stages in their lives. Like they always had to develop a new way of understanding death and how it affected them. I guess it's a lot for a kid. I don't know. That's why I try to protect Emma from further heartache. Logically, that's impossible, yet I try just the same."

Her heart pinched, recognizing his anguish all too well. Was he opening up to her because she understood the toll loss had on a person?

"It appears," she said, "you've done well handling everything you've gone through. The three of you are terrific people. A real inspiration for me."

Though she felt his remorse and the regret that often accompanies loss, it appeared he had moved past those feelings enough to live a successful life.

She wanted that for herself.

He raised his head and gazed into her eyes. "Emma's my reminder of where my priorities need to be. I'm so lucky to have her. She's my...my everything." He paused for a moment, then smiled sheepishly. "Wow. I haven't talked about this stuff for ages."

"It's probably good to talk about it occasionally." Who was she to give that advice? She's been closed-mouthed for years. "Could be we're comfortable doing so because we have so much in common." She felt safe with him and appreciated his honesty.

"Yeah, maybe so. What about your loss? Not just your dad, but your daughter and the divorce? That's a lot. How are you doing?"

Ugh. How much should she reveal about herself? "I'm afraid that the way I coped with my daughter's death, and then the collapse of my marriage, was to become a workaholic." She wrinkled her nose. "Distraction. Not necessarily a horrible thing, since my work success rebuilt my self-esteem...to some degree, anyway. The good thing was that work lessened the intensity of my day-to-day pain. Good, until withdrawing from the world became unhealthy."

As his eyes bore down on her, heat crept into her cheeks. She picked up her napkin and drew it under the table, nervously twisting it, while telling herself to keep going.

"My ex-husband, Frank, and I both held guilt over how our daughter, Maggie, died. However, he found it easier to blame me." She swallowed to dislodge the lump in her throat. "I think hating me helped Frank deny he hated himself. His grief, and possibly his self-blame, made him a different man from the one I'd married. All his hurt manifested as anger. He was angry with everything and everyone. Especially me." She paused. Cooper had been open with her, so she wanted to reciprocate. Sweat formed in her armpits.

"That...sucks." Cooper waited with soft, compassionate eyes.

"I swallowed the blame Frank dished out because I blamed myself. Because of that, I withdrew from family and friends." She tried to smile, but her lips barely moved.

Her voice grew steadier as she said, "It was my dad who stepped in to confront Frank about how he was treating me." She took a deep breath to calm herself before she could continue. "I'd never seen my dad so angry, or become physical with anyone. He slammed Frank against the wall. Got right in his face."

She raised her chin and squared her shoulders. "I didn't go home with Frank that night." She looked Cooper in the eye. "Having a failed marriage stung, though."

Cooper reached a hand across the table, palm side up, and she placed hers in his. He squeezed gently. "I'm sorry."

She focused on their clasped hands, trying to tamp down her anxiety. She wanted to tell him the story of how Maggie had died. What she'd said about Frank would make more sense then.

What would Cooper think of her afterward?

Her legs shook as she met his gaze. Seeing his clenched jaw, her eyes sprang wide with panic.

He noticed and took a deep breath to relax. "Pissed at Frank, is all. Go on." He smiled warmly, nodding for her to keep going.

"When Maggie—" She had to fill her lungs with a breath before she could speak. She kept her eyes glued to their hands. "We were at Frank's brother's house with a few other families. The men were building a workshop on the side of the garage. On that day, the trusses were going up. The kids were all playing in the front yard. Maggie was the youngest."

Her eyes filled with tears. She raised her head, beseeching Cooper to understand. "They had a sloped backyard with no fencing or landscaping to contain the kids, so we let them play out front." She lowered her head again. "I had been watching Maggie, but when it came time to get the lunches ready, my sister-in-law told her oldest son to watch Maggie while I helped in the kitchen." She licked her dry lips. "He was a good kid, so I thought Maggie would be okay." She paused and swallowed hard.

Cooper gently said, "You probably had every reason to think so."

His words helped her go on. "The kids were all running around playing tag. I guess it was Maggie's turn to be *it*. Apparently, she was chasing from behind, and, for some reason, she headed into the construction site. At that same time, a few of the men lost hold of a truss, causing some support braces to fall...on Maggie." She coughed as if something were lodged in her throat. "Frank was one of those men." With tight vocal cords, she said, "Her neck had been broken. She died instantly." Tears stung her eyes as she swallowed the lump of grief in the back of her throat.

Cooper stroked his thumb across her hand. "I'm so sorry. Horrible... just horrible."

She whispered, "So many people blamed themselves for what happened." She sat up taller. "I should have been there to stop her."

She squeezed his hand. "The *what-if game* has gone through my head a thousand times. I know I have to make peace with it, yet—" She gazed into Cooper's caring, non-judgmental eyes and felt safe. "You see, a large part of me believed I deserved Frank's blame and contempt. So grief-stricken, I didn't have the energy to stick up for myself."

She closed her eyes. When she opened them, Cooper's kind yet worried eyes met hers.

She wanted to assure him she was okay. "I'm planning a backbone-building exercise when I return to work. I'm way overdue for a more balanced life. There's so much I need to change about how I live my life. One step at a time—so they say."

"Definitely. One step at a time. Lora, I wish you'd be kinder to yourself."

She searched his face. Not encountering any disapproval, she felt strangely liberated. His attentiveness told her she was more than her past. She was a person worthy of being liked...and maybe even loved. Someday.

"Thank you for listening to me, Cooper, and for sharing, as well. My time with you, both today and last night, has given me an image of a family that has overcome a deep loss, then come out the other side. You'll be my reminder that brighter days are ahead."

"I'm so sorry that happened to you. And I'm angry as hell that Frank put all the blame on you." Cooper rubbed the back of her hand.

The warmth of his touch seeped in, caressing her vulnerable insides. A strength she thought she'd lost poked its head out. "My dad's dying wish was for me to let go of my past and start my life over. I'm finally going to take his advice."

She hoped Cooper could see her commitment was solid. "I've been trying to forgive Frank. He lost his child, and pretty much his relationship with his brother and most of his family. His anger and pain consumed him. He didn't know how to contain it, so he threw it at anyone who was near."

"I'm glad you left him."

"I am too."

"Lora, thank you for telling me. I know it wasn't easy. Healing takes time. Although you appear to be doing better."

"Trying my best."

After Cooper paid their bill, they walked the crushed oyster shell path to the bluff. The view from the edge was spectacular, and the saltwater spray invigorating.

Her time with Cooper had been transformative. He had given her the strength to take her hurts out of hiding, and his empathy allowed her to be empathetic toward herself.

This was a good start.

Cooper took her hand and pulled her around to face him. In his face, she saw a man who had grieved deeply. As she searched his face, she saw more—there was empathy, deep caring, and maybe—With his warm hands surrounding hers, she held his gaze, trying to decipher his feelings for her.

Pulling her closer, Cooper said in a low, tender voice, "Lora, I have a sense you're going to be just fine. No, better than fine. I honestly don't think you realize how wonderful you are." His thumb rubbed the back of her hand. "You're a beautiful and intelligent woman. And I—"

He gently caught a falling tear she hadn't noticed till then. She leaned into his touch.

"You deserve more than filling your days with work. That shouldn't be enough for you."

Watching his eyes as he spoke, hearing the sincerity in his words, her pulse kicked up. His words were like a soothing ointment, helping to heal the painful memories she'd shared with him. His nearness revved her heartbeat. Was he merely giving her a pep talk? Or?

Her skin warmed when his fingers caressed her face. Heat radiated through her body. She almost purred.

Slowly, he bent to place a gentle kiss on her lips. He lingered there, and she kissed him back. He tasted of blackberries and ice cream. His lips were soft and seductive. As the kiss deepened, her body heat rose.

Having nothing in her to hold it back, her hunger for intimate connection threatened to overwhelm her. A moan of pleasure escaped her lips. Wanting to touch his skin, she freed one arm from his embrace and slid it up to his chest, then to the back of his neck. She pulled his head down to deepen their kiss. He moaned, thrusting his fingers through her hair as he smashed his lips to hers.

Dazed by his reaction and her own need, she teetered. It had been so long since a man had wanted her this way, and for her to want, as well.

Cooper moved against her. She couldn't tell if he was responding to her need or his own.

And then—it was as if a switch had flipped. He stiffened and pulled away, separating their lips. He released a throaty groan.

Was he attempting to regain his wits and take back some control?

No, it was something else.

It was as if ice water had splashed her face. The hot, explosive energy between them swiftly receded, leaving an ache so intense she wanted to scream.

His abrupt change felt foreboding. She stepped back to explore his expression, forcing him to look at her. "What's wrong?"

With a resigned sigh, he leaned forward and placed his forehead on hers. His shoulders sagged as he released a sigh. Then he stepped farther away, dropping his arms to his sides as his face fell. "Lora, I'm...I'm sorry. I didn't mean to—"

"I don't understand."

He grumbled, "You're...you're going home tomorrow."

"What?" She shook her head. Was this really why he'd gone from sizzling hot to frostbite?

"Lora, I'm sorry. I tried a long-distance relationship a while back. It didn't work. It was too hard to manage the back-and-forth visits."

She squeaked out, "I'm only two hours away if traffic's good." Why did she say that?

He rubbed the back of his neck. "It's difficult to find a fair balance when you have a kid. When I was absent, I regretted missing out on what Emma was up to. I worried I was neglecting her. Also, I can't ask Mom to give more than she already has."

"Of course not, but—"

"I have to be here for Emma. And it wouldn't be fair to have the travel be one-sided. It would get old after a while. And there's no guarantee it would work out between us. Someone always gets hurt. I'm sorry. I am."

Her breath caught in her chest as the hurt of rejection spread through her. Why had she held such premature hope that something was developing between them? Now, Cooper's rejection was an affirmation that she wasn't worthy of his efforts to even try a relationship with her.

Tears threatened; she bit them back.

She sniffled. He won't even try.

Was it *really* because of his past experience, or was *she* the reason? Or could it be that he didn't want to try with *her*?

Cooper stuffed his hands in his pockets and said, "And, you probably haven't...you know, been dating much since the accident."

Meaning what, exactly?

He stepped up to put his hand on the small of her back, guiding her toward his SUV.

Don't cry. Don't let him see the hurt.

Why would he make the effort with *her*? Geez, she'd humiliated herself, acting like she was a wanton woman.

Don't cry.

The pressure and pain in her chest were nearly unbearable. What should she do? Continuing to be around him would be torturous.

As the SUV's engine came to life, she said, "Cooper, thank you for lunch, but I want to go back to the inn now."

"Are you sure? I could show you aro—"

"I'm sure." The detachment in his voice crushed her.

She turned away to peer out the window. To manufacture a façade of strength, she stiffened her posture.

She sensed his eyes upon her. "Lora, I'm sorry."

She kept her head turned and remained silent. If she spoke, tears might flow, or she might say something to embarrass herself even further. She had to get back to the inn as quickly as possible.

As they drove back, the cab was uncomfortably quiet. She sat up straight, determined to handle the situation with dignity.

Once she'd calmed down, she forced herself to examine the situation from Cooper's point of view. His explanation seemed somewhat reasonable. Still, it didn't seem adequate for the level of passion they'd shared.

Which meant...it had to be about her. She'd told him she'd failed as a mother and as a wife, all the while admitting she was still an emotional mess. Of course, he'd back away.

She swallowed and dug her fingernails into her palm, giving herself a different kind of pain to concentrate on.

Once she'd gained control again, she peered his way. Though he looked to be concentrating on the road, his expression held signs of distress.

She sighed inwardly. While in the restaurant, she was sure he had shown her genuine caring. He probably hadn't meant to hurt her with his rejection.

Not that this insight helped much.

When they arrived at the inn, he walked her to her door. She couldn't mask her sadness when she turned to say goodbye. He shook his head, sighed, and pulled her to him.

Unabashed, she laid her head on his chest. It felt like she was losing someone she'd known and loved for years.

He cleared his throat. His voice was husky with emotion when he said, "Lora, I know I keep saying I'm sorry, and I am. I just don't think a long-distance romance will work. It's better to stop now...to avoid hurting even worse later. I suppose—" He shook his head as a pained expression overtook his face. "I suppose maybe it's safer for *me* to do it this way. I just hate that —. Dang, I can only say I'm sorry."

As his chest expanded with a deep breath, her heavy head rose with it.

Stepping out of his arms, she said, "Please tell the girls how much I enjoyed meeting them, and your mom, too."

As she slipped through the door, her eyes were already tearing up.

Chapter 7
Lora

Lora shrugged off her coat, thankful her mom hadn't returned. She slipped into the bathroom and closed the door. As soon as she slumped onto the toilet seat, her head dropped into her hands. Her tears flowed as heavy sobs shook her body. Not long after, hiccups started, accompanied by chest pains with each eruption.

Why had she thought Cooper was the answer to her silent prayers? The universe wouldn't just drop a man like Cooper into her lap.

"He seemed so perfect! It all seemed so perfect." She sniffed and coughed, then blew her nose. Thankfully, her hiccups subsided. Spent from crying, her body deflated like a pricked balloon.

She whined, "I'd better think twice before telling my story to anyone again. How will I ever find a good man willing to take a chance on me?"

Grabbing more Kleenex, she blew her nose again. Her voice quivered with the disgust she felt for herself. "I made such a *big* fool of myself."

Her head raised when she caught a whiff of Old Spice.

She closed her eyes to focus on the scent. Occasionally, the smell of her dad's cologne alerted her to his presence. Sometimes, like now, she'd hear his voice in her head.

Shake it off. Focus on the next shot. With every loss, there's a gain.

Sports affirmations were his usual mode of offering support.

She considered his words, then sat up straighter and wiped her eyes. "You're right, Dad. There is a win in this. Cooper let me feel alive again, and desirable, for a few minutes at least."

She tapped her foot and swooped her arm. "After a bad swing, ya gotta step up to the plate again." She smiled. That was something Dad would have said.

At least this weekend had reminded her she missed people and missed having a man in her life. And beyond a doubt, she wanted to be part of a family.

Then there was Ivy. That girl took a spot in her mind and in her heart. She didn't know why, but she wished she lived closer to help her make her way in the world.

She threw up a hand. That's it! She'll focus on helping others to lessen her misery.

As quickly as it came, Dad's comforting scent disappeared. A slow smile rose on her lips. Dad's visits were weird. It was just like him to keep in touch, especially when she needed his advice or support.

"Thanks, Dad," she whispered.

With regained determination, she stood up to see her puffy eyes, and a swollen face in the mirror. What a mess she was. Before Mom gets back, she'll have to fix her face.

"Dad, as much as I cherish your visits, I'll keep them to myself."

***

After spending ten minutes on her face, she thought she'd done a bang-up job concealing the damage she'd done.

Mom noticed as soon as she came in the door.

"Lora, what happened?"

She tried to keep her voice neutral as she said, "I guess you could say I was overly sensitive to Cooper not wanting to further our relationship."

Mom looked her over for a few beats, then nodded. "Okay, I'll leave it at that."

Her legs felt weighted as they walked to a nearby restaurant for dinner. Once seated at their table, she relaxed. Mom overflowed with enthusiasm as she talked about her day.

"Claire has a wonderful apartment on the second floor of the complex. When she moved in with Cooper, she'd gotten rid of most of her furniture and household items. Now, her place looks updated without the forty years of *stuff* one would normally drag along."

"Nice." That was the extent of the response she could muster.

"The ladies in her quilting group were so wonderful. We sat around the quilt frame talking. It was...welcoming. I told them about my writing. They requested I put them on my email list. If I get my blog going."

"You will. Sounds like you had a good time."

"Claire participates in lots of the activities the complex offers. She said that after a move, it takes some effort to re-establish your social life." Mom smiled. "There's even a man or two interested in Claire."

With her chin resting in her hand, she murmured, "Good for her." Then she stared off into the distance, finding it difficult to engage in a conversation.

Mom backed off from talking until they'd finished their dinner. "Sweetheart, you seem out of sorts. You want to talk about it?"

She shook her head. "No. I don't want to talk about it. I'm just a little sad. Although I have enjoyed myself while we've been here." She reached for her mother's hand. "I think you have, too."

Mom frowned. "What happened between you and Cooper?"

"He's a pleasant person to be with, and I liked him a lot. For him...well, he thinks we live too far apart to start a relationship. I guess a previous long-distance experience didn't work out well."

The server came, and her mother took the check. "That's too bad. Claire and I were hoping—" She let the thought dangle. "You two seemed to have hit it off. Regardless, I'm proud of you for getting yourself out there. Keep it up."

"Thanks. I'll try."

***

The next day, heavy traffic slowed their commute time. It took over two and a half hours before they arrived at Mom's house. They hugged their goodbyes and agreed to see each other in three or four weeks.

It would be another twenty to thirty minutes before she reached her condo. As she drove north, dark clouds rolled in. The gloomy weather matched her mood. Not wanting to return to her empty condo, she turned off the freeway to stop by her office.

As she approached her desk, she sucked in a sudden burst of anger, then released it with a huge huff of frustration. Stacks of papers and multiple phone messages were stuck on the side of her inbox and computer screen.

Her fists and jaw clenched. "Rachael, this is how you handle my desk when I'm gone?"

She grabbed a pen and threw it across the room. "Seriously!" In a fury, she kicked her wastebasket. The sound of the metal cylinder hitting the wall echoed through the space.

She growled, "Rachael needs to step up. This is her company, after all!"

Her spine stiffened. She bounced her fist against her thigh as she stomped about the room. Her thoughts filled with overdue outrage.

After a few minutes, she calmed down.

This was silly and resolved nothing.

In business, she thought of herself as a practical, logical person. Her training had taught her to identify a problem, analyze the contributing factors, and make a plan of action toward a solution.

The issues at work were clear. So were the ways *she* let things get out of hand.

"It's time!" she declared.

She needed to stand up for herself and fix this. If she didn't, she'd never take back her life.

Staring at the results of her tantrum scattered across the floor, she cringed. She was better than that. As she picked up the floor, she wished all of life's messes were as easy to put back in order.

Tomorrow, she would schedule a meeting with the Goldens.

***

As she drove home, she reminded herself that after her world fell apart, the candy-distributing company had served an important purpose. It had been a relief when she found a job. She'd been out of the workforce for several years. Most importantly, her job provided a needed diversion from destructive thoughts and emotions. While rescuing the Goldens' failing business, she had gained valuable skills. While she saved their business from bankruptcy, she also saved herself.

A double win. Right?

However, those benefits had waned. Her resentment toward the Goldens had been escalating. Pete and Rachael continually handed substantial amounts of *their* responsibilities over to her. Initially, she found it helpful. A busy mind equated with noticing less emotional pain. Unfortunately, that practice morphed into workaholism, allowing the Goldens to take advantage of her. Small raises hardly compensated for all the hours she'd clocked, let alone the work taken home to fill her lonely weekends.

Now that the business was flourishing again, the Goldens were returning to living the high life by increasing their vacations and extending their holidays.

All thanks to her working her butt off.

It was getting harder to hold back sarcasm when they made their lazy requests.

On the flip side, she felt great about her accomplishments. She'd revived the company by refurbishing its business plan, installing a new inventory system, and revising the employee manual to tame the chaos. Initially, her request for the Goldens to spend only their designated salaries had worked. For a while, anyway.

She rubbed the ache in her diaphragm. Her bouts of heartburn had to be tied to the anger and resentment she'd suppressed.

Things needed to change. She'd love to just walk out the door. That wasn't her way, though. Before she'd allow herself to leave, she'd do what she could to stabilize the company...for the sake of the employees. She didn't need more guilt haunting her.

She set her jaw. First things first. Reasonable hours. Then—on to a life *outside* of work.

***

Her stomach felt on fire by the time she walked into her condo. She dropped her bag and hung up her coat in the hall closet. When she turned to face her living room, it was as if she saw it for the first time.

The place resembled a budget motel, minus the tacky artwork on the walls. Her walls were bare, and the room lacked personal touches to reflect who she was as a person. The space looked neglected, as if it were *temporary* housing for someone.

This wasn't temporary. It was the home she'd lived in for almost four years!

Why had she left it this way? Aesthetics had always been important to her. Yet, she'd never given her condo the love or attention it needed to become a *home*.

This was just another sign she'd let her past dictate whether she *deserved* to have pride in a comfortable, pleasing place to live.

Guess this was another area of her life she needed to address. Her only excuse was that when she'd bought the condo, she was barely functioning. A location close to work was the sole purpose of the purchase. When she'd moved in, she set up a functional space and called it good. Lord! She hadn't touched it since.

Who was she anymore? Her former self had loved decorating.

Okay, this is her blank canvas. How would she style this space to reflect who *she* was now? Gosh, there's the problem. She didn't know *who* she was anymore. Maybe it was better to think in terms of who she *wanted* to be?

Styling her space could parallel the transformations she wanted to make in her life.

Flutters of excitement swam through her chest. Her new mission would be *self-discovery*.

She plopped down on her ultra-sleek, uncomfortable couch and groaned. Nine years ago, Frank had picked out this couch, and she *hated* it. It definitely had to go.

If she were worthy of a new life, she was worthy of a new couch.

She glanced around the room again. If Cooper walked into her condo, what assumptions would he make about her? She winced. He would think she was a sad loser.

Geez Louise, why had she used Cooper as a reference? She rolled her eyes. *Because* there was no other male to pick from.

Loser!

Something bunched inside her like a cat ready to pounce. After seeing the problems more clearly, she wanted to attack them. Yet, decorating her condo was a minor task compared to the other areas in her life she had neglected.

Her excitement balloon deflated as her heart thumped in her chest. She'd need to address the part of herself that would self-sabotage.

Damm it! Her collapsed self-esteem affected *every* area of her life. She needed to do something. *Immediately!*

She ran to her laptop to search for therapists nearby. After reviewing their websites, she picked one and shot off a request for an appointment, along with a brief description of her history and problems.

A response came within a few minutes. The therapist had been online, dealing with a last-minute cancellation. Lucky for her, the flu and cold season opened up a spot for tomorrow afternoon.

A ragged sigh snaked through her. Telling her story again would be difficult, yet it had to be done. If she didn't do something, she'd never move beyond her past.

Exhausted, she crawled into bed early. Before turning off the lights, she wrote a short to-do list.

Buy some houseplants.

Unpack and hang her pictures.
Create a hiring proposal.
Set up a meeting with the Goldens.
Join some type of women's group, or volunteer (maybe with teens).
Buy a new couch and decorative pillows.

***

The next morning, for the first time in her career, she called in sick. She was taking a long-awaited and well-deserved mental health day. After breakfast, her mind filled with anxious chatter—what would she see on the therapist's face when she told her story? Would she judge her? Will she need therapy for the rest of her life to deal with all the garbage stuck inside her head?

To distract herself, she dumped two kitchen drawers onto the counter and reorganized them.

Once tidy, she still had time on her hands. She searched through packing boxes until she found a tattered, loose-spined copy of *The Bereaved Parent*. Years ago, a neighbor had handed it to her, saying it had helped her and her husband after they lost their child. She had never opened it.

Today, the chapter on *Bereavement and Guilt* called to her. She hardly blinked as she devoured the pages.

She was five minutes late for her appointment.

The therapist, Wendy Thompson, said, "I'm so glad I had the time to see you this afternoon. I read what you submitted. I can see why you're seeking counseling. How long ago was the accident?"

"About four years."

Once she'd answered a few more questions, her entire story spilled out. From the accident, to how she and Frank handled the aftermath of grief, to her father's dying request, to where she was now—wanting change.

Wendy interjected with observations, sometimes asked questions, or she would repeat something she'd said to emphasize her words. In doing so, her perceptions became clearer. While speaking to Wendy, she noted that some of her views had changed over time, while many remained steadfast.

Wendy shifted in her chair. "Frank was emotionally abusive. Did it go further than that?"

Her cheeks burned. "There were a few times he shoved me or grabbed my arm so tight it hurt."

"You seem embarrassed to say that."

"I'm ashamed I let it continue for so long."

"I imagine by the time Frank started the physical abuse, he'd already stripped you of your self-worth. That set you up to endure further abuse. You were even willing to sacrifice yourself to protect him from his pain. Both of you targeted *you* as responsible for your daughter's death, only because you had left her in someone else's care; someone you had trusted."

Wendy's eyes softened. "Thankfully, your father was intolerant of the verbal abuse he witnessed. And good for him for asking you to reevaluate your perception of the accident."

Wendy explained how Frank's need to deny any responsibility had caused him to distort his view of what had happened. He deflected his sense of guilt onto her while trying to survive his own pain, even while it devoured him. He needed her to be the bad parent to convince himself he wasn't.

As they talked, she gained some emotional distance, helping her view the unraveling of her marriage differently. Though looking back hurt, something heavy she'd carried dropped away. She felt lighter because of it. Silent tears slid down her cheeks. Her heart ached for her and Frank's misfortune. The accident had destroyed both of their lives.

Toward the end of the session, Wendy set aside her notepad and sat with a thoughtful expression. Then, with caring eyes, she said, "Tell me why you still hold the belief that Maggie's death was your fault?"

Her voice broke. "Because I was her mother. I should have been the one watching over her and keeping her safe." Her chin trembled as she fought back emotion.

"Had you ever left Maggie in the care of someone else before?"

"Yes, of course. Frank, my mom and dad, once Frank's parents, and a girlfriend of mine, a few times."

"Okay. Under their care, had Maggie ever gotten hurt? Say, a bruise, a pinched finger, choked on food, or even fell off the bed?"

"Yes. A few times." She remembered apologetic reports of minor injuries, which she understood to be typical for any child, especially one who had just become mobile.

"Did you blame those caregivers? Judging and blaming them for being irresponsible?"

"No. But, um...the things you mentioned happen to most kids at some point. They'd probably even occur under my care."

"Yes, that's true. Let's see. On the day Maggie died, you turned her care over to a twelve-year-old boy. Did you have any concerns that he wasn't capable of doing the job?"

She wound and unwound the edge of her cardigan sweater around her finger. "No, I knew Jacob to be a responsible boy. I believe my sister-in-law trusted him with Maggie because he regularly helped watch his younger siblings. I accepted her judgment."

Wendy nodded.

She reached up, grabbed a lock of her hair, tucked it behind her ear, then ran her fingers through it repeatedly. "Until the accident, the kids had stayed out of the construction site. We hadn't considered that that would change. However, when the kids were playing tag and it was Maggie's turn to be it, Jacob ran off to hide with the others. No one imagined Maggie would put herself in the exact spot where and when the braces dropped."

"Did you blame Jacob? Did you yell at him and tell him he was the one responsible for Maggie's death?"

"No! Of course not. The poor boy felt terrible about it. At the memorial service, he hung back from everyone, looking so sad and devastated. I had to assure him he held no responsibility for Maggie's death, that it had been a horrible *accident*. He needed to know I didn't think he was at fault. It would have been cruel to leave a child with that type of burden."

"Yes, so true. Then in your mind, Jacob, as a caretaker, was not at fault. Doesn't this confirm this tragedy was an *accident?* You also hadn't blamed Frank or the other men involved, either. Yet, *you've* carried the heavy burden of blame for over four years. Were you to blame? Did the truss slip from your hands so the braces would drop? Did you chase Maggie into the construction site with evil intent?"

She wanted to argue with Wendy's line of questioning. Wendy had boxed her in. There was no valid argument for being guilty of neglect. Or even the cause of Maggie's death. Nor could she blame the others for their part in the domino of circumstances leading up to Maggie's death.

Her shoulders slumped as a tear slid down her cheek. In a whisper, she said, "No, I'm not to blame."

"You are *not* to blame," affirmed Wendy. "An accident, a *tragic accident*, happened. It was unexpected and unforeseeable. One of the worst nightmares any parent could experience." Wendy's eyes were soft with understanding.

A warmth spread through her body as she accepted Maggie's death as an accident. There was no blame to be assigned.

You were right, Dad. It was never my fault.

A strange sensation coursed through her body. She had the odd sense of a thick, dark substance seeping out, leaving gaps behind. Sensing this ugly substance had been harmful to her, she assumed she'd feel relief. However, her focus turned to the empty spaces the release left behind.

Why wouldn't relief come? What would fill those voids?

No words could explain what she was experiencing. Troubled, she rubbed the dip on her neck.

Wendy's keen eyes watched her. "This might seem strange. Let's pretend for a moment that Maggie—she'd be about eight now, right?"

She nodded and leaned forward to grab a Kleenex from the table.

"Okay, then. If eight-year-old Maggie were sitting before us, what would she say to you about the accident?"

She shut her eyes, picturing a ten-year-old version of Maggie. In her head, she asked Maggie to tell her about the day of the accident. Once she quieted her mind, she heard the sweet voice of a young girl.

Mom, I made a mistake. Being a little kid, I thought I was tricking the other kids by going into where Daddy and the other men were. I didn't understand the game. Going in there was silly of me. Really dumb! Don't be mad at me or angry with anyone...even yourself. What happened was an accident. You couldn't have stopped it. Mom, I'm so sorry I had to leave you. I'm okay, though. Honest. I love, love, love you. I wish you and Daddy wouldn't be so sad. You were the best mommy ever! Mommy, remember to wish upon a star. Be happy again.

She sucked in a breath as Maggie's last words faded away. Keeping her eyes closed, she recalled how she would sing *When You Wish Upon a Star* to Maggie at bedtime. Afterward, they would make a wish for the next day, then indulge in one last hug.

Exhaustion came over her. As she slowly opened her eyes, another odd sensation zoomed through her chest. She put her hand there for a moment. When she was able, she told Wendy what she'd experienced.

"Nice," mumbled Wendy. "She asked you to be happy again. A similar request to your father's dying wish." Wendy glanced at the clock. "We don't have much time left. I want to teach you a technique called Box Breathing. I'll also send you home with a booklet on mindfulness exercises. You've had an excellent start toward acceptance and self-forgiveness. In the weeks to come, parts of that traumatic day, or those that followed, may surface. Often, they will be memories or images you've buried. We've opened up parts of that history for examination. If you experience feeling overwhelmed or anxious, you can calm yourself using this breathing technique. Also, try writing out whatever comes up in a journal every day."

"Okay," she said, her voice now an exhausted whisper.

This is good. Something concrete to do could be helpful. Her belly fluttered.

Was that hope returning?

At the end of the session, Wendy smiled reassuringly. "Don't worry, I'll see you again in a few days. Use the tools I've given you, and know I'll be expanding your toolbox as we go along. As you move your life forward, you'll soon have the tools to handle the past and whatever else comes along. We'll also explore what kind of life you'd like from here forward. When you can see yourself worthy of the good stuff again."

CHAPTER 8
LORA

When Lora returned to work the next day, a few warehouse workers asked about her trip. Not wanting to reveal too much, she fabricated a positive spin—which was *mostly* true.

"I had a lovely time with my mom. We met an amazing family, and they helped us get to know the area better."

To give herself a few days to catch up and prepare, she set the meeting with the Goldens for Friday.

***

When Friday came around, she stopped outside the Goldens' office door. Outside the door, she heard their raised voices.

Oh boy, they're in bad moods! She took a few calming breaths to slow down her racing heart. No need to be anxious. She was well prepared.

Now or never.

She knocked firmly on the door.

Their voices hushed. Rachael called out, "Come in!"

"Good afternoon," she said. With a forced smile, she walked into the room.

"Lora, we were just wonderin' what this meeting might be about. You're making us a little nervous." Rachael fluffed her teased hair as she bit the edge of her lip, smudging her tangerine lipstick. Then Rachael stood and tugged down her thigh-high pencil skirt.

"I didn't mean to cause you any stress. Thank you for seeing me. I'll get to the point so you can go home."

"We're all ears, so take your time," said Pete, eyeing the Krispy Kreme donut box open beside him. From the powdered sugar down the front of his shirt, he'd been indulging again. Pete patted the seat beside him, sending his wife a look that seemed to ask her not to get so ruffled.

Over the years, she'd learned Pete was a late-in-life baby; an only child coddled by parents who neglected to prepare him to inherit the candy-distributing company. Initially, she'd felt sorry for him. Those feelings faded as Pete avoided anything that made him uncomfortable. Attention to detail was his nemesis—along with his obsessive need to make his wife happy. Pete lavished Rachael with gifts and romantic trips. Making Rachael happy had put their business finances at risk.

Lora sat, then placed her notebook on her lap. "I've been working here for almost four years, and I can truthfully say I've contributed to your success and the expansion of the business. I think you know I'm stretched thin with all the duties I perform, working a fifty-plus hour workweek." She paused, then firmly said, "This has to change."

Pete and Rachael stared at her, bug-eyed.

Forcing an assertive tone, she said, "I have a draft of a job division proposal for you to look over. I'm suggesting an additional one to two people in the office. If you have any thoughts about this, I would appreciate your input."

Pete and Rachael turned to one another with raised eyebrows and erupted into nervous giggles. Rachael let out an enormous *whoosh* of relief. "Oh, Lora, we were worried you were gonna quit on us! You're so right; you need more help. We talked about this before you came in."

Pete nodded. "We want to offer you a percentage of the company. Though it's only ten percent, it's our way of saying thank you." Pete must have seen the confusion on her face, so he quickly said, "You can still add staff!"

Rachael twirled a loose strand from her updo. "You turned this company around when you came to work for us. You have a right to ask for more than what you're getting." She jiggled her body wildly as she bounced. "Hell, let's give you a new title and a pay raise, too. After all, you're gonna supervise the extras!"

A little red-faced, Pete nodded. "Your proposal of a job division is probably overdue. I'm sorry we didn't think of this earlier. We'll leave the decision of how many hires up to you. You know what their qualifications should be." He rubbed his chin. "You should do the hires. We trust you explicitly." He smiled, looking pleased with his idea.

Rachael cocked her head and gave her a wide-eyed stare. "How does that sound, honey?"

"Well, um...great, I guess. But that will require some extra work." Again, the Goldens had dumped their responsibility right back into *her* lap. "It will probably be worth it in the end, though."

She clenched her teeth. Something about their generosity was troubling.

"I should probably consult an attorney after you draw up a draft of the share transfer. Um, on second thought, how about you hold off until after the staff hires? Thanks, though. That's a generous offer."

"We should've been the ones to have gotten the ball rolling," said Pete. "We rely on you a lot. I think you know you're the brains of this company."

Rachael giggled as she paraded over to pull her into a hug. "You're our girl, Lora. Don't forget that!" Rachael's arms surrounding her felt suffocating. When Rachael let go, she asked, "You happy, honey?"

"Um...yeah, sure." This whole interaction didn't seem right on so many levels. "Let me think about everything. How about we talk more on Thursday next week? Say...one o'clock? I still want you to review the draft of the job divisions. We'll talk more about the rest then."

Rachael patted her hair. "Honey, how about 3:30? I got a salon appointment at 1:00."

***

That night, she sat in her kitchen and wrote out the pros and cons of the Goldens' offer. A percentage of the company bothered her. Even a small percentage of ownership would suck her into taking on more responsibility. Was that their plan? Working more wouldn't fit with her new goal of expanding her personal life. What she needed was more free time to create a more meaningful life than *just* work.

Now she had a crapload of work to get done, with hiring and training the new staff. She groaned. The Goldens kept handing over jobs *they* should be responsible for, or at least be involved in...always with big smiles on their faces. Why not? They'd ditched their work and put it in her lap.

Nope. She didn't want a percentage of the company. She only wanted to be an employee, with regular hours and clear responsibilities for the position she held. Boy, oh boy, that would require establishing healthier boundaries. Her sanity would depend on it if she were to continue working there.

She dropped her head onto her palm, questioning how solvent the business was. After the successful expansion of the business, she returned more financial control back to the Goldens. Now signs were showing things were slipping again. Over the past four months, angry suppliers claimed they hadn't received payment. She sent them over to Rachael, who was the one who would cut their checks. Hopefully, Pete's accountant would keep them abreast of the company's bottom line.

Crud. The hard truth was that she had no true control over her bosses' actions. She didn't want to return to a *parenting* role again. How silly of them to believe they had earned her loyalty. After she trained the new hires, she would consider a job change.

She raised her head from her hand. In situations like this, she would have called her dad for advice. What about Cooper? No, she couldn't call him. It would look like an excuse to contact him. That wouldn't be fair to either of them. They'd never spoken of staying in touch.

Regardless of the hurt he'd caused, she would follow through with arranging the shipping contact for him. She wanted him to succeed in his plan.

Why did her mind continue to float back to Cooper and his family? Even Ivy still wandered into her thoughts. Having met them shifted something in her, yet thinking of them only darkened her mood. She couldn't let herself get stuck in *if-only* thinking. She had to accept and move on.

CHAPTER 9
LORA

A few extra weeks flew by before Lora had a chance to visit her mom. En route, the traffic was slow, so she took the opportunity to mentally check off what she had accomplished from her personal to-do list. Taking work home had hindered her progress, although she was happy with her small achievements. Her condo was already looking *homier*. The green foliage of her new potted plants had softened the living room's hard edges and brought more pleasure than she expected.

It had been difficult to find the packing boxes with the pictures she wanted to hang. Most of the boxes were unlabeled. After selling the house, she'd thrown things in without marking the boxes. While she hunted through them, she'd discovered a hodgepodge of surprises. The holiday decorations had brought a heaviness to her chest. In the past few years, traditions and the magic of the holidays had all but vanished.

She squeezed the steering wheel. Not this year. She would create a special tribute to Maggie and her father's memory.

With her next breath, satisfaction freed the tightness in her chest.

When the traffic finally picked up speed, she figured it would be fifteen more minutes to her mom's house. When an SUV wedged in front of her, she was forced to stare at the back window decals depicting each family member as a Star Wars character. Her shoulders drooped as she slouched in her seat.

Would she and Frank have had more children if the accident hadn't happened? She'd been thinking more about their marriage lately. Therapy really had shaken things loose. Where was Frank now? There was no one she could ask. By the time he'd moved out, Frank's family had already ghosted her. Frank had said such cruel things to his family. Would it ever be possible for them to patch things up?

Inquiring would be too uncomfortable...and there really wasn't a reason to know.

She put her blinker on, wanting to merge into the right-hand lane. Therapy had been challenging but rewarding. Daily, she'd sensed she'd made progress. If anything, the stack of personal growth books on her nightstand revealed her commitment.

Some bittersweet moments came up when she'd found her *Maggie* box. Inside were the pared-down mementos of Maggie's favorite possessions, and some special items significant to her. She'd lost herself in touching, smelling, and caressing each one. After a few minutes of sadness, those feelings gave way to counting the blessings she'd received while being Maggie's mom.

Maggie's toddler years had been delightful. She'd been a vocal girl from day one. It had been surprising that when Maggie could form actual words, her vocabulary grew at lightning speed. Maggie was so good-natured and expressive. Her babble was adorable. That little girl was always eager to share whatever was significant to her. Her face would light up.

Would she ever be so lucky as to have a child like her again? Her fingers curled tight around the steering wheel.

She was getting older. Anyway, another child could never replace *her* Maggie.

Oh, sweet girl, you were the greatest joy of my life.

Wendy had told her grief had layers you had to peel your way through. Until recently, she hadn't even considered selling the home where she had built her family as another significant loss, layered within all the others. Selling the home had been lumped into *the one big consuming hurt.* Man, that was a difficult time.

As traffic slowed again, she drank from her water bottle. Weekend traffic was such a bear. She chuckled. Hadn't she offered to drive to Cooper's on the weekends?

Oh, no you don't! Not going down that rabbit hole!

Better think of something else. What more had she accomplished on her list? Not much. Her framed pictures still lined the hallway floor, awaiting their perfect spot to be revealed.

She had to give herself credit for writing in her journal nightly. This proved to be a helpful tool, along with all the other things Wendy had added to her therapeutic toolbox.

She gave herself a mental high-five for using them.

***

As she pulled up to her mom's house, her mouth flew open. Workers were covering shrubs with tarps, and a guy in paint-spattered overalls was unloading paint buckets from a van parked in the driveway.

Mom hadn't mentioned she was going to have the house painted. It didn't even look like it needed it.

Since the front door was ajar, she walked in calling, "Mom!"

"I'm back here, in the spare bedroom!"

She maneuvered around storage boxes stacked in the hallway, some with open lids and newspapers spilling over the sides. She lifted the paper in one and peered inside.

"What are you doing? Why are all these boxes out here?" Her brows pinched, noting her dad's things were inside the boxes. "Are you getting rid of Dad's stuff already?"

Mom's response was sharp. "After the memorial, I asked your brother if he wanted any of Dad's fishing gear. He didn't. So, the thought came to me — I should take it down to the fire station. The men might want it for themselves or their kids."

"Oh, okay. Why are you having the house painted? It doesn't appear to need it."

Out popped Mom's head from the closet. With a stern gaze, she brushed the hair out of her eyes. "I'm getting ready to put the house up for sale. I could probably stay longer, but it's too much to take care of." She shook her head. "It's more responsibility than I want right now."

"Okay, I get it, but where would you live then?" Her breathing quickened.

"Your brother asked me to come to Minnesota. Though I'm not sure that's the best place for me. Temporarily renting is always an option. I'm not sure yet." Mom looked at her with fire in her eyes. "I haven't decided. Please...can you trust that I'll do what's right for *me?*"

Mom gave a little laugh and shrugged. "Still exploring my options."

"But—Will—" She halted when Mom's palm popped up. Then she proceeded more cautiously. "Mom, may I ask if you've considered moving closer to me?" She let the question hang as she fidgeted with an open tin box of fishing lures sitting on a side table. She couldn't imagine Mom not living close by. If she chose Minnesota, would it mean she loved her brother more?

"Yes, sweetheart. I have. Minnesota isn't the only option I'm considering." Her eyes narrowed. "I don't want you and your brother to create any sort of jealousy over where I live. I know you've always thought I favored your brother, but don't forget, you were a daddy's girl!" She looked away.

It was true. Alliances had formed early in their household, especially since Mark showed no interest in sports while she possessed natural talent. Dad's favoritism gravitated toward where his interests lay. Her mother's empathetic heart turned to nurture Mark, whose self-esteem had always lagged hers.

Dad had been a softy with her. So, when she'd tried to assert herself in her teens, it was she and her mom who butted heads. It wasn't until college that she grew to appreciate her mother's influence on her.

Mom was back searching through the closet.

This time, she changed her approach by softening her tone. "Mom, if you plan to move, I would like you closer to me. I want to... be available to help when you need it."

Mom swerved around with pinched lips and sparks in her eyes. Yet, within a few beats, the frustration on her face receded. Mom sighed, walked straight over to her, and wrapped her in her arms. "I know," she said. "It would be hard for you not having any family around." She held her close and whispered in her ear. "Let me decide what to do. I have to figure this out myself."

"Okay. Okay." Yet anxiety still swarmed inside her chest.

***

They spent the rest of the day baking cookies to take to the fire department, along with the fishing gear. In memory of Dad, they made his favorite cookie—oatmeal raisin, with extra cinnamon. Before long, all tension between them vanished.

After they stacked the cookies in boxes and packed the fishing gear into the car, they headed off to the fire department's main headquarters. Most of the men greeted her and her mom by name, and many hugged them warmly. They joined the firefighters for coffee and a sampling of the cookies. The fishing gear sparked the telling of fishing stories. By the time they left the station, her jaw hurt from smiling.

When they got back into the car, she said, "Mom, coming here was not only good for us, but I think it was good for the guys, too. You heard how much they miss Dad. A few of them even teared up as they told their stories."

***

On Sunday morning, they worked alongside each other making a big breakfast, similar to what they'd done when she was a girl. Afterward, they leisurely sipped their coffee.

"Your dad was such a problem-solver and a protector. I imagine that's why he loved the fire service. He had a way with people. That came out so clearly from the testimonials at his memorial service."

"Those were special to hear."

Mom twirled her loose wedding ring on her finger. "I miss him. When something comes up that I'm confused about, I sit in his recliner and talk to him." She peered over at the urn sitting on the family room bookshelf. "I always feel better afterward. Though you know—" She drew in a breath and released it slowly. "Sometimes that man frustrated me. He meant well, I suppose, yet he didn't let me—or maybe he didn't *trust* I could do for myself. He was always steering me toward what he thought was best. That irritated me." She raised a shoulder. "Though often he was right."

She could relate. Dad had done the same with her often.

Mom's expression darkened. "I regret the day I lit into him. He was so very ill but kept talking about what *I* needed to do when he was...gone." She pushed the last word out as if it were a bitter pill. "That irked me!"

Mom's cheeks reddened. Was it from her anger or embarrassment? Outbursts were uncharacteristic of her.

"By then, I was so tired and full of anger. I just blew up. He didn't deserve that." She averted her eyes. As if to busy her hands, she swiped the breakfast crumbs off the table.

Mom's candor was rare, so she kept quiet, thinking Mom might need some space to process whatever was on her mind. This was their first woman-to-woman conversation. It seemed fragile in its beginning stage.

With a softened voice, Mom said, "I loved that man, although I depended on him too much. He seemed to like it, though. Dad needed to be needed."

This openness was such a change. Mom's blogging must have helped her become more comfortable revealing her inner thoughts.

Slowly, Mom stood, as if she were pushing against something that weighed her down. She gathered their dishes and proceeded to load the dishwasher. "Dad was always fun-loving, yet he preferred being commander-in-chief. That frustrated the hell out of me sometimes." She chuckled as she picked up the butter. "That's the messy stuff that comes from being married for so long."

What Mom said gave her a different view of the dynamic between her parents.

"Mom, I was lucky to have both of you as parents. Your two personalities created the balance I probably needed."

"Thanks, dear." Mom's words came out in an emotional whisper as she thumped the spot where her heart lay.

Seeing Mom's emotions triggered her own. She sprang from her chair to comfort her mom with her arms. There wasn't anything she needed to say. Her arms were an acknowledgment of her mom's emotional struggles and expressed how much love she had for her.

***

During her drive back to her condo, she thought about why her mom hadn't consulted her on the sale of the house. It irritated her that her brother was in the know first. Yet, of course, he would. He called Mom every Sunday. Shoot! She needed to do better in supporting Mom during this difficult time.

Mom revealing Dad's dominance helped her see why independent decision-making would be an important step for her. Mom deserved her respect; she was smart, capable, and had great judgment. From now on, she'd be more careful not to offer unsolicited advice.

It was probably best she held back on revealing how selling the family home was another horrendous loss for her. Mom's home was not *hers* to have influence over. Her focus should be on creating her own sense of *home* in the place she lives.

She slumped back into the seat. It seemed like every valued, tangible part of her past was disappearing. Without the people and things that made up her past, could she still connect with who she used to be? She felt her heart beat a little faster.

Today highlighted the strained relationship she had with her brother. She hadn't spoken to him since Dad's memorial. They'd hardly spoken in the years before that. On her end, she'd held a grudge ever since he hadn't bothered to come out for Maggie's memorial. To be honest, their history of jealousy was real. Long ago, a wedge had grown between them. The effort to remove it always seemed too exhausting.

CHAPTER 10
LORA

The following week, a text message pinged on Lora's phone as she was reading one of her many self-help books. It was from Cooper's daughter, Emma.

EMMA MARTIN: LORA, I WANTED YOU TO SEE THE QUILT I FINISHED FOR IVY. THIS PICTURE DOESN'T DO IT JUSTICE, BUT WHAT DO YOU THINK? IVY AND I WERE DISAPPOINTED WHEN YOU LEFT WITHOUT SAYING GOODBYE. WE HOPE THAT IF YOU EVER GET BACK THIS WAY, YOU'LL VISIT US AGAIN. DON'T MENTION THE QUILT TO IVY. IT'S A SURPRISE. SHE SAID SHE MIGHT TEXT OR EMAIL YOU SOMETIME. ~ EMMA

So unexpected. How should she respond? She couldn't imagine Cooper wanting Emma to develop a friendship with her. Keeping it simple would be best.

ME: EMMA, LOVE THE COLORS AND THE PATTERN YOU CHOSE. IT SEEMS PERFECT FOR IVY. YOUR FRIENDSHIP IS A SPECIAL GIFT TO BOTH OF YOU. I HOPE YOU HAVE A FANTASTIC UPCOMING SUMMER BREAK. I APOLOGIZE FOR NOT SAYING GOODBYE. PLEASE KNOW WE HAD A WONDERFUL TIME WITH YOUR FAMILY. YOU ARE AN IMPRESSIVE YOUNG LADY. I STILL REMEMBER THE TASTE OF THE SCRUMPTIOUS DESSERT YOU MADE. LET IVY KNOW I WOULD ENJOY HEARING FROM HER. ~ LORA

She tapped her foot on the floor, sighing. Just when she'd made progress putting Cooper out of her mind, Emma's text plopped him right back into her thoughts.

That night, she couldn't sleep. Her longing for Cooper and the girls was useless. They were another *past* she had to free herself from in order to move forward.

***

Bringing on extra staff was finally on the horizon. The Goldens had OK'd one full time and a part-time hire. She would bring the part-time staffer on later. Last-minute, she pitched to sponsor a marketing student from a nearby college for an internship. An intern would require extra work. Yet, she liked the idea of paying it forward. Her college internship had been invaluable. It would be rewarding to give a student a step up through actual work experience. A chance to collaborate would be a terrific experience for both of them. She only hoped that the additional staff would make coming to work more bearable.

She recruited two men from the warehouse to rearrange the office to accommodate the new furniture.

"If you use the diagram I sketched out, you'll only have to move things once. Trust me, you'll be back in the warehouse in no time."

When they were done, everything fit perfectly.

While setting up the new workstations, she discovered she had forgotten to order mouse pads. No problem. There was an office supply store within walking distance. She deserved some fresh air, anyway.

She popped her head into Rachael's office. "I'm walking to the office supply store to get a few things I forgot. Would you cover the office and phones?"

"Are you gonna be gone long? I don't wanna go out front. See these red splotches on my face? A cosmetic reaction." Her whiney voice was so irritating.

She wasn't going to argue. "I'll just switch the phones over then. See you soon."

Ever since she'd turned down shares in the company, Rachael had been upping her subtle, passive-aggressive behavior. Could Rachael be astute enough to notice her growing disdain?

She shrugged. Soon she'd be exploring new job options. Her heart fluttered, considering which business sector she'd like to investigate. She was so ready to move on.

Once outdoors, she turned her face to the sun. It felt wonderful.

She needed to keep her growing irritation with Rachael in check for a while longer. Her biggest victory was getting the Goldens fully on board with her staffing plan.

Once she'd trained the new hires, she'd reward herself with some needed time off. A vacation would do her nicely.

Wendy suggested focusing on creating a more exciting life, which would make it easier to let go of disappointments. If she continued her self-care and took steps to build new relationships, she'd have an exceptional life, making it possible to work for the Goldens a little while longer.

As she strolled up the hill toward the office supply store, she neared a furniture store display window. When she walked by, she perused the front window. Boy, she'd love to replace that horrible couch of hers.

Being dutiful, she continued up the hill, daydreaming about the color and style of the couch she might buy. She'd been watching a lot of HGTV lately to get ideas.

***

On the way back from the office supply store, she slowed her pace again to peer deeper into the furniture store window. After she passed the window, she quickened her steps to reach the next intersection. When she had to wait at the crosswalk, she looked back at the furniture store. It won't take that long for a quick walk-through. Ten more minutes wouldn't hurt...would it? She could consider it her coffee break.

She pivoted and race-walked back up the hill.

Buying a new couch would become her shining symbol of no longer being anchored to her past. Thanks to her therapy sessions, her shackles were gone. She would keep moving forward.

With a discerning eye, she whizzed through the furniture displays. Once she found a couch style she liked, she asked to take home a fabric sample book.

On the walk back to her office, a snappy tune popped into her head. She hummed and swayed to the beat. It kind of felt like she'd been playing hooky.

The furniture store prompted thoughts of Mom's move. If Mom moved farther away, she wasn't going to view her choice as a rejection; she'd see it more as her mom prioritizing what *she* needed and wanted in *her* life.

Gosh darn. When she wasn't so needy herself, it was easier to see what *others* needed from her.

As she slipped the borrowed fabric sampler alongside her file cabinet, she noticed the travel brochures at the corner of her desk. She had purposely placed them there as a reminder to focus on her future. Her travel savings account was gaining funds. A trip to Ireland should be possible in a year or two. If she had to live solo, she'd plan for something amazing to look forward to. She grinned. The world ahead was full of possibilities!

Rachael stuck her head out her office door. "Good. You're back. I'm switching the phone back over." Her face held a scowl.

"Sure."

She wouldn't let Rachael squelch her good mood.

When she turned down the shares in the company, she'd surprised the Goldens. This gave her the opening to ask for two extra weeks of vacation, a long overdue bonus, and reimbursement for a class on managing staff. They agreed to it all, seemingly happy to keep her on as an employee. However, as she made her requests, Rachael's demeanor clearly showed she was miffed. Things between them had been strained ever since. Now they avoided each other as much as possible.

***

In celebration of the first day of summer, she walked to work. It was glorious. When she arrived ten minutes early, she smiled her appreciation to her new hire, who was already there.

This was working out well.

"Hi, Meagan." She expected a cheerful response, yet none came. As she drew closer, she saw the distress on Meagan's face.

"I'm sensing something has gone terribly wrong."

"Um, you might say that?" Meagan wouldn't meet her eyes. "Um, remember I mentioned a while back I had a boyfriend stationed at Lewis-McChord?"

"Yeah, the romantic one your family loves. He's not being deployed, is he?"

"No, they *promoted* him. They're sending him to Fort Knox, Kentucky. So, he asked me to *marry* him. I said yes. I'm sorry. I have to give my notice."

"Oh." To tamp down her irritation and give her time before she responded, she took off her jacket and put her purse under her desk.

Meagan paced slowly in front of her. "We don't have much time to get the wedding arranged before he—I mean, *we* leave. Could you let me go ASAP? I'm sorry, Lora. I've really, really enjoyed working with you."

Oh crap! So soon? Her stomach lurched.

Meagan's pleading eyes said, *please let me go right now. I have a wedding to plan.*

"First, congratulations. Of course, I'm disappointed. You are a fast learner, and you've been perfect for the position." She let out a long sigh. "Let me see if my second-choice candidate is still available. I'll do my best to get you freed up as soon as possible."

She plopped into her desk chair. Things *had* been falling into place. The other candidate had definitely been her *second choice* for a reason. Darn. There wasn't time for another round of recruitment and interviews.

Okay, she had a call to make.

CHAPTER 11
IVY

As Ivy weaved her way through the crowded hallway at Orca High, she spotted Emma walking toward her, wearing a huge smile.

Well, she's happy about something.

"Ivy, guess what? Crissy's family asked me to go to Kauai with them this summer. Dad knows the family, so I think he'll let me go." Emma was bouncing like a bobblehead while waiting for her response.

Her spine stiffened. "Oh, great. You'll be gone most of the summer then." Sarcasm dripped from her every word.

Immediately, she dropped her head toward the floor. She was being a crappy friend. Aw, buggers. What was she gonna do with Emma gone so much of the summer? Shoot. Emma was going *everywhere* with *everyone* else.

She blurted out, "Well, I can see my summer's gonna suck."

When she looked up, Emma's face had fallen.

She quickly shrugged a shoulder. "Hey, it's okay. I gotta get a job anyway. Just haven't figured out how yet."

Emma smiled her relief. "Cool! What kind of job are you getting?"

"Any kind that pays me money."

They stood awkwardly as other students slithered around them.

"Gotta go," said Emma. "Hey, did you ever get in touch with Lora?"

"Nah, it was just one of those had-our-moment things."

"No, she's pretty cool, and she might have some job or money-making ideas." Emma waved and scurried down the almost empty corridor.

For a moment, she stood there, watching Emma with resentment building in her heart. As the ache in her chest grew, she hugged her notebook close. Then she turned and trudged off to class. Her summer would be a total bore, sitting around the house day after day. She'd have to listen to her dad yelling, or worse, deal with Derek's harassment. Her life sucked!

Her mood worsened as the day moved on. She'd switched from feeling discouraged to feeling anxious and depressed. The other kids were getting hyped about their summer break plans. She had nothing to be jazzed about. What kept nagging at her was that maybe Emma's other friends were becoming more important to her. It sucked depending on the Martins to help her feel ...what? Like she mattered to someone? If she lost Emma, what would she have?

***

A few days later, despair pulled her into the library during her study period to email Lora.

ME: HEY, LORA, IT'S ME, IVY. SCHOOL'S ALMOST OUT. I'M USING THE SCHOOL LIBRARY COMPUTER. WHEN SCHOOL IS OUT, I'LL HAVE NO PHONE OR COMPUTER EXCEPT FOR EMMA'S OR THE DOWNTOWN LIBRARY. IT'S BEEN A NO-GO FOR THE CRAFT BAZAAR. EMMA'S BEEN BUSY, WHICH MEANS I DON'T HAVE ANY PLACE TO WORK ON MY PROJECTS. THIS SUMMER EMMA'S GOING TO BE GONE A LOT—VACATIONING WITH HER DAD, AT A SPORTS CAMP, AND GOING TO KAUAI WITH A FRIEND. THEN THERE'S ME AND MY SUCKY LIFE! I WANT TO MAKE SOME MONEY, BUT I HAVE NO CAR, NO PHONE, AND NO ONE RELIABLE TO TAKE ME ANYWHERE. AGAIN, MY LIFE SUCKS! GOT ANY IDEAS ABOUT HOW I CAN MAKE SOME MONEY? YOU CAN USE THIS EMAIL UNTIL SCHOOL IS OUT, THEN I'LL OCCASIONALLY CHECK EMMA'S COMPUTER OR THE TOWN'S LIBRARY. THANKS, IVY

***

On Saturday morning, Mom was in the kitchen chopping carrots and throwing them into their garage-sale-find crockpot. Mom didn't look so good. The dark circles under her eyes were almost purple. It was warm, and she was wearing a sweater. Shit. She was hiding her arms. No need to ask why. She already knew.

"Mom, do you think Bernie would hire me for summer work?"

Mom stopped chopping and gave her a puzzled glance. "He doesn't hire much extra help in the summer. Besides, I think he's already got a senior from your school lined up."

"Dang! I should have thought of it sooner. It's gonna really suck to be in the house all summer. I wanna make some money so I can buy a few things for school next year."

The lines between Mom's brows deepened. "I don't know about summer work at your age. Why don't you come into town and hang out while I'm on shift today? I don't want you here all day either." Mom scooped up the remaining carrots and slid them into the crockpot. "Do you know what your dad and Derek are up to lately?"

"Yeah, I think it's kinda badass stuff. The kind that lands you in jail."

She wasn't sure what to say. No doubt Mom probably knew anyway. She stole a carrot chunk from the crockpot and popped it into her mouth.

"Derek's usin' again, and Dad always seems to have money for Jack Daniel's. There's money coming in from somewhere. Jake's around more often, too. The three go off on some *mission* every once in a while." She grabbed another slice of carrot. "Mom, we need to get outta here. You know Dad gets meaner when he's got more booze. Heck, he's mean even when he doesn't have it. Of course, being around Derek when he's high isn't fun, either."

Mom lowered her gaze. "The car isn't in good enough shape to trust going far." She walked to the sink and sighed. "Couldn't you stay with Emma more often over the summer?"

"Can't. She's gonna be gone a lot. Please, Mom, think about us leaving. How about when you see Dad with more money, you tell him the car needs fixing so it won't break down going to work? Once it's fixed, we could leave. You're a good waitress and could probably get a job anywhere. If we move and live in town, I could find some kinda work, too. I'm almost sixteen."

Mom's worried face suggested she shouldn't get her hopes up. Pleading had never worked. Yet, her gut had been telling her that the crap going on in their house was getting worse. Mom couldn't possibly be staying because she loved Dad anymore...not with those bruises she's hiding.

With Jake in the mix of things, whatever was happening wasn't good.

Lately, she wasn't so sure she was safe either. The advantages of being daddy's little girl or the little sister evaporated years ago. Someday, it wouldn't just be verbal crap slung her way. Dad and Derek were unpredictable. And mean.

Long ago, she'd learned that hiding in her room, quiet as a mouse, was her safest strategy. Invisibility had worked pretty well. Though this summer it would be more difficult. For sure, Dad would ask her to do more around the house so Mom could increase her hours. Then there's Jake. The attention he dished out felt creepy...and a bit of a turn-on.

"Look," said Mom, grimacing. "Since I'm only working a six-hour shift this afternoon, you can come with me. Go get a sweatshirt and your backpack. You can hang out at the library. Go on now. I don't wanna be late."

***

As she walked by the library's front counter, she whispered, "Hi, Mrs. Ackerman."

Mrs. Ackerman raised her head. Her customary frown peeked out between strings of greasy hair. From the scowl Mrs. Ackerman gave her, some might think she didn't like her. She knew differently. Her theory was that Mrs. Ackerman's permanent scowl resulted from a curse. That was her theory, anyway. Many feared Mrs. Ackerman. As a regular, she prided herself on getting on the good side of the sixty-something widow.

She mumbled to Mrs. Ackerman, "I'll check my emails, then take a table in the back for a while."

Mrs. Ackerman nodded, though she kept her eyes low, probably devouring one of those steamy romances she liked to read. Without raising her head, Mrs. Ackerman said, "A new art book came in. I'll bring it out in a few minutes."

When a computer became available, she took a seat and checked her emails. Seeing a response from Lora, she scooted to the edge of the chair.

LORA: IVY, IT WAS LOVELY TO HEAR FROM YOU. GETTING A SUMMER JOB WOULD BE A GREAT IDEA. REGARDLESS OF YOUR CHALLENGES, HERE ARE SOME SUGGESTIONS:

BEFORE SCHOOL ENDS, SEE THE SCHOOL COUNSELOR AND ASK ABOUT PROGRAMS FOR UNDERPRIVILEGED TEENS IN YOUR AREA. TELL ALL YOUR TEACHERS YOU'RE LOOKING FOR SUMMER JOBS AND WILL TAKE ANYTHING. YOU NEVER KNOW WHAT MIGHT COME UP. ASK THEM TO GET BACK TO YOU BEFORE SCHOOL ENDS OR TO LEAVE A MESSAGE VIA AN EMAIL ADDRESS YOU CAN ACCESS THROUGH THE LIBRARY. BECAUSE THEY KNOW YOU, THEY MIGHT PICK YOU UP AND TAKE YOU HOME.

MAKE FLYERS TO PUT UP AROUND TOWN. BE SURE TO MAKE IT CLEAR THAT THEY WOULD NEED TO PROVIDE TRANSPORTATION. LIST BABYSITTING, YARD WORK, WASHING WINDOWS, AND CLEANING OUT STORAGE SHEDS. GIVE THEM SOME IDEAS. COULD THEY CONTACT YOU THROUGH YOUR MOM WHILE SHE'S AT WORK?

DO THEY HIRE SUMMER STAFF WHERE YOUR MOM WORKS? IF YOU WERE ON THE SAME SHIFT, YOU COULD RIDE TOGETHER.

KEEP POSITIVE–YOU NEVER KNOW WHAT WILL TURN UP IN THE NEXT THREE MONTHS.

GOOD LUCK. LORA

A brief flutter of hope whirled through her. She'd check with the school counselor on Monday, although there were only three days of school left. The flyers might work. She could design one while she was here. Mrs. Ackerman might print some out if she offered to reshelve books. She knew of a few bulletin boards around town.

Dang! She slumped in her chair. No contact phone number. She stared at the ceiling until someone behind her cleared their throat, politely telling her they were waiting for the computer.

***

On the last day of school, she sent another email to Lora.

ME: LORA, THANKS FOR THE LIST. THE COUNSELOR IS LOOKING AT A GOVERNMENT PROGRAM. SHE THINKS I NEED TO BE SIXTEEN, THOUGH. BABYSITTING IS PROBABLY OUT. MY DAD AND BROTHER HAVE A NOT-SO-GREAT REP IN TOWN, SO PEOPLE MIGHT NOT WANT ME IN THEIR HOMES OR WITH THEIR KIDS. ALSO, THERE'S NO WAY DAD OR MY BROTHER WILL LET PEOPLE CONTACT ME THROUGH THEIR CELL PHONES. MOM DOESN'T HAVE ONE. MOM SAID SHE'D ASK SOME OF HER OLDER CUSTOMERS IF THEY HAD YARD WORK OR ODD JOBS TO BE DONE. I COULD DO IT WHILE SHE WAS WORKING A DAY SHIFT. HER BOSS HAS ALREADY HIRED EXTRA SUMMER HELP. I SHOULD HAVE ASKED EARLIER. VOLUNTEERING—MAYBE? YET I NEED $. ~ IVY

***

From the kitchen, she could hear the rumble of Jake's muffler. Nerves twisted in her stomach as she continued cleaning up from breakfast.

She kept her back to Jake when he came through the front door. As she wiped up the mess Derek had created frying bacon, she sensed Jake's eyes upon her. It flustered her, though sometimes she enjoyed the new attention he'd been giving her. It made her feel special. He was a hottie. Like, totally dope cute. Yet he could be creepy, *and* he was even older than her brother. He was always telling her she was sweet like candy, and other times she was spicy hot. Was she sexier than she realized? He sure made her think she might be.

When she glanced his way, their eyes met. They stared each other down until she broke contact. He nodded as he licked his lips. His eyes showed amusement. Heat shot to her cheeks.

Since a part of her wanted to stay around longer, she made them quesadillas. They were playing video games when she slid the plate of food onto the coffee table behind Jake. Jake immediately reached around and grabbed her leg. She froze as his hand slid up from her ankle. Heat radiated everywhere his fingers roamed.

He did a creepy thing with his tongue as he watched her response. Before Jake let go, he said, "Thanks, hot stuff." Then, his attention returned to his game.

She wanted to flirt back or say something clever, but she didn't. He was dangerous, but that made it kinda exciting. His interest made her life less boring.

Lots of rumors circulated at school about Jake being a supplier and a player. Although when he was here, he didn't seem so bad. Dad rarely liked anyone coming over, so it had surprised her when Jake started hanging out here. It was even weirder when Jake fell into the position of the head honcho in their macho threesome and not her dad. Even her dorky brother started acting like Jake's mini-me. Pathetic!

She glanced at the clock on the stove. Two more hours to burn before she could head to Emma's. Emma had some free time to bake, which meant the creative room was available.

She jotted *cheese* down on a grocery list, wondering when her mom would have enough money to go shopping. Dad demanded huge meals, yet hardly ever dished out cash to keep the house stocked. It wasn't fair. Mom had to hand over her money whenever he wanted it.

Jake sauntered into the kitchen. "Hey, wanna go into town? Gotta get some cigs."

Before she knew it, he'd pinned her into the corner with one arm. He leaned in so close his breath warmed her cheek. Her stomach somersaulted seeing what his eyes were asking. She knew what he was offering, and part of her was interested. He had a way of working her up.

She lowered her eyes, reminding herself he was way too old for her. "I'll pass this time. Thanks."

He raised her chin to read her face. Then he whispered, "Too bad. You're lookin' sexy today."

He gave her a peck on the cheek before he released her. She turned away. Heat spread from her cheeks to *other parts* of her body. He chuckled and walked back into the living room. She scurried to her bedroom, uncomfortable with the exchange.

Once she closed her door, she slid the slide lock into place. It was a habit whenever she entered her room. When she was thirteen, her brother came in one night wanting to *snuggle* with her. When his hands started to roam her body, she caused a ruckus by kneeing him in the balls. Afterward, her mother bought and installed the door lock, and for once, her dad hadn't complained about the extra money she'd spent.

***

By the first week of August, the temperature inside the house was miserable. The deep shade of the surrounding trees wasn't even helping to cool the house.

"Mom, could I go into town with you again today? Laundry's done, and I've mopped the kitchen floor." She would beg if she had to. "The library is air-conditioned, and I'll do some prep for the craft class I'm helping with tomorrow."

"Sure. Where did your dad and Derek go this morning?" Worry lines creased Mom's forehead.

"They don't tell me their business. I don't ask, and I don't wanna know. Someday they'll get caught doing whatever they're up to. Whatever it is, they sure get hyped up about it. You know... *when* they get caught, we'll end up on our own, anyway."

Of course, then she and Mom wouldn't be able to show their faces in town. They'd have to move away. Why not do it now?

She grabbed the lone apple from the fridge to eat later, hoping that at the end of Mom's shift, someone would offer her something to eat.

"Mom, shouldn't we get outta town before they drag us into it?" She filled a water bottle to take along with her.

"I don't know. Either way, it won't be easy for us." Mom glanced at the clock. "Get the rest of what you need. You'll have to stay until eight tonight, and tomorrow will be the same."

"Great. Anything to get out of this heat." She walked away, then turned. "Mom, we need to leave *soon* before something bad happens. It's our best option."

Mom avoided eye contact and didn't respond.

***

It had been a while since she'd written Lora, so while at the library, she emailed her.

ME: LORA, I GOT A FEW PAYING JOBS THIS SUMMER. TWO OF MOM'S CUSTOMERS HAD YARD WORK—$60. COOPER HAD ME SWEEP HIS GARAGE AND ORGANIZE IT—$75. AND I'M DOING A VOLUNTEER GIG HELPING WITH A FREE KIDS' SUMMER CRAFT PROGRAM AT THE LIBRARY. I'M HOPING MORE JOBS COME MY WAY, THOUGH I HAVE ENOUGH MONEY TO BUY A FEW THINGS FOR SCHOOL NOW. LAST WEEK, SOMEONE SEARCHED MY BEDROOM LOOKING FOR MY MONEY STASH. THAT TOTALLY SUCKED. LUCKILY, I ALWAYS TAKE MY MONEY WITH ME. I STILL HANG OUT AT EMMA'S WHEN I CAN. SHE MADE SOME AWESOME COOKIES WHILE I WORKED IN THE CREATIVE ROOM THE OTHER DAY. THANKS AGAIN FOR THE SUGGESTIONS. I APPRECIATE YOUR HELP. YOUR FRIEND, IVY

She pressed send and sat back in her chair. It felt good to consider Lora a friend now. Someone who might be there for her. One more person she'd add to her short list of adults she could trust. Too bad Lora and Mr. Martin hadn't hit it off.

Her summer was turning out okay, though she missed hanging out with the Martins as much as she used to. She'd never told anyone, but ever since grade school, she'd pretended Emma was her sister, Cooper, her dad, and Nana Claire, her grandma. Cooper paid attention to her, like a dad would. He asked about school, praised her artwork, made sure she had something to eat, and would joke her out of a bad mood. Well, that used to work. She would have to try harder not to be so grumpy around them.

Now that she was more grown up, she couldn't pretend her way out of the crappy life she had. The Martins weren't her family, and with their busy lives, she thought she was slowly losing them.

Her life sucked.

When she woke up this morning, there was a familiar heaviness in her chest, which rarely lifted anymore. Something bad was going to happen, and there wasn't anything she could do about it. If she told someone what was really going on in her house, she'd probably land in foster care. She knew a few kids in the system. Some said foster homes treat you shitty—only keeping you for the money. This new guy, whom she kinda liked, said his foster home was way better than where he'd come from.

She shrugged, then checked to see if anyone was waiting for the computer. Nope. Good. Searching Pinterest was her favorite way to pass the time.

CHAPTER 12
COOPER

An early October rain pelted Cooper's windshield. As he arrived at work, he noticed the "M" on the Martin Metal Works sign had a chip on it. Great! Rubbing his jaw, he thought about the dentist's recommendation of a mouthguard. He'd consider it, especially since clenching his teeth at night was contributing to his headaches. Scowling, he stomped through the front door.

"Hey, boss," Virginia Baker greeted him the same way she had for the past eighteen years.

Loved by all, Virginia was the mother hen of his company. He could admit she had become his most valued friend. Virginia was a straight shooter and, though irksome at times, he always knew she had his best interests at heart.

"Hey," he said, noticing for the first time Virginia's hair was thinning in the front and her wrinkles had deepened to reveal her senior citizen status. He wasn't concerned about her mind, though. She was as sharp and as insightful as ever.

He lumbered up the stairs to his office.

Fifteen minutes later, Virginia strolled in, clutching two coffee mugs in one hand.

He briefly acknowledged her by peering over his shoulder as he stood staring through the interior window overlooking the lower level of the manufacturing portion of his plant.

The coffee mugs clunked as they hit the top of his desk. He knew Virginia would sit in her customary chair at the front of his desk.

"Okay, what's up?" she asked.

He turned as she was leaning back, assessing him with an astute stare.

"Lots." He heaved a heavy sigh, knowing he'd feel better if he opened up. Since Karen's illness, Virginia had become his confidante, and today would be no different.

"Well, spill it," she said. "I ain't gettin' any younger." Though she wore a cantankerous façade, her eyes showed concern and empathy for whatever was fueling his distress.

"Let's see. A mom cornered me in the school parking lot when I dropped off Emma. Her sister's visiting from Chicago, and she wants me to go on a blind date with her." He ran a hand through his hair. "Why do ladies keep thinking I'm the most eligible bachelor in town?"

"Because you are!" exclaimed Virginia, peering over the top of her coffee mug. "You should have taken it as a compliment. She wanted to set her *sister* up with you." She raised an eyebrow and flipped out a hand. "I don't know. Maybe people think you're a nice guy or somethin'. Weird, right?" Her eyes twinkled.

He shook his head and snickered. "Okay, point taken." He sat down at his desk. "My blood pressure would've appreciated it if I'd seen it that way."

With that topic defused, he said, "I think something is going on with Emma and Ivy." He shook his head. "We're barely into the school year and we've got drama already."

"Oh?"

He took his first sip of coffee, loving the taste as it slid down his throat. "This morning, Ivy didn't come out when we were there to pick her up for school. Emma got out to check on her. Ivy had her pajamas on...or whatever it is she sleeps in. I had my window open a bit, so I heard some of what the girls were saying. Ivy told Em she wasn't feeling well. In an angry tone, Emma asked if Jake was there. Ivy got huffy and said he'd only been there in the evening. Em snapped back, 'Fine,' and stormed back to the truck."

"Doesn't sound good."

He rubbed his jaw, moving it from side to side, trying to release the ache. "I tried to ask Emma about it, but she clammed up. I got the silent treatment all the way to school."

Virginia wrinkled her nose. "I think that bad-seed brother of hers is hanging out with Jake Watson. Remember him? The kid who came lookin' for a job about seven years ago, after he dropped out of school his senior year." She gave a thumbs-down gesture.

"Right." He could barely picture him.

Virginia crossed her arms under her ample bosom, and she said, "It was a good thing we didn't hire him. Later, they caught him stealing beer at the grocery. Got off easy cuz he hadn't turned eighteen—his first offense and all." She rolled her eyes. "First time *caught* is more like it. I've heard he's been supplying liquor to minors...maybe drugs, too. Can't prove it, though Harry thought he saw him doing a drop-off, which confirms the rumors for me."

He narrowed his eyes. "Crap!"

"I would hate to think of Ivy hanging around him." Virginia pushed out a breath. "He could turn a young girl's head, though. Handsome kid, in a James Dean kind of way." She fanned herself, emphasizing her observation.

"Wow. That would explain it. If that were the case, Emma would be upset. Think I should talk to Judy?"

"You could, but I think Judy's lost any power she had in that household. She's become downright mousy. It's sad how she's changed. She was the town's *it* girl while she was in high school."

"Yeah, I think I remember that."

"Poor thing. She's the bread and butter of that family. Yet, do you think Ed shows her any respect?" Virginia's expression turned to disgust.

He agreed with the harsh assessment. "It's really none of my business, but I care about Ivy. She's like family. I'm sick about what's going on over there. And this Jake guy—" He got up and stared out the window again.

"I'm sure you'll figure out something after you think about it a bit."

He heard Virginia's chair creaking before she said, "Well, everything here's hunky-dory. Um. Except—"

He whipped around to see her pinched brows. "Except what?"

She huffed out her frustration. "Dagnabbit! It's Clark!" Avoiding eye contact, she stared down into her empty mug.

"Clark?" Had something happened to her recently retired husband?

"Just cuz he's retired, he wants me to retire, too." She wrinkled her nose. "When he retired last spring, I thought my honey-do list would last him *years*. He's checked 'em all off, but one!" She closed her eyes and drew in a deep breath before blowing out a burst of air. "He says he's *lonely* while I'm at work."

Where was this going? Sweat formed on his brow.

Virginia drummed her fingers on the wooden arm of her chair. "He's been putting cruise brochures on the coffee table. I keep ignoring them." She pressed her lips together in thought. "I've told him several times I don't want to retire for another five years. Senile. Old. Coot."

Panic pushed up into his throat. "Are you giving me your notice?"

"Nah, I'm going to hold him off a little longer. I would like to take a two-week vacation to appease him, though."

Relief whooshed through him. "Of course. Whatever time you need."

She tilted her head. "I figure I've got to find him a buddy, someone to hang out with and keep him off my back. He's been kind of a loner since old Stewart up and died. Maybe a volunteer job?" She rose. "Guess curing his loneliness is on my shoulders."

She sighed, picking up their empty coffee mugs. He swallowed back his panic when she left.

***

He had trouble focusing while reviewing work orders and overtime sheets, his thoughts looping back to the topics troubling him. He got up to pace. Could his mom talk to Ivy? Someone needs to tell Ivy that guys like Jake just wanna get in her pants!

He sat back down at his desk, trying to force himself to stay on task. When he caught himself staring off at nothing, he knew it was useless.

Why had he gotten so upset when someone asked him to date their sister? He shook his head, only to notice he had drawn loopy doodles across the top of a paper pad. He clenched his teeth. Those loops looked a lot like cursive Ls.

"What the devil?" he muttered.

Lora.

He couldn't seem to let her go, even though it had been months since he'd turned her away. When she'd left town, he'd moped around for weeks, making everyone feel sorry for him. Mom even tried to *cure* him by fixing him up with the cashier at the bank. The whole town probably heard about that fiasco. It'd be nice if everyone just left his love life alone.

He turned his chair around to face the interior window. No one had ever sparked his interest since Karen. Except for Lora. He'd made a colossal mistake with his one attempt at dating too soon after Karen's death. His head hadn't been on straight. It had been a disaster.

Lora.

He still felt terrible for hurting her. The intensity of his feelings and how quickly they'd formed had frightened him. He'd pulled away, even though he was drawn to her like a boy scout mesmerized by the flicker of a campfire.

Get too close and you get burned. Or that's what he told himself.

Before Lora, he'd been able to keep his emotional distance from a woman; a necessity for protecting his heart. What he'd felt for Lora had come so quickly, it scared the shit outta him. He'd panicked. Yowzers! Those feelings hadn't risen for years. He couldn't say he enjoyed having them back.

For chrissake, her eyes still haunted him. After learning Mom kept in touch with Rebecca, he'd wanted to ask about Lora. He hadn't. It would have spiked his mom's curiosity, and she would have mentioned it to Lora's mom.

Now, too much time has passed anyway, though he still wondered how she was doing.

***

At lunchtime, he ambled downstairs to find Virginia's desk empty. His gut twisted. He'd have to accept she'd retire someday. Emotionally, he might never be prepared for her leaving. He should probably talk to her more about it, though.

Dammit, he hated change.

He was still cranky when he waited in line to pick Emma up from school. He caught sight of Emma shifting her body from side to side. Her head was down, and she'd separated herself from the other kids. She was giving off an — *I-am-not-in-the-mood-to-be-chatty* vibe. When she noticed him approach the head of the line, she squared her shoulders and manifested a fake smile. By the time she'd walked the distance to the truck, her smile slipped away. After she yanked the door open, she threw her backpack on the floor and plopped into the passenger seat.

Uh-oh, she's in a great mood.

In a no-nonsense manner, she said, "Dad, I need to call Lora and invite her to my volleyball qualifying matches. While she's here, I want to talk with her about Ivy selling her art. They've kept in contact. Me too...a little." She stared at him with piercing eyes. "It's something that might help Ivy."

The request surprised him. Lora had been out of their lives for months. Then today she'd been on both of their minds. Though he admired Emma for wanting to help her friend, he had mixed feelings about seeing Lora again. Apparently, Emma considered Lora *the* person capable of accomplishing whatever her goal was for Ivy.

He tapped the steering wheel. Seems Emma's connection with Lora had stuck. His finger tapping advanced to heavy strumming. It would be hard to say no to a teenager who had faith in any adult to help with a teenage matter.

"Have you talked to Ivy about this? Is she still interested in selling her work?"

"I think so. She was excited when Lora brought it up before. She had even worked on new pieces for a while. It bummed her out when she couldn't work on them much this summer." She rolled her eyes in disdain. "Now she's *preoccupied*."

He pulled out onto the road and glanced her way. She was swallowing back tears.

"You okay?"

"If you haven't noticed, Dad, we haven't had Ivy over as much lately." Emma's eyes narrowed, and her voice sharpened. "When I'm busy, she's started hanging out with her loser brother and his loser friend." Emma swallowed hard. "Could you let her work on her stuff even if I'm not home?"

"I don't know, Em. Things are changing with Ivy. Heard she's hanging out with Jake Watson. I'm concerned that if she's at our house alone, he might come over. He's not to be trusted. Not him nor her brother."

Emma slumped in her seat as her head turned toward the passenger window. "Dad, I've told her not to hang out with Jake...that he's a *loser*. She doesn't listen to me. She thinks he likes her. He's a lot older, and he's a bad person."

He jumped right into his deepest concern. "Emma, if she has sex with him—" Heat crept up his neck. He was uncomfortable talking about this with his daughter, but it was necessary. "Well, that would be statutory rape. She's not sixteen yet. He could do jail time. Even worse, she could get pregnant."

Emma's face scrunched up, and tears were about to flow. "Yeah, I thought of that."

"Look, I understand your concern. She's certainly not thinking straight."

Tears started rolling down Emma's cheeks, so he pulled the truck over to console her.

Her heavy sobs were now coming up from the depths of her belly. It hurt to see her this way. He leaned in to give her a one-sided hug. "You're a good friend. I care about Ivy, too. I'll think more about it. Maybe I can come up with a solution."

In a few minutes, she calmed down, so he headed on home.

As he parked in the driveway, Emma turned to face him. Her eyes were bright with emotion. "I still want to talk with Lora and have her come to my match. After all, it's the play-offs, and it's a big deal for me to play varsity as a sophomore."

A swift exhale burst through his lips. Lora had made a big impression on them both.

"Okay." He relented. "Your team plays its first game at 1:00 p.m. on Saturday, right?"

She nodded. "Whether we play again will depend on how the team does. I'm hoping we'll do well. It might be late by the time your matches finish up."

He tapped his fingers on the steering wheel again. "And I suppose you'll want to talk privately with Lora before you meet with Ivy about *art*?"

Emma confirmed with an earnest nod. "Yeah."

"Then I imagine the meet-up with Ivy would have to be Sunday morning. Which means Lora will have to stay over Saturday night." He turned away for a moment. When he turned back. His voice was flat when he said, "I would prefer you not ask her to stay with us."

He watched his daughter's face as she processed this bit of information. With empathy in her eyes, she leaned over and hugged him. "Thanks, Dad. It's okay. Although... I think Lora can help." With her tears dried, optimism took hold. She hopped out of the truck and bounced her way to the back door.

He let out a low moan. *Great. Just great.*

As he walked behind her, his thoughts moved to seeing Lora again. Perhaps it wouldn't be so bad. Would he still find the hurt he'd caused in her eyes?

On impulse, he reached up and snapped off a low-hanging Japanese maple branch. As he tossed it to the side, he mumbled, "Dammit!" He rubbed his jaw; he was clenching again.

It had been sheer cowardice to turn Lora away. Would he always chicken out instead of risking loving someone?

CHAPTER 13
LORA

Lora's phone rang while she was applying her lip gloss in the mirror. Despite not recognizing the phone number, she picked up.

"Hi Lora, it's me, Emma."

"Emma, what a surprise! It's so good to hear from you, though." Had Cooper given Emma permission to call? Something must be up?

"I know it's late notice, but I wanted to invite you to my volleyball league play-offs this Saturday. A couple of weeks ago, I moved up to varsity after a player got injured. The match is in Bremerton. My first game is at 1:00 pm, though we could play more after, if we win."

"Oh. Well—"

"Then I was wondering if you'd meet with Ivy and me on Sunday morning to talk more about Ivy selling her art. I think it would be good for Ivy to get interested in it again."

She blinked, hearing in Emma's voice how important this was to her. What would have caused Ivy to lose interest in creating art?

"Moving up to varsity is pretty special, Emma. Good for you. On Saturday I was supposed to go to my mom's house, though I'm sure she wouldn't mind if I came to your game instead. Let me call you back tomorrow after I check in with her. You caught me right before heading off to my first quilt guild meeting. I'm trying to find the inspiration to get started again."

"Nana's coming to the game. Why don't you ask your mom to come? I'm sure they would enjoy seeing each other again."

"You're right. Mom often mentions Claire after they've talked. Is everything okay with Ivy? You seem concerned."

"Yeah, that's a big part of why I asked you to come. Could we talk about it before Sunday? I'm hoping she'll come to the play-offs, yet who knows?"

To ease the distress in Emma's voice, she said, "It's hard to see someone you care about having trouble. I'll call tomorrow to let you know if we're able to come."

"Would you be sure to call *my* cell phone?"

"Of course."

Emma was making it clear not to call Cooper's phone. Which was fine; she'd prefer postponing any awkward first moments.

***

The show-and-tell portion of the quilt guild meeting was inspirational. She was in awe of the talent within the group. The warm welcome she received affirmed the value of joining a women's group with similar interests. She connected with a few of the women and hoped to swap numbers at the next meeting. Mentally, she checked off "join a women's group" from her to-do list.

When she returned home, she called her mom.

"Hi, Mom. You'll never guess who called today!"

"Well, who, dear?"

"Emma. I was so surprised. It's been what, almost five... six months? She invited both of us to her volleyball league play-offs this Saturday. Then we'd stay over so I can connect with Ivy on Sunday. Would you mind? Or do you have something we need to tackle at the house?"

"Not really. I've been working steadily on it, so it's in pretty good shape. While I'm gone, I could have the realtor set up a showing. Seeing Claire again would be great."

"Good. The game is at 1:00 pm. It'll be crowded, so let's get there early. Since we'd be staying over till late Sunday morning, how about I book a room at the inn again?"

"Sure. We had so much fun last time."

"I'm not sure we'll be having Saturday dinner with the family or anything. It would be difficult for me...you know, with Cooper."

"Oh, yes. Will it be hard seeing him again?"

"Maybe."

"Honey, I'm sorry. Claire and I had hopes for the two of you."

"Well, we did initially hit it off but...well—"

"Hogwash! In my day, you'd give a long-distance relationship a try, then if it became too difficult, you either got married or ended it."

She snickered. "I would've liked those choices." To change the subject, she said, "I bet seeing Claire will be nice. You two talk often."

"Yes, it'll be wonderful to see her in person again. Her quilting bee works on charity quilts on Sundays. I'll call and see if she could arrange a meet-up with whoever is free for an early brunch beforehand."

She imagined her mom's eyes sparkling, anticipating the fun she'd have with the quilt ladies.

"I'll reserve a room. Let's be back on the road by 3:00 pm on Sunday. I'm not sure how long I'll be with the girls in the morning. If I'm free, I'll join you for brunch."

"Sounds good."

Her getting lost at the beach that day had serendipitously created new friendships and possibilities for Mom. Could that be all that was meant to happen?

***

The next night, she called Emma back. They chatted a bit, though neither of them mentioned Cooper. Whatever relationship she might establish with Emma would not include her father.

As she climbed into bed, she worried about how awkward it would be seeing Cooper again. Would he bring a date to the matches? She punched her pillow. How could someone she barely knew leave such an impression on her? Had it been a timing thing? He was the first man who'd warmed to her. Certainly, he touched her heart, being so empathetic while she revealed her past.

She stared at the ceiling.

A wicked idea popped into her head. She giggled as she made her plan.

What would be so wrong with making Cooper regret the decision he'd made?

***

The next day, she took the afternoon off. Since she'd trained the replacement hire, she could more easily take personal leave. The replacement for Meagan ended up having some unexpected talents. Patty's best attribute was that she was a computer whiz. She was like having their very own IT person. Over time, Patty's *other* superpower revealed itself. She could kid the Goldens in such a way that she kept them on task and productive.

Patty, however, had one major flaw. She had a rough-around-the-edges communication style with customers and the warehouse staff. Fortunately, she was willing to learn and took instructions well.

***

When she arrived at the office that morning, she told Patty she would be gone all afternoon. Immediately, she called a full-service salon and explained her situation. The understanding hostess squeezed her in for the works. She had a facial, manicure, and pedicure, followed by a hair stylist adding soft layers to her chin-length bob and a finishing product that added extra shine.

As the salon ladies worked their magic, her tension melted away. A few hours later, she noticed a new swagger in her step as she walked past a wall of windows. She raised her eyebrows. "Ooh, you sexy thing!" Her giggles came from deep within her belly.

Going with the momentum, she indulged herself further by addressing her wardrobe. Her weekend attire needed to be casual, though her primary goal was to look *hot,* without giving the impression she was trying too hard.

Her next stop was Tacoma's downtown boutiques. Feeling exhilarated and carefree, her first purchase was a pair of way-too-expensive designer jeans. After gazing at her backside in the mirror, she deemed them worthy of every penny spent. Then she added a pair of ankle boots, a short jacket, and a few new tops.

She snickered. This wasn't like her, yet it sure was fun. Gad, she was being as self-indulgent as the Goldens. She pushed aside the whispers of judgment coming from the fiscally conservative part of herself.

Hell yes! She deserved to pamper herself.

***

Sleep evaded her on Friday night. She tossed and turned, rehearsing every conversation she *might* have with Cooper.

When she opened one eye to peek at her bedside alarm clock, she flipped to her stomach and groaned. Determined to get some sleep, she pulled out a well-worn 3x5 index card from her nightstand. She read the handwritten words, first three times silently, then out loud with conviction.

"I am worthy of love. I will generously love and accept the gift of being loved. I deserve all the blessings my future holds."

The repetition helped her insecurities drain away as the truth in those words found a resting place in her heart.

At Wendy's suggestion, she had written the affirmation to squelch feelings of unworthiness. At first, she used the affirmation to replace destructive thought patterns. Over time, it became a declaration of faith that something extraordinary was on its way.

After diligently putting in the work, therapy helped her become more like her old self. She was proud of the changes she'd made and hopeful for her future, even though doubt occasionally slipped back in.

Wendy had told her she needed to first love and accept herself, despite her past, before she could be in an emotionally healthy relationship. Wendy had teased that once she accomplished this, she'd better watch out. Men would hone in on her like a hummingbird to sugar water. That hadn't happened yet, though the prospect created a flutter of anticipation.

"I *gotta* get some sleep," she whined.

Unfortunately, when she closed her eyes, she replayed the day Cooper backed away from her.

She rubbed the back of her neck. Tears stung her eyes.

In defiance of what had popped back into her head, she yelled, "I *am* a person someone would want to know and fall in love with!"

Her hands fisted. Knowing anger wouldn't get her where she wanted to be, she released her fingers. After a slow cleansing breath to relax her body, she repeated her affirmation again.

Wiggling further down under her comforter, she closed her eyes while focusing on slowing the rhythm of her breathing. As her body relaxed, she visualized a translucent stream of pink entering at the top of her head and spreading slowly through her body, down to her toes.

Fully relaxed, renewed confidence formed. She would handle any uncomfortable situation the weekend might bring.

CHAPTER 14
LORA

When Lora drove up to her mom's house, she had to admit the house looked fantastic with a fresh coat of paint. After knocking on the newly painted brick-red front door, she entered and announced her arrival.

"There in a minute." Mom called from the back of the house.

In the entry, the pictures of her brother and herself, at various stages in their development, had vanished from the walls. The living room coffee table was bare, and new decorative pillows nestled in the corners of the couch.

She called out, "Staging the place to sell, I see."

To squelch her disappointment, she attempted to view the space through a potential buyer's eyes. Yep, it would sell quickly. Then what? Hopefully, this weekend Mom would give her a clue about what her next steps might be.

"Meet me at the car when you're ready, Mom." She picked up the purple suitcase set out in the hall and headed toward the car. Wherever Mom landed, she would work on their mother-daughter relationship. The relationship was important to her.

A few moments later, Mom walked toward the car, looking healthy and happy.

As soon as the car door shut, she said, "Mom, the house looks great. I bet it'll go quickly."

"That's what the realtor says. I have mixed feelings, though I'm certain it's time to let the house go. Moving will make things easier as I get older. The work it takes to get it ready to sell deters a lot of older people from downsizing. They end up staying, and their house starts to fall apart around them when the maintenance gets too difficult and costly."

Mom tucked her purse down by her feet. "Doing the work now means I'll have a simpler life in my golden years." She chuckled. "No one knows what's ahead. We just have to bravely keep going."

"I agree with you there." She patted Mom's arm. "Mom, you're going to have lots of wonderful years ahead of you. I can't wait to see how you end up filling your days."

Mom smiled and nodded toward the road. "We better get going. Don't want to be late for the matches. It'll seem like the old days watching you. By the way, that fresh look of yours is terrific!"

A flutter of happiness danced through her, giving her a nice boost of confidence.

En route, they kept the conversation light, sharing bits of their lives since they'd seen each other last. When Mom's cell phone rang, her face lit up.

"Hello. Mary! That's wonderful. Keep me posted."

"My realtor booked three showings for today and three for tomorrow. I could have a bidding war by tomorrow night!"

She gulped down her reaction, then tried to keep her voice chipper when she said, "Good news. Are you ready for what's next?"

"Not completely. Though, I have some ideas. I'm going to talk a few over with Claire."

There she goes, excluding her *daughter* again.

"If there's anything I can help with, let me know, Mom."

"Nothing at the moment." Mom gazed off into the distance. "I've decided against living in Minnesota. I told your brother a few days ago. To soften the blow, I said I'd visit more often. Probably on the kids' birthdays. Then I'll rotate Thanksgiving and Christmas between the two of you."

"That seems fair." She reached over and squeezed her hand. "Selfishly, I'm glad you're not moving so far away from me."

"I know." Mom patted their joined hands with a sympathetic smile.

"Are you thinking of an adult community? Something like Claire's?"

"I'm leaning that way. Still in the research phase. Next week, I should be able to visit a few."

They reached Bremerton with thirty minutes left to get something to eat and find the gym. Concerned about parking and seating, they decided to eat later.

She was eager to see how Emma and her team performed. She'd loved playing high school volleyball.

As they pulled into the gymnasium parking lot, her mom received a text from Claire telling her where they'd saved seats.

As they entered the gym, the intensity of the crowd's excitement startled her. A referee's whistle blast called the end of the current game. Emma's team would be up next. When she peered into the stands, she spied Cooper. How she'd immediately spotted him among so many, she would never know.

Her stomach somersaulted. "Good grief," she muttered under her breath. To keep the colony of butterflies from ascending into her chest, she pulled her gaze away.

Snaking through the crowd, she headed toward Cooper and the seats Claire had saved. With her eyes elsewhere, she bumped hard against the front of a linebacker-sized man. She stumbled, and he caught her by the forearms while he choked back a few choice four-letter words. Once he'd set her upright, he leaned back for a better view. "Woo Wee. You okay?"

"Yeah, I think so."

His facial expression rapidly changed from irritation to an approving smile. As he loosened his grip, her first thought was how his plaid shirt and backward baseball cap suited him. When his smile broadened, his intimidating features transformed into one of those big teddy bear-type guys.

She couldn't help smiling back. "I am so sorry. I wasn't watching where I was going."

"No need to apologize." He looked her up and down. "Uh, I'm meeting up with my buddies now, but would you be free...say around 8:30? I could buy you a beer at White Oaks?" He cocked his head, waiting for a reply. The crowd was pushing against them, yet he held her steady with a soft grip.

His invitation stunned her. Was he asking her out? Her pulse quickened. "Thanks, but I'm here with my mom, and we're meeting up with friends."

He shrugged, released her, and gave her a farewell nod. The crowd swallowed him up as he walked toward the exit.

With her cheeks spread wide, she followed the stream of fans around the perimeter of the gym.

Well, that was a first-rate boost to the ego.

Mom was way ahead of her now. She heard Claire call out, letting them know they were sitting in the middle section of the bleachers.

She sucked in a breath. Here we go.

She avoided looking at Cooper as she climbed up to the fifth row; a feat made more difficult by the tight fit of her new skinny jeans. The fans in the bleachers barely made room as she wedged herself between them to reach her seat. Claire and Mom already had their heads together, talking. The only seat available was, of course, next to Cooper.

A quiver rattled through her as she sat down. Intent on keeping her cool, she hadn't acknowledged his greeting. When her arm brushed against him, she reflexively jerked away.

Embarrassing.

She shrugged off her jacket and stuffed it into the minuscule space between them.

Cooper greeted her again. "Thanks for coming, Lora. This is a big deal for Emma. Find the gym, okay?"

"Yep, GPS." She resisted making eye contact. "Can't wait to see Emma play."

When Emma's team bounded out of the locker room, Claire and Cooper jumped up and yelled, "Go Wildcats!"

Others around them joined in the cry, along with some aggressive foot-stomping.

She kept her eyes on Emma. Emma was the shortest member of her team, and probably the youngest. Before long, however, she marveled at how fast, aggressive, and strategically Emma played the game. As a result, the coach kept her in play.

"Cooper, Emma's a great player," she said, raising her voice above the crowd.

"Yeah, with two more years of high school, we'll see how her talent plays out. She loves soccer too. She's played since she was six. Who knows, a scholarship could come from either. Or both." He grinned at the possibility.

Emma scored again. She and Cooper leaped up to cheer. The atmosphere was tense, with only a few seconds remaining in a tied game. Caught up in the excitement, they turned toward each other, sharing the hope that Emma's team would break the tie. Their eyes locked. Everything but the two of them lost focus. He reached for her hand when the blast of the final buzzer broke their spell.

Game over.

She pulled her hand away and glanced back at the court to see Emma receiving high-fives from her teammates. Cooper seemed stunned for a second, then clapped and cheered along with the crowd.

Darn. He'll regret missing the winning play his daughter had made or assisted in.

The Orca Park Wildcats won their first match, with Emma breaking the tie.

When she turned, the mothers were looking her way with knowing smiles on their faces.

Fiddlesticks! The moms must have seen what happened between her and Cooper.

She flushed under their scrutiny. "Claire, where's the restrooms?" It was the first thing she thought of to escape their gaze.

Claire pointed to the double gymnasium doors. "Go out. Turn right. Probably a long line by now." Claire's grin only flustered her more.

"Thanks." Eager to get away, she tapped the person in front of her, showing she wanted through.

As she entered the crowded hallway, a group of teens were hanging out nearby. One of those teens was Ivy. She wore torn skinny jeans, a black stretched-out sweater, and a surplus Army jacket with a dark patch on the lower right where a pocket used to be. She'd lined her sullen eyes with black, while purple shadow covered her lids. Her hair was longer than when she had seen her last. Yet, those same angled bangs concealed much of her pretty face.

Regardless of Ivy's clothes or makeup choices, she was a striking beauty. There was something eye-catching about her lean, well-proportioned body and the remarkably symmetrical angles of her face. Hopefully, nothing too serious was going on with her.

When she neared the group, she made eye contact with Ivy.

"Hi, Ivy! See you tomorrow. I've got some exciting news and can't wait to see what you've been working on."

Ivy's reply was a slight nod. A brightening in her eyes was her only hint of enthusiasm.

She settled into the long line for the restroom.

Hopefully, Emma will fill her in beforehand about what's going on with Ivy that she's concerned about. As she cast a brief glance back at Ivy, a powerful longing filled her chest. She wanted to help Ivy; to do what she could to improve Ivy's chances of having a good life. Ivy had so much potential.

While inching forward in line, she closed her eyes and mentally reached out to her dad.

I could use your guidance here. You always helped kids, especially those who needed it the most. I want to help Ivy, but I'm not sure how.

When she exited the restroom, the teens were still there. This time, she merely nodded when walking past Ivy. Two boys in Ivy's group made inappropriate comments, and the others snickered. Ivy barked at them, putting them in their place.

Way to go, Ivy! She tucked her lips in, attempting to hold back her smile.

As she climbed the bleachers, she noticed Cooper staring down at her. Her swift physical response caused her to clench her teeth. Sure, she felt attracted to him, but she wouldn't pursue it. Her reason for coming was only to help the girls in whatever way they needed her. Cooper would be strictly off-limits.

Keeping Cooper off-limits proved difficult. As they continued watching the games, heat rose from their slightest touch. She begged herself not to weaken. It would be a mistake to open things up between them. Yet, she wouldn't mind if he seriously regretted rejecting her.

To be honest, she liked the interest he was showing her. Yet, she was determined not to show him *she* had any interest in *him*. Nope, not one bit.

Her voice was hoarse by the end of Emma's last game. The roar of the crowd made it impossible to talk to anyone. When Emma assisted with the winning score, the crowd went wild. The four of them joined in the fervor. Unexpectedly, Cooper grabbed her and bounced her up and down, with the bleachers rebounding under their feet.

As soon as their physicality registered, he pulled back, though he still held her arms as he gazed down upon her face. His facial expression registered a quick—*Oops!* Although in the blink of an eye, intensity darkened his eyes.

She knew that look. Even though she'd warned herself, those eyes drew her in. Fire ignited in her belly. Dammit!

Sensing how awkward the situation was, she took control. With a frustrated sigh, she twisted out of his arms.

She didn't want a fling. Why in the heck did she buy these friggin' jeans?

She turned toward the moms. Claire was leaning forward to get her attention. When Claire just wanted to affirm how exciting the game was, relief washed over her. Had they noticed?

Until the chaos died down, she remained trapped in her seat. Families, neighbors, and fellow students clogged the bleachers as they shared their favorite snippets of the games. Clutching her jacket to the front of her, she stood, feeling miserable.

All around her, spirits were high, yet despair sat in the pit of her stomach. Relief came when she caught a whiff of her father's cologne. She calmed as she focused inward, hoping the scent wasn't merely coming from a nearby fan.

Dad's voice was that low, soothing one he used when he knew she felt defeated after not playing her best game. *Don't give up, Cupcake. Don't become your own obstacle.*

She glanced over at her mom, who was completely engrossed in people-watching.

So, it looked like this father-daughter thing was for her ears only.

Dad, you've always been there as my coach, but this is different. I'm not sure I want to stay in this game. The risk could be too high.

Cooper was now highlighting the game with another man. His eyes sparkled as his hands gestured wildly. For her, the adrenaline from the game had already faded. She felt exhausted.

Even though she found Cooper appealing, she didn't want to win a man through the seduction game. Yet, having him awaken her sexually was a blessing. Having that part of herself come alive was exciting after such a long self-imposed celibacy. Though grateful he had liberated her, further involvement would only lead to heartache down the line.

Her best plan of action was to protect herself from being vulnerable to Cooper's charms.

She watched Cooper make his way down the bleachers to the gym floor. When he turned, he first glanced up at his preoccupied mother, then he made eye contact with her.

"Lora, tell everyone to meet out front by the flagpole."

She nodded, then moaned to herself. Why continue to think about an *us*, when they each wanted different things? She wasn't going to merely scratch someone's itch when she wanted the whole deal. She flung her crossbody bag over her shoulder.

"Mom. Claire. Are you ready to go?"

Her plan was to leave as soon as they congratulated Emma.

By the time they reached the flagpole, a sizeable crowd had gathered outside.

When could she talk to Emma about Ivy before they met tomorrow?

It was a relief having Cooper preoccupied with the male bonding ritual of back-slapping and handshaking. That alleviated standing around awkwardly with him while they waited.

Mom soon ventured off with Claire to speak with a few of Claire's friends.

Welcoming the solitude, she sat down on the low brick wall surrounding the flagpole and focused on the gymnasium door. Her stomach grumbled in need of food.

Finally, Emma strolled out, occupied in lively conversation with her teammates.

Observing Emma, pride swelled in her heart for how well Emma performed. She had once been like Emma, giving her all for her team, herself, and her dad.

Why was it that whenever she was around Emma and Ivy, she experienced the urge to nurture them?

As Emma and her teammates approached the crowd, they wore wide grins. Soon they broke apart to go to their respective families.

It was silly; Emma's invitation to the volleyball match had given her a warm sense of inclusion. Almost as if she were an important part of Emma's inner circle. It was unlikely that this was true. Probably some type of crazy wishful thinking on her part.

When Emma spotted her family, her smile broadened. Claire gave the first hug of congratulations. Emma closed her eyes and sank into her grandmother's arms. Next, Cooper strolled over; his parental pride clearly showing. He gave Emma a bear hug, and Emma giggled at the exuberance in his gesture. Then he swung his arm around her neck and gave her a knuckle rub on the top of her head. Something she had seen him do before. This time, judging by the look on Emma's face, his loving gesture had lost its mojo. Cooper hadn't a clue he was embarrassing his daughter. Emma was no longer his *little* girl. Certainly, if Emma's mother were alive, she would have set Cooper straight.

Once Emma noticed her and her mom waiting on the sidelines, she rushed over to give them both hugs and profusely thanked them for coming.

With everyone in high spirits, Claire announced she was taking them all to dinner. "And no arguments!"

Cooper scowled. She tried to protest. Emma pleaded. They conceded. To accommodate Emma's choice, the group would return to Orca Park to eat at Emma's favorite pizza parlor.

As they were about to leave, two women rushed toward them, one calling out, "Cooper!" The first had a tired toddler anchored to her hip. Her disheveled hair and pant leg marked with a wet glob of some unknown substance identified her as the toddler's mother. The other woman appeared unscathed, probably by avoiding contact with the overstimulated, cranky little boy. This woman's long brunette waves fell smoothly over one shoulder. Her flawless makeup and movie star features provided the surrounding men with some nice eye candy.

She blinked, then her eyes widened. This stunner's skillful hip action was amplifying the appeal of the same form-fitting designer jeans she was wearing.

Unbelievable! She twisted her lips while she shook her head. She could never replicate those moves in a million years. Nor was she sure she wanted to.

"Oh, Cooper!" yelled the toddler-toting woman, hurrying toward him.

The other woman sauntered up in a slow runway walk.

While shifting the toddler to her other hip, the mom said, "Boy, am I glad I caught you." She glanced toward the woman coming up alongside her. "This is my sister, Mindy Metcalf. The one I told you about."

Facing Cooper's back, she watched his shoulders move up, and down as he sighed. Did his sigh mean frustration or infatuation?

"Nice to meet you, Mindy." Cooper extended his hand in a greeting. "Pretty exciting game, wasn't it?"

Mindy tilted her head as she shook Cooper's hand. "You know it was! I heard your daughter assisted on more than one final score."

"Yeah, she played well today. Your sister said you were visiting. You in town long?"

Mindy turned her body sideways and twisted her head to look at Cooper over her shoulder. Her eyes intensified seductively as she said, "It all depends on whether someone is interesting enough to keep me in town."

She grimaced seeing the woman's Cheshire cat smile, but couldn't hear Cooper's response to her *invitation*. Her teeth clenched when Mindy said, "Why don't you give me your cell phone? I'll put my number in so you can call me later." While maintaining eye contact with Cooper, Mindy extended her arm and rolled her wrist to unfold her palm.

Cooper hesitated, glanced briefly in her direction, and then followed through by handing Mindy his phone. Mindy entered her number, then boldly stepped forward to pull back Cooper's sports coat lapel and placed the phone inside his interior pocket. Maintaining eye contact, she patted his chest where the phone now rested. "Call me," she said in a sultry voice.

Before Mindy stepped back, she peered over Cooper's shoulder, purposely making eye contact with her. The showoff tilted her head. It was clear the smug smile that spread across Mindy's face was meant for her.

Message received.

Mindy flipped her hair as she turned, then repeated her sexy runway walk away from their group, giving everyone a grand view of her impressive backside.

She was certain Cooper's eyes were following. It would be hard not to.

Her fists balled, while her nostrils flared as she sucked in a deep breath. *Whatever!*

Why should she care what Cooper thought...or wanted?

CHAPTER 15
LORA

Lora's anger barometer rose as she watched Mindy slink away. Luckily, Mom came to her rescue by jumping in to ask Claire for directions to the pizza parlor. Once received, Mom slid her arm through hers and steered her toward their parked car.

"Do you want to talk about it?"

"No!"

If smoke could really come out of someone's ears, she'd be emitting fumes all the way to their car.

So, loose bimbos are his taste. Fine. A man who liked that sort of woman wasn't for her.

Oh crap! She rolled her eyes upward. Hadn't *she* shown Cooper unabashed wanting after their first kiss? She was a first-class hypocrite!

Luckily, Mom respected her unspoken wish for silence while they headed back to Orca Park. She gasped when she read the speedometer and pulled up on the gas pedal. No reason to get in an accident over what...jealousy?

After she calmed down, she resolved to put her emotions in check for the rest of the evening. She wanted to keep her remaining dignity intact. After all, wasn't she there to support Emma and Ivy and nothing else?

They were the first to arrive at Wanda's Pizza Parlor, so they nabbed a half-moon booth in the back. When the rest of the group entered, Mom flagged them over. She, her mom, and Claire sat in the middle, giving the outside seats to Cooper and Emma, who continued to receive accolades from other customers. Emma sat beside her.

Once they settled, Cooper hailed a server and ordered three pizzas, giving the server a handsome tip to rush the order.

As they waited, she started a conversation with Emma. "For tomorrow, what time and where?"

"If you don't mind, 10:00 am at our house." Emma glanced at her dad. "We'll be hanging out in the creative room. Once Ivy knew you were coming, she's been working on new projects." Emma grinned with satisfaction. "That's what I'd hoped would happen."

"You said you've been worried about her?"

"Yeah." Emma glanced at her dad again. He was recapping the game with a guy wearing a polo shirt with Longfield Dental embroidered on the pocket. Mom and Claire were busy chatting, with Claire's hands dancing as the conversation picked up speed.

Emma turned her body toward her and whispered, "Ivy has been hanging out with a friend of her brother's. He's way older than her." Emma's voice tightened. "He's not a nice guy. Yet she's *so* into him." Emma frowned, and deep disgust filled her tone when she said, "I think she'd probably do *anything* he asked." Her innocent face expressed her concern.

Emma's breathing had sped up as she spoke. Wanting to calm her, she reached over and placed her hand on Emma's, sensing there was more. "Go on."

"I can't talk to her about it anymore. She gets mad if I say anything...trying to act so tough and grown-up. She's just being stupid."

When another customer interrupted to congratulate Emma, Emma smoothly shifted gears emotionally and graciously gave recognition to the entire team's efforts.

As soon as she could, Emma resumed their conversation. "I was hoping her art might keep her away from him." She sucked in a quick breath. "Her family doesn't put a stop to it either."

She shifted to hug Emma, who then dove into her arms. She closed her eyes as she patted Emma's back, murmuring support. Before their release, she battled to keep her own emotions under control.

As she sat back, a conviction formed. She'd do everything she could to help these two girls.

While she was in high school, a close teammate had fallen for a bad boy. She'd always believed the girl had tried to fill a void left by unavailable parents. The girl ended up pregnant, alone, and struggling to raise her son by herself. She didn't want that for Ivy—or any girl. Back then, she'd been powerless to help. Now she hoped she'd be able to turn things around for Ivy.

The pizza's arrival created a welcome distraction from the curious eyes around the table. Since everyone was hungry, the food quickly became their focus. As soon as they pulled the pizzas apart, her mouth watered and her stomach grumbled. She chose the house specialty—bacon, butternut squash, artichoke hearts, and leeks. It was the most satisfying pizza she'd ever eaten. There was little talk as the slices disappeared.

After everyone's bellies were full, Claire cleared her throat in the commanding way people used to get another's attention.

"While we're together, I thought we could discuss Ivy. I've spotted her in town, riding with Jake Watson. She's also been pulling away from friends she's had all her life. Ivy is headed for trouble." Claire leaned back in the booth, crossed her arms, and glanced around the table. "What can we do about it?"

Emma's face showed surprise.

Cooper was the first to respond. "I can't ground her. She's not my daughter. Though I wish I could. I hear Judy is powerless in that household, and her shitbag of a husband—excuse me, ladies—has no moral compass. People say he and his son are responsible for thefts all over the county. Though there's no evidence to prove it...yet." He leaned back to glance at Emma. "You need to stay away from that household."

"But Dad!" Emma slumped back into the booth.

Cooper shot her a look, shutting down any further objection.

"Mom," said Cooper, "do you think Ivy would listen to you?"

Claire put her chin in her hand and thought for a moment. "You can't forbid her from doing anything without the power to enforce it. A talk with

Ivy might have worked when she was younger. Now, I'm probably grouped into the uncool grandparent category. If I ever had that much status."

Emma said, "I've hoped Ivy would get back into her art so she wouldn't have time for Jake. The art thing — it's the only time I see her happy. And, you know, proud of herself. At least for what she's made."

Claire frowned. "Any ideas, Lora?"

She had a thought, but hesitated to bring it up. "Cooper, you've been a father figure for Ivy, and a father's job is to protect and show her how to protect herself." Her mom nodded knowingly.

She turned back to Cooper. "I imagine you love her like a second daughter. If you talked with her about your concerns, she'd grasp your good intentions, even though she might be upset initially."

Her words appeared to have agitated Cooper.

She continued anyway. "If you did it out of love, she'll feel your intent. Not to control her, but to protect her. To show her how much you care. Otherwise, you might come to regret not speaking up."

Cooper gave her a steely stare before he slowly nodded his agreement. "Yeah."

Now, it was time to reveal her plan. "I'd like to invite both girls for a weekend getaway. I've arranged for an art gallery owner in Seattle to look at the girls' work. Nothing may come of it, though she's willing to give the girls some pointers, which may be both beneficial and inspiring. I hope Ivy will renew her interest in art and learn how her artistic talents might benefit her in the future. Art could be her pathway to a better life."

Seeing Cooper's jaw tighten, she wondered if she'd overstepped.

Though her voice shook, she pressed on. "I know it's not my place to ask these things, and—" She stopped, cleared her throat, and glanced around the table. "I haven't known you all very long, yet here I am jumping right into this. Somehow, these girls, their friendship, Ivy being lost and neglected...well, it's all leaped into my heart."

When Emma placed her hand on her thigh, she reached down and squeezed it.

"Sure," said Cooper, "the girls would probably love a weekend away."

A sigh of relief erupted from her lungs. "I know all of us want to help in any way we can. If we could do it as a group, we'd be the most effective."

Mom spoke next; her eyes riveted lovingly on her daughter. "Your concern and your willingness to help remind me of how much you are your father's daughter. He had a soft spot for kids who struggled in families like Ivy's. I was always proud of him for that. You have the same heart as him, Lora." The warmth in her eyes came through as she spoke.

Claire validated the sentiment with a smile and a nod.

Cooper furrowed his brow and adjusted his folded arms. "About Ivy's art. Unfortunately, I can't give open access to the house. Jake might come around to see her."

He twisted his lips in thought. "Mom, maybe we could make a schedule? Give Ivy access on the days you cook dinner for us, regardless of whether Emma is home. Would that be possible?"

"Sure, we'll work something out." Claire took a sip of her water, then slowly put the glass down. "I'll stop by Judy's work—talk with her to get a sense of what she thinks about the situation."

"Lora," said Mom, "I've been wondering how I might help. I'd like to give you some money to make the weekend special for the girls. It might be fun for Ivy to have a makeover while in Seattle? How about buying her some new clothes? A makeover always gives a gal more confidence." She threw a private wink towards her.

Then Mom leaned toward Emma. "Honey, would you be upset if we made a big fuss over Ivy during that weekend? I wouldn't want you to feel left out."

Emma brightened. "No, it's a great idea! She's teased about her clothes at school. She doesn't have much." Emma smiled her gratitude. "That's so nice of you."

Cooper reached a hand across the table to his daughter, and she took hold.

"Kiddo, I'll give you some spending money, too." He glanced around the group. "This sounds like a good initial plan. Let's keep in touch and see how things progress."

The server asked if they wanted anything else. When everyone shook their heads, the server handed Cooper the bill. When Claire's hand reached out, he playfully swatted it away.

Not wanting him to pay for their meal, she said, "Cooper, please let me give you something for Mom's and my dinner."

"No, we appreciate your coming. Consider it a small thank you for your efforts in helping Ivy."

CHAPTER 16
LORA

Lora crumbled the napkin Cooper had drawn a map on the night before and tossed it into the passenger seat. "That was useless!" Since her GPS wasn't working in this remote area, she was on her own. It really was the boondocks. Cooper was right in saying she'd been lucky he'd found her that day.

Even though it hadn't worked out between her and Cooper, that weekend had been a turning point for her. The feelings Cooper and his family evoked were her guiding star for the future she wanted.

She slowed the car, sensing Cooper's driveway had to be nearby.

How would Ivy respond to her plan? If she goes along with it, it could spark a turning point in *her* life.

There it was. Peering out from behind an overgrown rhododendron was the sign that said *THE MARTINS.*

After parking the car, she walked toward the front door, jumping over sidewalk puddles too large to step over. The Pacific Northwest's early fall weather had done what it did best—dump gobs of precipitation. As she reached the front stoop, the door flew open. She stumbled back, gasping.

Emma grabbed her arm to pull her in. "Ivy's already here!"

Emma's hair was up in a messy bun. She wore black leggings and an oversized sweatshirt. After entering, Emma quickly shut the door. Immediately, Emma headed for the creative room. She followed, suppressing a giggle as Emma's thick, squishy-soled bunny slippers *faloop-faloop-falooped* across the hardwood floor.

Compared to Emma's outfit, she was a tad overdressed. She'd put on a new, heathered teal sweater that pulled out the blue in her eyes, along with the same designer jeans she'd worn yesterday. Still deflated from her encounter with her jean twin, Mindy, she'd put extra care into her appearance.

As they entered the creative room, they found Ivy, head down, concentrating on a project.

Ivy turned to them with a broad, open smile. Her dewy, fresh face revealed an innocence often hidden behind black-lined eyes.

"Hi, Lora. I was trying to get this one finished before you got here. It needs a little more...something. I've got two done, though." Then she lowered her head and returned to her painting.

She and Emma smiled at each other, pleased Ivy was back in her element.

Against the wall stood a row of canvases. She wandered over to view the series. Ivy had used repurposed paper as the background foundation. Each design was a representation of a woman's torso, and an evolution of the one before. All were uniquely different.

"Ivy, these are wonderful. I've seen quilters do this—use the same pattern or idea, then change some elements in the next—like color combinations or by adding different borders. They perfected one technique, then introduced another to freshen their work. Just like you've done."

Behind Ivy's half-hidden face, she caught a glimpse of a grin.

She peered down at what Ivy was currently working on. On a plain white canvas, Ivy had ink-blocked the background to create a light-gray cloudy effect. Then, by layering various torn, glued, gray-patterned scrapbook papers, she had created the shape of a woman's torso. She'd softened the torn edges with a light touch of a medium gray watercolor. The ghostly quality of the piece reminded her of the Celebration of the Dead art, though without the typical colorful qualities or distinct themed forms.

"Ivy, you amaze me! You have such a creative mind *and* lots of talent in those hands. Such exciting work!"

Ivy looked up, beaming. Today, compliments weren't pulling Ivy into her turtle shell. Also, her fresh-faced appearance was considerably different from the girl she'd seen at the gymnasium.

She liked the changes. Had she become a safe enough person for Ivy to eliminate the need to hide herself so much? She hoped so.

With a notebook in hand, Emma came up alongside her. "Ivy, may I show Lora your old sketchbook?"

Ivy twisted her lips, but nodded her permission.

Emma handed her the notebook. Inside were a series of cartoon caricatures. Each appealing in its simplicity while also capturing the subject's emotions and distinct personality. One or two caricatures showed up in the back of the book in a structured storyline, like those in a comic book.

Ivy clearly wasn't afraid to take chances in her art. It appeared she worked at something until she'd mastered the subject or a technique. This aspect of her personality would serve her well.

"I love these caricatures. Their expressions show their personalities. Wonderful! What had you planned to do with these?"

"I'd done a few cartoons for the school paper. Mostly I just kept myself busy while I hung out in my room or while waiting for my mom to get off shift. I always have a sketchbook with me."

"Well, you've used your time productively. At the back of the notebook, I see you filled the pages with line drawings of various subjects. I'm not sure what they call this? They're like those adult coloring books you'd see in grocery stores." She marveled at the detailed images filling the themed pages. "I bet you could draw just about anything, Ivy."

"Maybe." Ivy shrugged humbly as color rose on her cheeks. "Those coloring books gave me the idea." Her ears flushed red as she bent her spine, tucking her shoulders forward. That was Ivy's signal that she was uncomfortable.

She wanted Ivy to know her praise was genuine, not an attempt to boost her self-esteem. Ivy's talent was truly remarkable.

Pretending to think out loud, she wandered off. "Obviously, there are many directions your talents could take you. And lots of possibilities for eventually generating income. Especially since you're willing to put in the effort."

She casually glanced back, checking to see if she'd gotten Ivy's attention. Ivy's shoulders rose as she took a deep breath, then a wide grin spread across her face. Today, Ivy wasn't bothering to hide her emotions.

Over the next half-hour, she caught up with what was happening in the girls' lives. As expected, Emma was the most vocal. Ivy didn't mention Jake or her home life.

Eventually, Emma got around to showing her some of her finished jewelry pieces. Though Emma was creative, she didn't show the same passion for creating as Ivy. Probably since her life was already so full. Emma's participation seemed more about being a supportive companion to her friend.

Though it was enjoyable being with the girls, it was unclear how or if she could continue their relationship. Patience and time would reveal what her role would be in their lives. For right now, it was a privilege the girls trusted her enough to request her involvement. At the least, she would affirm the girls' talents and support their endeavors, just as many women had done for her throughout her life.

When she told Ivy about the Seattle weekend getaway, Ivy was initially excited. Once Ivy learned she needed parental permission, things changed. Ivy's face darkened, and her mouth stretched into a straight line.

"Look, if you suspect your mom will say no, I could call her now and ask."

"No. My mom's at work."

"It's not peak hours yet. She should be able to talk briefly."

Ivy's arms tightened against her chest. "Okay. I guess."

They all trooped to the kitchen phone. Ivy dialed. "Mom, I have Lora Hamilton with me, and she wants to talk to you. She's a friend of the Martins." Ivy handed her the phone.

Keeping her tone light and friendly, she said, "Judy, hi! I met Ivy a few months back and saw some of her artwork. Your daughter has genuine talent. Her love of art shows in her productivity. If you wouldn't mind, I'd like to take Ivy and Emma on a...well, something like a field trip...to an art gallery in Seattle. The owner said she'd look at the girls' art pieces and provide them with some feedback. Cooper would put them on the ferry next

Friday, and I'd pick them up at the other end. They'd stay with me at my condo in Tacoma. Saturday will be a full day in Seattle. The girls would return on Sunday, with Cooper bringing her home early afternoon." She held her breath as she waited for an answer.

None came. She walked away from the girls, not wanting them to hear what might be said.

Not sure of what was happening on the other end, she hurriedly said, "There will be no cost for Ivy to go. I wanted the girls to have a fun weekend and for Ivy to think of art as a potential career. My mom, who also believes Ivy has remarkable talent, has volunteered to cover expenses. Again, there's no cost to you."

"You think my daughter has talent?" Judy asked, with amazement in her voice. She also heard confusion and wonder. Had Ivy not shown her mother any of her drawings or art projects?

"Why, yes, I do. I'll make sure she brings home a few of the pieces she's created here at Emma's."

On the other end of the line was a "*Hmmm.*"

"What do you think? Can she go?"

When Judy muttered a tentative, "Okay." She walked back to where Emma and Ivy were waiting and gave them a thumbs-up. While the girls hugged and danced about, she provided more details to Judy. Afterward, she told the girls goodbye and headed to give Cooper the news.

***

She found Cooper in his office. She stood in the doorway watching him work. His head was bent and his hair disheveled, with one thick lock falling over an eye. Concentrating, the tip of his tongue moved to the edge of his lips as he read something on the screen. His outstretched bare feet extended beyond the front of the desk, which faced forward into the room. His feet rubbed rhythmically against each other.

Seeing him quickened her heart. Her breath caught from the intimacy of the setting. The longer she watched him, the more her body ached with longing—not just for him physically, but for everything he could offer.

Seeing him reminded her of what she couldn't have—from him, at least. She wanted to flee, yet she had a task to complete.

After taking a deep breath, she cleared her throat to get his attention.

His head snapped up.

"I talked to Judy. It's a go for next weekend. The girls are excited." She took a few steps in. "So, if you would take them to the Bremerton ferry next Friday after school, I'll pick them up on the other end. They'll return by ferry late Sunday morning. You okay with that?"

Cooper stood and walked around his desk, wearing well-worn jeans and a moss-green, V-neck, athletic-cut T-shirt.

He looked good.

He ran his fingers through his hair as he released a sigh. "I know they're gonna love it. Thank you. Have Emma call me when she gets off the ferry. Well, and every night to check in." He lifted a shoulder. "I get a tad anxious when she's away."

A spark of annoyance flared, and she spoke out without thinking. "Are you nervous about giving her some freedom, or is it they'll be under *my* care?" Heat rose instantly to her cheeks. Why had she said that?

She slung her purse over her shoulder, ready to escape the room. When she glanced at Cooper, there seemed to be confusion and hurt in his eyes.

He tilted his head. "*First*," he said sternly, "I know they need a little freedom to grow, and Emma's responsible enough to look after both her *and* Ivy if need be." He drew in a slow breath. "*Second*, I have no concern about how you will handle the responsibility of having the girls in your care. I know you'll keep them safe, to the best of your ability. I trust you, and I admire what you're doing for Ivy *and* Emma."

Her heart sped up as he walked closer. Then he reached out and gently placed his hand on her arm. She swallowed and closed her eyes briefly. Embarrassed by her outburst, tears welled in her eyes. She swiped them away quickly. "Okay."

"Lora, I have great respect for you. It's wonderful how the girls have taken to you. How could I *not* be happy about your giving the girls this opportunity?" His eyes pleaded with her to understand.

Captivated by his soothing tone, the warmth of his hand, and his affirming words, the tension in her chest dropped away. She croaked out a soft, "Thank you."

He was so close. Her body and heart responded. Those reactions weren't welcome. She turned away and hurried toward the front door.

Cooper followed, though he remained silent.

When she reached her car, she glanced back. He stood in the open front doorway with his arms slack at his sides. Before he turned away, she thought she saw regret on his face.

As she drove away, her belly knotted with self-disgust. She should have kept her mouth shut. She'd only made things more awkward between them.

CHAPTER 17
COOPER

Cooper went in search of a late afternoon snack for him and the girls. He headed for the kitchen to grab a bag of sweet potato chips when his mother came through the back door.

"Yoo-hoo! Brownie delivery." With her usual generous smile, Mom walked into the kitchen carrying a dinner-size plate of gooey brownies. As she looked about, her expression showed puzzlement. "I didn't see Lora's car out front. I'd hoped she'd still be here."

Instead of responding, he leaned his hips against the kitchen counter and stared down at his bare feet.

The brownie plate hit hard against the counter. Mom's sharp tone surprised him as she said, "So, Lora took care of things with the girls, then headed out?" When he didn't answer, she sighed loudly. "Nothing to keep her here, I suppose."

She jerked open the cupboard door, took out two glasses, and then walked to the refrigerator. After filling the glasses with milk, she placed them on a tray with a small plate of brownies.

"Lora's been wonderful with the girls. She's something, stepping up to help Ivy like that." She pivoted to go up the stairs. "Since Lora didn't meet up with her mom for brunch, did she eat here?"

"No." He let out a sigh.

Mom walked heavy-footed up the stairs; he stayed where he was. A corner of his lips raised hearing the girls' cheers of appreciation for the brownie delivery.

He was still leaning against the counter with his arms crossed when Mom walked back into the kitchen. She paced in front of him, though he refused to acknowledge her presence. An ass-chewin' was comin'. He probably needed one.

She threw down her arms and turned to him. "What are you doing, son? You have kept every woman at bay for years. Well, except for Cheryl." She shook her head. "That dimwit choice reinforced your belief that you and Emma would be better off *not* attaching to anyone again."

"Mom," he warned.

She moved closer. "I've seen the way you look at Lora, and she at you. You're making a mistake by not trying with that girl. Rebecca told me what an amazing person she had been before the accident. She's been making her way back to that person. She's a keeper!"

He ran a hand through his hair. "It's probably too late, Mom. She opened up to me about how her daughter had died and how her jerk of a husband treated her. Then, right after that, I backed off. I think she assumed I judged her poorly after what she told me." He uncrossed his arms and let them fall to his side.

"I'll admit, there *was* something between us. Then I...well, I got scared. Fear set my mind against trying." He shook his head. "I can't remember ever having such powerful feelings for a woman that fast. When I panicked, I told her I didn't want a long-distance relationship because—it doesn't matter. It's likely she believes I consider her damaged goods or something." He rubbed his chin roughly. "I hurt her. It's too late now."

Mom *hrumphed.*

He re-crossed his legs and arms and stared up at the ceiling. "I suppose I have wondered what scars might remain after what she went through. But I was—" He blew out a frustrated breath. "I *am* terrified to love again. I'm still attracted to her. However, she doesn't seem to want anything to do with me now."

Mom shook her head. "Omigod, son. You do know how to make a mess of things."

He walked to the cupboard to get a glass. At the refrigerator, he said, "Lora's strong and confident with the girls, and with everything else, yet around me she seems vulnerable. Today she accused me of not being comfortable entrusting her with the girls' safety on their trip."

Mom frowned. "How did you react?"

He poured some milk, drank deeply, and then refilled his glass. "I tried to tell her I trusted her. Yet I'm not sure what she was thinking when she left." He plopped down on one of the island's barstools and reached across the counter for a brownie. The brownie sat in his fingers while he stared off into space.

Mom took the stool two seats over. She sat in silence for a few moments before turning to him.

Her soft voice uttered, "You've lived in fear, expecting heartbreak around every corner. You talk about her scars; you've got some of your own." She patted his arm. "You've done a good job with Emma, though you're kidding yourself if you believe not marrying again had been the best thing for her *or* for you. Remarrying the *right* person would have made life richer for both of you." She got up and paced the area between the kitchen stove and the island.

He hung his head as his heart thumped in his chest. He didn't know what to say.

She leaned against the counter in front of him. "I know it isn't my place, yet I'm going to say it anyway. I know you've been on dates with ladies in the next town over. Ones *I* hadn't set up for you." She chuckled. "However, you've never talked about them or the dates you've had here in Orca Park. You're getting to be known around town as the one-date-wonder!"

He raised an eyebrow.

"Oh, my word. You are pitiful!" She sighed dramatically, although there was a smile on her face. She placed a hand on his arm. "You've fallen for Lora. Am I right?"

His shoulders slumped. There was that possibility.

"Son, even if you let yourself love Lora, there's no guarantee she or anyone else wouldn't be taken away from you. Even if you were together, it's likely you'd have challenges that bring discomfort. I imagine Lora might have similar fears and concerns. Heck, maybe even more complex than yours." She tapped his arm, requesting he look at her. "From what Rebecca told me, Lora's ready to take the risk. She wants, with all her heart, to love and to be loved again. You, Cooper Martin, are missing what loving someone provides. You'd have a partner to weather the tough times with and have the joy of making wonderful memories to carry with you the rest of your life."

A storm was brewing inside him. He didn't like being forced to look too deeply into himself.

Mom forged on. "Emma's gone in a few years. Will you be brave enough then? And you might consider the fact that Emma wanted *Lora* to help with her concerns about Ivy, *not* you or me. She has a strong connection to Lora, or she wants one. She trusts her." Mom's brows furrowed. "Son, if you wait too long, Lora won't be available. Rebecca said Lora's stronger now. She'll find the future she wants—a husband and a family."

"Mom, I—"

"Don't give me any excuses." Mom shook her head, then her face softened as she reached to give him a quick hug. "Just think about it."

He nodded. She made it sound so easy, but it wasn't.

As she headed toward the back door, she called over her shoulder, "Oh, by the way. I have two beaus at my adult living complex. It's quite fun!" She cackled as she shut the back door.

He let his mother's declaration sink in. Good for her. She deserved some romance in her life.

Well, maybe he did, too. She could be right. It would be ridiculous to wait until Emma was an adult before loving again.

He grabbed another brownie and returned to his office, refusing to dwell on the topic.

CHAPTER 18
LORA

Lora, along with the crowd waiting at Pier 66 for the 4:00 pm ferry, watched a group of screeching seagulls fight over food scraps.

An elderly man standing beside her, bundled in a heavy coat and stocking cap, asked, "Who you waitin' for?"

Good question. Who were these girls to her? She was not a mother, sister, or aunt to them. Friend? Yes.

"I have some young friends coming for a special outing in Seattle this weekend."

As soon as she caught sight of the girls strolling arm in arm down the off-ramp, she felt a surge of happiness. Emma was pointing out something to Ivy along the Seattle waterfront. Ivy's head swung from side to side, trying to see everything.

She sent a quick text to Cooper saying the girls had arrived safely. When the girls were close enough, she waved to catch their attention. They hurried toward her, grinning. Emma was the first to wrap her arms around her for a quick squeeze. Ivy held back. Hunched over, Ivy fiddled with her backpack straps.

Without hesitation, she lunged to give Ivy a quick embrace.

"So glad you're here!" Ivy rewarded her with a genuine smile. That smile brought an unexpected lump to her throat.

"Us too!" shouted the girls in unison.

"The car's parked in a lot nearby. We'll drop off your stuff, then walk up the hill to make a few stops. Since the traffic will be bad whenever we leave, we'll hang out around here for a while. Then have a late dinner. How 'bout it?"

"Sounds great!" said Emma.

Ivy, still rubbernecking, mumbled, "Yeah. Great."

After stashing everything in her trunk, they headed up the hill to downtown Seattle. To facilitate conversation, she turned around and walked backward.

"We have a few things to accomplish. Ivy, I have a surprise for you." She winked at Emma. "Emma's in on this, too."

Emma enthusiastically linked arms with Ivy as they trudged up the steep hill.

She squeezed in close beside the girls. "Ivy, you're already aware we'll be meeting with a gallery owner tomorrow. I'm so grateful she's doing this for us. Although please view this as a learning experience, especially if the pieces aren't as ready to sell as we hope. Everyone wants you to succeed and advance toward an art career someday. Is that what you want for yourself?"

Ivy nodded, smiling.

That smile sent a zing of joy through her. It was important for Ivy to see her potential as an artist. "With that line of thinking, we want you to look your best tomorrow."

Ivy's jaw tightened as she glanced down at her faded black jeans with colorful spatters near their worn hem. Someone had rubbed a black marker on the toe of her boot to hide a worn spot. Though Ivy carried off the grunge look well, the struggling artist vibe wasn't the image she wanted Ivy to present when meeting with the gallery owner.

With a tone meant to soothe, she said, "You have your own style, Ivy. Edgy is what I'd call it, and that's fine for a street artist. However, I suggest having a few items of clothing on hand for occasions like tomorrow. To represent yourself as a professional artist. To be taken seriously."

Ivy frowned and looked at the sidewalk.

Okay, she needed to sell her idea better. "I know a store a few blocks up where they have clothes you might like. I shopped there as a teen, during a time I insisted on wearing everything vintage."

Ivy's chin tucked lower, and her voice with it. "Um, thanks, but I can't afford new clothes."

The disappointment and embarrassment on Ivy's face said she'd jumped the gun. "I'm sorry! I forgot to tell you. You have a fairy godmother!"

She walked backward to observe Ivy's face. "Ivy, my mom gave me some money to help with expenses, like buying a few outfits for you."

Ivy kept her head down, staying mute.

Darn. She hadn't considered that Ivy wouldn't go along with the idea. This was supposed to be a positive experience for her.

Thinking on her feet, she said, "Mom's quite taken with you, Ivy. The thought of helping an aspiring artist get a leg up appealed to her."

Still only a scowl.

"Don't imagine it as trying to change you. Though lots of girls would consider a makeover appealing."

She blew out some frustration. "It's more about enhancing what's already wonderful about you."

No change. Oh darn.

"Um, it would be like representing new sides of yourself through your clothing. Oh, I don't know. It could be fun."

Again, no sign of receptivity.

"Down the road, if you would reciprocate with a signed piece of art, Mom would be thrilled. She would consider it a worthwhile *exchange* for her investment. She firmly believes that you will become an established artist someday. Her contribution isn't charity. It's more like bartering... a business deal."

Though subtle, Ivy's features changed. Then her chin trembled and her face scrunched up as tears flowed.

Boy, she needed to be cautious in the way she offered help from now on. She didn't want Ivy to interpret what she offered as charity. Gosh, she hadn't even considered how this might cause problems for Ivy at home. Inducing shame was not what she wanted Ivy to experience. Her goal was to raise Ivy up, not bring her down. From Ivy's response, she could see this was a delicate matter.

Emma grabbed Ivy's arm and quickened her pace, pulling Ivy along as if attempting to pull her concerns away.

"This is gonna to be great!" said Emma. "Dad gave me some money, too. I know that in the future you'll make something super-duper for Rachael, and she'll be so happy with it. You know, we've never been on a shopping trip together. Let's share a dressing room and model each outfit for Lora. She can give us a thumbs-up or thumbs-down."

Emma was almost skipping now. "I can't wait to see the shop Lora's taking us to."

While Emma babbled on, Ivy slowly regained her composure.

As she watched the girls walk side by side up the hill, she noticed a spring return to Ivy's step. A smile of triumph spread over her face.

Aware that the girls were approaching a busy intersection, her hand flew to her chest as her breathing constricted.

"Be careful at the intersection. Check for oncoming traffic, *even if* the light shows you can cross. Then turn left at the next block." Her heart hit hard against her chest. "Second Chances is three or four stores down on the left."

She took a deep breath, then exhaled slowly as the girls safely crossed the intersection.

***

As they stepped into Second Chances, honey-pear scented candles and contemporary music greeted them. Somewhere in the store, the owner's robust laughter made her feel as though she'd gone back in time.

By the expressions on the girls' faces, the creative displays, which made shopping at a second-hand store chic, had caught the girls' attention. The owner had a knack for stocking high-end, resale merchandise alongside new, moderately priced contemporary fashion.

Right away, she spotted a dress she wanted to try on. Holding it up in front of her, she said, "Hey, girls, how about this for me?" She laughed, reminding herself that the trip was for the girls' benefit. However, the gesture had broken the ice. The girls split up and started roaming the store.

After both girls picked out a variety of items, Emma took Ivy with her into a large corner dressing booth.

After she tried a few things on for herself, she waited in a nearby comfy chair. The girls' laughter drifted beneath the brocade-curtained booth. It warmed her heart to hear the girls support each other in their efforts to find their perfect outfits.

She had been a lot like Emma as a teen, naturally prone to nurturing her friends. She missed having close friends and meaningful relationships. In time, she would change that.

When the girls were ready, they dramatically swished back the booth's curtain to proceed with their best runway walks before striking a pose. Keeping their faces neutral, they mimicked the stoic stance of high-fashion models as they revealed outfit after outfit.

Before they decided what to keep, the dressing room became a haphazard pile of clothes. During their reveals, they each gave their opinions and a numerical vote. The potential recipient received double voting points. Some re-try-ons were necessary.

In the end, Ivy settled on a skater-style dress, a pair of skinny jeans, which looked brand new, three tops, and a bulky cardigan sweater. She also scored a moderately worn pair of cowboy boots, a discounted pair of sandals, and the deal of the day—a pair of newly arrived ankle boots.

Emma found a sweet, above-the-knee, cap-sleeved, blue floral dress, a denim jacket, and a vintage necklace she loved.

She was taking home a retro 1950s-style fitted sweater and a pendant necklace to go with a tunic and leggings she'd recently purchased.

Both girls profusely thanked her for the shopping trip. Ivy shyly said, "Please thank your mom for doing this for me. I'll remember to make her something amazing when I become a genuine artist."

Famished after shopping, they dropped their bags off at the car and headed to one of Seattle's most famous waterfront restaurants on the pier.

Soon after they ordered, Emma excused herself to call her dad.

What would Emma share about her day? Would Cooper ask about her?

Stop that! Don't consider Cooper in any way other than Emma's father. If she didn't, continuing a relationship with the girls would become difficult.

"Ivy, you can use my cell if you'd like to call home."

Ivy lowered her brows and pursed her lips. Without making eye contact, she said, "No thanks. Mom's working, and she doesn't have a cell phone."

"Well, let me know if you want to try another time."

What type of relationship did Ivy have with her mother? Ivy needed someone besides Emma to stand beside her. Could she be that person? How would that work, living so far away?

To melt Ivy's sudden frosty mood, she said, "I sure had a great time shopping. Returning to Second Chances brought back so many wonderful memories, and now you've given me some new ones. You were a good sport for going along with Mom's and my plan for treating you to a special experience."

Ivy gave her a weak smile, and her eyes read that she was back to worrying. She'd give her the space she needed. Besides, she was still on a high from their successful shopping trip and didn't want to suppress the joy she was experiencing.

She'd found that once she'd freed herself from the burden of guilt over Maggie's death, she'd had the desire to accept and then give as much joy as she was capable of. In retrospect, suppressing joy was like what happens when someone gives up their favorite food for Lent. You crave what you've restricted yourself from.

With that thought, she took a deep breath, which gave her the sensation of champagne bubbles floating through her chest. Funny how feelings of joy could pop up out of the blue over the simplest things. Accepting her tragic past and granting herself redemption had been the equivalent of putting on a pair of proverbial rose color glasses. There was joy to be found everywhere. Realistically, those glasses wouldn't always be on, but she could enjoy the moments when they were.

When she glanced at Ivy's face, her heart sank a little. Ivy retreated into her turtle shell again.

This girl sure pulled at her heartstrings. Ivy had so much potential. Someone had to help her become who she *could* be. What a blessing it had been for Ivy to find art. That passion gave her something positive to focus on. Ivy was also fortunate to have the Martins in her corner. She hoped she could be there, too.

Becoming more involved would complicate keeping her distance from Cooper. Yet, she didn't want this to hold her back from helping Ivy.

She reached over and squeezed Ivy's hand. When Ivy looked up, she said, "You're an amazing young lady. And a beautiful one at that."

A slight brightening skimmed Ivy's face. That was a start. Her silence had been making their time together awkward.

Emma bounced back to the table, wearing an enormous smile. Her energy seemed to perk up both her and Ivy. That and the fact the server swooped in to bring their meal.

Emma picked up her fork and said, "I told Dad what an amazing time we've been having. He said I owe you a big thank you. So, thanks, Lora. This has been so—awesomely cool! And we get another entire day tomorrow!"

"I'm glad you're having a good time. You two have made this one of the best days I've had in a long time." She raised her water glass and said, "Here's to tomorrow's adventure."

While Emma dominated the conversation throughout dinner, Ivy brought out a paper pad and started doodling. Emma rattled on about school and the clubs she wanted to join next year as a junior.

"And when Ivy and I are seniors, we need to choose a senior project. I'm freaking out about it already."

She asked a few questions, which Emma answered earnestly. It was clear Emma was the type of kid who eased her anxiety by crafting a well-thought-out plan.

She could relate. "Can I give you a little advice, Emma?"

"Sure."

"I've found that initial plans provide a certain amount of security and motivation, though as a project develops, plans often need to be changed...as they should, when appropriate."

Emma scrunched her brows and nodded. "Yeah, I've noticed that."

"I'm a bit of a planner myself, so I know the benefits and the pitfalls."

She wrung her hands under the table. Of course, all plans become void when tragedy strikes. Then, emotionally charged thinking messes with any further plans you might make.

She splayed her fingers, telling herself that was enough of looking backwards.

"Ivy, tell me about what you're doing in school. Are you planning to take any college prep classes?"

"I don't know." Ivy clicked the end of her pen in rapid-fire succession. "I'm probably not going, so why bother?"

Ivy twisted her mouth into a sour expression. To dismiss any further conversation, she picked up her pen and returned to her sketchbook. Her hand moved elegantly across her pad, creating an ink drawing of a couple embracing on the dock. She captured the essence of the figures with minimal strokes. Ivy had quickly returned to being consumed by the act of creating.

It was mesmerizing to watch her work. Such talent and versatility. Yet, to make a living as an artist, you need more than that. She would research careers where artistic talent was a major aspect of the job. That would broaden Ivy's career options. Most likely, Ivy wouldn't be aware of the possibilities out there. Graphic design?

She cleared her throat, and Ivy's head raised. "The woman we'll be seeing tomorrow told me about an art school that gives scholarships to students who need financial help. I'd be happy to get some information for you and maybe find other programs that do the same."

Ivy put her pen down and wove her fingers together. "You think I'm g-good enough for that?"

"Yes, I do. However, like any advanced schooling, there will be a grade point average and other requirements for getting in. Planning ahead will be important."

Ivy's shoulders curved forward again.

"It's certainly worth a try, Ivy. I'll help in any way I can."

Ivy didn't respond.

She released a frustrated breath. Having to deal with Ivy's emotions was like having hiccups while standing on a balance ball.

"Ivy, you're less than halfway through your sophomore year, so there's still lots of time before you'd have to apply. This is a goal that's within your reach. Don't sell yourself short or give up on viable options." Her heart melted as she watched a slew of emotions run across Ivy's face.

Ivy rapidly wiped the moisture from her eyes as her lips quivered. Softly, she said, "Yeah, I could try."

Her eyes stung with tears as she reached across the table to touch Ivy. She signaled to Emma to change seats with her.

Once she sat beside Ivy, she leaned in and whispered into Ivy's ear. "Let people help you. Everybody needs help from time to time. And later, as you become successful, you'll be in the position to help someone else." She gave Ivy a side hug.

With a shy smile, Ivy tilted her head onto her shoulder and said, "Thanks."

"Ivy," interjected Emma, "wouldn't it be great if we had careers where we could live together?"

That sparked an entire conversation about what their apartment would look like, who would do the cooking, and if they would get a pet.

Emotion caught her breath. Any future-focused thinking by these girls was another step toward manifesting a positive future.

***

Her two-bedroom condo was several blocks from Tacoma's downtown waterfront. The first thing the girls did was stretch themselves over the balcony railing to see her humble view. To them, it was marvelous. Lots of lights on the horizon provided some big-city glamor for these two small-town girls to gawk at.

After the girls explored their room, they laid out their clothes for the next day. Their appearing so happy made her happy. To give them some privacy, she wandered into the kitchen.

Watching the girls interact grew her desire for female friendships. She had been holding off on asking one of the quilt guild ladies for coffee. Friendships as an adult seemed a lot harder than when she was in high school or college. By now, most potential friends would already be mothers. They would talk about their experiences of being mothers, their children, and their relationships with their husbands. Would she have *anything* in common with women her age?

While she contemplated this, she made herself tea. There would be emotional hurdles to overcome if she wanted friends her own age. She tightened her fist. If people couldn't accept her crummy past, then she wouldn't want their friendship.

She squeezed her teabag out and put it on a plate.

No more hiding.

Ivy entered the kitchen wearing her new skinny jeans rolled at the cuff, ankle boots, a V-neck, jewel-toned T-shirt, and a bulky cable-knit cardigan. "What about my wearing this tomorrow?" She twirled with a big grin on her face.

"You look fabulous. Would you mind if I took your picture? I'll send it along with a text to Mom. She'd love to see what you bought."

After a slight hesitation, Ivy said, "Sure. And tell her thank you from me."

CHAPTER 19
IVY

Ivy opened her eyes and pulled in a steady breath to enjoy the smell of bacon cooking. Beside her, Emma was already sitting up in bed, stretching.

She shuffled down the hall, following Emma to the kitchen. Emma looked great in her cute flowered flannel pajama bottoms and a coordinated pink T-shirt. Her face drooped as she looked down at her boxer shorts. She squared them on her hips and ran her hand down her black faded hand-me-down T-shirt.

Whatever.

They entered the kitchen just as Lora pulled a huge, yummy-smelling, puffed-up pancake thingy out of the oven.

"I've made you girls a Dutch Baby pancake." Lora looked so pretty and at home in her kitchen. Lora scooped fresh berries into the hollowed center of the pancake, then sprinkled the top with powdered sugar.

Impressive. If she'd had a phone, she would've taken a picture.

They devoured their warm pancake slices in minutes. Lora and Emma gave her the last slice before they got up to make another.

At the kitchen counter, Emma hugged Lora. "It was nice of you to make us something so special."

Lora's face lit up.

Emma can be such a suck-up!

Darn, why hadn't *she* said thank you and gushed over Lora's breakfast? She didn't say thank you often enough. It rolled out of Emma's mouth so easily. It wasn't that she didn't appreciate things; she felt awkward saying it.

Lora was super nice. It was obvious she'd planned this trip mostly for *her*. She probably just felt sorry for her. Why would she even care, anyway?

All her life she'd been *poor, pitiful Ivy*. It was hard sometimes having a best friend who came from one of the cool families in town, when she came from the opposite.

A feeling of heaviness overcame her as Lora and Emma exchanged affections again. Uncomfortable, she longed for the escape a pencil and pad of paper could provide. Watching the *admiration duo* doing their cooking thing made her feel like an outsider. Kinda normal, though.

"What about using cardamom instead of cinnamon?" asked Emma. "And maybe leave out the berries and serve it with warm maple syrup or apple pie filling?"

Lora grinned. "Great ideas. I love cardamom."

What the heck was cardamom? Suddenly, her breakfast formed an uncomfortable solid lump in her belly. She could see it now; Lora and Emma were becoming friends. Real friends. Emma, the well-behaved girl from a respectable family, liked by everyone, had done it again. She rubbed her fingers between her eyebrows.

That sucks.

She croaked out, "Thanks Lora, this was delicious."

Lora paused and said, "You're welcome." Then she turned her attention back to Emma.

As the two continued chatting about Lora's cookbook collection, her jaw tensed. Why couldn't she have Lora all to herself? Emma had everyone.

She pushed her chair back with such force that the chair clunked against the wall. "I'm gonna go take a shower." She rushed out, knowing if she stayed much longer, she'd end up crying or saying something mean.

Why couldn't Emma see she was the one who needed Lora?

She slammed the bedroom door. Let it go. You've got today to look forward to. Don't screw it up by being a jealous grump. She hoped, though it seemed unrealistic, that the gallery owner would want to sell her art.

Wouldn't it be amazing if someday she became a famous artist? Like those in the books at the library.

Oh, sure...how stupid. Girls like her didn't get those kinda breaks.

No. Not true. Lots of people made it out of worse crud—rappers, movie stars, and even the guy who created Wendy's Drive-ins.

Why couldn't she?

***

They arrived at the gallery before any customers arrived. Carol was super cool. She looked really successful and high-class. When we brought out our art pieces, she asked us to tell her something about each piece. Afterward, she made suggestions for specific improvements.

"Emma, you have a good eye for what goes together, and you're very fortunate to have these vintage pieces as focal points. However, to make them high-end and get top dollar, you'll need to buy heavy-duty fasteners. Next, work to improve your soldering skills. You can't have something rough against a woman's skin. Overall, though, you have the right idea."

Her heart sped up like a machine gun in a *Tom and Jerry* cartoon as Carol turned to her.

"Ivy, I like your recent trio. You have some raw talent in design and composition, and I'm confident your skills will continue to develop. The finishing of your work needs some refinement. I'll give you a list of YouTube tutorials on how to finish multimedia work and acrylics so your pieces will hold up and have a more professional appearance."

Carol must have seen her embarrassment when she smiled and said, "Don't worry, I've given this same talk to other artists. So much energy goes into the creating phase that artists often neglect the finishing of the piece. If not done adequately, it might hold back a sale. It's worth putting the time in to get it right."

That wasn't exactly what she wanted to hear. Regardless, being surrounded by amazing art made her want to improve her skills and get to the level displayed before her.

"Okay." She swallowed her nerves before she asked, "What kind of art sells the best? I'd like to focus on what makes the most money."

Carol's eyes twinkled. "Ivy, there's no straightforward answer to that question. Art trends are forever changing. Some artists follow trends, while others prefer developing the medium they're most interested in or have a connection with. They go where their passions take them, resisting anything outside of who they know themselves to be as artists. To succeed, an artist has to create a customer following."

Her shoulders sank. Guess there's no easy or quick way to make money.

Carol touched her arm. "If you keep at it, Ivy, you'll know what works for you. Continue exploring and playing with a variety of art forms. Then see what takes off for you."

Since this was her and Emma's first time visiting an art gallery, Carol pointed out the specific artists who were her top sellers. She shared her theories about why some artists were successful and others weren't. She said that an artist and the gallery owner needed to form a relationship with their customers to establish a repeat customer base. Word of mouth and social media would also be important.

Wow, there was more to this than she thought. She already was fighting feelings of defeat. What if she was never good enough to become a successful artist?

Every once in a while, she'd glanced around to find Lora. Once she'd seen her dropping a card onto Carol's desk. Another time, Lora stood gazing at a watercolor of a Great Blue Heron.

Someday, she would like to paint Lora something awesome as a gift.

When a customer strolled in, Carol wrapped up their tour.

Once outside, Lora suggested a nearby cafe for lunch.

As they ate, Lora did something unexpected. "Ivy, I'd like to commission you to make a ballerina-themed art piece for my niece. It might become a Christmas present, or I'll keep it for when she performs in a dance recital. How about I give you fifty dollars in advance?"

Of course, she agreed. After she could hardly eat, even when the food was so delicious. Design ideas swirled through her head. This piece would definitely need to be one of her best.

Lora set a completion date and explained the importance in doing so for both the seller and the buyer. Lora was trying to teach her the business side of an art career.

"Ivy, here's my business card with my cell phone number on the back. Call if you have questions. Since you're just getting your business started, I'm willing to coach you with whatever you need to know to get your career going."

Her breath caught in her chest. Today, she had officially begun her career as an artist.

***

After lunch, they visited two more art galleries. Each had its own personality built around what types of art it featured and its display styles. The last gallery was an art co-op. The lady behind the counter had tons of enthusiasm. She explained how an art co-op worked. The concept seemed like it would be a great way to get your art seen and meet other artists.

"All co-op members create their own displays, work a certain number of hours in the gallery, and divide operation costs. Unlike the fancier galleries, we consider art more broadly, including all sorts of mediums. The skill levels of our artists vary. As a community, we make an effort to help each other learn."

Lora said, "Co-ops are a good way for developing artists to get their work displayed and gain business and marketing experience."

She didn't think Orca Park had one, though.

***

In the late afternoon, they headed back to Tacoma. She took out her sketchbook and jotted down notes of what she had learned during the day. There was so much she wanted to remember.

What a special day! She would never forget it.

"Girls, while we're in Tacoma, I'd like you to see the Washington State History Museum. Then, if we have time, we'll walk under the glass tunnel made by the blown-glass artist, Dale Chihuly, at the Museum of Glass. It's right next door. You up for it?"

"Sure!" she and Emma chorused.

This history museum was so, so cool. What a fantastic place to be inside. Only once had she ever been to a museum. She was pretty young, and the museum was a lot smaller. Nothing compared to this one.

One particular guest artist caught her attention—Amy Sherald, a Black painter based in Baltimore, Maryland, who painted oil portraits of Black Americans. She'd even earned a college degree in *painting*. Who knew you could do that?

While she was examining one of Amy's paintings, Lora came up beside her and asked what had caught her interest.

She struggled to find an answer. "It's the little things, I suppose. How the artist got the skin tones and shading just right, making the face look so real. It's pretty fantastic how she added, you know, the stuff that gives clues about what the person is into...to show their personality. Like their type of clothes. The colors she chose add to that, too. It made me curious about what the artist was trying to say about each person. Or maybe she was asking the viewer to come to his or her conclusions. You know, to make up their own story about the person in the portrait."

What she said made her feel sorta proud of herself, especially when Lora looked pleased with her answer.

"I'd like to do portraits like these. Bernie, the owner of the diner where my mom works, would make a great subject. I'd paint him wearing his stained apron with an onion in one hand and his cleaver in the other. And the flower lady, Miss Mabel. I'd paint her with a dirt smudge on her face, holding cut flowers in one hand and shears in the other."

Lora giggled and hugged her. "You have a true artist's mind, Ivy."

She grinned. *Cool.*

***

It was dark when the three of them walked arm-in-arm, eyes upward, through Chihuly's blown-glass tunnel. The tunnel's backlighting made every inch of the exhibit magical. There were amazing layers of colorful blown glass designs of all sizes and shapes, both translucent and opaque. Seeing them made her breath stick in her chest.

She would never forget those beautiful forms or the feelings they gave her.

Everyone was dragging by the time they made it back to Lora's condo. They were so hungry they ordered pizza.

While eating at the kitchen table, she wanted to tell Lora what the day had meant to her, even if that would be embarrassing.

"This whole day has been—" She searched for adequate words. "The best." Witnessing the happiness on Lora's face, she added. "I truly don't understand why you've done this for me."

A sob slipped out before she could bolt from her chair. Lora's arms wrapped around her, and she melted into the comfort of her warmth. Lora's hug was like slipping into clean sheets fresh out of the dryer. You wanted to snuggle in and stay there forever.

A cellphone rang in the distance.

"Emma," said Lora, "I left my phone in my coat pocket on my bed. Would you get it for me?"

Lora squeezed her tight before she released her. "Ivy, you may not see this in yourself, but there is something very special about you. It's not merely your artistic talent, though I'm envious of your ability to express yourself that way." Lora's smile reached her eyes. "You're pretty wonderful. I mean that."

Not knowing what to say, tears slid down her cheeks; the praise felt so good but also foreign.

Lora paused as if considering what to say; then, her face turned serious.

"There's something I wanted to talk to you about. I know it's a little motherly of me, but humor me." Lora reached over and gently brushed away her tears. "There's a...a *power* all young women feel when they reach an age when boys and men start to see them as sexual beings." Lora briefly hesitated. "That's when a young woman becomes an object of a man's desire. It's easy to misunderstand a man's intentions. A young woman might want to believe the man's interest is coming from a place of love. Sometimes it is. Often, it's only about sex."

Ugh, this was getting awkward. What brought all this on? Her eyes kept on her lap as she fidgeted with her fingers.

Lora didn't seem to notice. "Most young women start relationships with a certain amount of innocence about what love is. For some men, a young woman's innocence can be what appeals to them. Unfortunately, they might not behave in respectful ways. This puts her in a position where she needs to set limits to protect herself."

Lora's giving me the birds-and-bees talk! How embarrassing!

Lora's face had turned pink, yet she kept talking. "If a man she has feelings for is not respectful, a young woman might become confused. His actions might hurt her, or she could feel taken advantage of."

Someone must have told her about Jake. *Emma.* She turned her body further away from Lora. She did *not* want to hear any more of this.

"I've known girls who built their self-esteem and their dreams for a bright future on men being attracted to them. So, they neglected other aspects of themselves, which prevented them from fully developing their potential. My mom taught me that every woman needs to have a way of taking care of herself financially. In case a relationship doesn't work out as hoped. I agree with that. Not everyone gets their happily ever after."

Lora's face fell, then she cleared her throat. "Ivy, I wanted this weekend to inspire you to reach for an art career, so someday you can be financially independent."

Okay, now she understood. Lora was trying to help her. That wasn't so bad. Lora probably didn't want her to end up like her mom. If she could take care of herself, she wouldn't have to put up with some man bossing her around.

She nodded. "I want that, too."

Lora squeezed her hand. "I know this is awkward, and I'm probably not the person you'd want telling you this, but...I care about you. Be careful, Ivy. You're a beautiful girl. Some men might try to take advantage of you. I've seen lots of women make regrettable mistakes regarding men, and I don't want you to be one of them."

She squirmed in her chair. That advice was hitting a little too close to home.

"Okay. Thanks."

A sigh of relief came when Emma returned to give Lora her phone.

"Sorry, I didn't get to it in time. I'm gonna call my dad now, okay?"

"Of course."

Emma turned away quickly and left. Darn. Luckily, Lora seemed done with her...educational talk.

As soon as she could, she excused herself and headed to the bedroom to give Emma a piece of her mind. When she swung open the door, she knew something was wrong. Emma was curled up on the bed, looking sad.

"What's wrong?"

Emma sighed, then scootched up against the headboard. "When I was in Lora's room to get her phone, I saw a picture of a little girl sitting on Lora's lap on her nightstand. My dad said Lora had lost people in her life. I didn't know she'd lost her little girl. The little girl was about my age when I lost my mom."

With tears in her eyes, Emma touched her mother's cross, the one her dad had given her on her thirteenth birthday, which she'd worn ever since.

She sat down on the bed. "That's so sad. I didn't know. Who else did Lora lose?"

"Nana told me her dad died recently. She's single, so maybe her husband, too? That's a lot of people to lose. Yet, she doesn't go around acting depressed or anything." Emma gazed out the window. "The picture made me think about my mom and how Lora and I have like a reversed situation. Weird, huh?" Emma glanced over at her. "I didn't call Dad. I just texted him to say we had a fun day."

"Yeah, it was fun. Right up until Lora gave me a *sex talk*. Did you tell her about Jake?"

"Yeah, and Dad and Nana did too. Everyone is concerned about your getting mixed up with him."

"Well, don't be! I can handle myself." She grabbed the Ziplock bag holding her toothbrush and stomped to the bathroom.

So, they'd been talking about her. How freaking embarrassing! She wasn't stupid. Sometimes she just liked Jake's attention. What was wrong with that?

When she re-entered the bedroom, Emma was under the covers, acting like she was asleep. Fine. Being exhausted, she didn't want to talk, anyway.

***

They'd slept in on Sunday morning, although Lora must have gotten up early. Lora had a mound of French toast, a plate of breakfast sausages, and fresh cut-up pineapple sitting on the table when they came in. It looked *so good*. The only time she had food this darn good was when she ate at the Martins'.

With all the eating, packing, and getting themselves ready, they barely made it to the 11:00 am ferry. Luckily, they were walk-on passengers.

Lora gave each of them a big hug. Emma, of course, was first. She held Lora's hug for the longest time. When she pulled back, Emma said, "It's so frustrating my dad didn't start dating you. Anyway, I'd at least like *us* to be friends. If that's all right with you?"

"That would suit me just fine. You have my number. Call or text anytime." Lora gave Emma another quick hug.

When Lora turned to her, there was such tenderness in her eyes. Her heart rose in her chest.

"Ivy, you have my number, too. You can call me about anything." Lora drew her to her chest and hugged her firmly. "Anything at all."

Suddenly, not wanting to leave, she held on tighter to Lora, wishing she could stay. When Lora stepped back after one last quick squeeze, she found it difficult to swallow.

"Dream big, dear girl. Don't sell yourself short. You're more capable of making it happen than you think."

Why did Lora believe she deserved her big dreams?

"Now get going, or the two of you will miss getting a window seat."

She and Emma waved energetically as they walked onto the on-ramp. The smile she wore was fake.

Once settled on the ferry, they both pulled out their homework, although focusing was difficult. She kept staring out the window at the frothy waters and daydreaming. She was itching to get started on Lora's commissioned piece.

When they hit rough water, Emma said, "I'm having a hard time concentrating. I wish my dad would marry Lora. I know he likes her, and I think she likes him." Emma's lower lip pooched out. "He's so clueless sometimes!"

"She'd make a great mom. How about you tell him she's got a boyfriend? To make him jealous."

Emma scrunched up her nose and put down the pencil she'd been idly tapping. "Huh. If it would get Dad to date her, I'd do it." She grinned, then broke into giggles.

They both returned to their homework, although before long, she turned toward the window again.

"What are you thinking about?" asked Emma.

She blurted, "What Jake will say when he sees my new look."

Emma's judgmental expression led to a stare-down. Emma broke eye contact first. "Why can't you give it a rest?" Emma snarled. "He's no good for you. Can't you see that?"

"Don't tell me who I can like! Everybody thinks he's slime, but he's nice to me." She narrowed her eyes at Emma, not sure why she was even defending Jake. "It's none of your business anyway."

It hadn't been Lora's business either, but after she let what Lora had said sit a bit, she recognized the caring behind her words. Though embarrassing to hear, it was cool that Lora cared enough to caution her about guys.

It bugged her when people told others who they should or shouldn't hang out with. Once she'd overheard a few of Emma's teammates tell Emma to ditch her. Luckily, Emma hadn't listened.

Emma tagged her with her foot to get her attention. "People care about you. We're concerned you might ruin your life by getting mixed up with him."

When she kept silent, Emma got up and stomped away, fists at her sides.

Her jaw jetted for a second before she yelled out, "Shit, Emma, you're just jealous!"

What did that prissy girl know about boys? Heck, lots of guys liked her, yet she's too stupid to even see it.

When Emma eventually marched back to finish her homework, they gave each other the silent treatment for the rest of the ferry ride.

When they docked, Cooper was waiting to pick them up in his van. He must have sensed they were fighting because everyone stayed pretty quiet on the drive home. That was unusual. Normally, they'd be happily jabbering after having such a terrific time.

Emma should have kept her unwanted opinions to herself.

When they pulled up to her house, everyone's cars were out front, even Jake's. From the front seat, Emma said in a flat voice, "Great. He's here."

A scowl set on Cooper's face.

Who cared what they thought, anyway? Everyone was judgmental when it came to her and her family. She had had her fill of criticism from kids at school; she didn't need it from them, too.

It was tricky to get out of the van with all her bags. Cooper asked if he could help.

"No, I got it." She didn't want him coming to the door.

She walked penguin-style with her bags banging against the sides of her legs. That caused the overstuffed backpack slung over one shoulder to keep slipping. She readjusted the load as she stood outside the front door. Would everyone ask to hear about her weekend?

CHAPTER 20
IVY

As Ivy climbed onto the porch, she wondered if anyone would notice how much she'd changed. She felt like she had. A lot. It wasn't just the new clothes. Jake would probably be the only one to tell her how great she looked. Her family wasn't one to dish out compliments. She'd have to explain to her dad that the new clothes weren't charity but a barter arrangement with Rebecca. Hopefully, that would work. He might not even notice, though.

She turned her head to see Cooper's van leave the driveway. She'll ignore *perfect* Emma for a while. Emma would come around eventually. It was a stupid argument anyway.

Her chest ceased, taking her breath away. Would Emma really give up her BFF over Jake? Immediately, her heart rate sped up. Emma could easily dump her. She had lots of friends. Miss Social Queen Bee had lots of options for a new BFF.

Would she lose the only real friend she'd ever had? Jake wasn't worth it. He wasn't even an *actual* boyfriend anyway.

She stood outside the front door, expecting it to be locked. From inside, she heard the familiar booming gun blasts of Derek's video game. If she knocked, he would either ignore it or get pissed. She extended her fingertips to the doorknob to check if it was open. A bag swung forward as she turned the knob—the door opened a crack. *Good.* She repositioned her backpack with a shrug, then pushed the door open using the bottom of one of her bags.

Ear-deafening gunfire and bomb blasts from the video game filled the darkened room. Stepping inside, she back-kicked the door to avoid complaints about letting in the light. Derek whipped his head around to see who'd entered. Once he recognized her, he instantly dismissed her, swinging his head back to his game.

Sick! It smelled horrible in here—a mix of burned food, guy smell, and her dad's whiskey. Across the room was the bulky silhouette of her dad in his recliner. The side table held a bottle of booze. By the rhythm of his chest rising and falling, he had passed out.

Mom might never have told them where she'd been all weekend. Oh well.

Sensing movement to her left, she glanced over her shoulder to see a girl straddling a guy slumped on the sofa. A breathy moan escaped the girl's lips as she rocked back and forth on the guy's lap. The light from the video game created a strobe light effect, which traveled across the back of the girl's white shirt. As the guy's hands held her ass, the girl shifted, throwing her long hair over her shoulder to kiss the guy from a different angle.

To get a better look, she leaned forward. Did she know that girl? A guy's face peeked around the girl's back as the girl raised her arms to remove her shirt. That guy was *Jake.*

A gasp escaped her lips.

Jake's eyes narrowed into an icy stare. A second later, those eyes crinkled and danced with amusement. Jake locked eyes with her as he grabbed the girl's ass more tightly and pushed her harder against him, rocking her more aggressively. He studied her as he slid his hands up the girl's naked back.

The girl called out Jake's name.

She knew that thick, throaty voice. It was Yvonne Procter! Guys at school teased her, saying her sexy voice came from her giving blowjobs.

With a gasp, she squeezed the handles of her bags.

Why was she feeling Jake betrayed her? She had never been Jake's girlfriend. He was a known player. Some even said he traded sex for drugs.

Omigod! How could she ever have had a crush on a guy like Jake?

Jake smirked at her. That smirk made her feel like a stupid little kid. A big-time loser. It was disgusting his attention had ever flattered her. Jake was such a sleazebag; exactly the type of person Emma, Lora, and even her mother had warned her about.

Her self-loathing brought tears to spill down her cheeks. What a dumb, stupid, needy little girl she'd been. What a dork—feeling special because of his attention.

She hurried to her bedroom as Yvonne's moans grew louder.

As she scurried past the kitchen, she saw the source of the smell spread across the floor. There was brown gunk smeared everywhere. A saucepan lay sideways, spilling out its contents. *Barf!* They'll probably ask her to clean it up. No way was she doing that until Jake was outta there.

She dropped her bags and backpack onto her bed, then bolted for the bathroom. After she peed, she planned to stay in her room until Jake left.

In the hall, something sounding like a hurt animal came from her parents' bedroom. The hair on her neck rose. She raced to their room. Mom lay on her side, facing her. The curtain was up, so she immediately saw her black and blue, swollen face, with a pool of blood lying underneath her head.

Oh no! No, not again.

Though her breathing sped up, she still couldn't catch her breath. She dropped to her knees in front of her mom. Blood seeped from the cuts on her lip, by her eye, and on top of her cheekbone. She was so messed up, she didn't even look like Mom.

Mom opened one usable eye and peered at her as she struggled to say something. Her words came out in a garbled whisper. Mom winced. It had to be painful for her to speak.

To hear better, she leaned in closer.

Mom positioned a shaky hand gently under her jaw as she swallowed. This was the worst beating her mother had ever received.

Tears stung her eyes. Wanting to offer comfort, she reached up to touch the top of Mom's head. Her fingers sprang back when a slippery piece of scalp moved from her touch. Shocked, her fingers flew to her lips. The taste of Mom's blood made her gag. She swiped her sleeve across her mouth and wiped her bloody fingers on a pant leg.

She forced herself to take some slow, deep breaths to regain control of herself.

"Mom, I gotta get you outta here."

A guttural sound of defeat came from Mom's swollen lips. Struggling to speak, Mom said, "Purple socks. Dresser. Take it. Get out. Not safe."

She nodded and scurried to the dresser on the opposite wall. Deep down in the underwear and sock drawer were the purple socks. In them was a wad of cash, mostly ones and fives. Mom's tip money.

When she turned back, she spotted a huge, ugly purple patch peeking between Mom's black pants and her shirt. As she picked up the shirt, she gasped. This was so bad.

What should she do? She returned to crouch in front of her mom again. "Mom, you need help."

Mom's one eye seemed to plead with her. "Please. Go." Her raspy mumble showed how much effort it took for her to speak.

"I can't leave you."

Mom closed her eye, labored to swallow, and then focused on her again. "Go."

To hold back her tears, she put a hand over her mouth, but a whimper escaped her lips. She would sneak out to get the help Mom needed. With a nod, she left.

Quietly, she snuck into her room, gathered *her* hidden money, and repacked her bags. By the yelling coming from the living room, Dad had woken, raging at her brother or Jake.

Trembling, she slipped out the back door.

She crept behind the garage to grab her bike. Keeping to the far edge of the driveway, away from the living room window, she walked the bike out to the road. Once there, she hopped on her bike and turbo-speed pedaled. Certain they would come after her, she kept glancing over her shoulder. Every noise made her jump. Dad and Derek were mean and unpredictable.

Dad didn't like anyone uninvited coming into their house. Would he even allow medical help in?

She slowed as she neared Emma's driveway, then kept going. It didn't feel right to go there. Cooper had never asked, nor did he seem to want to know, what was going on in her home. She'd always thought that was a good thing. She hadn't wanted to lie to him. And now, it wouldn't be safe for them to come over. She didn't want either of them hurt.

How could Dad do that to Mom? He hadn't always been like he is now. Not when she was really little, anyway.

Had her brother even tried to stop him? The ass. He'd turn out to be just like Dad.

She pumped the bike pedals in a steady rhythm. Derek had tried to protect her once, when he was ten years old. Dad had flown into a rage after she'd made a mess with her toys. She'd clung to Derek, crying. Her being too scared to move made it difficult for Derek to get her out of the room fast enough. Her wailing made Dad even angrier. He yanked Derek's arm from hers. She heard the snap of Derek's arm.

As Derek cried in pain, Dad called him names. Dad shut them away in Derek's room until their mom came home. After that, Derek worked hard to please Dad. Once Dad lost his job, Derek became Dad's constant companion.

With time, her once softhearted brother had lost his heart.

She'd probably been able to keep hers because she'd had the Martins' home to go to. There weren't any monsters inside their house.

The image of Mom's bloody and battered body pushed her to blast out more pedal speed. What had happened before she'd come home? She didn't even want to imagine it.

She tightened her grip on the handlebars to pump even faster. Who should she get help from without making things worse?

Six miles down the road, she stopped and threw up. When she finished, she raised her head and shrieked like a crazed animal. Her head pounded, although emptying her stomach had made the cramping go away.

She got back on her bike and screamed up into the sky, "I never want to go back! I hate them! I hate all of them!"

Mom should have left. A long time ago, Mom seemed to want to go, but then the excuses came. Why had Mom kept taking more and more of Dad's shit?

The kids at school were right. They were white trash.

Her chin quivered. Was it fair to think so badly of Mom? She worked hard and did her best to protect her.

She coasted down the small hill she'd just climbed. It could be Mom hadn't wanted to take her away from the Martins. Or maybe if they had left, Dad would have come after them, like in the movies.

She'd probably been eleven when she figured out *she* would have to be the one to free herself from her crappy life. Lora thought art could be her way to a better life. Not likely at only fifteen, though.

Her legs were cramping up. To keep her mind off the pain, she focused on how lucky she'd been to have the Martins as her neighbors. They'd always been super nice to her, especially Emma. Claire was pretty cool, too. And now, through them, she had Lora.

A mile and a half from town, she skidded to a stop.

A car was coming.

Her heartbeat rocketed as she took cover in the trees. She crouched in the bushes, straining to hear where the car was.

Relief came when the car turned away from her. Quickly, she got back on the road. Lora would be the person she'd call when she reached town. Lora would know what to do.

She headed to the Starfish Diner to ask Bernie if she could use his phone.

Exhausted, she walked her bike through the alley to reach the back side of the diner. After leaning the bike against the wall, she pulled Lora's business card from her backpack. She was so sweaty her clothes stuck to her, and her eyes felt swollen and gritty. To hide her face, she pulled her hood up before banging on the diner's back door.

Mom had worked the day shift and some nights for Bernie ever since she was six. When she heard Bernie's heavy footsteps approaching the back door, she pulled the hood down further.

"Hey, Bernie. Um, could I use your cell phone?" Droplets of rain fell at her feet.

"Yeah." Bernie lifted the flap of his apron to reach into his front pocket. A strong whiff of onions came through the open door. It was likely Bernie was prepping for the dinner crowd. "Need a ride home or somethin'?"

"Just an important call to make." She bent, acting as if she were tying her shoe.

"Okay, but don't use all my minutes." He handed her his flip phone. Bernie believed in prepaid cell phones and often told her how prepaid phones would keep teenagers from abusing the privilege of having a cell phone.

She reached up to grab the phone but kept her face concealed. "I won't. I'll be out here."

He went back inside, and the rhythmic *chop, chop, chop* of Bernie's cleaver hitting the cutting board resumed.

She closed the back door, not wanting Bernie to hear her conversation. She sat trying to figure out what she could or should say.

Lora picked up on the third ring.

"Hello. Lora—" That was all she got out before she sobbed like a baby.

"Ivy?" Lora's voice was soft and caring, yet filled with concern. "I'm here. I'm here. Just breathe slowly. Slow, deep breaths in through your nose and out through your mouth." Lora waited for her to calm herself.

When she finally managed, she said, "Okay."

"Good. Now tell me what's happened."

"He beat her. Really bad this time. Mom made me leave. She said it wasn't safe." Gulping air, she pushed out more words. "Mom needs to go to the hospital. She might have a broken jaw, and she's got a patch of scalp ripped off."

The thought of Mom's blood threatened to gag her. "She's got an enormous bruise on her back, and...she's in a lot of pain."

"She's at home now?"

"Yeah. The thing is, when Dad drinks, he gets mean. Mom was lying in their bedroom when I got home. My brother and Jake are there too, though nobody helped her." She hiccupped, and a jolt of pain stabbed her chest.

"An ambulance needs to be called." Lora's voice was steady and firm.

"He might not let them in. Mom said it wasn't safe. It might not be safe for anyone to come in." Squeezing her lips tight, she tried to hold in a hiccup. It burst out, making a weird, high-pitched noise.

"If it's dangerous, for whatever reason, we need to get your mom to safety and get her medical attention. The police need to be called."

After more tears and hiccups, she said, "Okay."

"Where are you now?"

"The Starfish Diner."

"I'm going to call Cooper. If I reach him, I'll have him make the call. If I can't, I'll make the call myself. Someone will pick you up and take you to the hospital. Hang in there. We'll get you both taken care of."

She nodded into a disconnected phone.

Too unsteady to stand, she stayed seated on the stoop. Rain was now coming down in sheets. She tucked Bernie's phone inside her sweatshirt pocket and leaned back against the door. She was more tired than she'd ever been before.

The rain had soaked through her pant legs, though she didn't care. She stared across the alley at the graffiti on the adjacent cement wall. Last summer, she and a guy from art class had spray-painted a gigantic orange butterfly with red and aqua accent images onto a black background. If you looked closely inside the wings, you could see how the intricate interior lines created a series of skeletal faces.

Her shoulders slumped. Last summer seemed like a million years ago.

After today, everything was gonna change. Dad would go to jail, and probably her brother, too. She didn't care. They needed to pay for what they'd done.

What about her and Mom? Was Mom going to make it? She breathed in deeply to tuck in her emotions, not wanting to lose control again.

Once the rain slowed, the stench from the nearby dumpster assaulted her nostrils. She turned away just as Bernie opened the door. Though he didn't say a word, she felt his presence while she kept her face hidden. She tucked her head down further before she pulled Bernie's cell phone out of her pocket. She held it above her head.

"You okay, kid? It's been rainin'. You're soaked."

Bernie had a deep, gravelly voice, and a nose smooshed from his glory days in the Army. He was a good guy, as long as he didn't get mad at you. He wouldn't hurt you; he just runs his mouth off a bit and slams stuff around. Mom used to tell stories about him. She made it all sound funny—not scary.

Should she tell Bernie that Mom wouldn't be at work for a while?

No, not right now.

She turned slightly toward Bernie. "Could I borrow a towel? If I dry off, could I come in while I wait for my ride?"

"Sure, kid."

Bernie brought out two towels. "Dry off inside, then go out front." His tone had softened. "I'll bring you some hot chocolate and a piece of cake."

She nodded, hoping Bernie remembered her favorite was German chocolate.

CHAPTER 21
COOPER

"Lora, don't worry," said Cooper, as his heart thumped wildly against his chest. "I'll get the sheriff and the medics there right away. I'll see if Mom can pick up Ivy."

He wanted to assure her, ease her panic, though his own control was dwindling. Rage coursed through him as Lora described what had happened to Judy. The images he'd formed in his mind churned his stomach. It seemed too outrageous to believe. He cursed inwardly, ashamed he'd turned a blind eye to all the warning signs he'd seen.

Poor Judy. He really should have tried to do something. One hand balled into a fist as his stomach twisted.

"I'm going over to see if I can help Judy."

"No, Cooper! It's not safe until the sheriff gives the all-clear. Please don't go. Wait for the sheriff. Domestic violence situations can be so dangerous, even for the police."

Her caring concern washed away some of his physical tension.

"Okay. I'll stay back, though I'll see if I can ride in the ambulance with her. That way, she'll have someone she knows with her."

"Where will they take her?"

"Olympic Medical if it's not too serious, yet if it's as bad as you're saying, the Harrison Medical Center in Bremerton."

"I'm going to head to Bremerton as soon as I can. Call me if she's not taken there."

Immediately, his heart rate sped up again. She shouldn't drive while emotionally distraught.

"Please drive safely."

As soon as they hung up, he made a call to Sheriff Mark Collins. They had been friends since high school. He kept his voice steady as he passed on the information Lora had given him.

"You know," said Mark, his voice low with disappointment, "I saw this coming. Most of us in the department saw Judy regularly at the diner. We suspected Ed was abusing her, especially after his drinking started getting out of hand. We've known him as a mean drunk, and that boy of his didn't fall far from the tree. I'll get the team over there right away."

***

It was near dusk as he walked under his umbrella to the end of his driveway, waiting for the sheriff to arrive. The tension in his shoulders released when three sheriff cruisers and an ambulance slowed down as they passed his place. The Youngs lived just a quarter mile down the road.

A big swish of air left his belly. He returned to his house to reassure Emma that everything would be okay. "You'll be all right here on your own?"

"Dad, I'm almost sixteen."

"Right. Sorry."

"Please. Just see if Ivy's mom is going to be okay…but be safe, Dad." Her face was full of worry.

He used Ivy's path through the woods to get to the Young's house. Having never walked the full distance, he marveled at how brave six-year-old Ivy had been when she started trekking this path alone.

As he walked carefully through the path, he was aware of how much he loved Ivy. She was a great kid, despite having grown up in a home with such cruelty. He kicked a branch out of his way.

When he neared the house, he crouched behind a fallen tree, which gave him an excellent view of the front of the house. The sheriff's team had parked their vehicles away from the driveway. Four deputies approached the house, all armed and wearing Kevlar tactical vests. Two split off to go around to the back.

Sergeant Ferguson and a female officer, Deputy Perry, approached the front door. He knew Ferguson from his volunteering at summer festivals. Deputy Perry had only been in the community for about three years. Word about town was Perry had the skills to handle trouble-making kids, angry women, and big, burly guys. She'd gained a reputation for using spirited language. Apparently, she'd grown up with three older brothers on a Montana cattle ranch.

Ferguson rapped on the front door. "Sheriff's department! Open up, Ed! We heard your wife needs medical attention."

Less than a minute passed before Ferguson yelled the command again.

Still no response.

Each time Ferguson knocked on the door, it opened a little more. The two officers drew their guns and entered. Yelling ensued.

As he heard the commotion inside the house and then the ruckus behind the house, his mouth went dry. By the time all the scuffling ended, his temples throbbed and his legs shook.

They couldn't pay him enough to be a cop.

He paced the wooded pathway until two deputies brought a shirtless, tatted Derek from around back. They placed him in one of the patrol cars. Soon after, Deputy Perry escorted Ed out the front door and put him in the back seat of another patrol car, leaving the door open.

Sergeant Ferguson walked out the front door and messaged the medics that the scene was secure and safe to retrieve Judy. Ferguson made eye contact with him and nodded before going back inside. The ambulance drove up the driveway. Once parked, the doors sprang open, and two men rushed a gurney inside the house.

He eavesdropped on the officers discussing what had happened during their takedown. Ferguson had already called dispatch to arrange a telephonic search warrant. When they'd gone inside, they'd found lines of cocaine on the coffee table and suspected stolen electronics stuffed behind Ed's recliner. Though Jake's name came up, Jake hadn't been there when they arrived.

As the EMTs wheeled Judy out of the house, Ed called out from the patrol car. "I. Love. You." His thick tongue made the words come out in the start-stop fashion of a drunk. "Baby. I. Love. You."

Deputy Perry slammed the patrol car door shut on Ed's pathetic declaration of love, then rapped on his window. "Give it up, Ed. You dickhead. You gotta gol-darn asinine way of showin' you love her!"

He walked toward Perry, and she came forward to meet him. She nodded. "You the one called it in?"

"Yeah. I'd like to ride in the ambulance with Judy. She's my neighbor."

"I'll ask Ferguson, but it should be fine."

He waited behind the ambulance. One EMT made a few phone calls to the hospital; the other finished preparing Judy for the ride.

When he got the okay, he climbed into the back of the ambulance. The EMT said he'd already informed the hospital ER of their initial findings and received permission to administer pain medication. Sedated already, Judy appeared peaceful, despite her horrendous injuries. He scooted into the tight quarters alongside her, careful not to bump her IV drip.

As the ambulance flew down the road, Judy's eyes fluttered. He took her hand. "Judy, it's Cooper. I'm so sorry this happened to you. Don't worry about Ivy. She can stay with us until you're up and about." He patted Judy's hand. "You're strong. You'll get through this."

Her eyes fluttered once again before she returned to her drug-induced slumber. He'd never seen a face so battered. Was she going to make it?

Damn. He felt sick. He swallowed heavily to keep the contents of his stomach down.

The paramedic continued to monitor Judy's vitals and checked for more signs of trauma as the van sped through freeway traffic. Scrunched next to Judy, his imagination ran wild with what could have happened to the battered body before him.

What kind of human did this to someone they love? He'd been wrong about choosing not to get involved. He'd wanted to keep his and Emma's relationship with Ivy separate from what was going on with her family. Could he have changed this outcome if he hadn't done that?

On the drive to Bremerton, Judy moaned. He took her hand again and gazed down at their clasped fingers. Dried blood caked around Judy's fingernails. Her face was almost unrecognizable. Blood matted her hair. What horrors had she gone through?

He turned away, his mind swirling with questions. If Judy didn't make it, then what? Poor Ivy, to see this when she arrived home.

The young EMT said, "We're approaching the entrance to the hospital. Once we stop, they'll open the back of the van. I need you to be ready to hop out quickly and stand aside." He leaned in closer, his brows drawn together in concern. "You okay, buddy?"

He bobbed his head. "Yeah, just concerned about her."

"It was nice of you to come along." The EMT patted his arm. "She'll come through this. The docs here are great."

He tried to smile. He wasn't sure how convincing he was, though. Feeling so helpless was something he hated.

When the van slowed down to make the turn into the hospital, he went on alert. Gently squeezing Judy's hand, he said, "We're approaching the hospital. You'll be in excellent hands. I promise I'll bring Ivy to you soon."

CHAPTER 22
COOPER

The van stopped, the doors opened, and Cooper jumped out. He stepped aside as two nurses hustled over with a gurney. They transferred Judy onto the gurney and swiftly rolled her toward the entrance, all the while talking to her in a calm, matter-of-fact manner.

As he followed them through the first set of doors, his heartbeat sped up, and he struggled for air. While he inched his way to the second set of sliders, he broke into a sweat. When the automatic doors opened, the smells from the ER assaulted him. He shuffled back to stay behind the doors. As lightheadedness made him sway, he leaned against the wall. He was having difficulty breathing.

"Shit," he croaked through tight vocal cords. "What's happening?" He kept his eyes closed, willing himself to slow down his breathing. Thankfully, the wall held him upright as memories overtook him.

He was riding in the ambulance with Karen. En route to the hospital, she struggled to hide her pain from him. It had taken all he had not to break down when her face contorted and her breathing halted for a second. He'd done his best to hide his fear and the helplessness he felt as pain racked through her body. All he could do was hold her hand and mumble words of encouragement.

They'd stayed in the ER for just over six hours before they sent Karen home to die.

Hospice arrived the next morning, giving him his first break from her bedside for almost two days. Tired and numb, he aimlessly roamed the house, eventually finding himself on the back deck. In a fatigued stupor, he gazed out at the water, his arms limp at his sides.

"Please take her," he pleaded through tears.

When he lifted his eyes, he watched a bald eagle swoop down toward the shoreline. Its high-pitched squeal echoed through the stillness. The eagle's cry conveyed the pain he felt. Yet, he was too weary to utter a sound.

He paced the deck, pulling at the neckline of his T-shirt. How would Emma handle the loss of her mother? His mind flipped from one idea to the next for how he would tell Emma her mother had died. Would he do it wrong? Why hadn't he researched how to tell a kid her age?

As the morning sun rose, he continued to pace, tormented by restlessness. Exhausted, he tripped on the edge of the chaise lounge and slumped down onto its dewy cushion. His heavy eyes closed, but not for long. He gave up after a few minutes.

He straddled the lounge and leaned forward, then slammed a clenched fist into the cushion. The release felt good. He spread his thighs wider and rapidly pummeled the cushion with his fists. If he could have, he would have screamed his anguish, yet nothing would escape his parched throat. He continued to pound feverishly until something shifted inside him.

It was as if dark clouds had slid aside to reveal the grace of the sun.

A profound sense of acceptance came over him. As he leaned back into the cushion, his mind and body calmed. He closed his eyes to let those feelings soak in. Exhaustion finally won over.

He awoke two hours later with an overpowering need to hold his daughter. He wanted the comfort of her little arms around him. Yet he held off, knowing how his tender-hearted child sensed the feelings of others. Before he saw her, he would need to be stronger.

Karen died two days later. Afterward, his greatest desire was to help Emma mend after losing her mom.

***

As his memories receded, his present situation came into focus. Perspiration covered his brow as he peeled himself off the wall of the emergency entrance. The residual feelings from the memory of Karen's last days remained. His legs wobbled as he pulled himself away from the entrance wall to head out for some fresh air.

If he was going to help Ivy and Judy in the hours ahead, he'd have to pull himself together. Once outside, he sucked in a few deep breaths before walking toward the perimeter of the hospital. As he walked, his fists clenched from the primal desire to avenge Judy, though he wasn't the type of man to act upon those feelings.

Tormented, he continued walking to clear his mind. When he reached the entrance to the Reflection Garden, he went in.

He'd taken Emma there as a toddler. It was the day Karen had a catheter inserted. The PICC line allowed fluids and medications to be administered to avoid additional needle insertions. For him, the PICC line had meant they were a step closer to losing the battle.

He and Emma waited for Karen in the Reflective Garden. Karen had requested they have a fun day after her appointment, knowing she soon wouldn't have the strength for family outings. They'd learned about a children's play area near the hospital, so they'd brought along a picnic lunch his mom had made.

Tonight, the garden path was lit by solar lights. Since his mom, Ivy, and Lora wouldn't be arriving for a good while, he sat on a relatively concealed bench flanked by overgrown shrubs. He slumped down, then drew in a deep drag of moist fall air.

His eyelids closed involuntarily. Images of being there with Emma turned up his lips. Her two-year-old curiosity had been a wonderful distraction from his weighty concerns that day. He'd laughed when she hunted for the magical fairies he'd told her he *thought* he'd seen underneath the shrubbery.

With her high-pitched, sweet voice, she'd called, "Come out, fwaries," as she teetered while squatting down to peek under the bushes. Her bulbous diaper bottom touched the ground as she bent low. The strain of her mother's illness had delayed potty training.

He sighed. His sweet daughter had continued to be a blessing to him. She always provided much-needed emotional relief.

Mom once suggested he'd given Emma the role of being his emotional caretaker, which could eventually be a burden to her. He'd quickly pushed the idea aside. Although he could see now that it could be true. Emma was acutely sensitive to his moods. She often took it upon herself to cheer him up.

Did he rely upon her that way? Had he reinforced that role by showing appreciation for changing his mood? Or had she simply noticed when and how she had succeeded?

He tapped his heel in rapid succession. Since Emma was such a cheerful, undemanding kid, he'd assumed losing her mother hadn't affected her. She rarely brought up her mother, except lately when mentioning her baking goals.

Watching Emma interact with Lora made him wonder if Emma had missed out.

Had he done wrong by Emma? He had always believed he and his mom were all she needed to fill in the gaps made by the loss of her mother.

He supposed he'd wanted to believe *she* was all *he* needed, as well.

Could he have been using Emma to avoid the discomfort and fear attached to loving someone? He exhaled a long breath. Over the years, people had given him the honorable badge of a self-sacrificing, child-centered, single father. That would be a sham if he'd used Emma to avoid the risks involved in deeply loving someone.

"Blast it!" He scraped a hand over his face and groaned.

His temples pounded as he struggled with an avalanche of insights and feelings. With a grunt, he jabbed the tip of his shoe at a pebble. It rocketed into the bushes.

"I'm a darn fool!"

Mechanically, he got up and walked to the gift shop in search of aspirin and something to wash it down with.

After stuffing the small bottle of aspirin into his pocket, he headed to the emergency room waiting area. He spotted Mom and Ivy once he entered.

Ivy was lying across two chairs with her back toward him. Mom rose to meet him.

"How's Ivy?"

"Dazed and detached." Mom lifted her hand to his chest, staring solidly into his eyes. "What's going on with you?"

He placed his hand over hers, knowing she would see right through him if he lied. Ivy stirred just as he was about to speak. "Hold on a moment, Mom."

Ivy looked haggard. As she sat up, her body slumped in the chair. Her eyes appeared vacant.

He sat down beside her and put his hand on her knee, wanting to comfort her though not sure how.

"You and your mom will get through this. The EMT stabilized your mom by the time she got here. She's a tough gal. I told her you could stay with us until things got figured out. Her injuries are pretty extensive, so she'll be in there for a while. She'll get good care, though. There are skilled doctors here."

When he gave her a side hug, her body melted into his. He swallowed hard, trying to keep it together. He shrugged off his jacket to drape it across Ivy's shoulders.

"Thank you," she whispered.

"Mom, would you give Ivy your cell phone while you and I step outside?"

"Of course."

"Ivy, I figured you'd like to talk to Emma alone. Emma's a worrier, and you know she'll want to hear from you about how you're doing. Lora will be here as soon as she can. Call if anything comes up or if you need us for *any* reason. We won't be far or gone very long."

"Okay." Ivy's head bobbled.

He took his mom's arm to steer her outside. "Walk with me, and I'll fill you in."

He told her about the scene at the Youngs' house and what he'd learned after the sheriff's department took Ed and Derek into custody.

"This goes well beyond the assault on Judy. There were drugs and stolen goods in the home. Judy's injuries were so severe, I wondered if she was going to live. The EMT thought she'd pull through, though. Never in my life have I seen anyone in such terrible shape. It was awful for Ivy to find her mom like that. I'm certain it wasn't the first time Ed had beaten her, though."

He shook his head. "I should have known and helped Judy and Ivy before this happened."

Mom touched his arm. "Stop. I am sure others must have suspected it too. Helping in domestic violence situations can be difficult. The important thing is what you're doing now. You said Ivy could stay with you. That'll help both Judy and Ivy. Ivy's comfortable at your place. It's her second home, and she'll feel safe and supported there."

"Yeah. It's the least I can do for now."

They walked around the side of the hospital. He sighed heavily, then said, "When I got here, I followed Judy into the emergency room entrance. I didn't make it in. I had...something like an anxiety attack. Later, I connected it to the last time I brought Karen here. Right before hospice was called."

Mom patted his arm again and hummed a sympathetic response.

"Mom, I finally really understood that losing Karen has been why I've avoided loving another woman. I get it now."

"Well, good. Now you can do something about it."

"Yep, though there's more to correct. You told me once that I was letting Emma take care of me emotionally. Today I recognized I had. I've messed up."

"Maybe. Yes, she is sensitive to your moods and has always wanted to make her daddy happy. Yet, son, her being so connected to you wasn't all bad. She's successful both academically and socially, and she's got a kind heart. Those qualities grew out of that, too. That said, she shouldn't be stuck in that role forever. She'd have to give up too much of herself if she did. I know you want her to become a healthy, emotionally strong woman who has clear boundaries."

"I do. Remedying my mistakes will be my top priority."

They walked in silence for a while.

Mom wrapped her arm around him. "Like you, Emma might suppress uncomfortable feelings. The two of you both avoid things that might disrupt your status quo. It could be helpful to talk with her."

"Let me think about it. Right now, my noggin's full." He groaned. "Life has suddenly gotten pretty complicated."

As they walked back to the ER, movement in the parking lot caught his eye. It was Lora getting out of her car. He squeezed his mom's arm to get her attention, then jerked his head Lora's way. "And here comes another complication to deal with."

Mom's words had a soft, reprimanding quality when she said, "It doesn't have to be complicated if you'd only follow your heart."

CHAPTER 23
LORA

As Lora got out of her car, the lights in the hospital parking lot revealed soggy clumps of fallen leaves scattered about the pavement. She spotted Cooper as he stepped away from the sidewalk, sauntering toward her with his hands stuffed in his pants pockets.

Quickening her pace, she muttered to herself, "Oh, thank God, he's okay." She could only imagine what a difficult evening he'd been having.

She tried to watch where she stepped, telling herself, *Don't fall,* as her eyes kept seeking reassurance that Cooper was there, safe and sound.

As she sped toward him, she tripped over a crack in the pavement. He instinctively swung his arms out to steady her. She too, had extended an arm, catching Cooper around the waist. His heavy sigh whizzed past her ear. Their bodies mutually relaxed as they moved closer to give each other a firm hug.

Oh, his arms felt so good.

As she held him, she sent up a prayer asking for Cooper to find relief from whatever horrors he had seen.

"Thanks for coming," he whispered.

With her face cradled against his collarbone, she said, "I'm so glad you're all right. I worried all the way here, imagining you might do something heroic and g-get yourself h-hurt." She tried to swallow back the emotions those words evoked.

"No, I'm a big coward." He squeezed her briefly, then pulled back.

She stepped back as well. When she saw Cooper's puffy, red-rimmed eyes, whatever relief she had felt vanished. "Cooper, what is it? What's wrong?"

He winced. "I'm all right. After seeing what happened to Judy, then coming here to the hospital…it triggered some stuff connected to Karen and Emma. It was probably good that it surfaced. Painful to look at, though."

He took her arm, steering her toward the ER. "Let's stay focused on Judy and Ivy right now. Judy's bad off, and Ivy has shut down."

Then he looked down at her. "I'm really glad you came."

***

When she and Cooper walked in, Ivy had her back to them, now lying on one of the waiting room couches.

Cooper's mom acknowledged them with a nod and rose from the chair closest to Ivy. "So good of you to come." She rushed over to embrace her and, with emotion choking her voice, Claire whispered into her ear. "Both Ivy *and* Coop need you." When she drew back, tears glistened in her eyes.

"Lora?" croaked Ivy as she slowly pushed herself to a seated position.

As soon as she had sat down, Ivy collapsed into her arms. It was as if Ivy had been holding it together until she arrived. Ivy's slender body trembled as she held her tight.

Poor thing. What a terrible experience!

"Ivy, I'm so sorry." She rubbed Ivy's back. "We're all here for you and your mom. We'll stay to get you through this. You won't have to do it alone."

Deep sobs shook Ivy's body. Eventually, when they slowed, she scooped Ivy closer so she could rock her back and forth. Ivy's sobs eventually softened into whimpers.

While she held on to Ivy, she closed her eyes to focus on Ivy and keep out the distraction of the emergency waiting area. Before long, she had a sense Ivy was absorbing the comfort she offered, like a neglected plant soaking in needed water. When Ivy's breathing synchronized with hers, it reminded her of when she would rock Maggie to sleep. Maggie's breathing would eventually match hers. She'd always thought this synchronization was a part of their bonding process.

With each exhale, she sent her love into this wounded young woman. Before long, she had the feeling that the love she'd shared was being looped back toward her. She hugged Ivy tighter to show she had received that love and welcomed it.

Claire left to get everyone something to eat and to buy Ivy some dry clothes. She, Cooper, and Ivy remained huddled in a corner, away from the comings and goings of the busy emergency waiting room. Cooper read a magazine a few chairs away, but she often felt his eyes upon them. Sometimes when she glanced up, they made eye contact, and he would smile. Once he gave her a thumbs up and mouthed, *Good job*. She appreciated the gesture. She didn't know what to do for Ivy other than to be with her and affirm that things would eventually be okay.

The ER doctor came looking for Ivy. "Hello, I am Dr. Ruth Schaffer. I've been taking care of Judy Young in the emergency room. Why don't you tell me who you all are? Family?"

Cooper looked at Ivy and then spoke. "Ivy is Judy's daughter. She's fifteen, with no other family able to be here. Could we accompany her when you tell her about her mother's condition? She's the one who found Judy and sought help. I don't think she's functioning well right now."

"And the two of you are?"

"I'm Cooper Martin, neighbor. My daughter and I are like a second family to Ivy. This is another friend of Ivy's, Lora Hamilton."

"Why don't the three of you follow me into the consultation room?"

When they were all seated, Dr. Schaffer said, "We have completed a CT scan of Judy's head, neck, and abdomen. She has a bruised kidney. We repaired the scalp laceration. Because of the facial trauma, we'll bring in a dental specialist and any other specialists she might need as we complete further tests and assessments. They'll be the ones to talk to you about further treatment plans and any therapies she might need. She'll be moved out of the ER now that she's been admitted into the hospital."

Ivy cried softly. Seeing the emotional pain Ivy was enduring ripped her heart, making her chest ache. She'd kept her arm around Ivy, whose body seemed to liquefy.

Dr. Schaffer's face showed her concern for Ivy. "Ivy, I understand how painful this has been for you. I've had domestic violence occur in my extended family, so I am aware of the devastation it has on a family. We'll get a social worker in to talk with your mom and you…and anyone else involved. The social worker will probably be Becky Wilcox. She'll also help in finding the resources you might need. You'll be able to go in and see your mom soon. However, because of the heavy pain control administered and her dental injuries, she probably won't be able to talk."

Dr. Schaffer scanned their faces. "I can't tell you what's ahead for Judy, but she will get the care and help she needs while she's here." Then Dr. Schaffer focused on her and Cooper. "I am glad you're here with Ivy. Make sure she gets the emotional support she needs. What's ahead for Judy, and maybe even Ivy, could be a slow recovery process."

"We'll help in any way we can," said Cooper.

Dr. Schaffer said her goodbyes and headed back into the belly of the hospital.

Grateful for the time and care Dr. Schaffer had given them, she called out, "Thank you, doctor!"

What she heard soured her stomach. As they walked back to the waiting area, her concern was for Ivy, who seemed close to collapsing.

With Ivy settled, Cooper laid a comforting hand on her shoulder for a few seconds. It seemed a gesture of support. His presence had a steadying effect on her. How was she going to help Ivy?

Ivy seemed to have chosen her to lean on; that responsibility was weighty. She would do her best, though. Was she capable of giving Ivy what she needed? She was still recovering from her own traumatic past. Thank heavens a social worker would be available to Ivy.

Regardless, she would do whatever she could.

***

When Claire returned, Ivy robotically walked down the hall to change into dry clothes. Later, as they ate their burgers, the adults attempted small talk while Ivy picked at her food. When Cooper sent Claire home, Claire's face showed relief. He called Emma to give her another update and asked her to go to bed. It would be hours before they would return to his house.

There were still so many unanswered questions hanging in the air. When the nurse called Ivy's name to say Judy was ready for visitors, Ivy gave her and Cooper a blank stare. Recognizing Ivy's need, she asked if they could come along. Once they received the okay, she wrapped an arm around Ivy's waist to support her as she shuffled down the hall.

They stopped just inside Judy's door, shocked to see Judy's battered facial features. Judy focused on Ivy with her one usable eye.

Ivy swallowed down her sobs. "Mom. Mom...I'm—" She crept closer, holding one hand to her throat. "I was so afraid you wouldn't make it." When she reached the bed, she gently took her mother's limp hand. "I told Bernie you wouldn't be in for a while." She swallowed like a pelican gulping down a fish. "He said to get better and not worry about a thing."

Cooper joined Ivy and bent down close. "Ivy did the right thing in getting you help. She's a brave, smart girl. Ed and Derek are now in police custody. Besides the assault charges, there will be additional charges for illegal drugs and possession of stolen property. The sheriff will sort all that out in time."

Judy's eye sought her daughter's face before glancing back at Cooper.

Had Judy and Ivy known about the stolen property? It seemed likely they had. It was probably necessary to keep quiet for their survival. To confront the men in that household would, no doubt, have been dangerous.

Cooper patted Judy's arm. "I'll contact someone to apply for emergency guardianship of Ivy, so she'll be able to stay with us. If that's something you're okay with?"

Judy approved with a slight nod.

"We'll take good care of her for as long as you need us to." He smiled reassuringly. When he returned to stand beside her, he leaned in and whispered, "Did I give too much information too soon?"

Absorbed in how grotesque Judy's face looked, she hadn't responded. An unwanted memory captured her mind.

Frank had come home smelling of whisky a few months after Maggie's death and found her boxing up their daughter's belongings. She'd planned to donate them to a women's shelter. Frank went ballistic, escalating quickly as he screamed at her. "You unfeeling bitch!"

Like a wild man, he whipped Maggie's things out of the boxes and stuffed them back into the dresser drawers before slamming them shut.

Her attempts to calm him only made the situation worse. At one point, she'd clasped her hands over her ears while her body trembled. She backed out of the room into the hallway and seriously considered leaving him. His manic behavior had her fearing for her safety. Yet, she couldn't leave. She sensed that if she left, Frank would harm himself. The thought of losing him scared her. As a result, she took on the responsibility of protecting him from himself. She also couldn't handle affirming that she was the unfeeling bitch Frank claimed her to be.

So, she had stayed. Which cost her dearly. Over the next two months, the emotional battering eroded her self-esteem to the point that she believed she deserved whatever he dished out.

Numb to the constant verbal attacks, she endured the gradual escalation of his physical abuse. Emotionally, she was on a downward spiral. Her isolation was her attempt to hide the ugly truth of her collapsing marriage.

When Cooper's arm bumped hers, she blinked the memory away. Being such a significant memory, it would be something she would share with Wendy during their next session. Wendy had already given her literature on spousal abuse. After reading it, she'd known how lucky she'd been. Staying with Frank could have resulted in something like what happened to Judy.

Empathy for Judy engulfed her.

Cooper said softly, "Should we leave them alone for a while?"

When she hadn't answered, he leaned in and whispered, "Are you okay, Lora?"

She closed her eyes and took a deep breath, telling herself to relax. "Yeah. Give me a minute." She stepped up to Judy's bedside. "Hi, Judy, I'm Lora. We talked on the phone. I'm the one who took the girls on the trip to Seattle." She kept her hands clasped, afraid to cause Judy pain if she touched her.

"I'm so sorry this happened to you. You didn't deserve any of it." She glanced over at Ivy, whose eyes looked vacant.

Turning back to Judy, she said, "As a mother, you might be worried about your daughter, but don't be. Cooper will take good care of her. I'll be there for her too, in any way I can."

Judy blinked an acknowledgment.

"Stay strong, Judy. Things *will* get better for you. Trust they will. Keep focused on your recovery." She peered over at Ivy, whose sad eyes blinked back into focus. To Judy, she said, "I'll stop by again another time. For now, get some rest."

She and Cooper left the room. Cooper placed a gentle hand on her lower back as they exited, guiding her down the hall. Although the touch was welcome, she wondered if it was merely a gentlemanly gesture, the type he might have offered to anyone.

He would make a wonderful life partner...to someone.

Cooper leaned over and said, "I assume you're planning to spend the night. Stay with us. We have a guest room. And besides, having you nearby might be good for Ivy. I know Emma would love to see you."

"Are you sure you're comfortable with that?"

His voice warmed when he said, "I am."

Later, as she drove Ivy and Cooper back to the Martins', she played soothing instrumental music on the radio. Ivy was sitting up front with her, and in no time, fell asleep. In the back seat, Cooper was silent, seemingly mulling something over.

CHAPTER 24
COOPER

Cooper took a quick glance at his cell phone when they rolled up to his house. It was after 2:00 am when they walked through the front door. They found Emma asleep on the couch. Her head popped up as soon as the door closed. Sleepy-eyed, Emma shuffled over to Ivy to throw her arms around her. The impact made Ivy teeter on her feet. As soon as Emma stepped away, she did the same with Lora.

"Girls," he said, through vocal cords constricted by emotion. "I'll call the school and excuse you both for tomorrow. Or, I guess that's today, actually. Go up and get some sleep. Save your talking for later. Ivy, the sheriff, wants to take your statement late morning. We'll try to get you back to see your mom sometime tomorrow. Do you want something to eat before bed?"

"I'll get it for her, Dad. To keep myself busy, I baked Ivy's favorite—cowboy cookies." Emma grinned over at Ivy. "We'll take some up to *our* room."

With glazed-over eyes, Ivy nodded.

"Save some for Lora and me," he said jokingly, then turned to Lora. "Before you go upstairs, how about we hang out in the kitchen for a minute while we eat our cookies? If you don't mind?"

"Sure, that's fine." She dropped her bag by the stairwell.

He tried to sound parental when he said, "I recommend we all try to sleep in tomorrow."

The girls nodded, then took their plate of cookies and glasses of milk upstairs.

"Lora, would you like milk or something else to drink with your cookies?"

"Milk is great." Lora sat down at the island and slowly bent her elbow to drop her head into her hand.

"To tell you the truth, I don't know if I can even chew. I'm so tired."

He should let her go, but he had things he wanted to clear up with her. Tonight, as he'd watched Lora with Ivy, he'd gained a deeper understanding of who Lora was at her core. She had a big heart, even though she'd gone through a lot herself. Or possibly because of it. It still wrenched his gut when thinking she believed he pulled away because he judged her poorly as a mother. Or worse, that she had any responsibility for her daughter's death.

Lora stifled a yawn. "Ivy said we don't need to worry about Jake anymore. She despises him, and for good reason."

Lora took a cookie from the plate and held it limply in her hand. "It's just so awful that Ivy saw what happened to her mom by her own father's hands." She shook her head. "It makes me nauseous just *thinking* about it. I pray Ivy and her mom get through this okay."

"God. Me, too."

Lora bit into her cookie and chewed slowly. "You never know, though. Living in that household might have made Ivy stronger in ways we can't comprehend. I hope she'll accept the counseling when it's offered. And Judy, too." She yawned and took another bite of the cookie in slow motion.

He came around the counter and sat beside her. They companionably munched their cookies.

He rested his hand on Lora's arm. "You're being there tonight helped Ivy. She responds to you. I think...she would benefit from whatever time you have available. That's a big ask, though."

"The thing is, I want to help her." She stared off in thought.

He needed Lora to understand why he'd pulled away before. If he told her about his revelation at the hospital, might she think better of him? But the timing?

He cleared his throat before he plunged ahead. "When you first saw me tonight at the hospital, you asked what was wrong. Well, I'd just had a kind of meltdown."

Somewhat embarrassed, he kept his head forward to avoid eye contact. "I'd ridden in the ambulance with Judy. When we got there, I started following the gurney inside the emergency entrance. I...I couldn't go in. I had something like an anxiety attack. Karen's last visit there came flooding back."

"Oh, Cooper." She put a hand on his arm.

"Seems the emotion of not knowing if Judy would make it was probably the trigger. That's my guess, anyway. I've had attacks before. Not like this, for a very long time. When I peeled myself off the entry wall, I took a walk. I ended up at the hospital's Reflection Garden. I sat down and let the impact of Karen's last days gut-punch me." He turned to look into her eyes and saw only compassion there. Seeing it was comforting.

"Cooper, that must have been so hard on you."

"Yeah." He nodded repeatedly, giving himself a moment. "I recognized that ever since I lost Karen, I've been trying to protect myself from the devastating pain of losing someone I loved."

This was harder than he'd expected. He exhaled in frustration.

He drummed his fingers on the counter. "I've figured out that the strategies I've been using to protect Emma and myself have stopped me from having a genuine relationship with any woman. I've been in denial about what I have been doing. Seeing how Emma's so taken with you showed me I haven't done Emma any favors by keeping a woman out of her life. Not only that, I'm seeing ways I've messed up with how I've parented her."

Lora blinked, as if his words surprised her. When she lowered her head and didn't comment, he bit his lip while his right knee bounced.

He cleared his throat. "I, um...I'm concerned now that I, unconsciously of course, let Emma take on the role of my emotional caretaker. I didn't mean to do that. But I can now see how that's playing out."

He put his elbows on the counter, clasped his hands, and let out a chuckle. "It's my hope I haven't set her up to marry some *needy* loser, because she's become comfortable in the role of taking care of someone emotionally."

"Oh, Cooper, I'm not sure you've messed Emma up. She's an amazing young lady."

"Well, one thing I now understand is that my fear of romantic attachment wasn't so much about protecting Emma. It was about *me* trying to feel safe...because that kind of pain—well, I haven't felt capable of handling something like that again. That earlier long-distance relationship I mentioned? I can't say I ever really gave her, or anyone else, a chance. Being a coward has had its consequences."

Lora glanced into her lap briefly before meeting his gaze. "Don't be so hard on yourself. You did the best you could, considering what happened. Emma had been lucky. She grew up with you and your mom's full attention and love. Lots of kids never even have that."

"I suppose."

She shook her head. "No one does parenting perfectly, Cooper. Yet, based on your results, you did a darn good job." She rested her hand on his arm. He reached over and patted it.

"Thank you." That was reassuring.

"By chance," said Lora, "are you planning to do something with these new insights? Talk to Emma about them? Giving her a voice might reveal something you've never considered." She removed her hand and smiled. "She *is* a great kid. You didn't do half bad." She bumped her shoulder playfully against his.

He smiled and took her hand to kiss it lightly. "I also owe you an apology. For the same reason I pulled away from all the other women who'd come along, I pulled away from you. You see, the chemistry between us hit me with a hefty punch. I panicked. I was afraid that if I let those feelings grow, I could open myself up to the pain of loss again."

She furrowed her brow.

"I got scared, Lora. Unconsciously, I think I connect any powerful feelings for a woman with the potential for devastating loss. It wasn't about how far apart we lived. It was about my being chicken."

He searched her eyes, afraid of what he might see there. There was no disgust, as he would have expected.

"If you thought it was for any other reason, I'm sorry. I didn't intend to hurt you, though I know I did."

His gaze held hers. She remained silent, as if mulling over what he had said. His heartbeat sped up.

"Lora, I made a mistake. Can you forgive me? Give me a second chance to see where we might take this?"

She appeared surprised. Maybe as surprised as he was by making the request. As if wanting privacy, she turned her head away and drank the last of her milk, giving herself more time to think.

When she turned back, her eyes looked determined. "You've been through a lot today. We both have. I'm dead on my feet. I appreciate what you shared, but my brain's not functioning at its best. Let's talk tomorrow, okay?"

Her droopy eyelids confirmed how exhausted she was.

"You're right." He stifled a yawn with the back of his hand. "Let's both get some sleep. Tomorrow we can talk."

He picked up their dishes and put them in the sink. Disappointment swam with his exhaustion.

"Good night, Lora. Sleep well."

She lumbered up a few steps on the stairs before she softly called over her shoulder. "Let the girls know if they need anything, they can come get me."

Her desperation for sleep showed in her voice and on her face. What a schmuck. He'd kept her up just to dump more crap on her.

It was possible he'd hurt her too deeply for him to be given a second chance. And, being the dumbass he was, he'd just revealed a crapload of personal baggage. What was she thinking of him now?

Heck, was he even sure he wanted all the changes that came with developing a new relationship?

He yawned. He'd think about it tomorrow. Right now, he needed sleep. Fatigue had a way of scrambling your thought processes.

CHAPTER 25
LORA

Lora lingered in bed, not wanting to leave the comfort of Cooper's deluxe sheets and mattress. When she finally rose, the bathroom mirror revealed dark half-circles under her eyes. As tired as she'd been last night, she hadn't been able to fall asleep. Yesterday's events, Cooper's surprising confession, and then his request for a second chance kept running through her head.

Once downstairs, she said good morning to everyone. Next, she headed straight for the coffeemaker. Cooper smiled when she came in, yet he kept himself busy cleaning up the kitchen. With a closer look, it appeared Cooper probably hadn't slept well, either. He was keeping his distance, but took sidelong glances at her often.

Was he feeling awkward about what he'd said last night?

She was more confused than ever about what she wanted anymore. It wouldn't surprise her if Cooper wasn't sure either. Aside from helping Ivy, her original goal of protecting herself from heartbreak might remain a wise goal.

Cooper picked up the serving plate with the remnants of the girls' banana chocolate chip pancakes.

"Lora, would you like me to warm these last two in the microwave for you?"

"No, thanks. I have to hit the road soon. I'll stick with coffee." She had to get back to Tacoma. By the time she drove to work, most of her Monday would be gone. She had a packed week ahead of her.

"Ivy," said Cooper. "I had a call from the sheriff's department. They'll be here in about 20 minutes to take your statement. Just do your best. Be honest and keep to the facts."

Ivy rubbed an arm and glanced at the clock. When Cooper turned away, she started whispering to Emma.

Cooper drifted back to the counter to pick up the syrup and the butter. With his brows knitted, he said to Ivy, "Don't be nervous. They'll want to know what you saw, anything your mom said to you, and if you know what your dad and brother were up to."

Ivy nodded, averting her eyes.

Cooper then turned to her. "Lora, it would be a big help to me if you could stay while Ivy makes her statement. Then, on your way back to Tacoma, could you drop Ivy off at the hospital? I'm sorry to ask, but there is a pressing matter at the plant. Would that work out for you at all?"

She didn't want to cancel her first meeting with her new intern. "Sure, but I need to make it back to my office by three-thirty."

"Dad, can I go with Ivy since I'm staying home from school?"

Cooper hesitated. "Okay. You can be Ivy's support person before and after seeing her mom, although I don't want you seeing Judy just yet. Let Ivy go in alone. Both of you should take any homework with you in case I'm delayed picking you up. If that's the case, I'll see if Nana could do it."

Cooper sipped his coffee, thinking, then pulled out his wallet. "Here's some money for the two of you to eat in the cafeteria if you get hungry. Take along some of those cookies from last night."

He smiled at Emma. "They were *delicious*."

A few minutes later, she waved goodbye to Cooper from the front door. Thankfully, there hadn't been time to discuss his request from last night. It was her opinion they both needed time for yesterday's events to settle and for their heads to clear.

Despite his request, she wasn't convinced he was ready for a committed relationship. From the way he acted this morning, he might be regretting he opened up to her. He'll have a lot on his plate after taking in Ivy and dealing with all the messy stuff connected to her. Besides, having an epiphany didn't mean he'd be able to banish his anxieties about loving.

Therapy taught her that ah-ha moments didn't automatically pull down the subconscious walls a person built after experiencing trauma. Nor would they banish the irrational habits you develop to fortify your protective walls. Walls like that were difficult to deconstruct and could persist despite one's best efforts.

Gad, she'd thought befriending the girls might complicate things between herself and Cooper. Now, her new commitment to help Ivy, while Ivy lived with Cooper, brought that complication up to a whole new level.

***

When the sheriff and a deputy came to interview Ivy, she stayed close by to lend support. Both officers made efforts to put Ivy at ease. Within an hour, the interview was complete.

She hugged Ivy when they left. "I'm so proud of you."

After listening to what Ivy had told them, she'd learned just how bad Ivy's family life had been. What a horrible environment to grow up in!

When she released Ivy from her hug, Ivy let out an enormous breath. "Thanks for staying with me."

Knowing they were on a time crunch, Ivy ran upstairs to get Emma so they could leave for the hospital.

Once they arrived, she suggested going to the gift shop. The girls chose a stuffed puppy whose big, crystal eyes seemed to radiate love.

"Perfect," she said.

They left Emma in the waiting area as she escorted Ivy to her mother's room. Judy appeared much the same. After saying a few words to Judy, she hugged Ivy goodbye. It was hard to leave, not knowing when she'd be able to return.

***

By Wednesday evening, she had already received separate phone calls from Ivy, Emma, and Cooper. They all needed a sounding board. She listened, asked questions, and occasionally gave advice. What she'd learned and experienced in therapy helped her know how to respond. After their talks, she jotted down a few questions to ask Wendy during their weekly session.

Their calls reminded her of experiences she had as a teen and college student when peers gravitated toward her to confide in. Most often, all she had to do was listen and give witness to their struggles.

In hindsight, after Maggie's accident, she wished *she* had gone to talk with someone. Instead, she barricaded her emotions.

Thankfully, she had Wendy as a resource to guide her through whatever she needed as she continued on her journey, and for helping Ivy and the others.

***

During her next counseling session, Wendy asked, "Do you have any concerns about how extensive your involvement might become while helping Ivy? Would you back out if it got too much?"

She closed her eyes to contemplate the question. She knew she was making a difference in Ivy's life. True, there was the risk of getting more involved with Cooper. Yet, she had made herself available to the *whole* family in their time of need. She cared about each of them.

"No," she said. "I don't want to back out if it gets tough. Absolutely not. I want to be there for them. If it gets too hard on me, I think I could talk to them and set up some parameters. Time will tell where things go with Cooper. I'll have to let that play out." She shrugged her shoulders, giving their situation over to fate.

By Friday night, her hectic work week had left her exhausted. Once home in her condo, she changed into comfy clothes. When her phone rang, it went to voicemail before she could fish it out of her purse. As she listened to the message, she heard the urgency in Emma's voice when she requested a call back. Her pulse sped up as she pressed Emma on her contact list.

Emma immediately answered. "Lora, I'm putting you on speakerphone so Ivy can hear."

She frowned. "Okay."

Emma's words raced out. "I almost got into a fistfight today. Yvonne Procter's friends got in my face, saying Ivy was a snitch for getting Yvonne in trouble and putting Jake in jail. One girl pushed me, and I pushed back. Luckily, a teacher came along and broke it up. It would have been four girls against me."

A rush of alarm hit her. "That had to be a scary situation. Are you being harassed, too, Ivy?"

"Yeah. Mostly name-calling, though. Only a few kids are doing this kinda stuff."

"Was Jake those girls' dealer for alcohol and drugs?"

"Most likely," said Ivy.

"Right. I imagine they see you as the cause of all their problems. It figures you'd be a target for gossip. You've given them something to get worked up about. I hope that as soon as something more gossip-worthy comes along, you'll become old news."

For their sake, she hoped it would be soon.

"Not soon enough," Ivy grumbled.

"I suggest letting someone in authority at the school know what's going on. When you're in the halls, stay in a group with your friends around you. Assign a specific person to get help if things escalate. At lunch, do the same thing. Avoid engaging with the troublemakers...if at all possible."

The girls muttered their agreement. "Yeah, that might work."

"Even though you might not like the idea, Cooper needs to know, too. He's your parent, Emma, and your guardian, Ivy, so he needs to be informed. I won't keep secrets that could compromise your safety."

"Okay," said Ivy.

"When you talk to him," said Emma, "would you let him know *we'll* get a handle on it?"

"I will," she promised. "Ivy, so much of what's been going on is outside your control. It's time to focus on yourself and the things *you* can control. What you *can* control is where you put your time, energy, and attention. Those choices will create the future you want. Don't get sidetracked by those mean girls or your family. Whatever is going on with them is outside your control. And it always has been."

Ivy's voice carried hurt when she said, "True. None of my family is showing any concern for me or my future...for sure."

She sat silently with Ivy to honor the hurt within her words.

"Um," said Ivy. "The school counselor took me out-of-class yesterday. She talked to me about creating something like a group of people who would support me in what I want or need currently and into my future life. You know, cuz I'm sorta on my own now."

"That's a great idea." Did Ivy still feel she was on her own? How would this group assist in Ivy's future?

"Um, there's something else. I haven't told you or Cooper, but I want to become emancipated. I never want my dad or mom to come back into my life, tearing down what I'd built back up for myself. Emancipation will make it so they can't dictate what I do or where I live from here on out. I can't apply until after January, when I'm sixteen. However, the counselor said that forming this group now could make it easier for the court to grant permission. The counselor will meet with me next week while Emma's at volleyball practice. I'm supposed to be putting together a list of names for my team."

"That's wonderful. Tell her I'd like to hear more and will help in any way I can. You can give her my number."

"Cool. Emma and I are hoping to see you soon."

"Yeah," said Emma, "and thanks for the suggestion on safety. Shoot, Dad's calling us down for dinner."

"Alright. Ask your dad to call me tonight when he has time. Bye, girls."

***

Later that evening, Cooper called.

"Did the girls tell you why I wanted to talk with you?"

"Nope, I'm clueless."

She filled him in on what they'd told her and shared the advice she'd given.

"I don't like this," said Cooper. "I'll follow up with the principal and have her inform the teachers and staff to keep a better eye on the girls."

"Good idea."

"So, I was wondering," said Cooper, "what do you think about decreasing Ivy's visits to her mom to once a week? Every time Ivy comes back from seeing Judy, she says her mom doesn't even try to talk to her."

"Really?" Wasn't Judy more capable of speaking by now?"

"And it's a heck of a drive on weeknights. I'd like to keep visits to Sunday afternoons. Of course, she can call her mom as often as she likes. If Judy would only pick up the phone. Judy's able to talk better now, but she's not even trying to connect with Ivy."

What was going on with Judy? "Cooper, I'm sorry you're burdened with all the transportation."

"I'm dealing with it. Mom helps some, too."

"Anyway, I don't see a problem with once a week and keeping the visits short. That will give Ivy more time to focus on herself. I wouldn't want her to get behind in school or get bogged down worrying about her mother. There's nothing she can do, especially if Judy isn't attempting to connect. Did Ivy tell you the school counselor is helping her set up some kind of support team? I'd like to be involved. Ivy told me she plans to petition for emancipation."

"First, I've heard about this."

"Cooper, it has nothing to do with you. She just doesn't want either parent disrupting her last years of high school. She wants to take back control of her life."

During the rest of their phone call, they shared their thoughts about Ivy's request for emancipation and her desire to become independent from her family.

When it was time to hang up, Cooper said, "Hey. Thanks for filling me in."

"Happy to help."

***

Over the weekend, she thought a lot about how she could help the girls. All her therapy tools had been helping her. Even minor acts of self-care made a difference. Choosing to practice them affirmed she saw herself as worthy of the effort. If she shared some of those tools with the girls, their stress levels might be lowered.

For Ivy, she'd suggest keeping a gratitude journal to offset all the negative events happening in her life. Breathwork might also help her keep centered and calm.

For Emma, who was sensitive to Ivy's moods and concerned about her friend's future, she'd suggest visualization. Emma could hold Ivy in her mind's eye and envision her growing emotionally stronger and finding success in a future of Ivy designs.

Both girls might benefit from using the Serenity Prayer.

Later that day, she talked on the phone separately to the girls. Both girls were receptive of her ideas.

She found that her involvement with Ivy and Emma provided a sense of purpose outside of work. She had grown to love them both. The girls would never replace Maggie in her heart, but taking part in their lives had become a rewarding experience.

Her feelings toward Cooper were still a mixed bag. He hadn't brought up the second-chance topic again. Yet, during each of their phone calls, he opened up more—giving her a deeper sense of who he was. He struggled with how to respond to Ivy's rollercoaster of emotions. Not surprisingly, the baggage Ivy carried for years was now unlatched. Everyone was rocked by their exposure to what had once been hidden.

It was admirable how conscientious Cooper was when considering Ivy's unique needs.

***

On Monday, for the first time, she had made it out of the office by five o'clock. What a novelty to be the *first* to leave! A smile stayed on her face for the whole soggy short drive home. Hopefully, her days of working past quitting time were over.

Things were running smoothly enough. Her replacement hire had mellowed, though an unusual relationship had formed between the replacement and Rachael. Since Rachael stopped speaking to her, the new hire became the go-between. So far, she wasn't too concerned. Yet it would be wise to keep a watch on the situation.

With how improved things were at work, she would consider staying with the company longer.

Since she arrived home at a reasonable hour, she put on music, changed clothes, and pulled out the ingredients to make a ground turkey curry dinner. Cooking for one and eating alone wasn't where she wanted to be in her life. She yearned for someone to share a meal with...and a life.

Her involvement with Ivy had waylaid her efforts to develop friendships. Her priorities had changed. Friendships could stay on her to-do list for a while longer.

Ivy called almost every day, often upset. Fortunately, Ivy liked the counselor assigned to her. Poor Ivy. She had so much to unpack while dealing with her present circumstances.

The following Tuesday, Cooper called, chuckling. "Okay, I know the counselor is helping Ivy, but I walked into the great room after dinner, and there was Ivy, sitting by the fireplace, tapping her head and face while chanting something. What kind of voodoo are they teaching her?"

She recognized what he was describing. "Don't worry. That's a technique to help Ivy manage her emotions by stimulating acupressure points. It's called *tapping,* a mind-body thing used to relieve stress and anxiety. I assume it's part of her trauma work."

"Did you use it during your therapy?"

"Yep, I did. Rarely anymore, although it's in my therapeutic toolbox. Is Ivy still having nightmares disrupting her sleep?"

"She might, though she doesn't bring it up to me."

"Cooper, you should know Ivy worries about her being occasionally *temperamental.* She thinks a lot of you. I'm sure she even loves you. You've been a blessing to her since she was a little girl."

"Hmm," said Cooper. "She's special to me, too."

"You know, I've been reading more about PTSD. I believe that Ivy— well, all of us—can overcome our trauma and be okay."

"Yeah. But it's tough making your way to the other end."

Cooper was most likely speaking for himself.

"Cooper, you should also know that when Ivy has a lousy day and doesn't do well in controlling her emotions, she worries you'll abandon her. She's concerned she'll become too much of a burden for you."

"No way. I'd better fix that. I expected getting her emotions under control would take time. She is doing better. Heck, she is not as difficult as she thinks."

"Good to hear."

"You'll like this. Sometimes she'll read her gratitude journal to us. It's often about teachers, fellow students, and long-time friends who've been kind or encouraging. Sometimes it's about you. I think that practice has helped Ivy turn a corner. She's recognizing lots of people value and believe in her."

"That's wonderful. I'm glad it's helped."

***

It was a big surprise when she received an enormous bouquet of daisies and mums at work. Each person in the Martin household had written a personal note of gratitude for her involvement in their lives. To hide the tears pooling in her eyes, she walked away from her desk to finish reading the note.

Though what the girls wrote touched her, Cooper stunned her by writing how her coming into their lives had been the most wonderful gift he could imagine. He thanked her for generously giving of her time, her compassion, and her sensibilities with the girls. He also asked her to dinner as a thank you.

***

She met Cooper for dinner in Port Orchard the following Thursday night.

Immediately, he declared, "Tonight, let's focus on us and not the girls."

"I'll give it my best try!" Could she really stick to that plan? The girls were such a big part of her life now.

They sat at a romantic corner table overlooking the Puget Sound. The building's twinkling lights reflected across the ripples in the indigo waters. Since it was a weeknight, they had the place almost to themselves.

"Excellent choice, Coop."

They talked about their experiences at the University of Washington, then the conversation moved onto their first romantic relationships.

She laughed until her cheeks hurt. "Cooper, you are an excellent storyteller, and certainly a man comfortable revealing his flaws."

He tilted his head with a reflective look on his face. "It wasn't always that way, believe me. Age has helped with that."

They moved on to discussing how their views on marriage had changed with maturity.

"Since I'd come from a small, conservative town," said Cooper, "I followed the same traditional gender roles my parents modeled. If Karen had lived longer, that would have changed eventually. When I lost her and became a single dad, I often functioned in both parental roles, or negotiated with Mom on how she could fill in. With every stage of Emma's development, there were lessons to be learned. I think all first-time parents are anxious about *winging it* through all of their child's stages. Especially a single dad with a daughter. Mom taught me that a guy's ideas on parenting could often differ from those of a woman." He shook his head. "Mom and I butt heads sometimes."

"I can imagine." She chuckled.

His eyes twinkled with amusement.

"After Dad died, Mom found her voice while forced to run the business he left behind. When she came to live with us, she had no problem making her opinions known."

He became serious. "I'm more open now about how couples and families function. I suspect everyone has to customize how they operate based on their unique circumstances and needs. There are no rulebooks. You are stuck with having to figure it out as you go."

"I agree." She enjoyed hearing his insights.

If they continued their relationship, what would their individual roles be with Emma and within the household look like? Even with his mom,

Cooper was the one who called the shots as Emma's parent. However, it boded well that he and Claire had a history of working things out. That showed they could respect each other's perspectives.

Gosh, it was hard not to fall for this guy.

Though they both had to go to work in the morning, they lingered at the table for as long as possible. When Cooper walked her to her car, a crescent moon lit the night sky, and the crisp air smelled of fall. The leaves in the parking lot crunched underfoot.

When they reached her car, she turned around, and his eager lips were waiting. She wrapped her arms around his neck to pull him closer. They enjoyed a mini make-out session right there in the parking lot. By the time they pulled apart, their chests were heaving as they gasped for air.

He took her hand and squeezed. "If we keep this up, we'll end up in the back seat of your car." He glanced up at the parking lot security light beaming down on them. "Probably a bad idea." He grinned, then took her hand and kissed the back of it. "Until we meet again, my fair maiden."

As she drove home, her smile continued to broaden. The residual heat from their kissing kept her warm until the car heater kicked in. Geez Louise, when he kissed her, she lost all sensibility. He was such a good kisser. When her mind wandered to the bedroom, her eyes sprang wide.

Whoa, girl! Dial that down.

"Oh, my gosh!" Hadn't her passion just shown Cooper she'd given him a second chance?

She laughed and shrugged. Okay, then. Second chances it is!

***

The next night, she picked up Cooper's call by the third ring. After their perfect evening, she'd been expecting his call.

"Hey, babe. How about we have another date soon?"

"The first chance we get." Her lips curved at the thought of their next meeting.

"Can't wait," said Cooper. "Hey, I hadn't wanted to bring this up during our romantic dinner, but I got a call from Judy's social worker. Judy had given her permission. The social worker told me Judy's emotional and physical abuse had been happening for more than a decade. They've diagnosed Judy with PTSD. Once she's discharged, Judy will need ongoing therapy and some help with household tasks as she continues to physically heal. Currently, her biggest problem is depression, which has been hindering her recovery."

"I might have guessed that would be the case."

"Yeah. The social worker has been exploring Judy's after-care options. She contacted Judy's only sister, Helen, in Arizona. At first, Helen was hesitant to get involved. She was bitter that Judy had abandoned their family, leaving Helen as caregiver to their elderly parents, making Helen less inclined to take on more."

"Sounds like a tough situation."

"Helen has softened, though, after learning of Judy's history of domestic violence. Helen then found resources for Judy in her hometown. Now she's reconsidering taking Judy in."

"Will she take Ivy, too?" A lump formed in her throat.

"She hasn't decided yet. I'd miss Ivy if she had to leave. And isn't this the very reason Ivy wants emancipation? I'm going to call the social worker back and say I'd be willing to keep Ivy on a more permanent basis."

"That's wonderful. I honestly believe your home is the best place for her."

After finishing their conversation, they said their tender goodbyes.

In the middle of the night, she awoke with her heart beating like a barking Chihuahua. If Ivy had to leave the Martins, would her reason for being involved in Cooper's life vanish? Would this lead to the relationship running its course?

She pressed her fingers to her heart. No, that was silly. It was just her fear talking.

CHAPTER 26
IVY

Mom and Aunt Helen said their goodbyes to Ivy and then drove away. Aunt Helen had stopped by prior to explain why she couldn't take her back to Arizona with her and Mom. Her aunt, however, invited her to visit whenever she could.

Maybe someday she would. After all, she had never met her grandparents.

Not going with them did kinda bother her. It shouldn't have. Her relatives were strangers to her. Mom seemed like a stranger now, too. When she hugged Mom goodbye, Mom didn't even seem to care that she was leaving her. Her eyes were vacant, as if no one was really there.

Staying with the Martins was the best thing for her. Wasn't that what she'd always wished for, anyway?

Though she would like to call Lora, emailing would be easier to say what's on her mind.

ME: HI LORA! I HOPE YOU CAN VISIT SOON. I MET MY AUNT HELEN TODAY FOR THE FIRST TIME. SHE KEPT APOLOGIZING FOR NOT TAKING ME BACK TO ARIZONA WITH HER AND MOM. SHE PROBABLY FIGURED MOM WAS ENOUGH TO DEAL WITH, THOUGH I THINK I COULD HAVE HELPED. MOM LOOKS BETTER ON THE OUTSIDE, BUT SHE'S QUIET AND KINDA NOT THERE. I'M NOT SURE IF IT'S HER

PAIN MEDS, OR...? MOM WON'T BE GOOD COMPANY FOR MY AUNT ON THE DRIVE. MAYBE THE ARIZONA SUN WILL HELP HER. HOPE SO.

YOU WON'T BELIEVE IT. SOMEONE IN TOWN STARTED A GO FUND ME ACCOUNT FOR MOM AND THE ORAL SURGEON AND OPTHALMOLOGIST DISCOUNTED THEIR FEES. CRIME VICTIMS ALSO HELPED FINANCIALLY. MOM WON'T OWE MUCH TO THE HOSPITAL AT ALL. MAYBE THIS MOVE WILL GIVE HER A FRESH START. DO YOU THINK SHE'LL EVER RETURN? COOPER SAID MOM GAVE THE HOUSE BACK TO THE BANK. CLAIRE TOOK ME TO THE HOUSE TO GET A FEW THINGS BEFORE THAT HAPPENED. THERE WASN'T MUCH I WANTED THOUGH.

THINGS AREN'T AS AWFUL AT SCHOOL. THE STARES AND GOSSIP LET UP AFTER KIDS DISCOVERED KATE PORTER WAS PREGNANT AND NOT JUST GETTING FAT! THE MARTINS HAVE BEEN GREAT. COOPER TALKS TO ME LIKE AN ADULT. THAT'S COOL. EMMA AND I ARE TIGHT. MY GRADES ARE BACK UP, MOSTLY THANKS TO EMMA'S NAGGING. I HOPE MY GRADES ARE GOOD ENOUGH FOR AN ART SCHOOL SCHOLARSHIP. IT'S A LONGSHOT. I'M TRYING NOT TO COUNT ON IT.

SOMEONE TOLD ME HOW LUCKY I WAS NOT TO GO INTO FOSTER CARE. THAT REMINDED ME TO BE GRATEFUL FOR THE MARTINS. I WROTE THAT IN MY GRATITUDE JOURNAL.

CLAIRE TOLD ME YOUR MOM IS MOVING INTO THE SAME BUILDING SHE LIVES IN. WHICH MEANS EVERY TIME YOU VISIT HER, YOU CAN SEE ME TOO. HINT, HINT!

I'LL SEE YOU FRIDAY AT THE WRAPAROUND MEETING. THANKS FOR WORKING WITH THE SCHOOL COUNSELOR TO SET UP MY COMMUNITY SUPPORT TEAM. MY DAD HATED THE IDEA OF TAKING CHARITY AND HAVING PEOPLE FEEL SORRY FOR US. I KNOW THIS IS KINDA LIKE THAT, BUT THANKS TO YOU AND MISS MURPHY, I

CONSIDER IT MORE LIKE NEIGHBORS HELPING HEIGHBORS. MISS MURPHY SAID PEOPLE FEEL GOOD ABOUT HELPING SOMEONE ELSE. MY VOLUNTEER GIG OVER THE SUMMER TAUGHT ME THAT, TOO.

ANYWAY, SEE YOU SOON.

IVY

***

She'd been nervous all day and more so sitting at the table as her team came into the room. Already there were Cooper, Claire, Emma, her art teacher - Mrs. Allen, Bernie, and Miss Murphy. Lora texted she would be a few minutes late.

Nerves were making it hard to sit still. She trusted Miss Murphy knew what she was doing. She said she had had previous experience developing and working with this type of team before she moved here. Miss Murphy assured her it would be a positive experience.

Things were great with Cooper as her temporary guardian, so she was glad he wasn't upset that she wanted to petition for emancipation as soon as possible. It was the only way her life would be free from future disruption. Emancipation would require a lot from her, although Miss Murphy said her team would help with that. She hoped she'd be ready in two and a half months, so she could file shortly after her birthday.

Lora rushed in, then took the chair beside her. She gave her leg a quick squeeze and smiled. Having her so close helped calm her nerves. However, as always, she sure wished she had the power of invisibility. The best she could do was wrap her arms around her waist and avoid looking at anyone.

When Miss Murphy got up to start the meeting, Lora leaned over and whispered, "Relax. This will be great!"

"Thank you all for coming," said Miss Murphy. "You were hand-picked by Ivy to become a part of her WrapAround team. The team's purpose is to help Ivy live and thrive within this community while preparing her to venture out on her own when she's ready and able. Her goal is to become emancipated. This means she will need to show the court she can support herself financially, have housing, demonstrate she's capable of making good decisions, and attend school through graduation."

Miss Murphy glanced her way and nodded. "Our first task today is to determine what Ivy's strengths are. These are the attributes Ivy possesses that can help her succeed. Next, we'll define what her current and future needs might be. From there, we will look for ways Ivy can use her strengths and her team as a resource for meeting her needs and future goals."

A rumble of approval spread through the group.

Miss Murphy taped two enormous sheets of plain paper onto the white bulletin board behind her. "We'll start by identifying Ivy's strengths. As you call them out, I'll write them down."

Mrs. Allen jumped right in. "There is no doubt about it. Ivy has artistic talent. She's not afraid to try new techniques, and she's great at finishing projects. Also, she's wonderful with other students, encouraging them to try new things and offers her support. I'd say she's one of the most talented art students I've had."

Wow, that was super nice to hear!

Miss Murphy wrote a summary of what Mrs. Allen said on the paper labeled "Strengths". Then she waited for others to speak up. Everyone shifted in their seats.

Great. Didn't anyone else think she had any strengths?

Nana Claire finally spoke up. "I've known Ivy since she was in grade school, and I've always known her to be an honest person. *No* cheating to win." She smiled warmly at her.

"If she lost in a game, she was a good sport. She's also been a wonderful friend to my granddaughter, Emma, and their small circle of friends. Even though she's been less fortunate than the other kids, she's never shown ugly jealousy or been mean. I agree she has artistic talent. She spends a great deal of time in the creative space Cooper made for her and Emma."

Nana Claire winked at her. "She's a good kid and a free spirit, not afraid to express her artistic style. I hear she volunteered at the library's summer art program for kids, and the kids and their parents loved her."

Nana Claire looked directly at her. "It's hard to come from a troubled home. Ivy, you did a wonderful job separating yourself from that."

Claire glanced about the room. "Ivy has shown real resilience during adversity. She also has the strength of character to admit when she makes mistakes. This shows maturity. She's curious, enthusiastic, fun-loving, empathetic toward her mother's situation, and expresses her feelings well through her art. Sometimes she amazes me with how well she can articulate her thoughts."

She chuckled. "Well, we have to remember she's a teenager and give her a little slack sometimes."

The group laughed and nodded their agreement.

Heat rose from her neck to her cheeks, even though she liked what Nana Claire had said. Claire had been the only grandmother figure she had ever known. Like a loving grandmother, Claire was generous with her hugs and would often make special after-school treats for them.

As the room quieted, everyone focused on her, making her want to hide under the table. Their approving smiles felt good, though.

Emma's face was already pink when she spoke up next. With a steady voice, she said, "I've been Ivy's friend since first grade. She was the kind of kid teachers liked because she was quiet and nice to all the other kids. Even in first grade, we saw she had artistic talent. Kids would gather around her desk to check out what she was creating during art period or to admire the doodles she was *always* making. To this day, she carries paper and a pencil with her *everywhere*."

She lifted the pad and paper she had on her lap, and everyone laughed.

Emma made a silly face at her, then continued. "When we got older, they assigned group projects to us in school. She always had *amazing* ideas and was respectful of the ideas of others. What I'm saying is she never insisted things had to go her way. Another good thing was that she always followed through on her part of the assignment. When we played sports together, she was a valued member of our team. She never lost her temper when things didn't go well."

Emma looked at her. "The team was sad when she left."

For a moment, Emma paused, but everyone waited. It was clear she was thinking about what to say next.

"I know last year she got a little off track in school. However, now she has a goal, so I know she'll finish strong."

Immediately, Cooper scooted his chair back. "We've had Ivy over since she was little, and more so as the girls got older. I wouldn't have agreed if Ivy had been a difficult kid. She pitches in, helping with meals and cleanup like a family member. And she keeps her space in the creative room tidy. Mostly, she's a lot of fun to be around. She's a good kid who's had some tough breaks. I'd like to see her succeed in whatever she desires. She's welcome in our home while she works to accomplish that." Cooper nodded in her direction with tenderness in his eyes.

All this attention was embarrassing. What they said about her was overwhelming. Yet, hearing those nice things was pretty cool, too. She hugged her belly again as she looked around to see if anyone else would speak.

Bernie pushed up a sleeve and cleared his throat. "Ivy showed up with her ma on weekends sometimes since she was a little tyke. Normally, that kind of thing wouldn't work out, but Ivy was a good kid and no trouble. She liked puttin' the silverware and napkins on the tables, wipin' them off...that kinda stuff. I paid her with a piece of cake."

Everyone chuckled.

"Ivy would go sit in the back drawing...real quiet." A grin crept over his face. "Being there gave her ma better tips, I think!"

Again, everyone chuckled. Bernie scanned the group with a broad smile, revealing his missing tooth. He'd told her once he'd lost his tooth, courtesy of the misguided path he'd taken early in his life.

After a moment, Bernie spoke again. "Judy always said Ivy was a big help at home too, real proud-like. We all miss Judy. I'd like to help her daughter if I could." He cleared his throat, appearing newly uncomfortable.

Miss Murphy finished writing everything on the "Strengths" paper and turned to the group.

"We have found some admirable strengths which will help Ivy reach her goals. Now let's assess her needs. What does an almost sixteen-year-old, who is homeless and without a family's support, need?"

On another sheet of paper, Miss Murphy wrote at the top, *NEEDS*. Next, she drew a circle in the middle of the paper and then wrote *Ivy* inside. Off that, she drew branches with smaller circles attached. Inside one circle, she wrote "homeless".

Cooper spoke up quickly. "I've got her covered for a place to live. She's got shelter and food, and some extras. Right now, I have temporary custody, but I understand Ivy's reasoning for wanting emancipation. Anyway, we've always said she's like part of our family, and I want her to always feel welcome with us. And most of all, safe."

Nana Claire said, "I've always thought kids need to learn how to take care of themselves before they become adults. They need to know how to do things like...well, like how to do their laundry, take care of a car, budget their money, and how a bank works. Skills to help them become independent adults."

Miss Murphy made a "self-sufficiency" circle on the *Needs* paper, then added the skills Nana Claire had mentioned on branches coming off the circle.

Lora said, "I haven't known Ivy long, but she could use her artistic talent and build a career by going to an art school after graduation. There is one in Washington and several in California with top ratings. She'll need to build a portfolio to submit with her application. She might need to apply for a low-income scholarship or a work internship. I believe this is doable for Ivy."

Mrs. Allen said, "I'm familiar with the art school admissions process. I'm willing to help. Ivy should apply to at least four programs. Even though Ivy has genuine talent, there is considerable competition. To build a portfolio, she'll need a camera and to get her work out in the public eye."

"Thank you, everyone. Excellent suggestions," said Miss Murphy. "Ivy, what do you think your current needs are? And what do you think they might be in the future? Be as specific as you can."

All eyes turned to her, and her face flushed hot. "This seems a bit like when you're a kid and they ask you to write a wish list for Santa."

Everyone laughed, which helped her relax.

She thought for a moment, then said, "I would like to earn my own money while living with the Martins. You know, to buy my own clothes and any stuff I might need. After I turn sixteen, I'd like to petition for emancipation, though still live with the Martins, of course."

She smiled at Cooper in gratitude, then noticed the concerned faces around the room. "Don't worry, I'll stay in school and do my best. I should be able to work and still keep my grades up. Other kids have done it. I appreciate living with the Martins, yet it should only be until I graduate. After that, I should be on my own. I'd love to go to art school...if I could. It seems an impossibility, but I wanna try."

She took a deep breath as her legs bounced up and down from nerves. "There are so many things I need to learn before I graduate. When I move out, I'll have to buy a car and get insurance. I'll need a computer for school and for doing some of my art stuff. The list just gets bigger and bigger the more I think about it." She grimaced.

Lora took her hand and squeezed.

"Thank you, Ivy," said Miss Murphy. "The more specific you are, the better we can meet your needs."

Miss Murphy glanced around the group. "Ivy has the same dilemma I've seen for teens who are in foster care, yet Ivy isn't in foster care. She's fortunate to have the Martin family and all of you to wrap your support around her."

Cooper caught her eye. "I want you to know we care about you. Even when you go off to college, you will always have a place to come home to. I'd like you to feel okay about asking for a few bucks if you need it, or to call if something goes wrong and you need help. Our family can be in your life for as long as you want us to be. What you do with your future is your decision. I'm available to talk to if you're ever having trouble figuring things out." He turned back to the group. "I believe Ivy *can* make a future she'll be proud of."

While she listened to Cooper, she had to swallow several times. Being close to tears, she lowered her head, embarrassed that others might see her get emotional. What Cooper said felt huge.

The Martins considered her *family*.

Miss Murphy tacked up another big sheet of paper and wrote at the top: *ACTION STEPS*. "Now we'll address how the team can help fulfill Ivy's needs."

Everyone called out what they were willing to do.

Mrs. Allen said, "I'll volunteer once a week to help Ivy work on her art portfolio at lunch and occasionally after school."

"I have a digital camera Ivy can have, and I'll teach her how to use it," said Nana Claire.

"She can load her pictures on my computer until she can get one of her own," said Emma. "I'll also nag—Er, *encourage* her to keep her grades up."

"Since the legal paperwork will probably be tricky," said Cooper, "I'll help Ivy with the emancipation process. We'll also see about getting her name changed at the same time. That's something she's always talked about doing."

Her heart thumped in her chest. He remembered.

The conference room was buzzing, and Miss Murphy was having difficulty writing down everything people were saying.

"Everyone, slow down and speak one at a time? Your enthusiasm is wonderful; however, I can't write that fast. I don't want to miss anything important."

Under the table, she squeezed her hands together. It was awesome to have everyone want to help her. Warmth spread through her chest. She could tell she *mattered* to them.

Nana Claire said, "I'll take Ivy to the bank and help her open a savings and checking account. We'll have to locate her social security number. I'll help with that, too."

Bernie raised his hand. "Ivy could work the Sunday after-church shift at the diner, possibly some Saturday nights, too...if she'd like. Shouldn't be too much, you know, to get her behind in school. The holidays are comin'. Tips are usually good then."

"That would be great," she said. How cool. She could make her own money.

Nana Claire volunteered to help her get her food worker card as soon as possible.

When the room quieted, Lora said, "I've seen some towns where all the businesses have their windows painted for the holidays. Though it's November 3rd, there's still time for Ivy to start a holiday window-painting business...if she'd like. It could continue to other seasons once she establishes a regular clientele. She could build her portfolio from the window displays. What do you think, Ivy?"

"That would be pretty amazing! I've seen painted windows on Pinterest. It's like painting on a huge canvas. I'd love to do that!" She squirmed excitedly as her mind filled with images of window possibilities.

Cooper said, "In that case, she'll need a business license. If not now, eventually. I'll help with that."

"When the business takes off, I'll help Ivy set up a simple bookkeeping program," said Lora.

Cooper nodded. "Sounds good."

"I like that idea!" said Bernie, turning toward her. "I'll hire you right now to do the two center windows while you're waitin' to get your food worker card. Come up with some ideas, and we'll settle on a price."

The happiness bubbling inside her was freaking her out. She wrapped her arms around her waist. She could scarcely believe this was happening. "Cool. I'll work on that tonight and come by tomorrow!" Her head was about to explode. She was so pumped. Was this for real?

With a little chuckle, Mrs. Allen said, "I love your enthusiasm, Ivy. I assume you'll need some painting supplies. When I get home, I'll sort through mine. I know I have a few brushes and some acrylic paints you can have. That might be enough to get you started."

Miss Murphy summarized what each team member had volunteered to do and wrote it all down on the *ACTION PLAN* paper. With everything settled, they set another group meeting for the Friday before Thanksgiving break.

"Thank you all for coming," said Miss Murphy. "Ivy is a lucky girl to have all of you wonderful people supporting her."

Everyone was slow to leave the room. They all lingered to say something to her or Miss Murphy.

She heard Cooper invite Lora and Nana Claire over for dinner. Nana Claire said she had a date and zipped out the door.

Lora shook her head, looking sad. "I promised to help Mom do some unpacking. It's only been four days since she moved into Claire's building, and she's already stressing out."

Hesitating before she spoke, Lora said to Cooper, "The movers put gobs of boxes into Mom's guest room. Would it be possible to stay at your place?"

Mentally, she crossed her fingers; she wanted to be around Lora as much as possible.

Thankfully, Cooper said, "Sure, the guest room is yours for as long as you need it. Let me know if your mom could use some muscle."

She wanted to volunteer to help, but she had window designs to come up with. How cool was that?

CHAPTER 27
COOPER

To keep from falling asleep, Cooper read an action novel while in bed. He had cracked his window open so he could hear when Lora arrived back at the house.

As soon as he heard her car pull up, he pulled a T-shirt on over his boxers and headed downstairs. He found her in the kitchen, getting a glass of water.

He sauntered up behind her. "Hey. How'd everything go?"

From the dark circles under her eyes and her glazed-over look, she was exhausted.

"The good news is we finished setting up Mom's bedroom and her closet. Next is the kitchen. She'll need to downsize even more." Lora yawned into her hand. "She's going to need my help for a while. Could I use your guest room again?"

"Sure." He took her hand, pulled her to him, and wrapped his arms around her.

Lora skimmed her palms over his chest as her eyes held his. "You don't mind?"

His voice lowered. "No complaints."

He lowered his head to trail kisses along the side of her neck. She raised her chin and turned her head. He took this as a sign she wanted more. When their lips met, familiar fireworks shot through his belly. Her moan instantly aroused him.

Damn, she felt so good.

Desperately needing to touch her skin, he lowered his arms and slid his hands under her shirt, splaying his fingers around her waist to tug her even closer. The kisses progressed to tongues mingling, hands roaming, and bodies grinding. He couldn't get enough of her.

Then the hairs on his arms rose with the sudden urge to flee from Lora's arms. He needed...breathing room. Shit, was he gonna have a panic attack? His heart raced uncomfortably. This was ridiculous. Not again!

This shit is irrational. He needed to get a grip on himself.

To ease the squeezing pressure in his chest, he stepped back to take some breaths. He clenched his teeth. This panic was so random and unpredictable. He threaded his fingers through his hair, afraid to look at Lora.

He didn't want to ruin this.

When he finally glanced at her, her eyes were scanning his face.

Her shoulders slumped when she said, "We're not ready for this, are we, Cooper? It's too soon. Before we take the next step, we need to be sure. And ready to risk it all."

She was right. Being able to risk loving again was something they both had to be okay with. He wanted it, but something was holding him back. He didn't want to hurt her again if he found he couldn't handle it.

To bring some levity, he peered down at his bulging boxers and said, "Someone thought we were ready." He grinned, shrugging. Humor was his attempt to hide his embarrassment.

She giggled and shook her head.

He shuffled his feet. "You're probably right, but...heck, when we kiss, I rocket right out of control." He knew the grin on his face had turned crooked.

She laughed and took a step back. "That's the danger. We have no problem with chemistry. Obviously, that's the easiest part of what's happening between us. Let's slow down and see if there's a realistic future for us." She leaned in and kissed his cheek. "Good night, Cooper. I'll see you in the morning."

***

When he awoke, he assumed Lora would be sleeping in. Needing coffee, he wandered toward the kitchen, yawning and stretching. He found Lora there, teaching Emma her secret recipe for Dutch babies.

Good grief, the kitchen smelled amazing! His stomach growled with anticipation as the first pancake came out of the oven.

Before entering, he further observed Lora and Emma. Yes, Emma would have gained something if he'd given her a new mom early on. Heck, maybe she still needed a mom? Emma and Lora's interactions seemed so natural; companionable cooks with an easy banter between them. Lora fit into their lives so effortlessly.

What would it be like if it were permanent?

Wow! What a leap—after only two dates and a few dozen phone calls. No, that wasn't fair. It had been a lot more than that. He'd already learned she was a wonderful person. She was thoughtful, smart, kind-hearted, and patient with the girls...and perhaps with him, as well.

The idea of having Lora permanently present in their lives had entered his mind before.

He shook his head and walked into the kitchen. "Your taste tester is here!"

"Only if you do the dishes!" Emma said sternly, but with a smile in her eyes.

His growling stomach decided for him. "Deal."

Ivy was sitting at the far end of the kitchen island, working on Bernie's window sketches.

He approached and peered over her shoulder. "Great job."

The colored-pencil sketches showed a couple of elves carrying food. One held the Starfish Diner's traditional red plastic serving basket with its red-and-white checked paper liner, loaded with a burger and fries. The other elf carried a platter filled with holiday baked goods. The elves had impish faces, big pointy ears, and bulbous noses. Their smiles radiated delight at what they were about to serve.

"Ivy, these are amazing. Does Bernie carry some of the baked goods you've included in your drawing? If he doesn't, he should."

"I don't think so."

Emma stopped rolling a pizza cutter through the hot Dutch baby. "Dad, could I make and sell holiday baked goods to Bernie?"

He shook his head. "That would be a lot of work. Stick to concentrating on school and sports."

"It would just be during the holidays," grumbled Emma with an unusually sharp tone. Her mouth opened to say something more, but she scowled and closed it quickly.

He ignored her and walked to the fridge to pull out the orange juice carton. When he turned around, Emma's face still held a scowl. She was being ridiculous, wanting to add more to an already full schedule.

Emma opened her mouth again to say something, then stopped. As she lowered her head, her nostrils flared.

It was unlike her to get so huffy. He'd said no for her own good.

Then Lora touched Emma's shoulder to console her.

What? Was he the bad guy now?

He ignored Emma's glum face as he ate a slice of the pancake. It was truly delicious.

After checking with the girls, he learned he and Lora would be alone for the evening. Emma had a movie and pizza night with her teammates. Ivy would be over at Rebecca's, setting up her computer and jazzing up Rebecca's website. Afterward, Rebecca was taking Ivy to dinner at Bernie's so Ivy could present her Christmas window design. He'd have Lora all to himself.

***

That night, when Lora returned from her mom's, he'd set the stage for a romantic dinner. Soft jazz was playing when Lora came in the door. After she showered, they leisurely prepped enchiladas together, chatting while they worked. He poured himself a beer; Lora unwound with a glass of wine.

"Mom seems unable to decide what to keep and where things should go. I understand, though it's frustrating how little we accomplish."

He saluted her with his beer. "In my mind, that's great news. I enjoy having you here." He gave her a smooch on the cheek before heading to the pantry.

He liked how they worked smoothly in the kitchen together. With the enchiladas in the oven, they assembled a tossed salad before going into the great room.

"How's training the intern going?" he asked.

"She's impressive. She has great ideas and is nonstop in telling me how grateful she is to be working with us. Nice to hear, though now her academic advisor has asked me to take on another intern next quarter."

"Isn't that a lot of work?"

"It'll be easier next time around. I've figured out how to sequence the learning to help an intern understand our operation. After that, they'll have the freedom to suggest and implement their own ideas."

"Sounds smart. She's lucky to have you." He tapped his foot while considering his work situation. "I've got a bugger of a problem developing at work. My invaluable office manager, Virginia, will need to retire before I'm ready to let her go. She doesn't want to leave yet, but she's dealing with pressure from her recently retired husband."

"She's your only office staff?"

He nodded.

"That's the risk in having only one person managing an office. When you lose them, it can be devastating. I'm wondering...since she's of great value and not fully ready to retire, have you thought about hiring a full-time replacement and having Virginia go part-time? That way, Virginia could ease out while she trains the person stepping into her shoes. Another thought might be—You are planning to expand, right?"

"Yeah."

"You're probably going to need more office staff. Hire one or two full-time staff while Virginia is still available to train them. Later, if you're both willing, assign her a single task or a larger ongoing project which would allow her flexible part-time hours."

"Hmm, both good ideas. I'll talk them over with Virginia. Right now, she's so frustrated with our new inventory system, I'm afraid she'll up and quit on me."

Boy, that would be a disaster.

They sipped their drinks in silent reflection.

Lora was sure savvy about business. Those ideas should have come from him. Crap! He had a problem with the people he was attached to leaving. His cowardly choice was to avoid thinking about it.

Lora asked, "What system is Virginia having trouble with?"

"Our *Stock Smart System* software. The newest version."

"We use that system too, although an older version. It has some quirks and a steep learning curve. I'd be happy to help Virginia figure it out. Yet, other than Ivy's next team meeting, I'm not sure when I'll be back. Definitely not during the week."

"Hmm, I bet Virginia would appreciate your help. She might even be willing to come in tomorrow, before you go back home. Would that work for you?"

"Sure. How about in the morning? Mom needs to do more sorting before we can continue organizing her rooms." Lora blew out a breath. "Letting go of what you think connects you with your past is hard. She keeps asking me if I want some of her things, but I really don't."

He picked up his empty beer bottle and picked at the label. "I imagine with your mom moving here and you helping Ivy, you'll be around more."

"Normally, I visit Mom once a month. She's farther away, but I plan to continue with that. When I'm back, would you mind if I checked in with the girls?"

"From my perspective, whatever relationship you continue to develop with those girls, especially Ivy, would be great."

He shifted his body toward Lora, put down his beer bottle, and took her hand. "I'm hoping *we* can see more of each other, too. It's been a mistake keeping myself from having a serious relationship."

He rubbed the back of her hand with his thumb. "Lora, I'm attracted to you. No surprise there. I have been ever since the day I saw you mopping the kitchen floor with your foot, and more so after I've gotten to know you. I admire you...for so many reasons." He gazed deep into the warmth of her eyes.

"I've seen how you are with the girls, so I can only imagine you were an amazing mom to your little girl."

Lora's eyes moistened as she whispered, "Thanks for saying that. I can see you're a wonderful father, too."

He squeezed her hand. "Lora, I think falling in love with you would be darn easy."

She squeezed his hand back. There was tenderness in her eyes. Her voice was soft when she said, "Cooper, the attraction is mutual. I asked to slow down because we both have baggage to deal with. And since we've both denied ourselves loving relationships for so long, a premature hop into bed would be too easy. Afterward, we might have regrets. Anyway, for the type of relationship I want, at least, sex shouldn't come prematurely. It's best we take our time. Make sure we are ready for a lasting commitment."

He sighed. "Okay. You're probably right."

"Cooper, I like the person I'm getting to know in you." She put her wineglass on the coffee table. "Then there's the girls. I have to say, being involved with them puts back something I've missed." She tilted her head. "For now, I don't mind being the one commuting. At least once a month, for sure." She lifted a shoulder. "More, if possible."

"I'll take what I can get, though I'd love to see you more frequently."

She grew quiet for a moment. "If we move forward with our relationship, you'll have to think about how you'd incorporate me into the way your life functions. Could you share the decision-making for Emma and Ivy? If we were ever to get married, I'd want to co-parent—to share all aspects of parenting, even financially. I'd like to contribute a woman's point of view to their next phase in life. Knowing how I might step into your established family would be helpful."

The muscles in his stomach tightened, forcing him to take a deeper breath to relax. This was serious stuff.

"As I see it," she raised her eyes and shook her head, "being a part of your family would be amazing."

His brows hiked. *Wow!* Lora just set some terms for how their relationship could move forward. Fair enough, I guess.

Shoot. Seeing each other once a month would be difficult. He wanted more of her. Trying to control the heat between them would be agonizing. He'd have to think more about the rest.

Lora lowered her gaze. "Though I believe being part of your family would be wonderful, I also think it wouldn't be easy. I would be an outsider. We'd have to figure out how I'd mesh with you as a parent beforehand...as much as we could, anyway." She sought his eyes. "There's a lot of *what-ifs*, aren't there? Most of them are probably born out of fear. We'll have to learn to trust each other. That only comes with time."

He smiled to hide his nerves. "You've given this a lot of thought. I thank you for that. I'm okay with taking it slow, as long as I know you'll give me a fair chance. From what you've said, you want—shoot, I could mess this up pretty easily. You'll tell me, won't you, if I mess up? I'll need your help."

She leaned in and kissed him, a sweet, lingering kiss.

"Mmm, I like your kisses," he said. "Could more kissing be one of our next steps in getting to know each other?" He kissed her again.

She giggled into his lips, then pulled away. "You make me feel like a teenager." She ran her fingers through her hair. "Cooper, I'm going to mess up, too. This will be unfamiliar territory for both of us. If we want this badly enough, we'll work it out."

He gave a wry chuckle. "We're not teenagers anymore, so we know what's ahead of us, at least on the physical end of things. Going slow might be tough." His face grimaced with disappointment. "Though I also think it could be fun, too." He leaned over and nuzzled her neck.

In a breathy whisper, Lora said, "Same here."

He pulled her close to kiss the top of her head. She snuggled in close and sighed.

With a voice turned husky from need, he said, "Oh yeah, slow can be a lot of fun." He gently put his fingers under her chin and brought her lips to his. They enjoyed another full six minutes of kissing before the stove timer startled Lora out of his arms.

He groaned. "Guess it's dinnertime."

"It smells so good." She followed him into the kitchen. "Mom said your mom finally chose between her two suitors. I hear her relationship with the winner is getting pretty serious."

His eyes popped wide. This was the first he'd heard about it. "Guess I should find out more about this guy." His voice sounded gruff from disappointment that he hadn't been informed. "Obviously, I'd like to see Mom happy. I just need to know this fella's not a jerk."

Lora set out the serving utensils. "I met him yesterday, and they're adorable together, acting like love-struck kids. He can't keep his eyes or his hands off her. They're planning a trip together in the spring."

"Didn't know that either. I'm not sure how I feel about their going off together so soon." He rubbed the back of his neck. "She never dated much after Dad died. Moving into an over-fifty community made finding love easier, I guess. Mom deserves happiness. She basically gave up her life to take care of us." He removed the enchiladas from the oven. "Seems like I held everyone back from having significant relationships."

Lora came up behind him and hugged him around his middle. "I'm sure that's not true. You're a good man, Cooper Martin. Don't you forget it."

He smiled before twisting around and laying a warm kiss on her lips. When he pulled back, what he saw in her eyes made his heart thump. There was unmistakable love there.

Satisfaction spread a big grin over his face. "Thanks. 'Preciate that." He hugged her tightly, then stepped back. "Enchilada time!"

He took the enchilada pan off the stovetop. Its spicy, cheesy aroma spread throughout the room. He headed for the kitchen island. "Watch out, girl! Hot stuff comin' through." He winked as he passed her by, placing the steaming dish on a trivet.

They dished up and ate beside each other, exchanging flirtatious banter and sappy grins.

Eventually, he brought the conversation back to his mother. "You know, I've missed having Mom in the house as much. I guess I'm a guy who enjoys keeping things status quo." He blinked, then raised a hand. "Wow, probably shouldn't have said *that*." He raised his brows and rolled his eyes. "Personal change has been difficult for me. Shocker, I know."

She smiled her understanding.

"Cooper, you mentioned once that you came to realize Emma took on the role of an emotional caretaker for you...and possibly at her own expense?"

He nodded, wondering where this was going.

"You never mentioned whether you've talked to her about it yet." She hesitated. "Stop me if I'm out of line." She watched for his okay.

He nodded. "No worries."

"I was wondering if you might ask Emma the same thing Miss Murphy asked Ivy? You know—what does she want and need for the future *she* desires?"

He had a sudden urge to defend himself. Instead, he stood up to give himself time to calm down. Slowly, he walked over to retrieve the wine bottle from the counter and returned to fill Lora's empty glass.

"Do you have a reason for asking?"

"Well, yes. As an example, earlier Emma asked if she could bake Christmas pastries for Bernie's diner. You shut down the idea quickly, without giving her the respect of exploring what she had in mind. I saw her disappointment and how she stuffed down her feelings to let the topic go. At her age, teens often fight for what they want and question their parents' boundaries. Emma gave up so easily. That's not really a good thing. You wouldn't want her to stage an all-out rebellion because she wants more independence in her choices."

Crap. The need to argue his side nearly overrode his good sense to pause and think this through. Okay, calm down. Hear her out. If he planned to have a relationship with Lora, he needed to listen to her.

He shoved the wine stopper back in the bottle and paced the floor. "You're right. I did shut it down quickly. Though it's not like I've set everything for her future in concrete." He shook his head. "Although— okay, I might have pushed the University of Washington." He rubbed the back of his head. "And, could be I've verbalized my hope she'll get a sports scholarship." He grimaced. "No, you're right, I haven't asked her what she wants to be when she grows up."

Not for a long time, anyway. Or even what college prep interests she'd like to pursue in her junior and senior years. He rubbed his jaw. Wow! Being called out on how he was parenting was uncomfortable.

He resumed his pacing. "Okay. So, I'm an ass for assuming she's on the same wavelength as me."

Lora put an elbow on the counter and rested her chin on her palm. "Oh, you're probably like lots of parents who've guided their kids in the direction *they* think would be best for them. Unfortunately, that doesn't always match where their child's interests or talents lie. I'm sure you know that when kids or *anyone* makes their own choices, they're more energized and invested in the outcome."

He mulled that over. "Makes...sense."

She kept her voice light. "You also might consider that, like Ivy, Emma might benefit from being taught the independence skills Claire mentioned."

That was true. He'd be doing Emma a disservice if he didn't.

Why had he avoided doing so? Did he *want* her to need him?

Geez.

"You're hitting some sore spots here. What you've said has merit." Though he may not like hearing it.

He sighed heavily. "Parenting a teen or a *young* adult is more challenging than when she was a little girl." He wiggled his eyebrows. "When I was the *all-knowing* one."

Lora laughed. "I bet she'll surprise you when you ask about her future wants. She's a kid who organizes her life and plans ahead."

He picked up their dishes and rinsed them in the sink before turning back to her. "Thanks, um, for your thoughts."

This was the troublesome part of having a relationship. It required him to be open to another person's opinion. He'd managed with his mom, yet it hadn't always been easy. With a glance at Lora, he decided he'd have to see how this goes.

He loaded the dishwasher as Lora finished her wine. "You still game for helping Virginia with the inventory software tomorrow morning? If so, I'll call her."

"Sure."

He had the sense she was watching him to gauge where he was emotionally.

To be honest, he was still a bit rattled.

While he called Virginia, Lora hunted for a movie they could snuggle up on the couch to watch. He liked the domestic quality of their evening together. It helped him relax into accepting that there would be adjustments if they stayed together for the long haul.

***

The next day, they drove in separate cars to meet Virginia at his office on the outskirts of town. He was curious to see what Lora would think of his business.

A chain-link fence enclosed the exterior of his two-story industrial building. The outside didn't look like much, but the setup inside the plant might impress her. His office was on the second floor, though they were meeting Virginia on the lower level. As they walked from the parking lot, he gave Lora a brief history of the business from inception to his current efforts to expand.

As he opened the main entry door, the welcoming aroma of freshly brewed coffee signaled Virginia's presence.

Virginia stood behind the long reception counter, wearing an enormous grin. "Hey, boss." She pushed her purple acrylic glasses down to look Lora over. "And *you* must be the angel who's gonna show me how to run our blasted inventory system!"

"Lora, meet my right-hand gal, Virginia. We go way back, so she tries to push me around whenever she can." He laughed as he walked around the counter to give his favorite employee a quick hug.

Virginia grumbled and pushed him away, still grinning. She nodded her head toward the coffeepot. "Lora, get yourself some coffee and have a seat by my computer. Boss, get some, too. You probably have enough work upstairs to keep you out of our hair."

With a flick of her finger, Virginia feigned disgust when she said, "It did *not* please my hubby when I left this mornin'. So, you owe me lunch tomorrow for havin' to take his guff." She turned and walked to her desk with a raised hand. "Omigod, can that man whine!"

He winked at Lora as he left to do as he'd been *told*.

An hour later, Lora walked into his office, giving him a thumbs-up. "You're up and running. Virginia has it mastered now."

Lora leaned a hip on the side of his desk. "Would you mind giving me directions to the nearest craft store? I offered to pick up a few supplies for Ivy before I leave." She smiled sweetly as she batted her eyelashes. "If you'd tag along, you could take them back so I could get on the road. ASAP. Ivy is an eager beaver to start on Bernie's windows. The prospect of making her own money seems pretty motivating for her."

"Yeah, I've seen that too. Thanks to you, the sullen teenager has become a young female entrepreneur. That was a great idea."

He walked over and kissed her on the cheek. "You're pretty amazing, you know." He saw his words pleased her.

"It won't be long before it's lunchtime. Could you stick around a little longer, and I'll treat you to a burger at Bernie's?"

"Sorry. Wish I could." She returned his kiss, this time on the lips.

He grinned. It had been a long time since he'd been *this* happy. He pulled back. "Wanna neck?"

She playfully slapped his shoulder. "You're horrible!"

"Only around you." He grabbed one of her hands and walked her downstairs.

Virginia jumped up as they passed her desk. "Boss, your gal truly is an angel! How 'bout you hire her and let me go part time? As I see it, it would solve *both* our problems."

Lora turned pink.

He narrowed his eyes in surprise. He hadn't talked to Virginia about this, nor did he think Lora had either. "I, uh—"

"Oops!" She raised her palms. "Sorry, didn't have my filter in place. Still, you might consider it! Both of you." She gave them a hopeful smile.

He rolled his eyes at Virginia, then walked Lora out the door.

Maybe he *should* consider the idea.

CHAPTER 28
IVY

As soon as Ivy sketched the elf figures onto Bernie's windows late Sunday afternoon, she drew onlookers. Mostly families stopping by after church. They hovered around to watch and ask questions. Their interest in what she was doing made her stomach jumpy. After all, she wasn't a *real* artist. This was her very first attempt at painting a window. She would have to learn as the project progressed. Painting something this large was intimidating. Could she get the scale and proportions right?

As the elf figures took shape, the encouragement and compliments from passersby kept coming. Though she could see the completed window in her mind's eye, she didn't know if she could pull it off. Regardless, she was so jazzed she was hyper. If she *could* paint the window as she imagined, it would be amazing. People would love it.

It still astonished her she was actually going to make money from a real grown-up job. Lora even thought it could turn into an actual business. An artist's career would sure beat being a server or working a drudge job. Art was her jam. She lost herself in it. All the bad stuff faded away while she was creating.

While she finished up for the day, Mr. Owen, the owner of the drugstore, stopped by.

"You're doing a great job here, Ivy. Could you come up with some ideas for my windows? Something more traditional, incorporating a drugstore theme while keeping it Christmassy?"

Excitement surged through her. "Um, of course. I could have some ideas for you by…Tuesday. I could come by after school."

"Looking forward to seeing your ideas, Ivy."

While she was bent over, boxing up her supplies, something dawned on her. How was she going to get home from her meeting with Mr. Owen? She could walk there, but she'd need a ride back to Cooper's. It was too far to ride her bike to school, and it'd be dark on the way home.

Darn it. She'd have to ask Cooper. Ugh! She didn't want to be more of a burden than she already was. But she had no choice.

Thankfully, tonight Bernie had offered to give her a ride home.

On the way, Bernie said, "Hey, kid, I'm sure happy with the windows. The looky-loos are often coming in to buy at least coffee and a piece of pie."

"Thanks. I'm loving doing it."

Her mind busied with ideas for how to add more detail to Bernie's windows. The elves needed shading to give them more depth. How was she going to show movement in the elves? Before bed, she needed to do some research.

When Bernie dropped her off, her insides vibrated with a forgotten kind of excitement. She put her supply box on the utility room floor, then washed out her brushes before she headed into the kitchen.

Lora said once—*you can choose where you put your attention*. If you look for and focus on the good stuff, you'll be a happier person. Lora was right. There was a lot of good stuff happening these days. She couldn't wait to show Lora the finished windows when she came back. Would Lora see that she had what it took to make something of her life?

She burst into the kitchen, eager to share her day.

"I *see* you've had a great day!" said Cooper. He glanced down at his empty plate and frowned. "Sorry. We didn't know when you'd be home, so we ate."

"However, we put a plate in the fridge for you," said Emma.

"Great. I can smell what you made—porcupine meatballs. Right?"

Emma gave Cooper a cheeky grin.

"Microwave your dinner," said Cooper, "then tell us how your painting went."

She walked toward the fridge, then froze as emotions overtook her.

"What's the matter?" asked Emma.

Her tears spilled over. "I don't know," she blubbered. "Everything that happened today made me so happy. Then you asked me about my day and...and...you fixed one of my favorite meals." She sniffled as her cheeks heated. "It just hit me how nice this is—having everyone care so much about me. It's all so...totally...unbelievable."

She was sure that the smile she offered was so wonky it looked like what she'd draw on a cartoon character.

In slippered feet, Emma shuffled over and gave her an enormous hug. "Of *course,* we care. We *want* to know all about your day. We're so excited for you."

Cooper embraced them both in a group hug. "You girls baffle me!"

She and Emma smiled at each other and laughed.

She was so lucky to have them. Being here was like having the family she'd always wanted.

While she ate the savory meatballs smothered in a rich tomato sauce, she told them about all the attention she'd received while working on the windows.

"Mr. Owen came by and asked me to design something for his drugstore. I told him I'd come by Tuesday after school. But...um, Cooper, would it be possible to get a ride home afterward? I'm uncertain about the time, though."

"No problem. Emma could go with you. I'll meet the two of you for dinner. Burgers or pizza?"

Cooper squeezed her shoulder. "I'm so proud of you, Ivy. Your talent has already hooked another potential client. Let me know if there's any other way I can help." He made a face when her waterworks returned. "No need for all that."

"Sorry," she said, as she wiped her tears with her sleeve. "I could use your help with pricing. I'm not sure what to charge Mr. Owen for his windows if he hires me."

Too excited to eat any more, she pushed her plate away. "Boy, there's a ton of stuff I've gotta get done tonight *and* tomorrow." She fidgeted with her fork.

"I'll help if I can," said Emma, beaming at her.

Cooper crossed his arms. "Ivy, you're going to need a cell phone for your business and for contacting us. Also, don't worry about what to charge until he decides on a design. It would probably be best if you could give him a couple of options. Then figure out your time and the supplies needed."

"Dad, could the WrapAround team add a cell phone to Ivy's *Needs* list during the next meeting?"

"We could solve that problem pretty easily. Ivy, you could buy an inexpensive prepaid phone with the money Bernie gives you and pay for a few hours of use each month. Just a cheap phone could get you by. One with no contract or any bells and whistles. Do a little research and let me know."

He paused for a moment. "You know what? Since it would help me a lot by not having to worry about how you'd get in touch with me, the phone is on me. You can buy the minutes as you need them."

"Thanks, Cooper!"

Wow! Her own phone! Now, people who want windows painted could call her. As soon as she gets her number, she'll make a flyer.

After he walked away, Cooper turned around. "Heck, now that you're a businesswoman, you can write off the phone expenses on your taxes. This coming week, we'll do the paperwork to get you a business license. Meanwhile, think of a name for that new business of yours!"

For real? Was this really happening?

She squealed after Cooper left the room. A name for *her business!* How was she going to sleep tonight? Can't wait to design a cool business card.

To get it all done, she'd need to set priorities.

She glanced over at Emma, doing her homework at the counter. Though she'd be interrupting her, she just had to say it. "Your dad's great, though I'm worried I might be causing him too much trouble."

Emma waved away her concerns. "No. He cares about you. Helping you start a business might take him a little time, but he doesn't seem stressed about it. I'll let you know if that changes. Don't worry. Lora will help when she can, too. Just think, you'll probably be the first kid at school to have a business license!"

"Hmm. Yeah, probably. Got any ideas for my business name?"

"It shouldn't be something that focuses only on painting windows. You'll probably sell other types of art later, right? I'll give it some thought, though." Emma peered down at her math book. "Hey, I've figured out those two bonus math problems if you want some help. They could help raise your grade."

"Maybe later." She avoided looking at Emma, ashamed she didn't want to put the effort into raising her math grade. She preferred to be brainstorming business names.

Right then, her priority was researching how to shade Bernie's windows and then finding some traditional Christmas images she could use for the drugstore. Antique pharmaceutical equipment might work.

Tomorrow she'd call Lora. She might have ideas for a good business name.

CHAPTER 29
COOPER

When the morning sun streamed through cracks in Cooper's window shade, he flipped onto his back, resting his forearm over his brow, thinking. Normally, he'd hop out of bed to get his day started. Today, Lora's voice from last night's phone call replayed in his head.

"You're getting a reputation for rescuing damsels in distress," she'd said, referring to his offer to buy Ivy a pre-paid phone and how he had to deal with her emotional meltdown.

The fact Ivy missed out on so much because of her home life soured his stomach. His decision to give her a phone was a small thing to him, but seeing her response was everything. He could afford it, so why not? Besides, that eliminated his worry about her ability to contact him in an emergency.

He threw the covers off his chest and swung his body up to sit on the edge of the bed. Those nightly chats with Lora, sharing daily joys and struggles, had brought them closer. True, sometimes when he gauged how far he'd already fallen for her, he freaked out. She constantly occupied his thoughts.

If he lost her today, there would be a huge, bottomless void in his and Emma's lives. Wasn't that always the risk of letting someone in?

She'd changed their lives already. Big changes normally bothered him. He hoped that wasn't true any longer. Knowing Lora would be by his side for whatever life dished out was comforting.

He smiled. Then, of course, there was the pleasurable ache that ran through him whenever she was near. He had fallen in love, all right.

Was *she* sure about *him*? How could she be, after his past fleeing episode? He still had times he felt anxious about loving in that all-consuming way he'd experienced with Karen.

He'd have to work at convincing Lora he wouldn't run away from her again. A marriage proposal? That would definitely be a statement of his commitment to a future together.

He drew his eyebrows in. There were some details they needed to address first.

If they got to the point where she accepted a proposal, he'd want her to move in with them. Would she give up her job?

And she was only thirty-four. It was possible she'd want a child of her own again. Could he offer her that? She seemed okay with taking on Emma and Ivy to raise. There was no doubt she loved the girls.

Dang, co-parenting could be challenging for *him*. Heck, he didn't even know how co-parenting was supposed to go.

Complicated.

It was time for them to have a discussion about some of the more difficult topics.

He popped his knuckles, then stretched his fingers out. What if something turned south after bringing those things up? Or what if they ran into one of those make-or-break issues?

There's no getting around it. They needed those uncomfortable talks to keep their momentum.

*****

When he stepped into the kitchen, his mouth watered at the sight of Emma's cinnamon coconut coffee cake sitting on the counter. She must have made it last night while keeping Ivy company while she worked on her sketches.

Emma had always nurtured others through her baking. She gave people baked goodies to celebrate special occasions or provide a supportive *I'm-*

thinking-about-you gesture. That's how she showed others they mattered to her. Was she using baking as a stress reliever lately?

Was Ivy living with them, causing Emma stress? Would Emma even tell him if he asked?

With the house still quiet, he brewed coffee and sliced himself a piece of coffee cake. Mmm, so good!

He still hadn't talked to Emma, as Lora had suggested. He knew his daughter was level-headed, but talking with her differed from talking with Ivy. As Emma's father, he was naturally more protective of her. As her parent, he didn't want regrets or harm to come to her from poor decisions. Crap! Wasn't that a justification for controlling her choices? How could he know what was best for her in all areas of her life? Especially at this stage.

Hypocrite! That's what he was. Wasn't he proud of Ivy for working hard on the goals *she* determined all on her own? Didn't Emma deserve the same chance?

Emma wasn't a little girl anymore, and he needed to show her he recognized that.

He mumbled and scratched his sideburn, "Dang, I'm so thick-headed."

He licked a finger to pick up the last crumbs off his plate. What was Emma's purpose in that crazy Karen's Recipe Challenge all about? And then why hadn't he ever asked?

Honestly, Lora was right. He neglected asking Emma what was on her mind.

***

Before taking the girls to school Friday morning, he said to Emma, "How about I pick you up after school? We'll hang out together at Bernie's while we're waiting for Ivy to go over the final sketch changes with Mr. Owen."

Emma grinned. "Oh boy, a daddy date!"

"Well, more like a checking-in-with-my-little-girl-who's-growing-up-*way*-too-fast date." His belly tightened, wondering what he should disclose or ask about?

After getting in the car, he noticed Ivy was being unusually quiet. She appeared to be running on empty this morning. She'd either stayed up late or hadn't slept well. He had to give her credit, though; her determination to get her business up and running was admirable. He'd better watch her, though. She might run herself ragged.

After drop-off, the girls merged quickly with a group of girls. Ivy joined in the conversation.

Good. Ivy was back in the pack.

***

He and Emma took a back booth at Bernie's, while Ivy was at the drugstore. The other teens coming in gave them some privacy by taking seats up front.

"What will you have besides hot cocoa, Em?"

"The coconut cream pie is supposed to be fantastic this week." She scooted her backpack out of the way while she waved to a group of girls who had just arrived.

"I'll take your recommendation. This is a popular after-school spot." The number of patrons at the diner swelled as kids wandered in.

"Yeah, everybody likes hanging out here. All the food is great."

When the doorbell dinged, she craned her neck to see who'd come in. As soon as she saw, she ducked down a little.

This made him curious, so he turned to get a better look. Three teenage boys had entered. "One of those guys interest you?" he asked casually.

She took a deep breath and let it out in a burst of frustration. "Sorta. He's a guy in my math class. It's nothing."

"Hmm, which one?"

"The one in the blue parka. It's not a big deal, Dad."

"Okay." He let it drop since their hot cocoa and coconut cream pie had arrived. He'd check on that later—not his purpose for today.

After a few bites of pie tempered his afternoon hunger, he said, "Part of this daddy date is to give you an apology, Em. A long overdue one."

His daughter's surprised expression made him wonder if he rarely admitted to making a mistake. That could be another issue he needed to ponder.

"Let's see, where do I start?" He drummed his fingers on the table. "Well, it's come to my attention recently that after your mom died, I made an unconscious decision not to let myself love again. Romantically, I mean. Basically, I didn't want either you or me to be hurt by losing someone we loved again."

"Understandable, I guess," she muttered.

He ran a finger around the rim of his mug. "I tried it once when you were little. Do you remember Cheryl?"

Emma shrugged. "Not really."

"It ended badly, so I never let myself get too close to any woman after that."

Emma's brows furrowed.

He gritted his teeth, knowing he was fumbling. "Besides protecting myself, I also wanted to protect you. I saw how difficult it was for you after your mom died. Since I basically fell apart, I probably didn't do a great job helping you feel secure." He smiled weakly. "You were like Velcro when I came home."

"Well, I probably missed you," she said, her face pink.

"The thing is...because of that big heart of yours, you started taking care of me—emotionally, at some point. I admit I liked your hugs, warm snuggles and laughing at those adorable antics you'd do to cheer me up. Yet, it became more than that. You started working *too hard* to please me or make me happy."

Emma's eyes stayed steady on his, though she didn't comment.

He swallowed. "You were, and are, such a sweetheart. Although, you are still trying too hard to please me. Sometimes that effort is at your own expense. I'm so sorry if I set you up to do that."

Emma had watched him intensely as he spoke, though now her face had softened. She reached over to still his restless hands, stopping his nervous habit of twirling his fork on the table.

"Dad, don't apologize. As I got older, I understood how hard it must have been for you to lose Mom. I think in reality, we were both trying to comfort each other. I needed to be close to you. You were the only parent I had left."

"Yeah, but I—"

"I read in a book once where the dad had trouble looking at his daughter. Cuz, she looked like the mom who left them. Sometimes, I wondered if I reminded you of Mom, and that made you sad. Then sometimes, I thought you were afraid of losing me, just like I was afraid of losing you. I know you worry a lot about me, and you're always trying to protect me."

He nodded. "I have. I do."

"Dad, this may sound weird, but I always felt better knowing I had the power to make you happier." She shrugged her shoulders. "That made me happy...and, somehow, feel more secure." She smiled reassuringly.

"Well, wise little one, that may have been true. However, I don't want you picking loser guys to date because they need you to make them happy. You forgot about the part where you've given up what you want in order not to upset me. For instance, baking pastries for Bernie's."

Her mouth dropped open, then she snapped it shut. "Hmm, I see your point."

"Also, there's still the part about me holding off on having a serious romantic relationship. I never gave you another mother. You missed out because of that. Because I was too chicken to take a risk." He took a sip of his hot cocoa.

A cascade of expressions slid over his daughter's face.

He quickly said, "And by the way, looking at you didn't make me sad. You have traits from both sides of the family, which makes you uniquely you." He smiled widely to show his pride in who she was.

"Thanks, Dad. I did okay without a mom. I had you and Nana, and most of the time, that was great. Lately, after spending time with Lora, I've wondered what I *might* have missed out on."

"You and Lora have become pretty close."

With a twinkle in her eye, Emma raised an eyebrow. "Same for you, Dad."

He grinned. "It's that easy to see, huh?"

With an adamant nod, she said, "Yes! Are you gonna do something about it?"

He laughed. "Any suggestions?"

She tilted her head with a smirk on her face. "Your generation calls it...*courting.*"

He almost choked on his pie before he considered she was messing with him. "Okay, I'll work on it." He hesitated, then plunged on. "Speaking of Lora, she had a good idea. At Ivy's meeting, we were supporting Ivy on what *she* wanted for her future and what she might need to get there. Lora suggested I ask you what *you* want and need."

"Oh." Again, he'd caught her by surprise.

"So, have you thought about what you want for your future?"

She caught her lower lip between her teeth and thought. "Thank you for asking, Dad...cuz there is something I've wanted to talk to you about." She swallowed hard and glanced down at her hands. "I would like to go to—"

"Just say it, honey."

"I want to go to a culinary school this summer. There's one in New York City, at the International Culinary Center. It's a two-week pastry camp. It's expensive, though it could help me decide if I want to become a pastry chef."

Once Emma started talking, she lost all hesitation. She told him of her initial research into the program geared toward high school students who were exploring culinary career options.

Immediately, the urge to criticize and say no took hold. He stopped himself. Without committing, he said, "The summer camp might be doable. Are you considering skipping college and going straight to culinary school after you graduate high school?"

She shrugged. "Maybe. It's something I really enjoy. They say if you do something you love, it won't feel like work...and I *love* baking."

"I thought you'd go to the University of Washington like your mom and me." He sounded whiny and immediately regretted what he'd said.

"That's why it would be great to try the culinary program first," she said reasonably. "To help me decide. I'd still take college prep classes, just in case.

I've even thought about doing the Running Start Program during my senior year."

He squeezed his fingers together, trying to squelch the impulse to argue that a culinary career wouldn't be a good choice. Could being a pastry chef be a viable career? He was clueless. Lora would have advised him not to make snap judgments or shut down Emma's ideas simply because they didn't fit his vision for his daughter's future. Lora was right; he needed to show his daughter respect for investigating where her passion might lead her.

"Okay. Give me the information, and I'll look into it." His smile wavered as he thought of his young daughter living in a big city, thousands of miles away, for two weeks, all on her own.

"Cool." She leaned back in her seat and squirmed a little. "Thanks, Dad."

His phone vibrated with a text message. "Time to pick up Ivy."

He scooted out of the booth to pay their bill. He glanced back and saw Emma beaming from ear to ear.

Lord, give him strength. This was only the first phase of loosening his parental strings. Even though what they talked about gave him the heebie-jeebies, he felt he was on the right track. This had gone better than he'd expected. Though by no means culinary school was a done deal.

However, there was one consolation if he gave Emma his blessing to go to New York City this summer. She'd be three thousand miles away from that boy in the blue parka. That boy had given his daughter goo-goo eyes ever since he'd come into the diner. Luckily, Emma was oblivious.

CHAPTER 30
LORA

On the Friday before Thanksgiving, Lora speed-walked down the high school corridor toward Ivy's second WrapAround meeting.

As she entered, she said, "So sorry. Traffic again."

The group was already giving Ivy positive feedback on her windows. After she sat down, they officially began the meeting.

Mrs. Allen reported that the photos of Ivy's windows were an impressive addition to Ivy's portfolio, and that Ivy had started a challenging project during her lunch period.

Bernie said, "I love my windows. So, I'd like to do something with a Valentine's Day theme starting in early January. Ivy's first day at the diner with her food worker card could be this coming Sunday. However, if she's too busy painting windows, she should stick with that. She'd make more money."

Ivy smiled at Bernie. "Thanks for your flexibility. I have two more window inquiries—the Dairy Queen and the flower shop. The flower shop wants something more permanent and less seasonal, though."

Claire piped in, "We located Ivy's social security card, and when she changes her name, we'll make sure we keep everything straight. She also has a checking and savings account set up."

"Ivy has a cell phone now," reported Cooper, "which should help her in scheduling clients, and it'll make transportation arrangements with me easier. We sent in her application for her business license, so she should get that soon."

"Ivy, what's your business name?" asked Bernie.

"An Artist's Tale, because there is a story within each piece of art."

There were murmurs of approval throughout the room, which brought color to Ivy's cheeks.

Everyone was pleased with Ivy's progress and congratulated her on her hard work. They set up another meeting for after the holidays, with the goal of continuing to assess her ever-changing needs.

After the meeting, Cooper and Claire wandered toward her while the girls chatted with the school counselor.

"Would you two like to come for dinner?" asked Cooper. "We could go over the Thanksgiving menu."

Cooper had already asked her to come for Thanksgiving by saying his mom had invited a special guy friend, so he wanted to invite his special gal. He'd sweetened the deal when he said, "This fair damsel has captured my heart."

"Going over the menu is a good idea. We can divvy up the meal prep." She looked at Cooper. "But first, I want to go see the finished windows at Bernie's and what she's done at the drugstore. I can't wait to see them in person."

After dinner that evening, they discussed their Thanksgiving menu and made a grocery list. Cooper was hosting the get-together, and he took his responsibility seriously.

"Cooper, I haven't strapped on an apron in a while. Yet I want to do my fair share of cooking for this massive feast."

"Thanks, I'll take you up on that. The girls want to help, too." He rubbed his hands together, grinning. "With all the extra helpers, I might even get to watch some football this year."

"Just an FYI. Mom asked me to meet her at the Bremerton Mall this Sunday morning. She wants me to purchase my Christmas presents for my brother's family so she can take them on the plane with her."

"So, you'll leave for home after?"

"Yeah, that's the plan."

***

The next morning, she left with Ivy to help her finish up the drugstore windows. On the job site, she took on the role she nicknamed *sous-painter*. She cleaned brushes, followed instructions on simple painting tasks, and did a coffee and refreshment run. Because it was Ivy's second window, she appeared organized and confident. When onlookers stopped to watch, Ivy politely smiled and answered their questions.

However, when one of her male classmates came by, Ivy slanted her body away from the boy, and her ears turned red when he asked her a question. A possible spark between them?

A countywide newspaper reporter came by unexpectedly in the late afternoon. She asked to interview Ivy. The young reporter was friendly and inquisitive while still putting Ivy at ease. After the interview, the reporter took pictures of the drugstore window and said she had taken photos of Bernie's windows earlier.

Before the reporter left, she asked Lora for a statement.

"Ivy's windows showcase just a fraction of her talent. She's developing an art portfolio, hoping to win a scholarship to an art school. I'm very proud of this community for the support they've given her. The quality of her work truly warrants the praise she's received. These holiday windows are charming and add to the community's holiday festivities. Ivy is a wonderful, talented young woman. Art is her passion, and I hope more businesses use her services."

Once the reporter left, Ivy sighed with relief. "I was worried she'd ask questions about my family. Luckily, she only seemed interested in me as an artist. She's from the next town over, so it's possible she didn't know about them."

She gave Ivy a hug. "You should be happy. This article will give you countywide exposure and hopefully expand your business."

Quickly, she sent Cooper a text saying they had cleanup to do before going for pizza, as planned. Cooper replied that Emma was out with friends and that he was meeting a buddy for drinks. Don't wait up.

Huh. That was strange. He hadn't mentioned his plans earlier. Could be he's not used to reporting in with anyone?

Things were moving pretty fast between them. Was his anxiety kicking in? He'd somewhat warned her it could happen again.

When her pizza arrived at the restaurant, she wasn't as hungry as expected. What she could eat stomped down on her belly like a combat boot. Something about Cooper's text didn't feel right.

***

Though stressed out, she'd fallen asleep before Cooper came home. She woke with a headache and took a painkiller before she made banana pancakes for the girls. The pounding in her head got worse as Cooper skulked into the kitchen. He headed straight for the coffeepot. Had Cooper drunk too much last night? She would have never guessed that was his MO. The girls took one look at him and stopped talking, probably also noticing the tension in the air. Immediately, they lowered their gaze to their plates and kept them there.

Once she served the girls their pancakes, she offered to make Cooper a plate. He shook his head, still not speaking. She felt the negative energy radiate off him.

Enough of this.

She stepped in front of Cooper. "Could we take our coffee and sit out back?"

Cooper grumbled, "Sure."

They grabbed their warm coats before heading outside. They sat in a pair of Adirondack chairs facing the beauty of the inlet. The air was chilly, and a haze hung over the water below.

The awkward silence lingered between them until she couldn't stand it any longer. "Something's bothering you. Please tell me."

"Sorry. Yeah, you're right." He tucked in his lips and rocked his torso for a moment. Then he took a deep breath and angled his body slightly toward her.

"Something happened at work Friday afternoon that's...giving me some issues. An employee came in asking for a leave of absence. Doctors diagnosed his wife with breast cancer. Thank heavens they caught it early enough."

"Thank goodness."

"However, they're a blended family with three kids, and their teenager from the wife's first marriage is freaking out. She's more aware of the terrible possibilities than her younger siblings. She's *not* dealing well."

He ran his fingers through his hair. "I couldn't help it, Lora. That guy's pain and what his family was going through stuck with me. That's who I had drinks with last night. The pain and fear that family is going through...it got lodged somewhere in my brain and chest, *squeezing* out my hopes for our future." He felt his face distort from the distress of even talking about it. He turned away.

"I keep considering what might happen if we became a family and the same thing happened to us."

She moaned, not liking where this was going.

They sat in silence for a while. Though she had empathy for his pain, she was also angry.

"I can see how much this is affecting you. One thing I learned in counseling is that there is always a choice after experiencing trauma. You can let it consume you, or you can battle it down. Right now, you've wrapped yourself in the terrible hurt you remember, and you've absorbed the hurt happening in that man's family. You're afraid what happened in the past could repeat itself for you. Am I right?"

"Yeah, I suppose."

"I understand. That man's hardship is a reminder of the unpredictable nature of life. You're focused on the unpleasant possibilities instead of the love and joy ahead of us."

By his expression, fear still consumed him.

"Cooper, I know loving me is a risk for you."

Her teeth clenched, angry at his remaining silence. Had he even heard what she said?

"I'm sorry, Cooper. There are no guarantees. I can't give you the security you need."

His silence made her stomach churn.

"Have you considered that I *also* fear losing the people I love? I especially fear I might *cause* a loss."

To her, his fear was compromising his ability to be with her in the present, let alone the future.

"I love you, and I love the girls. I view sharing my remaining days on earth with you as a privilege; one where I will share all of who I am with you and the girls. It saddens me you see my presence in your life as a potential danger."

He continued to stare out at the water, stuck in his anxious chatter.

Her chest constricted as her irritation grew. "Cooper, right now, your fear is crippling your ability to love. Somehow, you think withholding love can protect you. It won't. It will only give you a lonely, unhappy life."

This was what she'd been afraid of. His anxiety made the risk of loving too great. This could put an end to everything. The past was suffocating his—*their*—potential for happiness.

She turned toward him and placed a hand on his arm to get his attention. "You'll have to make your decision on your own."

Her voice became steely. "Cooper, I know I am worthy of being loved. If you're not fully ready to take the risk, then I'm *not* willing to draw this out to the inevitable end. However, if you decide you want to take the risk, I'll be right beside you to offer comfort and support through whatever challenges we might face. I want a partner who faces hard times with me without resentment, blame, or withdrawal."

His face remained clouded. He was hurting her again. Her body slumped with disappointment.

In a shaky whisper, she said, "I have to go now. Call when you've decided." She stood up. "I won't wait forever."

For the first time, he faced her. "I'll think all this through. You'd better get going, so you won't be late to meet your mom."

He followed her back into the kitchen. She put her coffee mug in the sink and hugged the girls goodbye.

"See you soon for Thanksgiving," said Emma, then glanced with worried eyes toward her dad.

Cooper shuffled his feet, avoiding eye contact. "Yeah, until Thanksgiving. Careful on the road."

Her overnight bag hung heavy on her shoulder as she walked to her car. The girls followed her to the front porch. Although they waved with their usual zeal, their faces showed concern.

As she drove out of the driveway, tears fell. Eventually, she couldn't see to drive safely, so before she reached the main road, she pulled over.

Frustrated, she slammed her palm into the steering wheel and threw herself against the back of her seat.

"Dammit, Cooper!"

Would he call tonight to end things?

Would the girls be gone from her life, too?

She shivered and struggled to catch her breath.

No! Enough! Stop thinking like that.

It wasn't helpful for her to catastrophize. In doing so, she would be doing the same as what Cooper was doing. It's possible he'll need more time to process what she'd said. He might reconsider what he's losing by giving her up, or he might have a breakthrough in resolving his fears. Those are the thoughts she should entertain!

She closed her eyes and focused on her breathing for a few minutes. After drying her tears, she felt safe enough to drive again.

She'd been brutally honest with him. A marriage wouldn't work if he was always guarding his heart, fearing some kind of painful loss was imminent.

Oh, what a mess they were in.

***

As soon as she walked into her condo, she made a beeline to the hall closet to search the pockets of the coat she'd worn to the beach months ago.

"It's got to be here somewhere." It took a second pass through to find it.

Clenching the sea glass in her fist as she sent a prayer into the Universe. "If you brought Cooper to me before, bring him back to me again, prepared to love freely with his whole heart."

That night, the loneliness of her condo felt amplified. Cooper hadn't called. Nor did her dad come to provide his wisdom. The sea glass was her only tangible symbol of hope. She gently placed the sea glass on the nightstand, knowing in her gut that the type of relationship she wanted with Cooper would require more than luck.

CHAPTER 31
COOPER

When Cooper lumbered into the plant Monday morning, Virginia was standing at the reception counter. He kept his head down to bypass her inquiries. He grumbled a *good morning* as he made his way up to his office.

Naturally, she followed. "Am I gonna havta pull it out of ya, or are ya gonna spill it?" She sat down in her customary chair and waited.

He plopped into his chair. "I'm not sure how to say it."

"Start wherever. I'll catch on."

"Brian came in the other day to tell me about his wife's cancer. The situation had freaked out their teenage daughter. His story took me back to dealing with Karen's illness. My fears about having this happen to me again exploded."

"And?"

He steepled his fingers. "Well, let's just say I didn't handle the situation well with Lora. When I told her why, she got upset."

The weight of it all had him drop his head. "Now she's saying she doesn't want to be with me unless I resolve my fears. She's worried my anxiety about loving someone will prevent me from fully committing to our relationship...or that I'd hold back my love in order to protect myself."

Virginia squinted at him.

Yeah, he sounded pathetic.

"I get what she's saying. It sure wouldn't be fair to her if I kept riding the fence and get toppled over so easily."

"Wow. So, you're saying you're too chicken to fully love her? Yet, I know you love her already. Damn, Cooper. This means you could lose her."

He ran a hand over his face and groaned. "Yeah, that's the gist of it. She thinks I'm a flight risk."

Virginia snorted. "Is she wrong? Seriously, Cooper, are you really going to let her slip away?"

"I don't want to, yet...I'm not sure how to fix...me."

How could he remedy a fear that could overtake him so easily? He couldn't even reason with himself when he was in the middle of it. Man, oh, man. He was in a bind. He loved Lora. He'd already imagined growing old with her. He also couldn't stop ruminating about what would happen if he lost her.

His body stiffened. Hell, he was already losing her. He was creating the very disaster he feared.

If he pushed her away to protect himself, he would drop himself right into the same painful heartbreak he was trying to avoid. This time, it wouldn't be outside forces taking someone he loved away. It would all be his doing. He rolled his eyes at his own stupidity.

Virginia had been silently studying him. "Boss, I'm gonna tell you a story about my friend Margie. Her losing her hubby, Bill, utterly devastated her. Then Henry came along. She could easily have passed up that opportunity, and almost—"

He waved a hand. "I don't want—"

"Stop right there, boss! I've been with you during and after Karen, and through all those years you'd blocked yourself from loving someone. Lora has been like a spring rain that cleaned out your clogged gutters. You're finally runnin' on all cylinders. I'm not letting you sit back and have misery invade that heart of yours. You may hide it well from others, but not from your mama and me."

"I don't—"

"Now listen to me. What I was saying about Margie—she had a rough go taking care of her hubby before he died. Then her dang teenage kids took his death as an opportunity to act out, especially her son. When she met Henry, he was the assistant coach on her son's baseball team. Henry saw what was happening with her son and offered his help. He turned her son around and, while he was doing it, he fell in love with Margie. When he told Margie, she ran. Just like you're doing. However, Margie confided in me that she thought she loved Henry. Since she really didn't want to lose him, I pushed her into talkin' to him. He understood how vulnerable she felt loving again. See, the darn thing was, it was *love* that pulled her back to him."

With a look of frustration, Virginia shook her head as she tapped the arm of her chair. "Let your love guide you, boss. Easy as that!"

With a cocky smirk on her face, Virginia said, "Margie and Henry have had fourteen wonderful years together. She'd probably say they were the best years of her life."

He sighed. "It's not easy, Virginia! If it was, I'd be asking Lora to marry me instead of cowering like a jackass."

Virginia leaned forward. "You've taken your first step. You've admitted your fears to yourself, to Lora, and now to me. The *why* is something you are well aware of, *and* the behaviors you've used to protect yourself. You *can* fix this."

She rubbed her chin. "You know, you could do what they do on those cooking shows."

"What?" His eyebrows squished together.

"They deconstruct a dish—examine all the parts, or the ingredients that make up a particular dish. Then change their perspective on it."

"I don't get it."

"Okay, wrong approach. You're good at problem-solving, right? You could analyze your fears the way you would when the gears in our machinery get jammed."

What the hell was she talking about?

"Heck, if you can't figure it out, consult an expert if you have to. Just don't sit there staring at the walls, sinking deeper into that crap-hole of your own makin'."

"Yeah, thanks for your support," he grumbled, feeling worse by the minute.

"Heavens-to-Betsy! You should talk to Lora, cuz you probably freaked her out. From what you've said, she's pretty attached to your sorry ass and your two girls. You'll have to fix this together. If you are willing to have a *together*!"

"Son, you gotta remember, you're tougher now than you were in your twenties and thirties."

He clenched his teeth as he kept his head down.

"Good grief," he moaned. " I'd like to think so, but this panic stuff has shot down my confidence."

Virginia cursed under her breath. "Didya not know everybody has anxiety when they start givin' their hearts away? Yah gotta focus on the benefits outweighing the risks."

She stomped her feet on the floor and stood up. "I gotta get back to work. Who knows...with Lora by your side, you might be able to dust off that damn superhero cape of confidence you've put in storage? A sidekick makes it easier to weather whatever shit might be ahead of you."

Virginia was sure givin' it to him, and she was getting awful riled up as she got going. He needed some peace and quiet to think.

"Guess I've got some thinking to do."

"Boss, I've got things covered here at work. Why don't you take the day off? Decide if you want your irrational fears to hijack the incredible hours, days, and years you *could* have with Lora." With that parting shot, Virginia strolled out of his office.

As soon as she left, he pivoted his chair to gaze through the window overlooking the manufacturing plant.

Someday, he'd sell the business. Emma and Ivy would be in college or already building their own lives. He would most likely outlive Virginia and his mom. All the people he loved would eventually leave him.

There he'd be, with no one to share it with. *Depressing!*

Why wouldn't he open his arms to the chance of having as many days as possible with the woman he loved and who loved him? Why wouldn't he?

***

He took Virginia's suggestion and knocked off early. When he opened the door to his home, the emptiness brought profound sadness. With a heavy heart and heavier steps, he walked into his office in search of an empty spiral notebook.

With a pen in hand, words poured out of him.

First, he wrote a letter to Karen, thanking her for helping him shape his dreams as a young man. Then he thanked her for her contribution in designing their home, and how he still loved living there. With tears dropping onto the paper, he forgave her for becoming ill and leaving them.

Next, he expressed his gratitude for her giving him Emma and explained his need to change his parenting practices, promising to support Emma's dreams and choices.

When it came time to write about Lora, he paused. Loving Lora made him question if he was dishonoring the love he'd had for Karen. However, while he wrote to Karen about his fears of loving again after the pain of losing her, he'd gotten a gut feeling that finding someone again would please Karen. He went back and wrote more about how he wanted to marry Lora and that Lora would be an amazing mother to Emma. Matter-of-fact, he was sure a woman like Lora would benefit Emma's growth as a young woman more than he could.

Next, he wrote an apology to Lora.

When he felt finished, he put his pen down. With a heavy sigh, he let his eyes close. He searched his body, exploring what he was feeling and what those feelings were telling him. His limbs relaxed, and his breathing slowed. He pictured a warm light hovering around the top of his skull. As he focused on its warmth, an intense sense of knowing everything would be alright came to him. Tears of gratitude welled in his eyes.

Lora coming into his life wasn't luck; it was a blessing for both himself and Emma. Now, he needed to do *something*, so that blessing didn't slip away. He had a responsibility to himself and Emma to take action.

Instantly, he knew that if he held heartfelt gratitude for Lora coming into their lives, there wouldn't be any space for anxiety.

A surge of energy rushed through his body as a plan formed for what to do.

He drove to the florist. With some careful decision-making, he selected flower arrangements to be sent to Virginia and his mom, along with a gigantic bouquet for Lora. He made sure Lora's bouquet included some daisies. She'd once told him how happy daisies made her feel. He recalled that old childhood game of picking petals off daisies while saying—*she loves me; she loves me not*. On his card to Lora, he made sure she knew he was professing his everlasting love to her. He wrote that every day he planned to show her she was worth the risk of loving her.

***

He bought one more bouquet and drove to Karen's gravesite. Since her funeral, he'd avoided going to her grave, thinking the pain would be too great. Today it was different. After writing his letter to her, he knew from then on, the pain of losing Karen would be less. Soon, he would take Emma to her mother's gravesite. Emma needed the chance to acknowledge her mother's life and say goodbye. They could make a ritual of bringing flowers to Karen's gravesite on Karen's birthday.

Knowing both of the girls were anxious about what was happening between him and Lora, he had his mom pick them up from school and bring them home. When they arrived, he asked everyone to sit at the dinner table. As he explained what had occurred that Sunday morning before Lora left, he saw the concern on their faces. He also informed them of his breakthrough that day and how he planned to set things straight with Lora. They thanked him for letting them know, then they informed him how much they wanted Lora in their lives.

Mom said, "Go fix this, son." She saluted him with crossed fingers before she left the house.

When he figured Lora would be home, he called. She didn't pick up; he left a message. When two hours had passed, he called again.

He immediately heard the distress in Lora's voice when she said *hello*.

"Lora, I'm so sorry. I know how much the girls and I mean to you, so that ultimatum you made must have been hard. You risked losing all of us. If you can be that brave, I can match that by loving you in the way you deserve."

"Do you really mean that, Cooper?"

"Yes." He switched the phone to his other hand and leaned back on his bed.

"I haven't been very good at showing you how serious I am about us. Babe, I love you. I can't say anxiety won't come up from time to time, but when it does, we'll talk it out. I don't want fear or anxiety to make my decisions or pull me away from you. You deserve all the love I have to give."

"I'm so relieved. I want my future to be with you, Cooper. Are you ready?"

"Yes, Lora. I'm ready." Then he shared all that had occurred that day, which had helped him to *become* ready.

***

The next day, he walked into the office whistling.

"Hey boss, you musta got things settled with Lora."

"Yeah. We're back on track. I've renewed my trust in the Universe, so to speak. I'm even giving Em that summer pastry program she wants as a Christmas gift. Mums the word, though."

Virginia zipped her lips with two fingers. "Wonderful! She'll love it. Hey, I saw the article about Ivy in the paper. That was a fantastic way to get the word out about her business. Ivy sure is talented."

"She is. Lora will read it online. Unfortunately, that reporter discovered and revealed that Ivy was working toward emancipation, and had a community team helping her. Ivy didn't want her personal stuff in the public's eye."

He unzipped his jacket and put it over his arm. "Nothing we can do about that now. Regardless, it was good press for her business."

"Gotta say, though, she has the type of personal interest story papers love. It was nice they included her hopes for an art school scholarship. Lora gave a nice plug for her business, too."

***

Two days after Ivy's newspaper article was posted, a member of the local Lion's Club approached him. The club wanted to set up a scholarship fund for Ivy. Thrilled, he called Lora to tell her the news, though he wouldn't tell Ivy until it was all set.

"Lora, I bought a few extra copies of the newspaper and suggested Ivy mail her mom a copy. She seemed uncomfortable with the idea. I don't believe she's followed through. You know, I'm pretty sure her mom has never contacted her since she left. Would you mind checking in with Ivy to see what's going on between them?"

"Sure, if there's a natural way to bring it up in conversation."

"I'd appreciate it. You should see her, Lora. Ivy is more radiant every day. She's not wearing heavy, dark eye makeup anymore, and she's asking tons of questions about operating a business. I don't know if it's because of the money she's making or what, but her entire demeanor has changed. She's definitely focused on what's ahead of her instead of what happened in her past."

"I'm so proud of her. How are you doing with all the extra driving connected to Ivy's jobs?"

"I'm okay. It's so worth it. When Ivy climbs into the truck, I'm rewarded by her enthusiasm for what she's completed that day." He wouldn't complain, but the extra trips were becoming a drag.

"The reason I asked is, over Thanksgiving, Mom is going to ask my brother if he wants Dad's old truck. If he doesn't, she wants to give it to Ivy. We both are hoping he doesn't want it. Ivy turns sixteen on March 12th, and if it works out, the truck would be a combo Christmas and birthday gift from Mom. There's even a truck canopy where she can lock and store her painting supplies. What do you think?"

"Hallelujah! It would be like I'd gotten a Christmas present, too. I was wondering how I would swing two vehicles next year. The truck would be a godsend. I don't see her painting gigs slowing down. Some of the town's business owners have expressed an interest in keeping themed windows going throughout the year. The Chamber of Commerce is exploring how to support the addition of murals on the more visible buildings in town, as well."

"Wonderful!"

"Hmm. I could work some driving lessons in for the girls during Thanksgiving break. They've both been chomping at the bit to get their permits. It would be amazing if the truck works out. Thank your mom for even considering Ivy." He crossed his fingers.

"Mom's very fond of her. Ivy did a fantastic job setting up Mom's blog. Witnessing their collaboration was absolutely adorable, and her design was really fantastic. By the way, Mom has some exciting news. A large adult-living community in Bremerton asked her to give a talk on later-in-life transitions. She's going for it. Who knew my mom had all this in her? I'm so proud of her."

"Lotta good stuff happenin'. Babe, I've gotta go. Pick up duty."

***

Only a few days later, his three ladies were in his kitchen preparing their Thanksgiving dinner. They'd sent him off to watch football. No argument there. At half-time, frustration with his team led him to head for the kitchen.

The girls were giggling as they shared their most embarrassing moments. He stopped to eavesdrop.

Emma was just finishing up hers—a story he knew well.

Lora spoke up next. "My prom date was a real chick-magnet. Even though he was every girl's heartthrob, that status hadn't swollen his head. I'd been thrilled to be his date. And I have to say, I looked pretty elegant in my long, peach, empire-waisted gown with green velvet ribbons flowing down the back." Lora giggled as she struck a pose. "I felt so grown up as we dined at a fancy restaurant on the waterfront.".

He waited for what else was to come.

"I felt very grown-up and sophisticated." Lora's eyes sparkled, and a mischievous grin curved her lips. "After we ate, I excused myself to use the restroom. As I was walking back, I noticed a friend sitting at another table, trying to get my attention. Confused, it took me a while to figure out what she was pointing at. Yet, those around me *knew*."

The girls already started snickering.

"My friend kept whispering 'your shoe'. I glanced behind me."

Lora rolled her eyes in disgust. "I was dragging a streamer of toilet paper behind me, stuck to my shoe." Her expression captured the humiliation a teenage girl would experience.

Emma and Ivy cracked up again. Then Emma declared, "Oh, you poor thing!"

Lora held up a finger. "It doesn't end there. When I'd glanced behind me, I also saw that my velvet ribbons must have fallen into the toilet. They were a darker shade of green one third of the way up, and underneath them, my dress looked wet." She covered her mouth in feigned horror.

The girls laughed so hard their squeals morphed into what sounded like hungry sea lions barking.

By the time the girls gained control of themselves, Lora had calmly gone back to kneading the sweet potato bread dough.

"Girls," Lora said to get their attention. "This story goes to show life has its humiliating moments, yet it doesn't have to scar you forever. Later, you can look back and have a good laugh about it. Sharing these moments can be a bonding experience. It shows others you've accepted how human and imperfect you are."

He couldn't help himself; a laugh erupted from his belly. He had seen that she'd spotted him right before saying this. Was this a life lesson also meant for him?

Emma and Ivy turned his way. "Dad," said Emma, "tell us one of your embarrassing stories! Please, please!"

Caught off guard, he blurted, "You're asking me to humiliate myself in front of the woman I love?"

He saw the immediate shock on the girls' faces before those faces slid into big grins.

He made a beeline for the back door.

"I'm gettin' some more firewood."

CHAPTER 32
LORA

Lora's floured hands stopped mid-air above the bread dough she'd been kneading when Cooper made his unexpected public declaration. After the back door shut with a *snick,* the kitchen fell silent.

Emma lunged forward and wrapped her arms around her. When Emma wouldn't let go, she attempted to hug her back, being careful not to smudge Emma's clothes with her floured hands.

She heard Emma swallow. Was Emma forcing down tears?

When Emma finally stepped out of her arms, Emma smiled happily and said, "I've been hoping he would fall in love with you. Then you could be with us *forever.*"

She and Cooper hadn't talked directly about marriage. She didn't want Emma to get her hopes up.

Cautiously, she said, "Emma, I'm honored you would want me to be a permanent part of your life. Be patient. Things with your dad and me have a way to go yet."

"Oh, okay." Disappointment clouded Emma's face.

She tucked a lock of Emma's hair behind her ear. "Just give us some time to figure things out, honey."

Emma appeared somewhat appeased. "Okay, but beware. Dad can be a real dork sometimes."

She and Ivy chuckled over Emma's statement about her dad.

Ivy slid in beside Lora and swung her arm around her shoulders. "Ditto for me. I want forever, too. Well, I mean, you being in my life forever."

Their declaration felt wonderful to receive. "Girls, I'm sure that will happen no matter what the future holds for Cooper and me."

Her smile felt like it was reaching up to her ears. Was this the type of smile a mom would have after reading one of those sweet, sappy Mother's Day cards? The girl's declaration touched her heart.

No time for lingering on mushy sentiment.

"Nana Claire and her friend should arrive soon, so we'd better get back to work. We have a feast to prepare!"

She wanted this Thanksgiving to be exceptional, especially for Ivy and for Claire's special someone. The girls and Cooper would meet him for the first time.

This was her first holiday with the family as well. She glanced at the girls peeling potatoes at the sink. Such beautiful helpers. She loved them as if they were already her own . How thankful she was to have them as part of her life.

***

Thirty minutes after the football game ended, the front door swung open. Claire called out, "Happy Thanksgiving!"

Claire strolled into the great room, followed by a tall, distinguished-looking man with thick, white, wavy hair carrying Claire's famous cornbread stuffing. His expression was open and warm.

Claire linked her arm through his and said, "This is my friend, Will. Will, this is the whole family, except for Lora's mom, Rebecca, who will join us at Christmas."

Claire gestured to each of them in turn. "That's my handsome son, Cooper. The ponytail-ed gal is my granddaughter, Emma. Beside her is Ivy, her talented artistic friend I told you about. And this beautiful woman is Lora, Rebecca's daughter, whom you met a while ago. She's probably worked her fingers to the bone making our dinner. She's fairly new to us, yet she's already family." Claire winked at her.

"Nice to see you again, Will. Claire gave me too much credit for the dinner. Everyone helped out. Let me take the stuffing. I'll put it in the oven."

Her heart had skipped a beat when Claire claimed her as *family*. She glanced at Cooper, who was gazing at her with a thoughtful expression.

Claire released Will's arm so she could hug the girls.

After they all chatted for a few minutes, Cooper joined her in the kitchen. "What can I do to help? I usually carve the turkey and mash the potatoes, but what if we ask Will to mash and Mom to make the gravy?"

"Great idea. I'll get some extra aprons. The girls can put the cold things on the table and dress the salad."

"I'll take the turkey out and let it rest."

She looked about the kitchen to see if they'd forgotten anything. "If you give everyone their assignments, what will my job be?"

"How about you pour the wine and whatever the girls want to drink? Then, take a moment to relax. You deserve it." He leaned over and kissed her cheek.

Her heart fluttered as she smiled up at him. At that moment, she felt that this was exactly where she belonged.

***

After eating a delicious Thanksgiving dinner, they sat around the table as Will entertained them with stories of his many travels. He'd been a man of the sea—first as a sailor in the Navy, then after college, he did research as a marine biologist. Later, he'd switched careers to become a tugboat captain.

"My greatest regret is that my time at sea caused me to lose my family. However, my daughter and I have been speaking a lot lately, and I'm planning a spring trip to meet my grandson for the first time. I hope Claire will join me." His face beamed at the prospect.

Will and Claire reached for each other's hands. Their eyes tenderly met in that secret connection of lovers. They made the cutest couple.

Cooper's initial conversations with Will sounded more like an inquisition. Thankfully, Will was a good sport, appearing unscathed by Cooper's probing questions.

After receiving a reprimanding glare from his mother, Cooper backed off.

Two scrumptious desserts were enthusiastically dug into a while later. After Cooper declared he would do the dishes. Will volunteered to help. While everyone cleared the table, Will sheepishly asked Emma if he could take home an extra slice of the pumpkin cheesecake.

Emma grinned proudly. "Of course." She packed him up a gigantic piece.

While the men took on the mighty task of cleaning the kitchen, she and Claire started a Christmas movie in the great room while the girls headed upstairs.

Before long, the commotion in the kitchen caught her and Claire's attention. As they watched their two guys getting along splendidly, they shared a smile.

"Lora, I'm head over heels in love with that man." Claire's eyes sparkled with adoration. "He's so good to me. When I made my choice between my two beaus, Will wanted to assure me I had made a sound choice. Knowing my history with Cooper's father, Will disclosed his finances before we progressed any further with our relationship. He told me he had set up a trust for his children, but if we were to get married, he'd make sure I was financially secure as well."

She glanced at Will again. "I have no concerns about Will."

"It sounds like his intentions are honorable *and* serious."

"I think he might ask me to marry him soon." Claire caught Will's eye as he stood drying dishes. He gave her an affectionate smile, and Claire blushed.

"Lora, I'm going to say yes."

"I'm so happy for you. He seems like a wonderful man, and I can tell he adores you."

"If we marry, we'll continue to live in our senior community. We love all our friends there—your mom included. I'm so proud of Rebecca. She's doing a magnificent job of writing her blog. Her newest project is to interview other seniors so they can tell their stories. It's so validating for them, and for her readers."

"I'm proud of her, too. She's surprised me with how she's put herself out there."

***

At breakfast the next day, she enjoyed the girls' efforts to critique Thanksgiving. Though mostly positive remarks, they suggested that next year they incorporate a between-dinner-and-dessert activity.

Cooper nodded. "Sounds good. I hope that means you're volunteering to set that up?"

He turned to her. "Babe, you did a fantastic job with the dinner. Everything tasted great, and you made it look easy. I'm usually a frazzled mess."

"We can't leave out praise for Emma's most fabulous Thanksgiving desserts imaginable." Emma beamed as she mouthed a *thanks*.

"Dad, I was wondering if you remember Mom ever making that pumpkin cheesecake? She'd had it starred."

"No, can't say that I had. She might not have had a chance to get around to it."

Emma lowered her voice and her head. "Then I'm glad I made it for her."

To elevator Emma's spirits, she asked, "Girls, what should we do for the rest of this holiday weekend? Any ideas?"

"Eat leftovers?" suggested Ivy. Everyone laughed and groaned at the same time.

"How about we get a Christmas tree and decorate it?" said Emma. "Lora won't be back with us until Christmas Eve. Since this will be Ivy and Lora's first Christmas with us, we should decorate while we're all together."

"Excellent idea!" exclaimed Cooper. "How about chopping down our own tree this year? I heard about a tree farm where there's snow on the ground. Would that be Christmassy enough?"

"Perfect!" was the unanimous shout.

Everyone changed into warm outdoor clothes. When Cooper strolled in wearing a plaid shirt, jeans and a stocking cap, she thought he looked just like a cute Paul Bunyan.

It was a perfect, crisp, cloudless day for a trip to the mountains. The tree farm had accumulated a foot of snow on the ground. Their search was extensive, but after close inspection, they found the perfect tree—a ten-foot noble fir.

Once back at the house, Cooper fetched their family's ornaments. As they hung them, Emma and Cooper told stories attached to many of them.

Emma placed the last ornament on the tree and stood back. "Perfection!"

"It's more than perfect," said Ivy. "It's the most beautiful tree I have ever seen."

I would agree," said Lora, as Cooper came up and put his arm over her shoulder.

"Girls," said Cooper. "If you turn off the lights, we'll let Lora do the honor of switching the tree lights on."

The honor of being given the controls brought a huge smile to her face.

"Okay," she said. "Here's the countdown: 5...4...3...2...1."

A collective "ahh" of admiration was spoken when the tree lit up in all its glory.

After a few moments of admiration, Emma said, "Ivy, let's go upstairs and strategize what to give our friends for Christmas. And thanks, Dad, for letting us get the tree a little early this year."

"Hey, it was a *great* idea."

***

A few hours later, she called the girls down for a dinner of turkey sandwiches and leftover pie.

They sat in a row at the kitchen island. Cooper turned to Emma. "Honey, I've researched the laws governing a home-based cooking business. I'm sorry, you won't be able to sell baked goods at the Starfish Diner. There are too many rules and hoops to go through, which we can't accommodate."

Emma's face drooped. "Thanks, I appreciate you taking the time to check it out, though."

"However," said Cooper. "You *could* sell directly to customers at craft fairs or festivals. That said, I have two direct customer sales for Christmas desserts. One is Virginia, and the other is Chuck, my foreperson. They both want something chocolatey and fancy. Does that sound doable?"

Emma's response was to cheer and lunge at him with a hug. "Thanks, Dad. You're the best!"

Later, when the girls were out of sight, she kissed Cooper's cheek. "You just earned yourself a few points...from me *and* Emma." She kissed him again for good measure.

***

On Saturday, Emma announced, "Why don't we go to the mall for some Christmas shopping? The holiday decorations will be up, and the Christmas music will get us into the spirit."

Everyone agreed.

***

Once at the mall, the girls ventured out on their own, promising to meet later for lunch at the food court. Cooper tasked her with helping him pick out presents for Virginia, his mom, her mom, and Will. It was also fun to shop for stocking-stuffers for the girls. She'd found loads of cute girly stuff.

Who would consider shopping to be so romantic? With her hand intertwined with Cooper's and their spontaneous kissing, her holiday spirit soared. They were meshing nicely as a couple, and that made her so happy.

Please, don't let me lose him again.

CHAPTER 33
IVY

Ivy felt Cooper's eyes on her as she read her dad's letter. The envelope had the official return stamp from the prison where her dad was incarcerated. Angry heat spread from her chest to her face as she read it through. Her hands shook. By the look on Cooper's face, her reaction was making him uncomfortable. She couldn't help it. She was furious.

"Cooper, I need to talk to Lora. In person. Tomorrow. Please. I need to see her."

"Okay. I'll make the call." He hadn't even asked why. Good. Right then, she couldn't discuss anything with him. She feared she would lose control of herself.

It would probably be best to hide out in her room. To blow off steam, she picked up her pillow and threw it against the wall as hard as she could. Over and over again. Not being hungry, she skipped dinner. When Emma came up to bed, she'd hugged her without saying a word, then crawled into bed.

For her, sleep came in fits, with long periods of staring at the ceiling. She was afraid to close her eyes. The images her mind manufactured terrified her.

***

After Cooper and Emma left for the day, she walked through the empty house. She was alone in the house for the first time. She loved it there. Dad sending a letter to the one place she felt safe was an intrusion. Her fists balled. The letter confirmed he didn't care about her, or anybody else except himself.

Life had been going so well. She hadn't even thought about the messiness of her family lately. More and more, the Martins felt like her family.

She'd acted badly yesterday. More than anything, she didn't want Cooper to regret taking her in. She wanted to make it up to him somehow.

Pacing the floor seemed the only way she could tamp down her anger as she waited for Lora.

When Lora came through the front door, her love and concern were obvious. Lora's expression of caring filled her eyes to the brim with tears.

They rushed together. Lora pulled her into her arms. "Let's go sit down." Lora guided her to the couch.

"Cooper said you received a letter from your dad. Can you tell me what your dad said that has upset you so much?"

She wiped her tears. "He must have read the article in the paper about me. He demanded that I bring him some cash and a bunch of other stuff to the prison. I don't think he's supposed to have any contact with Mom, but he asked for her address." Her voice was sharp with hatred.

"The jerk!"

"You're right. There's a no-contact order."

Lora took her hand in her's. "I'm sorry he contacted you for such selfish reasons." She pulled a Kleenex from the console behind the couch and handed it to her. "Your dad placed a heavy burden on you by doing so. It wasn't fair of him."

She clenched her teeth. Since when had Dad *ever* been fair? Neither parent nor Derek had shown any concern for *her*. It felt like everyone had essentially abandoned her. Fine. She didn't want them in her life anyway!

"I hate him, you know. That asshole didn't even say he was sorry for what he did to Mom. Nor did he ask how Mom was or how I was. Now I'm stuck not knowing what to do. Someday he'll get out...and he holds grudges. He might come after me. Because I ratted on him, he wrote I owed him and

Derek. He didn't even express any remorse for what he'd done. I'd hoped he was sitting in his cell thinking about the harm he'd done to Mom and me."

"I'm so sorry, Ivy." Lora leaned back, and a heavy breath escaped her lips.

"You know, when Cooper called to tell me what happened, I suggested you take out a restraining order on your dad and Derek. What do you think?"

That idea felt satisfying and might allow her to feel safer.

"You mean that neither of them can ever come near me? That would be awesome! I never want to see or talk to their butt-faces again."

"Cooper will help you get that taken care of. I don't know how long a restraining order lasts, but he'll find out for you. Do you want one for Jake, too? I heard his family moved away. He may not come back when he gets out." Lora squeezed her hand. "Cooper plans to ask if the sheriff would tell your dad and Derek that they're not welcome in this town any longer. There's no home here to return to anyway."

"I probably don't need one for Jake. However, I'd like the sheriff to tell Dad and Derek that." She grimaced, not sure if that would make a difference.

"Oh, honey, it's your dad's mistake, thinking you owe him. Don't get pulled down by his actions."

"I'll try not to."

"What about your mom? Cooper said neither of you have attempted to contact each other."

She shrugged, pushing down the hurt that leaped from the mention of her mom. "When Mom didn't call or write to tell me how she was doing, I figured I didn't matter to her anymore. I wondered if she thought...you know...with me being with the Martins, that I didn't need her anymore."

Lora sat quietly for a while. "I can see how you might think that. You said your mom was like a zombie when she left, though. Remember?"

"Yeah, she didn't talk, and she seemed really out of it. I've thought maybe she's still not doing well mentally."

"That could be true. It's also possible she's having difficulty adjusting to living with her sister. Then, it could also be her PTSD or maybe even her pain pills affecting her. Most likely, she needs more time. Try to be patient with her."

"I suppose. Cooper suggested I send her the newspaper article about me. I guess I can do that. Then she'll know I'm doing okay and won't worry. If she doesn't write back, I can always write to my aunt to check up on her. Do you think Mom will be upset when she reads I want Emancipation?"

"No. I think she might be proud you're brave enough to take charge of your life. Most likely, she knows Cooper and I are available to help. You've done an amazing job dealing with everything that's come your way, Ivy. Think about it. In a short time, you rescued your mom, you've settled into a new home, faced town gossip, dealt with flak from taking a drug dealer out of circulation, started a rapidly expanding business, and brought your grades up while juggling a hectic schedule. Everyone's so proud of you."

"Thanks. When you say it like that, I guess I'm proud of *myself.*" She rubbed her forehead. "I still get upset if people ask or say something about my brother or dad. I don't want people thinking I'm *anything* like them."

"My mom once told me people do the best they can in the circumstances they find themselves in. I think most people would do better if they *knew* better. Thinking that way helped me be more understanding. Your family might have been trying to survive, but couldn't find a healthy way to do so. You didn't contribute to your family's choices that got them where they are. Let's face it, no one has control over another person's choices. Don't take ownership of anything they did. None of that is on you. You can't fix any of it. With time, most people in this town will come to know you by your actions from here on out."

"I guess." She hoped Lora was right.

"You know, you're getting some fantastic positive attention for your Christmas windows. This will widen the recognition of your artistic talent. Have you thought about setting up your own website? The one you made for my mom was fantastic."

"Thanks." Her shoulders naturally tucked in with the discomfort of hearing Lora's praise. The website was a great idea, though. Since she had a boatload of homework to finish up before Christmas break, she wouldn't get to it anytime soon.

"Yeah, I might later. I'm kinda on overload now."

As embarrassing as Lora's praise was, it felt good. Just as she'd always wanted Cooper to be her real dad, she now wished Lora could be her mom. Both of them were exactly how she imagined loving parents would be.

Should she tell Lora about the nightmare she had after getting the letter? Even thinking about it made her sick to her stomach. She picked nervously at her cuticle.

Lora gently pulled her hand away when it started bleeding. "What is it, Ivy?"

"Um, last night I had a bad dream. Dad and Derek were chasing me with an ax, *screaming* at me. I woke up all sweaty and couldn't go back to sleep. Dad's *scary* when he's angry, to the point that he might kill someone. The dream seemed so real to me."

"That does sound scary. You're afraid he'll come after you to retaliate, aren't you?

She nodded mutely.

"I get it. His letter disrupted your peace of mind. Don't worry, we'll take measures to make sure they can't harm you."

She really, really wanted to believe that was true.

Lora leaned over to give her a shoulder hug. Her warmth and reassurance were helping her to believe she would be safe.

Still holding her, Lora said, "When I leave, remember to use the tools your counselor gave you. Don't be passive about this, Ivy. If you're upset, fight back to regain control of your emotional life."

Lora was right. She couldn't let the bad stuff take her down. And she wouldn't. She would not be a passive doormat like her mom.

Her mom.

Uninvited tears filled her eyes. Lora said she should be patient with her mom. That could be right, but patience wouldn't make the hurt go away.

"Mom didn't even call on Thanksgiving. That really hurt."

"I'm sure it did. Maybe she couldn't, for whatever reason. In her traumatized state, she might have convinced herself it was better not to. Regardless, I hate that you're feeling abandoned by her."

"Well, you've helped me think differently about it. When Mom left, I could tell she wasn't caring much about anything. I know she's been through a lot. I won't hold her silence against her anymore. Like you said, she needs time."

Lora sighed. "How about you view your mom's situation more in terms of her abandoning *herself*? I'm sure she holds you in her heart. She might even have the false opinion that she doesn't *deserve* you. Or that she let you down too often for *you* to care about her."

She blinked. She'd never thought of that possibility. Mom might have similar feelings to hers, that she deserved little from others. Until recently, part of her felt undeserving of anything good coming her way. Thanks to the Martins and Lora, and her WrapAround team, she now knew better now. She deserved good things to happen to her, and she deserved to *be* happy.

And so did her mom.

Mom deserved a daughter who would be patient as she healed. Doing that might show her the love and support she needed to recover.

"I know Mom didn't purposely let me down. I know she always did the best she could."

"It's good you can see that. Your dad's abuse probably took away much of her confidence and self-respect."

"Yeah, that sounds about right."

Now she was feeling more sorry than angry at her mom.

Lora's eyes locked with hers. "It'll take time for her to reconnect with who she really is, to regain her confidence. Only then will she be able to return to you...to be your mother, in whatever way the two of you arrange."

"Yeah. I get it now."

She couldn't imagine what was going on in her mom's head after what she'd been through. She probably never would. Yet, *she* could do the right thing and be supportive. There was no reason she couldn't reach out first.

"Ivy, it's time for you to focus on the blessings you have right now. You have a family here in the Martin household. I believe it will be a forever one. In the next few years, everyone will see you as a talented young woman who worked hard to make her future brighter."

She sniffled a little, then her lips turned up into a smile. "Thank you for coming today. Talking with you helped."

"Anytime. I'm glad it made a difference."

Lora grinned. "Hey, before I go, are there any of Emma's baked goods hanging around? I'd love something yummy before I get back on the road."

Relieved and feeling about a zillion pounds lighter, she jumped up from the couch.

"I know where she stashes the best ones. Want some milk, too?"

"Certainly do!"

She carried in a tray with two glasses of milk and a plate of cookies. "You'll love these." She pointed to the triple chocolate chip cookies. "They're a little frozen, cuz she keeps them in the freezer."

Lora took one, held it in her hand, and a funny grin came across her face. Then she blurted, "Ivy, I think Cooper and I have fallen in love!" Instantly, Lora's eyes widened, and she slapped a hand over her mouth.

"Oops. I didn't mean to share that. But gosh, I'm so happy!"

She gawked at Lora in surprise. Then she threw her arms around Lora's neck, laughing with delight. "That's so awesome! It's what Emma and I have been hoping for." She pulled back. "Are you getting married? You're gonna let me tell Emma, aren't you?"

"Oh, I'm such a nincompoop! I shouldn't have said anything yet. We haven't gotten past the *I-love-you* part. However, Coop did mention that he was a packaged deal and both Emma and *you* were part of that package."

She whooped. What the what! They *were* talking about marriage.

"Works for me!" She got up and jumped around. "O.M.G. This is the best news ever!"

She couldn't wait to tell Emma as soon as she got home!

CHAPTER 34
COOPER

As Cooper settled in at his desk, he chuckled to himself. It was ridiculous. He couldn't stop whistling, humming, and singing lovesick country-and-western songs or sentimental Christmas carols ever since he and Lora proclaimed their love. Once Lora spilled the beans to Ivy, he'd been dealing with two ecstatic teenage girls.

Each day passing gave him another day closer to Christmas Eve when he could hold Lora in his arms.

Though he'd bought a few things for her Christmas stocking, her bigger gifts stumped him. Those he wanted to be special.

Virginia strolled into his office. "Okay, boss. What's up with the Forrest Gump got-a-box-of-chocolate look on your face?"

"I was thinking about Lora and the girls. The girls are acting weird since they found out Lora and I are officially a couple." He tapped his fingers on his desk to the tune of a song stuck in his head.

"So, what's your next step? Hmm...Christmas would be a romantic time to get engaged." Virginia picked up his coffee cup to head back downstairs. "Just sayin', boss. Unless you think she might turn down an ornery, close-minded, stick-in-the-mud like you?"

Jeepers, she shouldn't even plant *that* in his head. Was she right about a Christmas engagement, though? Were they ready for the next step...either of them?

***

While around the kitchen island the next morning, the girls made their lunches, suspiciously whispering.

Emma stopped what she was doing and exclaimed, "Dad, you should ask Lora to marry you at Christmas. But listen...you've got to build up to it. Know what I mean? To ensure she says yes." With a flushed face, she lowered her head and focused on shoving her sandwich into a baggie.

Ivy kept her eyes averted.

He pulled his lips in tight to keep from smiling. "So, you want Lora to become your stepmom? And now is the time to ask her?"

"Da-a-ad, I never want to use the term *stepmom* for Lora. It's such a bummer word. She'll just be Mom or Lora. And yeah, she's like family already. Why wait any longer?"

Emma stuffed her lunch into her backpack. "However, you've *got* to do the whole thing up right. I know you're older and probably out of practice. Women like some romance. The proposal needs to be special...memorable. Whaddya say, Dad?" She gave him her best puppy dog look.

He glanced over at Ivy, who was nodding her head, her brows knitted with concern.

"And I suppose you girls have some suggestions on how to do this correctly?" He tried to maintain a sober face. "I could probably use some help. I like the idea of bringing Lora into our family as soon as possible. However, there are a few grown-up things she and I haven't discussed yet."

"So, when can you discuss them?" Emma asked. "We don't have much time, Dad! How about by tomorrow? Then you can start with the romantic stuff, to be ready to pop the question on Christmas Eve."

Emma bounced on her heels, giggling nervously. "Gosh, I'm so excited I won't be able to sit still in class today."

He hiked his brows in amusement and would have rolled his eyes, but he'd never appreciated that gesture from the girls. "Pop the question? What are you...like sixty?"

"Ha, ha, Dad."

The girls hugged and then continued to speak in whispers all the way out to the truck.

He snorted out a laugh. Heaven help him. This should be interesting.

Heck, he had no problem upping the romance. Lately, his phone calls with Lora had gotten decidedly steamy—heading toward cold-shower-level.

With a travel mug in hand, he followed the girls out.

What the girls had in mind wasn't exactly the same type of romance he'd been picturing. But what-the-hay. He'd let them have some fun with it.

***

That night, he obeyed Emma's request by calling Lora to ask her some *hypothetical* questions. After a few easy ones, he asked, "If we married, would you be willing to give up your job?"

After a brief pause, Lora said, "Yes. However, if we were to marry, I'd like to find a less demanding job. One where I could be more available to the girls during their last years of high school."

"I see no problem with that. That would probably be good for all of us."

They talked a little more before he had the courage to ask the question he was most anxious about.

"Would you want another child?"

This time, Lora's pause was longer. "No child would replace Maggie. What's most important now is for the four of us to bond as a family. Another child isn't necessary for my happiness. Besides, we might be getting too old for babies and the lifestyle changes that go along with them. What are your views on that?"

"Same." He hadn't realized he'd been holding his breath until Lora gave him the answer he'd hoped for. He breathed a sigh of relief. In May, he'd be turning forty-four. A baby coming in another one or two years would be a challenge.

He closed his eyes and took a deep breath. Most of the big stuff was out of the way now. They'd both been financially responsible, so there wasn't unreasonable debt on either side. He had complete trust in Lora and knew they'd both do their best to make their marriage work.

***

The next evening at dinner, he sensed the girl's anxiety. "Girls, I talked to Lora, and you are free to put those proposal plans into action."

They jumped around, squealing before embracing him.

When they settled down, Emma said, "Okay, Dad. The first thing you have to do is send flowers to her office with a mushy note. A few days later, she should receive one of those expensive Christmas cards at the drugstore, with a handwritten note. Do you want us to help you figure out what to write?"

He struggled to keep a straight face. "Nah, I can handle it."

"I know Lora likes chocolate," said Ivy. "How about you have some delivered? The really fantastic ones. They *can't* be any brand her company distributes, though."

He nodded his compliance. "Okay, yeah."

Emma brightened. "Oh! It would be so cool if you hired Christmas carolers to go to her office or her condo."

He crossed his arms. "Nope. That's a hard no."

Emma and Ivy put on their pouty faces.

He rolled his eyes. Darn, he hadn't meant to do that. They headed out to the garage. Was all this fuss overkill?

The next morning, he said to the girls, "Lora's coming Christmas Eve and we'll have our big dinner with her, Nana, Will, and Rebecca. As per our tradition, we'll open one present on Christmas Eve—"

"Yeah, yeah, new pajamas," interrupted Emma in a tone of disgust.

"Ha, ha. No, this year will be different. I'm going to ask Lora to marry me. If she says yes, one of my Christmas gifts to everyone will be a brief stay at a resort of Lora's choosing for our wedding. Hopefully, the ceremony can be mid-February over Presidents' Day weekend."

The girls' eyes grew enormous, and smiles erupted on their faces. "Yay!"

"Ivy, that includes you, of course. We are giving Lora a new family, and we are asking her to accept *all* of us."

Ivy's face beamed as her eyes filled with tears. "Thanks for including me, Mr. Martin. I've never been to a resort or a fancy wedding before. Did you get her a ring?"

"First, no more of this Mr. Martin stuff. Call me Cooper or Coop. You're family now, so no need for formality. If you were younger, I would have given you the option of calling me Dad. And second, I already called Rebecca for Lora's ring size. I hope you two will go ring shopping with me tomorrow after school. We only have four more days before she gets here."

"Count me in," said Emma, happy tears glistening her eyes.

"Me too!" said Ivy.

Emma hugged him. "I love you, Dad. This is so amazing! Though, Dad, I think we need to put up more twinkly lights. *Everywhere.* They create the feeling of Christmas magic."

He nodded, smiling. "Okay. Good to know."

Emma excused herself and skipped upstairs to finish a pressing school assignment.

Ivy took her time putting their dinner dishes into the dishwasher. She hung around awkwardly, seeming to have something on her mind. Finally, she said, "Being included is, like, super incredible for me, Mr. — Er, Cooper. I'm so happy for you and Lora. She really loves you. I can tell. I'm...I'm so thankful you took me in. You've always been like my second family."

She dipped her head. "And if you ever have problems with anxiety again, I could teach you the tapping technique I learned from my therapist." She smiled up at him shyly before rushing off.

He called out after her, "Thanks, Ivy." *Boy, is everyone worried I'm going to blow this again?*

It seemed silly that he was so overjoyed to have the girls' acceptance and support. He knew they'd both blossom having Lora in their home. Sure, he might feel a little jealous over Emma's affections shifting to Lora. That would probably be normal, though. He'd cure that by holding gratitude for having a wonderful woman like Lora in his life.

As he wiped down the kitchen counters, a lightness spread through his body. A quote from Richard Bach, read long ago in a high school English class, came to mind.

The bond that links your true family is not one of blood, but of respect and joy in each other's life.

My gosh. Soon he'd be a lone man in a sea of women. Since he loved all the ladies in his life, he wanted to be the type of man who showed his respect by applauding the success each one made from their own choices. He couldn't wait to see how everyone's futures would unfold.

***

He was eager to tell Virginia about his plans for a Christmas Eve proposal when he arrived at work the next day. Though he knew she'd be happy for him, he hadn't expected she would have a million ideas on how he could do the asking.

Why did everyone think he needed so much help with these things?

Virginia again brought up the idea of Lora working for the company. He said he'd give it some thought.

He did. So much so, he found it difficult to focus on anything else. As each scenario ran through his mind, he could feel his resistance growing. Wouldn't they have enough adjustments incorporating Lora into their lives at home? Adding her to his work environment might present too many challenges to sort out.

Would Lora even want to be his employee? She certainly was business-smart and would be an asset. But dang! The company was *his* baby. He wasn't sure how much sharing he wanted to do. Besides, hadn't he heard family-run businesses could be problematic?

CHAPTER 35
LORA

From her waist, Lora tilted her upper back from side to side, trying to loosen her stiff muscles while sitting in the driver's seat. With all the red taillights ahead of her and the headlights behind her, the backup would take time to clear.

"Shoot!" She would be late for Christmas Eve dinner.

Yep, and so would everyone else in this annoying traffic jam.

She jabbed the phone call button on the steering wheel.

"Cooper, I'm sorry, but I'm stuck in a huge traffic backup. There's probably an accident up ahead. Why don't you turn off everything and serve the appetizers? I'll be there as soon as I can."

From the car speaker, the tension in Cooper's voice came through. "I've been watching the weather. The roads are pretty bad, aren't they? I suspected that's what caused the traffic jam. There's got to be a pretty terrible accident ahead of you."

There was a pause before Cooper spoke again. "Hon, don't hurry or take *any* unnecessary risks. Pay attention to your surroundings. There's always some yahoo in a big rush who'll do somethin' stupid. *Please* be safe." His voice quivered as he spoke his last words.

"I will. Don't worry. I'm a cautious diver. See you soon."

"I'll be waiting for you. Again. Be safe!"

She frowned. There was so much distress in his voice. She understood his concern. The roads were terrible. She'd white-knuckled it in a few spots where compacted snow lay in patches on the road. However, his reaction had been more pronounced than she'd expected. Her call had frightened him. She'd heard it in his voice.

What was going on in his head? Had fear taken hold of him again? Would he be shaken enough to run from their relationship again?

She was still moving at a crawl when she neared the accident site. It was hard not to gawk as she passed. Bodies were being carried away from three mangled vehicles. Four ambulances were on the scene, along with countless first responders. She turned her head away. How horrible for the families if they'd lost loved ones during the holidays.

Life was so fragile. You could lose someone in an instant. She knew that too well.

She pushed her fingers into her lips, trying to suppress her building emotions. Losing Cooper or one of the girls would be devastating. As she breathed in, she felt her chest squeezing down into her lungs. It was a frightening feeling.

This is probably what Cooper experiences...but his would be more intense.

Every day apart this past month had gotten harder.

Feeling overheated suddenly, she adjusted the heater. A few minutes later, the restriction in her chest gave way to buoyancy.

Well, why not? No need to delay starting her life with Cooper. Hadn't he been asking her all those what-if questions? He must be considering marriage.

Oh, no! She'd told him she wanted to go slow. He probably thinks she needed more time.

No. No, she didn't. She was sure of that now. She loved him, and she was certain he loved her.

Keeping a cautious eye on the car ahead, she mulled this over.

No need to wait.

****

As soon as she parked the car, Cooper was there, opening her door. With urgency, he took her into his arms.

"You made it safe and sound." Relief dripped from his every word.

"I'm sorry I kept everyone waiting. You probably worried too much because—"

He raised her chin to crush his mouth to hers.

"Oh! Oh-h-h...mmm..." She swayed in his arms as he deepened their kiss. She felt his lips curve up as she released a soft moan that vibrated between their lips.

Their hunger for each other pulled them closer.

"D-a-a-ad!" yelled Emma from the front door, the frustration in her voice noticeable.

Aware the family waited; Cooper broke away first. "Let's get you inside. I bet you're starved."

With locked fingers, they sprinted to the front door, laughing.

***

Throughout their meal, Cooper kept his eyes on her from the opposite end of the table. Every time their eyes locked, her stomach danced with excitement.

The family was a noisy bunch—everyone happy and enjoying each other's company. This was exactly the close family experience she'd longed for.

Cooper looked so darn handsome. With each gaze, warmth shot through her body. *Pop the question...pop the question*, she told herself. A four-espresso kind of jittery anticipation was hyping her up. Holy Moly, was she really going to do this?

Now! Do it now!

Abruptly, she stood up, with her chair scraping across the floor.

Around the table, surprised faces peered up at her. Cooper's mouth gaped like an open oven door.

"Um...I have something to say," she announced. "This came to me tonight after seeing that horrible accident on my way here."

She focused her eyes on the man she loved. "I don't want to waste another minute of my life without you, Cooper."

His eyes bugged out. "I—That's—"

"Shush. I'm trying to do something here." She walked around the table toward him. "Will you marry me? Preferably as soon as possible? I love you. I love the girls, and I believe we're ready."

For a few seconds, the room quieted, other than a small choking sound coming from Cooper.

Then Cooper's mouth snapped shut as he regained his composure. He stood up and walked to meet her. Looking inscrutable, he took her hand to steer her into the great room.

With a wave of murmurs, everyone followed. The girls raced ahead to turn off the overhead lighting, bathing them in the glow of Christmas lights from the tree and the decorated mantel.

What was going on? Cooper still hadn't answered. Had she totally misunderstood his feelings toward her?

With a wry expression, Cooper said, "Babe, I can't believe you beat me to this." He dropped to one knee.

It was her turn to gape. "Oh!"

"I've been planning this proposal for a while, but damn, you beat me to it. Lora, I love you with my whole heart. Make me the happiest man by becoming my wife."

All the air left her lungs. In an emotional quiver, she said. "Oh, Cooper." She pulled him up to stand as she continued to hold his hands in hers.

"Cooper, I've been such a sad, lonely person for so long. Loving you and these two wonderful girls has given my life meaning again." She glanced over at the girls to send love their way as emotions ricocheted through her body.

"Yes, Cooper Martin. I would be thrilled to become your wife."

Her mother, Claire, and Will all cheered. Cooper pulled her into his arms for a deep kiss.

When they came up for air, he said, "Hold on. There's more." He cleared his throat and stepped back. "Lora, you came to me as a damsel in distress. However, your involvement in our lives awakened me from a deep sleep. You coming into my—*our*—lives made what was good so much better."

Cooper reached over to bring the girls in close. "We didn't even know we needed you. Yet we did." He squeezed her hand. "Lora Hamilton, we can't wait for you to become part of our family."

She couldn't speak. There was an enormous lump of happiness lodged in her throat.

Emma made a weird face at Cooper. He nodded and whipped out a hand. "Wait, wait! I forgot something!" He reached into his pocket and pulled out a small velvet box. "The girls and I picked this out together. We hope you like it." He opened the box, then extended it toward her.

She gasped in awe. Inside was a glistening double-halo, platinum square-set diamond ring. Utterly gorgeous.

"It's perfect," she said in an emotional whisper.

Cooper slipped the ring on her finger before giving her a kiss that claimed her as his.

She turned to the girls. "Thank you, girls. You helped pick out the most beautiful ring I could have ever wished for." She hugged them. Their exuberant return embrace showed their happiness.

Then the rest of the family rushed in to join in a group hug.

When the excitement died down, everyone headed back to the table. Emma served her first-ever Yule Log cake, with peppermint whipped cream. They all pulled out their cell phones to snap a picture of the cake to share on social media. Emma's cake was magazine-worthy from the outside and fit for royalty on the inside.

They had shifted chairs at the table so she could sit close to Cooper. Her heart drummed in her chest as they discussed wedding plans. It was a unanimous decision their destination wedding would be held at a Jamaican resort during Presidents' Day weekend. She asked her mother to walk her down the aisle and the girls to stand beside her and Cooper during the ceremony.

Would Jamaica have daisies? Would they be in bloom in Texas in February? She'd splurge to have a few flown in if they could find them. Some might think daisies weren't regal enough for a wedding bouquet, but to her, they held a special meaning.

After they'd sketched out their plans, she had more she wanted to say. She clinked her fork on her water glass, then stood up. "From this moment on, I am officially starting my new life with this fantastic family. You are my priority, so I plan to give my notice after the New Year."

Cooper smiled and gave her a thumbs-up. "Good plan."

"I want time to make the wedding arrangements, find the perfect wedding dress, and take the girls shopping for their dresses. Oh yes, and sell my condo!" She grinned. "Meaning no more commute!"

Emma and Ivy gave each other high-fives and squealed.

"I love all of you so much. I want to be with you all as soon as possible." Her gaze floated from face to face, then landed on Cooper's. "Cooper, you rescued me shortly after I had decided to give loving someone another try. Somehow, after I met you, I thought the Universe had answered my prayers."

She chuckled and wryly lifted a shoulder. "Yet, it turned out neither of us were ready right then. We both had...some work to do before accepting the risks attached to loving again with our whole hearts. Cooper, you have my whole heart."

She turned to the girls. "As do you, Emma and Ivy. By the way, I owe you two girls a big thank you. You brought Cooper and me back together. Though, admittedly, there were some bumps along the road before we arrived at where we are now."

She took Cooper's hand. "I take nothing for granted anymore. Therefore, I plan to approach every day, recognizing what a blessing you are to me."

She leaned in to kiss him. He surprised her by swinging her onto his lap for a proper kiss.

Her mom, Claire, and Will clapped in delight. The girls yelled, "Ew, gross!"

Cooper looked down at her, grinned from ear to ear. "Damn, girl. How did I get so lucky?"

A short time later, the moms and Will left, though they would return the next morning.

As they all pitched in to clean up the kitchen, her eyes kept drifting between Cooper and her engagement ring. It all seemed so dream-like.

She had a family again.

Happiness bubbled inside her. Even more so when she caught a whiff of Old Spice.

She smiled and closed her eyes.

I did it, Dad. I won't be alone, so you won't have to worry about me. I have a family now, with Cooper and the girls. Mom's a part of this family now, too. We'll take good care of her. Please know that you and Maggie will always be with us in our hearts.

As she wandered back into the great room, she noticed someone had hung four brand new red and white wool Christmas stockings from the mantel. Thrilled, she pulled Ivy over to the fireplace. They stood shoulder to shoulder, admiring them.

With her arm wrapped around Ivy's waist, she said, "There is no better symbol than those Christmas stockings to show we have now become family. We belong."

Ivy tilted her head toward her and said with a sigh, "Yeah."

Cooper came over, swung his arm around her shoulder, and kissed her cheek. Emma stepped up beside Ivy, worked her way in close to put her arm around Ivy's waist, stacking it on top of hers.

With the room glowing from the immense amount of Christmas lights, they stood gazing at the stockings and the festively decorated mantel. She welcomed the warmth of happiness spreading through her body. It had to be what overwhelming joy felt like. She glanced at the three precious people snugged in around her.

Linked by love and appreciation, that was the best bond any family could have.

When she turned to Cooper, his soft, adoring eyes met hers, communicating his love.

"See?" said Emma. "There *is* magic in twinkly Christmas lights."

THE END

Acknowledgments

It takes a multitude of gracious people's involvement for a writer's ideas to blossom into a publishable story. For me, there were years of rewrites and revisions. That said, acknowledgements are in order.

First up is the wonderful man I married. My husband, George, has been my first and most frequent proofreader and beta reader. Most importantly, he willingly gave me the space needed to immerse myself in the creative process. He also accepted that I am prone to losing all track of time while working on any writing project. A book's journey to publication can be a long, arduous one. With my husband as my cheerleader, the journey became more sustainable. His warm hugs and willingness to pick up household tasks I had neglected kept me motivated to continue. He deserves my praise.

I think all writers will tell you that learning the craft is an ongoing process. Along the way, you discover you don't know what you don't know. After classes, workshops, articles read, and anything free I could learn from, I would return to editing the manuscript—over and over again. Luckily, I love the revision/editing process. When reading the changes out loud, I could hear the improvement.

Many early readers helped this book come to life. My apologizes if your name does not appear on this list. Early readers need a big thanks because they gave their time to a piece of writing that was far from being ready for publication: Annette Millar, Leslie Miller, Cathy Carnes, Karen Nickel, Sandy Sewell, Tawn Wolfe, and my lovely neighbor, Connie Russell, who put her eagle eyes on it twice. I also want to thank J.D. Young from the Olympia Fire Department's Honor Guard for educating me on the procedural protocol of a formal ceremony given for a fallen firefighter. Unfortunately, as often goes for new writers, I discovered this intended first chapter was not where the story should start. This was not the only piece of writing chopped. Abigail Raeke, writer, book coach, and workshop presenter, helped me see how I could eliminate one of my characters. Amazing! I didn't need him after all!

Paid services also played a role in helping me along the way. Early on, I used the services of Spun Yarn, a professional beta reader service that provided a thirty-page report written by the founder and three women readers in different demographics across the US. Then there was Kimberly Taylor, who provided a developmental review of the manuscript, followed by a copy edit by Nina Bruhns. Nina's encouraging words kept me motivated through the next round of edits. At one point, my publisher even sent the manuscript through ProWritingAid Software for an AI analysis. I also used ProWritingAid while writing since I am horrible at spelling and grammar. Unfortunately, as a writer, I have a love/hate relationship with technology.

A thank you goes to book coach Jocelyn Lindsay, whose services came early on when I was a recipient of The Women's Fiction Writers Association's mentorship program. Those three months of collaborative work were inspirational. The Women's Fiction Writers Association is an amazing international organization, run by volunteers. Their mission is to help writers improve their craft and succeed in the business aspects of publishing. I have learned so much through them and from the Women in Publishing Summits, organized by Alex Haddock. The best money I ever spent in terms of value.

My thanks to my cover designer, Michael Verdum, for creating the perfect cover design, along with the help of BRW's David King. David was particularly patient when I continued to want more time to edit my manuscript. Next time, I will hire a line editor.

Finally, a big thank you to my publisher, Black Rose Writing, for giving this book the opportunity to be placed in the hands of readers. Another resource attached to Black Rose Writing is their authors' private Facebook group; I am honored to be among their ranks.

Dear Reader: I write a monthly newsletter containing an article on the broad topic of life transitions, a book review, and any pertinent news about my writing projects. Consider subscribing by visiting https://conniemorganwriter.com

The back of this book has discussion questions for book clubs. If you are in a book club, I would love to join either in person or virtually by Zoom. Please contact me at conniemorganwriter@comcast.net.

Book reviews are the lifeblood of books. If you love or even like this book, please leave a review online on Amazon, Barnes & Noble , and/or Goodreads. Even a one or two sentence statement is enough. Another way to support an author is to share the books you read on your social media accounts. Help others discover *MORE THAN LUCK REQUIRED* by snapping a picture while smiling and holding up the book. Then post it. That would be wonderful. Thank you!

Book Club Discussion Questions

- Is there a place, like Lora's Orca Park, where you go to find comfort and inspiration?
- How did Lora's and Rebecca's relationship change over the course of the story?
- Could you relate to any of the characters? If so, who and why?
- Did you learn anything of value from the characters in this story?
- What was your take on Cooper's relationship with his daughter, Emma?
- What do you think contributed to the special bond between Emma and Ivy? Between Lora and Emma, and between Lora and Ivy?
- Were the descriptions of the traumatic events too troubling for you, or were they necessary for telling the story?
- Did Lora's emotional and behavioral reaction to the death of her daughter and the collapse of her marriage seem realistic to you?
- What was your experience of being with Lora during her therapy session with Wendy?
- After Cooper asked for a second chance, did you agree with Lora's request to slow down the pace of the relationship?
- Ivy hides a great deal of what she'd gone through. Because of her home environment, her life could have gone down a different path. What kept her on the better path?
- Who was your favorite secondary character? Why?
- Did you cry or laugh at any point in the story?
- Did anything stay with you after reading this book?

ABOUT THE AUTHOR

Connie writes under the pen name Connie Morgan. Even before she became a licensed mental health counselor, Connie was a story collector—both fictional and real. Fascinated by life stories of any type, Connie is especially drawn to transformational and second chance stories. She has a passion for understanding the inner workings of people and the *why* behind their behavior. Connie worked with children and adults in the mental health field for twenty years in various capacities. More than likely, in every book she writes, you will find a mental health component encouraging the reader to be their most courageous self.

She is a Washington state native who lives with her husband, George, a retired assistant chief/fire marshal. From their back deck, they enjoy a view of Mt. Hood and Connie's organic raised-bed garden.

Note from Connie Morgan

Word-of-mouth is crucial for any author to succeed. If you enjoyed *More Than Luck Required*, please leave a review online—anywhere you are able. Even if it's just a sentence or two. It would make all the difference and would be much appreciated.

Thanks!
Connie Morgan

We hope you enjoyed reading this title from:

www.blackrosewriting.com

Subscribe to our mailing list – *The Rosevine* – and receive **FREE** books, daily
deals, and stay current with news about upcoming
releases and our hottest authors.
Scan the QR code below to sign up.

Already a subscriber? Please accept a sincere thank you for being a fan of
Black Rose Writing authors.

View other Black Rose Writing titles at
www.blackrosewriting.com/books and use promo code
PRINT to receive a **20% discount** when purchasing.